Her Hungers

Mary Winter

PPB

Pink Petal Books

Pink Petal Books, an imprint of Jupiter Gardens Press, publishes romance novels where the relationship is primary. It doesn't matter if you want to read super erotic or sweet inspirational books. Pink Petal Books believes that love is a beautiful thing, no matter what form it takes. For more information about Pink Petal Books visit http://www.pinkpetalbooks.com/.

HER HUNGERS
ISBN# 9780982543559

Edited by Mary Ann Haverlack

Electronic Publication Date: April 2009
Print Publication Date: September 2009

For more information to learn to more about this, or any other author's work, please visit http://www.pinkpetalbooks.com/

Additional Books by the Author

Good Medicine (e)

Juli's Choice (e)

Passionate Practice (print anthology of the previous two stories)

The Purrfect Man (e)

Stray Cat Strut (print anthology containing "The Purrfect Man")

StarMyst: Prodigal Son (e and print)

StarMyst: Forgiven (e and print)

Dangerous Spirits Book 1 :Ghost Touch (e and print)

Dangerous Spirits Book 2: Ghost Redeemed (e and print)

Ursa Major (e and print)

Two In Hand (e)

The Marksman (e)

(e = electronic book)

PPB

Chapter One

Strong hands gripped Lilah's waist and kept her pinned between Adrian's hard, muscled body and her dresser. She gripped the corner so tightly the wood bit into her palms. His cock pressed against her slick labia, demanding entrance. She wouldn't let him. Not yet.

"God I want to fuck you." Adrian's husky words rasped across her ears. His fingers splayed across her hip. "You know you want it."

Damn Adrian for being right. If only...She clenched her jaw. *Focus on the moment.* Lilah closed her eyes and leaned forward, baring the back of her neck to him. Her long curtain of mahogany brown hair shielded her face from view. "You know what I am--what happened to me." She expelled a harsh breath. Her pussy begged for the thick length of his cock inside her, her nipples diamond hard with need. Beneath the surface, her twin hungers roared. Her wolf beast sought the domination from being pinned beneath an alpha male. Her vampire lust for blood filled her with a desire for the tang of life's elixir.

Adrian didn't like her wolf.

Lilah's canines lengthened and a lust for blood mingled with the sexual desire in her veins. Her body's hunger or her soul's hunger, Adrian accepted half of her dual nature. Feeding both the vampire and the wolf's hunger would drive him away. He understood her vampire. Her wolf repulsed him. Inside her, the wolf's need to run beneath the moon and track prey demanded its time, and Lilah suppressed her canine instincts.

His hand slid over her side, fingers sure against her ribs. Cupping the weight of a breast in his palm, he pinched her nipple.

Lilah gasped. The tug went straight to her pussy, and it clenched in response. Thrusting her ass back, she rubbed against him like a bitch in heat. "Please," she begged as the fingers of his other hand slid toward her damp curls. "Please."

Adrian scraped his teeth against the side of her throat.

Lilah shuddered. She bit her lip hard enough to draw blood, and the coppery taste flooded her mouth. Oh yes, she thrust against his cock, feeling Adrian flick his fingers over her clit. Moaning, she arched her neck, baring her vein to him. She wanted him to take her, body and soul.

He licked the side of her neck, drawing the skin between his lips and sucking. His left hand pinched her nipple as his right strummed her clit and labia. The twin sensations drew her tight as pleasure arced through her body.

Lilah whimpered, the sound building into a frustrated growl that rumbled in the back of her throat. She wanted to be fucked hard and fast. Adrian wouldn't give her that. No, he'd devour her in little nibbles, a slow seduction of many little deaths that would keep her writhing wet and needy for hours. For a moment, just a moment, she remembered the rough passion of his brother, the way he consumed her, made her into his image. She ran her tongue over her fangs, all too vividly aware of what he'd done to her.

Adrian pulled his cock away to better thrust two fingers deep inside her.

"Please. God, Adrian, please just fuck me." Lilah hated begging.

He stroked her sweet spot, and a long, low moan of pleasure erupted from her throat. Shudders ravaged her body. She clenched her fingers onto the edge of the dresser, hearing the crunch of wood. The front bit into her flesh, metal pulls cold against her naked skin. Her chin nearly touched the dresser's top, and only the warm, wet suction of Adrian's mouth on her neck kept her from letting the furniture support her.

Her nails lengthened, scouring the hardwood dresser top. Reaching behind her, she cupped his ass, fighting hard not to bury her emerging claws into his flesh and force his cock inside her. Her beasts warred. The base of her spine tingled. The change hovered so close to the surface and she shoved it away.

"So rough, so fast. You don't savor my cock stroking deep inside your wet, tight pussy. Don't you want to feel every inch of me as I slide into you?" Adrian's words evoked an image of sweat-slick bodies.

The smell of sex hung in the air. Sliding her hand from his hip, she reached between her legs, her fingers caressing his shaft. Silky skin met her touch, and she carefully curled her fingers around his girth, guiding him toward her pussy.

Adrian added a third finger. He tweaked her nipple, the pleasure-pain bringing her back to the present.

She thrust against his fingers, her movements rough. "Fuck you," she growled, feeling her anger rising along with her lust. Pressed against the dresser she couldn't pull away, couldn't turn in his arms and shove him back and down against the floor, where her twin beasts would overcome his vampire strength. Then, she'd ride him until they both screamed their release and she would collapse, fully sated, on top of him.

"You always want it rough. Fine, I'll give you rough. But then, I'll tie you up and make you wait for me." Adrian grabbed her hips, aligning her pussy with his hard cock. A single thrust sheathed him deep inside her clenching channel.

Lilah screamed her pleasure. Adrian knew how to give her what she wanted. Exactly what she wanted. Each and every time. He pulled out, not the slow, gentle withdrawal to which she had become accustomed, but a quick slide that had her pussy contracting around him, trying to hold him inside. Then he shoved forward again. And again. Her cries of pleasure turned into low, keening moans. Reaching between her legs, Adrian smashed his finger against her clit.

Lilah's orgasm tore through her. Head thrown back, she wailed loud enough to be heard outside the house. She struggled to remain upright as her body shuddered and convulsed. Only Adrian's hand on her hip kept her from crumpling to the floor. And he wasn't finished.

"Yes," she snarled. "Give it to me!"

As if her challenge roused something primal deep inside him, he thrust through her orgasm, not giving her a chance to catch her breath before he drove her toward the peak again. Her juices dripped down her legs, and the wet sounds of sex filled the room.

"Come for me again," He stepped forward, pressing her front against the wood and metal of the dresser. The hand on her hip slid to her pussy, gathering up her juices on his fingers, and then he pressed them against her anus.

Lilah moaned. She'd dreamed of this, of his big cock penetrating her so deep she had no idea where she ended and he began. His thick digit pressed against the tight ring of muscle, and her pussy clamped down on his cock.

"Oh yeah, you like it, don't you?" He growled, his pace never slacking.

She could only whimper in response as a single finger slid into her. At last, some measure of control must have broken, for Adrian fucked her mercilessly. He grunted, his balls slapping against her sex, adding rhythmic bursts of pleasure to the harsh pounding. Splinters of wood gouged beneath her fingernails. The pain drove her hunger. Her beasts reveled in the sex, the hunger, the fury. They roared to life inside her.

Adrian stiffened as he thrust into her. He growled, his cock jerking as he came. Warm splashes of seed bathed her channel, and Lilah shuddered as she orgasmed again. Slumped against him, she felt Adrian slowly lower her to the floor. The hardwood should have cooled her heated body. It didn't.

Fingers curled into claws, shifting and shaping into pads and toes. Legs bent, changed, as one beast emerged dominant over the other.

Lilah rolled away. She curled into the fetal position, battling the change. Behind her, Adrian sat up, one leg bent. "What is it?"

"The change." Pain stabbed through her, a fierce ache in her temples as she fought the beast within. "I'm sorry." Still wearing human form, she rose onto all fours and crawled into the corner of the room.

Adrian stood. He grabbed his jeans and pulled them on.

Looking up at him through her hair, Lilah saw revulsion in his eyes. Adrian swallowed hard, battling his inner demons as much as she. Damn him. She tore her gaze away and concentrated on stopping the change.

Her sensitive hearing heard the crunch of boots against dried grass. Her enhanced lupine senses, so close to the surface, allowed her to sense the intruders. Three of them made their way across the yard, one alongside the house, two in front. Lilah didn't like it. She hadn't stayed alive by ignoring her instincts.

"Lilah," Adrian said. He opened his mouth to continue to speak.

She held up her hand and cocked her head toward the outside wall. Flaring her nostrils, she scented the men. Tobacco hung heavily in the air around them and mingled with the bite of alcohol. Lilah frowned. She doubted these were professionals. She'd evaded members of the werewolf's Luna Guard sent to protect pack secrets. Even those sent by the vampire's Immortal Council had been smarter than these men. She let the beast out, shifting in a single move from woman to wolf.

Adrian stepped back.

Raising her muzzle to the ceiling, Lilah ignored him. Instead, she padded on soft paws to the door. A tiny growl erupted from her throat, lips pulled back to reveal sharp teeth. Hair rose on the back of her neck as she inhaled the intruder's scent. The urge to squat and piss to mark her territory nearly overtook her, until she shook her head and loped toward the front door.

Patience didn't come easily to the wolf, though Lilah retained enough of her human senses to know better than to rush outside. They thought to catch her asleep during the day, unable to move. Even now, she heard Adrian pull on clothes, cautious during the daylight hours. Lilah padded to the closed door and growled. They wouldn't get in here, not into her territory. Adrian and she had struggled long and hard to find a sanctuary, a place where she could feel safe.

She didn't ask for her dual nature, didn't want it, but now that she had two beasts she fought just to stay alive. The werewolves among whom she'd spent her human childhood hated her vampire side, and the vampires hated her recently-acquired wolf. If she ever saw Adrian's brother again, she'd kill him for starting all of this with a single bite. Sadly, the men outside weren't connected to the foolish, immature young vampire. In her werewolf form, she couldn't speak with Adrian to relay her plan. Not that she had one, but it would have been nice to communicate with her vampire lover. The men outside emitted the distinct smell of human and that made them dangerous to both of her and Adrian.

Lilah padded back to the bedroom, careful to keep her claws from clicking on the hardwood floors.

Her violet eyes locked with Adrian's rich, amber gaze, her look silently urging him to let her handle things. She doubted he'd obey, but she had to try. If he got hurt protecting her, she'd never forgive herself.

The door rattled. Behind the heavy, darkening curtains, the window crashed.

Instinctively, Lilah threw herself between the window and her lover, knowing her lupine body couldn't completely shield him from the sun.

The intruder spilled through the broken glass and torn fabric.

Lilah leapt. Fangs bared she bowled the man onto his back. Glass crunched beneath him. His heart pounded, the blood in his veins calling to her. Trapped in her wolf form, her canines couldn't lengthen, but she wanted to sink her teeth into his veins and taste the hot spray of his blood.

She pounced. Paws pressed to his shoulders, hind legs straddling his hips, she lowered her muzzle. A growl rumbled from her throat. Saliva dripped from her maw as she opened her mouth.

"Lilah! The door!" Adrian whirled to face the man, the heavy darkening curtains once again in place over the window.

In her bloodlust, she hadn't heard the pounding on the door, but now the sounds of wood giving away filled her ears. With a nip at the man's neck, she whirled off of him and into the living room. Claws gouged into the floor. Just as she stepped into the foyer, the door burst open and two men rushed through.

Lilah charged.

"Holy shit! It's a wolf!" The leader said, his gun leveled at her chest.

Lilah leapt.

The gun fired, the bullet so close it brushed her fur. A growl rose deep in her throat, as she brought the man down. Jaws snatched onto sleeves, arms, anything she could reach. Behind him, another man hurried forward and shoved at her. From the bedroom, she heard the sounds of Adrian and the other man scuffling. She couldn't focus on that. A man kicked her in the stomach, and she whined with pain.

"Stupid bitch." The man beneath her spat.

Lilah closed her jaws around the man's arm and bit down. She tasted fabric, and skin ripe with the unwashed taste of a dirty body. She nearly released him, her enhanced wolf senses gagging with the smell. Instead, she tugged hard, tearing a rent in his arm. Blood poured freely.

Oh the blood. The vampire in her relished the hot liquid filling her mouth. Lilah struggled not to swallow greedily.

Out of the corner of her eye, she saw the other man point a gun at her. Tearing her jaws away, she whirled and leapt against him. He stumbled, but didn't fall. Damn it, powerful reflexes and strength meant nothing when she longed to grab the gun in her hands and train it on them. Who where they? Who sent them? Questions she couldn't voice swirled in her mind.

She snapped at him, jaws closing a millimeter shy of his leg. Powerful muscles sent her bowling against the man. He hit the wall, the gun wavering. Behind her, she saw the other man rising to his feet. His own gun lay in the corner.

Two men with guns. She didn't want to chance that the bullets might be silver, and a gunshot wound hurt like hell, even if they weren't. Neither group she knew would send humans after her. *Fuck.* She tussled with the man, trying to get a good grip on him with her teeth or rake him with her claws. At last, she knocked him to the ground.

The man twisted beneath her. Lilah curled her paws against his shoulders, her jaws gaping perilously close to his neck. Claws snagged in clothing, fists pounded against fur-covered flesh. Lilah worked to stay on top, trying to use her superior reflexes to keep the man pinned down. His partner came up behind her, shoving at her, and kicking her. Bone crunched. Lilah whined.

Behind her, a gun shot rang out. The bullet exited through the door in a splinter of wood. Sunlight streamed in through the hole.

Another shot.

She whirled from her target to face the shooter. From the bedroom, the sound of a body hitting the floor echoed. Lilah hoped it wasn't Adrian, but didn't have time to check. She leapt for the man, teeth closing around his throat. A jerk of her head, and he fell backward in a spray of blood. Eyes wide, breath gurgling from his throat, he collapsed onto the floor. Lilah spun back toward the man she'd been attacking, to find herself looking down the barrel of a gun.

"Don't move," the man ordered.

Her muscles twitched. Shit, wasn't this just the way it would end? She'd taken out one man only to be shot by his partner. And they were human. Not werewolf, not vampire, but just human. She exhaled a breath. Her speed against the man's speed. If it were a straight-out contest, she knew she'd win, but the question was, could she be faster than a speeding bullet?

She'd take the chance. Tired of running, tired of hiding, Lilah figured she'd take her opportunity. Never breaking eye contact with the man, she ducked low and rushed him.

He fired. The gunshot echoed in the room, plowing into the floor and throwing up a plume of woodchips and dust. The slivers abraded her flesh, digging in and drawing tiny points of blood. Lilah ran into his shins, sending the man staggering. He fired again, and again, each time missing her. Clamping her jaws around his gun arm, she forced him to drop the gun and then sent him to the ground.

Feral growls erupted from her throat. No longer able to keep contained, she let the beast loose. Snapping and growling, she fought with him, until her teeth closed around his throat, crushing his windpipe. He reached for her, fingers tangling in her fur. His face turned purple, his breath wheezing in his throat.

Lilah bit harder. She didn't care. These men hunted her, tried to kill her. They deserved no less than she gave them. The lust for blood roared through her veins. Kill. Feed. Her beasts rose in unison, one wanting flesh, the other wanting blood. Lilah sank her teeth just a little deeper into the man's throat, tasting the blood oozing up from the wounds.

His eyes bulged.

"Lilah!" Adrian's sharp voice cut through the room.

Relief flooded Lilah's veins. He was alive. Her muscles tensed to jump up and run to him. She stilled. The hunt wasn't over, and Adrian wasn't her alpha. She didn't have to obey his unspoken command. Yet the authority in his words caused her to pause and wait for further direction. *No! He's vampire, not were.* She didn't have to listen.

Growling, she tightened her grip on the man, her heavy paws pressing against his shoulders, hind feet curling into his thighs. Beneath the pads of her feet, she felt the sticky slide of blood soaking the fabric of his jeans. *Hunt. Kill.* She ran in a pack of one, beta to no one's alpha.

"Lilah!" Adrian yelled. "If you kill him we can't find out who sent them." He softened his voice and stepped forward.

Lilah growled. *Mine.* She'd downed her kill, and now she would finish it off. A warning glare kept Adrian from advancing any closer. Beneath her, the man whimpered.

Foolish, foolish human. He thought he could come in here with his guns and kill her. For whom, she wondered, Adrian's words sinking into her lupine mind. With a snarl, she released his throat, but kept her paws on his chest. She'd fight tooth-and-nail against Adrian being her alpha, but she'd obey. She sat, her tail thumping the floor with a heavy beat. Let Adrian interrogate all he wanted. She wouldn't move, because when he finished, she hoped he would let her take care of the intruder once and for all.

~* * *~

Adrian stared at his lover, watched her slow capitulation as she released the intruder's neck and sat back on her haunches. He struggled to keep his feelings locked deep inside. Ever since she'd returned to him and told him of her dual nature, he'd struggled. The woman he loved – a vampire and a wolf. Unspeakable, but he'd do whatever it took to keep her safe.

Adrian strode forward. He stared down at the man, blood oozing from numerous cuts and bites. The tangy scent filled the air. Incisors lengthened, and he longed to sink his fangs and drink his fill. Iron-will would keep his bloodlust under control until he found the answers he sought. Then, for trying to harm Lilah, he'd take care of this bastard once and for all.

"Who are you?" he asked. Out of the corner of his eye, he saw the gun lying on the floor. He hated firearms, hated the lack of finesse and subtlety they represented. Still, men like the one lying before him respected their power.

The man swallowed hard and said nothing.

Stopping by their captive's prone body, Adrian glared at Lilah. She still sat on the man's legs. He scowled at her. She might change, then again, she might remain wolf. She seemed to revel in her beasts. He wondered where the sweet innocent his brother had turned had gone. He remembered her then, new to the vampire's world, trembling at what she'd become. Lilah cowered no longer. Maybe he loved an illusion, a veneer Lilah no longer possessed. He nodded to her, telling her in unspoken words to get off the man.

Lilah curled her lip, revealing a hint of fang.

"Lilah, off!" He pointed to the corner, commanding her as one might the family dog.

She rose to all fours, shook herself, and padded into the corner, where she sat with a growl to remind him she wasn't about to be ordered around.

Adrian stepped forward. He paused by the man's prone figure and kicked him in the ribs. The man winced and struggled into a seated position. Adrian stepped forward, boot planted in the middle of the man's chest. "You don't move until I tell you to." He summoned the haughty presence of one used to being obeyed. "Who hired you?"

"I don't know," the man stammered. "I don't know." He shook, fear radiating from him in waves. The primal emotion called to Adrian's vampire, demanded he change, give into the hunger, and drink the scum dry. He dared not glance back to Lilah, not wanting to know what the man's fear did to her twin beasts.

"You know." He stepped down, just a little, until he felt bone start to give way.

The man's face turned purple. He sucked in air. "Look, we were just after the bitch."

Adrian slid his boot to the man's throat. Such strong-armed tactics disgusted him. But then again, the lengths the vampire and werewolf communities would go to in order to kill Lilah disgusted him too. He had vowed to keep her safe. If it meant turning into something he didn't like, he would.

“I think you know who hired you. You’re just not telling.” He grinned, letting just a hint of his own fangs show.

His eyes didn’t glow, forehead didn’t change shape like on television, but his vampiric nature came to the fore. Civilization fell away, the veneer of niceties that kept man from killing one another.

“I don’t know. Seriously, I don’t. He hired us to kill the bitch. Didn’t tell us she was a wolf. Didn’t tell us she’d kill. Paid in cash. Worked through an agent. I don’t know who hired us. I don’t know,” the man babbled on the floor.

Adrian believed him. Damn it, but he did. He glanced up at Lilah. She sat in the corner, jaws open. She snapped her mouth closed, a clear indicator of what she wanted to do with the man. He shook his head.

“Who was the agent? Who did the business? Who paid you?” Adrian doubted these men hadn’t seen who had handed over the cash.

The man shook his head. “I don’t know. The man you killed, he did all the work.”

An easy excuse, and one Adrian was quickly growing tired of. “Then if you know nothing, you can die.” He removed his foot and stepped back.

The man shivered. Blood had congealed, clotting against wounds, but the lingering coppery tang filled the air with a sweet elixir. Saliva dripped from Lilah’s maw, the wolf in her hungry to kill. Looking at her like that, he struggled to remember the soft girl his younger brother had brought home. Then, Mikhail’s jealousy destroyed her life, and he turned her without preamble, without permission. He frowned. No, he wouldn’t let Lilah kill. She’d done too much, taken too many lives, in her struggle to stay alive. The werewolf community hated vampires. The vampire community hated the werewolves, and Lilah, the only woman he knew to be both, was stuck in the middle.

Adrian stepped forward. It disgusted him, the action he was about to take. Life wasn’t shades of gray anymore, just black and more black. Who would believe this pitiful human, if he were to return with tales of a wolf that attacked them? Adrian looked around the house they’d bought, a place where they thought they could stay safe. If someone did believe him it would be the end of their life there, and he wasn’t sure he wanted to go on the run again. He knew Lilah was tired of running. A place to make a stand, she’d said when they purchased this place.

Sympathy. Compassion. Two human virtues he thought long gone. Yet looking at Lilah, watching her struggle with her beast, he forgot about their prey lying on the floor in front of him. Instead, he only wanted to see Lilah safely out of here. He stepped away from the man. "Go! You're not worth my killing."

He scrambled back, toward the door. He crawled on all fours, struggling to his feet. Wobbling, he made it to the door, not even pausing as he opened it and rushed outside.

Adrian watched, out of the path of sunlight spilling in through the open door, until their once-attacker slammed it behind him. Then, Adrian turned and looked at his lover.

"Look," he dragged his fingers through his hair. "He wasn't worth killing. We don't kill for sport. All right?"

Lilah growled. She rose to all fours and leapt.

Chapter Two

Sitting in the corner, watching Adrian let her attacker go free, she battled the urge to give chase. She didn't. Instead, she leapt at Adrian. Paws outstretched, she tackled him to the ground.

Prey. Prey. Prey. The mantra ran through her mind, making her growl low in her throat. Her hackles rose as wolf and man toppled to the ground. She clung tenaciously to him, rolling with him as he tried to overpower her. One instant, she straddled him, her paws heavy on his shoulders. The next minute he flipped her onto her back. A quick twist, and she righted herself and charged him again.

Mine. Mine. Mine. She nipped at him, tiny bites meant to leave bruises, but not break the skin. Like an alpha female chastising the members of her pack, she herded Adrian into the corner and pinned him against the wall. He sat there, back against the wall, and glared at her. With growls and bites, she kept him still, held him, punished him for letting her quarry escape.

That man tried to kill her, and Adrian let him get away. Lilah nipped Adrian's ankles.

"Stop it!" he said. She sensed the anger, the fury building inside him, but he wouldn't do anything to harm her.

Still Lilah pushed him. Fire, passion, an impetuousness—things that drew her to his younger brother Mikhail—she longed to see them in Adrian. Instead, she saw his fierce need to wrap her in cotton and keep her safe. Except she could keep herself safe and hadn't relied on anyone since her turning and subsequent transformation. Hell, he hadn't even known the latter had happened until she showed up, bloody and wounded from being attacked by rogue werewolves. And then he learned the truth.

Did he accept it? Lilah didn't know. She demanded a lover who accepted all of her, who understood both her beasts. Adrian hated her wolf. She saw the revulsion in his eyes as she rubbed against him. Her anger turned to stubbornness. She'd make him accept her beast. She butted her head against his legs, felt his rock-hard body. Her tongue lolled out of her mouth in a wolfish grin.

She rose onto her hind paws, front legs balanced on his knees. Dropping her muzzle, she sniffed his crotch. He still smelled like sex and the heat of adrenaline. She inhaled deeply, and then drew her tongue over his chest.

Adrian stilled.

Battle lust changed into a different kind of lust as she lapped at his lightly furred skin. Between his pectorals, over his navel, tracing the ridge of each one of his abs, she laved him with her tongue. Her paws rested on his rock-hard thighs, and beneath the pads, she felt the muscles flexing. If only she had fingers, hands, so she could open his jeans and take the length of his cock into her mouth. She suppressed the urge to change, wanting Adrian to face her wolf.

She braced her back legs, tail high in invitation. She wanted to turn around, to thrust her hind end at him and make him see just how much she wanted him in either form. No, it'd be too much, and she whined with the knowledge. Nipping the fly of his jeans, she felt his cock harden, and inside, she triumphed.

He wanted her. Now, like this, with her wolf tongue curling against his denim-covered shaft, then between his legs to find his balls high and tight against his body. He spread his legs.

Lilah rubbed against him, her paws rising to his shoulders. Belly-to-belly she rubbed against him, the need to shift into human form roaring through her. No, not yet, not until she got the response she wanted. Someone needed to break Adrian out of his stuffy, immortal box, and she'd be the wolf to do it.

She nipped his ear.

Adrian growled.

The primal sound reverberated through her. Strong hands came around her ribs, ruffling through her thick, ebony fur. Lilah thrust against him as if she were human, knowing she wanted, needed something more. His palms flattened against her ribs. She wanted him to fuck her, to take her as a wolf. To show his acceptance of her other form. Instead, as if she were human, his fingers strayed down, between her hind legs.

Lilah slid from his shoulders. She moved between his legs, turning over so she lay with all four canine feet in the air, her rear paws brushing his chest. With a thought, she shifted forms. Her legs lengthened turning into silky smooth skin as her ankles slid over his shoulders. She lay naked between his legs. His cock thrust against her back, an insistent pulse that matched the one in her pussy. Moisture filled her, and Adrian looked at her sex, so close. His nostrils flared.

Strong hands grabbed her ass and hauled her pussy closer to his mouth. He dipped his head and drew his tongue along the length of her labia, a long, sure lick like the ones she'd given him. Lilah's head fell back. She grabbed his knees, her cry of pleasure echoing in the room. Another lick, another moan. Fingers kneaded the flesh of her ass, thumbs working toward the puckered bud of her anus.

Sensation washed over her. The hunter became the prey, her need to dominate him, to make him see her as she faded beneath his sensual onslaught. The scent of her juices hung in the air, her channel clenching on something that wasn't there. Adrian parted her folds, and licked her clit.

Lilah screamed. Her hips bucked. Adrian buried his face in her pussy, licking and sucking only her clit, not touching anything else, until she whimpered and twisted her hips in an attempt to get something, anything inside her. Sliding her hands up his legs, she curled her fingers into his thighs, struggling to reach behind her and touch his cock.

His ministrations slowed. No longer devouring her, he gently pressed the flat of his tongue to her clit, and then laved it with soft, gentle laps. His hands relaxed, his touch turning into a caress instead of a demand.

In his lap, Lilah writhed. Her nipples drew into tiny points. Locking her ankles behind his head, she longed to hold him against her pussy forever. Her fingers curled into his hard thighs. She needed something to steady herself as a slow burn of arousal pumped through her veins.

Adrian held her firm, not letting her take control. He nibbled on her inner thigh, his fangs scraping against her sensitized skin. The smell of her arousal filled the air, his fingers entering her drenched channel. Torn between the need for a good hard fuck and the desire to ride the wave of passion coursing through her, Lilah felt as if she were a bowstring drawn taught by a master archer.

His cock rubbed against her back. Unable to reach for it, she fisted her hands against the hardwood floor. He took her beast and tamed it, drawing the need to fight, the need for revenge and channeling it into the need to have his cock filling her, fucking her.

Adrian slid her from his lap. Lilah made tiny whimpers, not wanting to be parted from her lover. She pressed her face against his chest and closed her eyes. He rose to his feet, scooped her up in his arms, and careful to avoid the sunlight spilling into the room from the open door, carried her into the bedroom. He set her on the bed, and the clink of metal filled the room.

Restraints. Lilah growled. She pulled against them.

"Let me go," she said, thrashing to try to get free. The bonds, specially made for vampiric strength, held fast. She looked up at Adrian, eyes wide with the fact he'd finally taken control.

She snarled, demanding that he cater to her sexual needs.

"No." Adrian said. He straddled her hips, his muscled thighs in reach if she had the use of her hands. His cock rose tantalizingly close so thick and hard. Slowly, he caressed the length of her arms, sliding his fingers down over her shoulders to the plump mounds of her breasts. "I want you to enjoy this, and I want to savor you."

Her anger drained away with the tender touch of his fingers against her skin. It was for her, all for her, and she couldn't be mad. Frustrated, yes. Horny as hell, damn straight! But she couldn't be mad. She flexed her arms against her bonds, testing them. They didn't budge.

Adrian bent his head. His hair slid over his cheek and as he dipped his head, the short, silky strands caressed her breasts. Just a little touch that had her womb quivering and her hips arching up to meet his cock that wasn't there. Inside, her wolf howled with joy. Yes, here was a mate who would master, conquer, and be strong enough to protect her. Her vampire flashed angry eyes and demanded control.

Wet lips closed around her nipple, drawing it into the warm cavern of Adrian's mouth. Lilah moaned, eyelids fluttering closed. She let her beasts war, felt the battle in her blood. She rode it like a tide. Lust filled her veins, her teeth elongated as her vampire battled for control over the wolf. She didn't shift, though her skin crawled with each suck on her nipple.

"Adrian, please." She wasn't the type to beg, not usually, but her pussy ached.

He pinched her other nipple. Back bowed, she cried out. She was burning up inside, a fiery inferno from which she'd never emerge. Vampire to vampire, his mind touched hers, gently, making her feel the heaviness in his balls, the throbbing in his cock. Just as softly as the mental communication came, it dissipated. His head lifted, and in his eyes, hunger blazed.

"When you're ready," he replied, licking his lips.

"I'm ready now!"

Adrian flashed the self-satisfied smile of a man who could reduce a woman to the consistency of a wet dishrag with fabulous sex. "Not yet." His fingers trailed closer to her navel. "Not yet." His nostrils flared, the scent of her arousal heavy in the air. "But you're close."

Lilah whimpered with frustration.

Adrian looked down at her. Beneath the surface she knew he sensed her natures, the vampire and the werewolf, and she watched him shiver. She wanted him to turn her hands loose, let her go, and see how hard and how wild she fucked him. No, she would play his game, allow him to give her the tenderness she denied herself.

He bent his head to her flat stomach so fast she almost missed his snarl. Did he think of her with another man? She'd been with him for so long and he'd tried to block out her life before him. She knew what he believed. That she'd never wanted him, only his piss ant of a brother, but here she was shackled, pussy soaked, ready for him. Frankly, that should tell him something. It should tell him that she wanted him far more than she had ever wanted Mikhail. He battled a satisfied grin. Even if they'd been human, he bet he and his brother would have competed for her.

He moved down by her feet, and she spread her legs. Her pussy, lips glistening with moisture, called to him, yet he ignored its siren song. He moved lower, past her knees to her feet and then slowly, kissed along the arch of her foot. With his tongue, he licked the sensitive skin.

Lilah rattled her bonds and swiftly inhaled, but made no move to pull away. A soft moan erupted from her lips as he swirled his tongue around her big toe before drawing it deeply into his mouth.

Lilah never knew how erogenous her toes really were, but each pull of Adrian's lips around her metatarsals had her biting back moans. The answering tug deep in her pussy only made her ache more for the good, hard fucking it seemed he was determined to deny her. *Bastard.*

As if he heard her, Adrian's self-assured smile grew.

Lilah yanked against her bonds, harder now that he drew her second and third toes into his mouth. Her frustrated growls emerged as moans.

"Damn you, Adrian," she cursed. If she shifted, if she wrenched control away from him, she could have him exactly as she wanted him. Closing her eyes, she gulped air and struggled to surrender to the will of the man holding her slender ankle in his big hand. *Be careful what you wish for*. She sucked deep breaths, reminding herself she wanted Adrian to be strong enough to dominate her. Yet giving him control meant putting her life in his hands. Right now, she didn't trust him with it. Not yet. With a savage snarl, she shifted her hands just enough to slide the gray paws from the shackles, then shifted them back into human form.

Lilah reared up.

Adrian leaned back, censure in his gaze. "We were playing my game," he said. "You cheated."

"You're not fucking me," she snapped. His earlier words, that he wanted to enjoy her, savor her, hummed in her mind, and for a moment, she regretted her harsh actions. No, he had to earn her submission. She pushed on his shoulders, sending them both toppling over the bed.

She landed on top of him. Knees straddling his hips, his hard cock brushing her slick folds, she had him exactly where she wanted him. Lilah leaned forward. She nipped his shoulder, marking him with her possession. "Mine," she whispered. "Mine."

He lifted his hips to plunge his cock into her, and Lilah rose off of him. "You called the shots once before." She stilled him with a finger against his lips and then shimmied down his body.

Adrian spread his legs.

As she sat on her heels, she admired the thick, full cock rising from the nest of dark curls between his thighs. His balls hung heavy and full, the crown of his penis fully extended from the foreskin. Mouth watering, she leaned forward and licked the length of him.

Adrian moaned.

With one hand, she fondled his balls, the other she held around his base, until his shaft, wet with saliva, slid easily past the back of her throat. She deep-throated him, loving his salty nectar taste and knowing that she, and she alone, brought him to such states of hardness. He grabbed the back of her hair, shoving his cock deeper into her mouth. Only now, when he slipped past the muscles of her throat and fucked her mouth as far as he could, did his restraint slip away. Guttural cries of encouragement echoed from his throat, and then she tugged on his balls, stilling his impending climax.

He cursed her in his native language. She didn't recognize the words, but their sharp tones clarified their meaning.

Rising above him, nipples pointed toward his face, back arched to give him the best view, Lilah slid her labia over the head of his cock. A single plunge and he rested balls-deep inside her. Contracting her inner muscles, she wrung a groan from him and smiled. She leaned back, bracing her hands on his legs, and gave him an eyeful of her pert breasts, his cock buried deep in her pussy. And then she began to move with a long, leisurely slide, as slow and torturous as he wanted to give her.

At the apex of her stroke, she halted with him just inside her pussy. Now who has control, she wanted to ask. Now who has the power? She did, and with two preternatural nations wanting her dead, she knew she had to keep it.

A twist of her hips on the way down, a little bit harder and a little bit quicker, and both of them moaned at the exquisite sensation. So full, so deep, every time Adrian took her, every damn time, he made her feel like this, and a little part of her hated him for it. Her alpha bitch looked for a mate, a male to share dominance with. Too much of her feared that, just like now, she'd dominate Adrian forever.

With a shake of her head, she shoved the thoughts away and concentrated solely on the experience of his thick shaft between her legs. In and out. In and out. Harder. Deeper. Faster. The primal need to mate, to claim life after destruction, roared in her veins. Her nipples tightened, so hard they ached, and she released her grip on his leg to pinch one between her fingers. Her other hand went between her legs.

Her juices soaked the finger she strummed against her clit. Tiny electric charges darted through her body, starting at her clit and working their way outward. Her breath came in tiny pants. The smell of her own juices filled her nostrils, made her even hornier as she ground down against Adrian's penis. His hands came around her hips, trying to set the pace, and yet, he couldn't, for she constantly changed it, a little bit harder, sometimes slower, a little twist here, an extra thrust there, always staying one step ahead of him.

Her head fell forward. She curled deep inside herself, past both her beasts, to that place where she knew one more thrust, one more stroke, and she'd fly apart. Lilah ground down against her clit with her fingers, rammed Adrian home one more time, and screamed as shockwaves poured through her body.

She leaned back, nearly collapsing on his legs with the force of her release. Her body exploded, her wolf howling its pleasure, her vampire drinking in the lust like sweet blood. Lights flashed behind her eyelids, and she thought she flew apart, never to regain herself again.

Beneath her, Adrian bucked. With a savage growl, he came, his hot seed coating her channel. His hands forced her forward, her mouth to his, and kissed her. His tongue slid between her lips, plundering, claiming her as much as any man could. At last, she pulled back and sucked in a breath of air, then rolled to the side on the hard floor. Her breathing echoed in her ears, a counterpoint to Adrian's ragged breaths.

The front door slammed open.

Lilah bolted to her feet. She rushed to the edge of the door and pressed against the wall. With her hand, she motioned for Adrian to slide around the side of the bed out of view. She wanted the element of surprise, and she reached for a weapon that wasn't there.

Her nudity didn't bother her, not when she could shift into wolf. But she wouldn't shift, not yet, not until she determined whether it was human, vampire or were coming across her threshold. She sniffed. The scent of a pine forest, fresh with dew on a sun-dappled morning filled her nostrils. She inhaled deeply thinking of home, the woods where she grew up and the pack that lived there. They'd found her, and she'd have a hell of a fight on her hands. The need to shift prickled along her skin, and as the first footfalls vibrated along the floorboards, she burst from her hiding place straight for the intruder.

And skidded to a stop as she saw the last man she ever expected to see.

"Roarke?" his name came out in a croak. She stood there, another man's seed dripping down the inside of her thigh, and stared at the one man who held the power to rock her world. She'd expected the werewolves to come for her, expected the Luna Guard with all its stern military types and orders. She never expected Roarke.

He stood there, wearing a button-down shirt and jeans that molded to legs and thighs. A pair of work boots replaced military jump boots, and she saw no weapons. Of course, as the alpha in the pack, he needed no weapon except himself. Broad shoulders, lean hips, and dark brown hair her fingers itched to caress. A childhood crush, now something more, and never realized. If the Luna Guard had to send anyone after her, why did they have to send him? She could accept being found, accept being caught, and even accept her death, but she never imagined it would be at the hands of the man she once loved.

~* * *~

The sight of Lilah drove the breath from Roarke's lungs. He'd crossed the country, searching for her, fearing he'd be too late. He hadn't been, and now she stood before him. Roarke let his gaze take in her disheveled hair, her pert breasts with their pointed nipples, the flare of her hips, her long legs...and the smell of another man on her. He lifted his lip in a snarl.

"Lilah." He breathed her name like a benediction and closed the door behind him. "I found you. Whoever is hiding in the bedroom can come out too. I'm not here to kill you." He held his hands open at his sides, though his fingers twitched with the need to reach out and touch her, to draw her frame against his and never let go.

Lilah didn't move. He didn't expect her to. It had been too many years, and he'd not made any overtures when she'd been last in his territory. Now she stood there, stinking of another man, their mingled juices running down her thigh.

Since her attack had come in his territory, he felt somewhat responsible for the wolf bitch that hovered beneath her skin, and hover it did. Like her tail waving in the air, announcing her presence to all the males in sight, the sweet scent of her cream filled his nostrils and tightened his cock. It took all his willpower not to step forward.

"How do I know that?" She must have recovered from her shock for her voice held those same low, seductive tones he knew so well. Her fighting stance didn't ease. She licked her lips, her gaze traveling the length of his body, lingering on his aching cock and balls. "Why are you here?"

"Yeah," called the man from the bedroom.

Roarke heard rustling, and he figured the man must have stepped into some jeans, for he strode into the living room, taking care to avoid the hints of sunlight on the floor. Vampire? Roarke struggled to decipher what the hell was going on here. He inhaled deeply and caught Lilah's scent, different, but still unmistakably hers. Had he turned her? His anger flared, the need to rip out this vampire's throat pulsing in his veins.

"Lilah, get dressed," the vampire ordered as he moved in front of Lilah, blocking her body from his view. He turned his attention to Roarke. "Why the hell are you here?"

Her eyes widened as if she wasn't used to being ordered about by this man, but the need for modesty must have overcome her objections for she whirled and hurried into the bedroom. Moments later, she emerged dressed in an oversized t-shirt that hit her at mid-thigh. The vampire's shirt, he wondered, the thought of her wearing anything belonging to a bloodsucker rankling. The vampires wanted her dead too. What was she doing here with this undead creature? He intended to find out.

"Yeah. Why are you here?" Lilah elbowed her way in front of the vampire.

"Why do you think I'm here?" he said. "I'm here to protect you."

"The hell you are," Lilah snarled as she leapt forward with the vampire right behind.

Chapter Three

Adrian tried to push Lilah out of the way, as he rushed the man she called Roarke. The werewolf stood there, strong and possessive, and he'd smelled the way her body reacted to him. She might have just finished having sex with him, but from the rush of juices in her cunt, she wanted this werewolf too. He'd be damned if he let some overgrown dog take her away from him.

With his shoulder, he barreled into Roarke, sending the other man flying back. Lilah darted in from the side, half trying to push him away, half trying to get at the werewolf. She used her preternatural strength and held nothing back. Neither did he. And both of them managed to pin Roarke to the ground. A shove of his hand sent her scrambling off of Roarke. Adrian wanted the werewolf to himself. A solid right-hook cracked satisfyingly against the werewolf's jaw.

Brawling. Vampires never brawled. Adrian wondered where the animal instinct to battle this man for Lilah had come from. Another blow landed against Roarke's face, and then another, until he realized Roarke defended himself, but didn't fight back.

Adrian leaned off of him, only to have Lilah dart into the space between them. "You bastard," she snarled, and she slapped Roarke. "Why didn't you come sooner? You let me almost die, and then you show up. You fucking bastard." She slapped him again, leaving a large red handprint on his face.

Roarke reached up and grabbed her wrist. "Wait."

One word stilled the chaos.

Adrian moved to the other side of Lilah, not ashamed that he'd punched Roarke. He snagged Lilah's other wrist so the two men held her between them, suspended, caught between both worlds. Which, Adrian mused, she was. Lilah looked at him, her expression unreadable. "Let's get dressed and discuss this like civilized people," he offered.

"We're not *civilized people*." Lilah tugged her wrist away from him, and then from Roarke. Spinning on her heel, she stormed back to the bedroom.

"No, I guess we're not." Roarke's wry grin unsettled him. "Mind if I get up?"

Adrian moved to the side, not wanting to step back into the beams of light penetrating the room. Too close, that had been too damn close, and he'd been too caught up in Lilah and Roarke's battle to even realize the danger to himself. The old house at the end of the overgrown drive needed work, more so now that the front walls had been peppered with bullet holes and glass broken out of the window. Sitting on a two-acre lot, untamed foliage shielded the home from the street and curious neighbors. He needed, more importantly Lilah needed, somewhere more secure for them to talk, and he opened up the door to a room with boarded-over windows. Turning on the bare bulb hanging from the ceiling, he gestured Roarke into a ratty chair.

"Being on the run makes it hard to offer hospitality." With that explanation, he sank into a threadbare couch that faced the boarded-up window. "So who are you?"

"Roarke Connelly," Lilah answered for Roarke. She emerged in the doorway wearing a short, black spaghetti-strap shirt with tight, black jeans. "Alpha of the Northwoods pack, master's degree in engineering with a minor in geology. My father worked with his family, and I grew up with the pack." Boots covered her feet, and he had no doubt she had a knife, maybe two, secreted on her person somewhere. The faintest bulge at the base of her spine showed him the location of one weapon.

She strode into the room, commanding both men's attention as she grabbed the other chair, hauled it across the floor, and sank into it.

"Don't say you're here to protect me. You couldn't save me from a broken leg when I was ten, and with a pack to run, it's not like you can hide out with us. So tell me, Roary, what are you doing here?"

Dressed and armed, Lilah sounded much better. Bringing up the broken leg was just her being a bitch, though her use of his childhood nickname softened the blow. She'd never blamed him for the tumble out of a tree he'd told her not to climb, and neither did her family. But, they had a history, one he suspected Adrian resented. Let him stew. He sensed Lilah's alpha bitch wanted Roarke around, needed an alpha male as strong and determined as she. He grinned.

"Pretty damn convenient, isn't it? We're ambushed by some men, and then you stroll in and say 'hey baby, I'm here to protect you.'" She frowned. "Of course you could have paid those men to attack, and then waltzed in here like a savior. Then again, you're obviously close enough. I didn't hear any car engine. Makes me wonder why you didn't come in here and take them out yourself." She caught Adrian's questioning gaze and knew he had to be thinking the exact same thing.

"Can't hunt by scent in a car. I knew you were in the area, but not exactly where. As far as the men, why don't you show me the body? I didn't look at it too much as I entered, and I'll tell you what I know." Roarke said.

"You could know a lot if you hired them. The Luna Guard are after me. A good member of the greater pack such as yourself shouldn't be caught with a bad girl like me." She dropped her booted foot to the floor with a thud and leaned forward, elbows braced on her knees. "Then again, I never was good enough for the prince of the Northwoods."

Roarke flinched at the vehemence in her words. About the time she'd gone off to college, the pack had paraded eligible bitches in front of him. He hadn't wanted any of them. No doubt, Lilah expected him to be hip-deep in pups by now. Especially when he'd sent her away to college without even a farewell kiss.

Lilah curled her fingers into her palm. "Why don't we go look at the body? And then you can help me dispose of it. This is my world, Roary. Welcome to it." Sarcasm dripped from her voice.

Roarke watched Lilah rise to her feet. She paused long enough to tell Adrian to stay there, no sense in him endangering himself to look at already dead men, and although he grumbled, he remained seated. Roarke bristled at the thought of her stepping out there, but it was her home, and she'd already defeated one attack today. If he expected to protect Lilah, he knew he'd have to work with her.

Her long, mahogany brown hair hung in a ponytail that hit the middle of her back. Slim shoulders with creamy white skin revealed by the thin straps of her shirt. Her body was curved, muscled like a warrior's. He inhaled deeply, filling his lungs with her scent. He still smelled Adrian, and the wolf in him growled at the smell of another man on her skin. Floral, warm, sunlight, all those things he needed in his life, because since the Dark Moon Dogs had made their presence known and split his pack, he'd lived far too long in the dark.

His gaze trailed down her spine to the curve of her hips. His palms itched to cup her ass and haul her against his body, let her feel the pulse of his cock against her skin. In his jeans, his shaft hardened, balls drawn tight against his body, painfully tight.

She stopped so quickly that he nearly ran into her. He steadied himself with a hand on her shoulder. Sparks leapt from her skin into his, and deep inside, his wolf threw back its head and howled. *His.* She belonged to him, he knew it in his bones, though he'd never said anything, never done anything to claim her. He'd rectify that as soon as possible.

Roarke knelt by the corpse, noting the bite marks too carnivorous to be a vampire. He glanced at Lilah, but the last he knew she was human. She didn't fight human or smell human, but whatever she was, probably couldn't have made these teeth marks. Blood dripped down one arm, nearly obscuring a dark tattoo. He looked up at her, noticing that Lilah looked as sexy from this angle as she did from the back. With her arms crossed beneath her chest, plumping her breasts, she scowled at him.

"Do you have a rag or something? I want a better look at this tattoo."

She shrugged and said nothing as she turned away and hurried into the kitchen. Moments later, she returned with a towel and tossed it at him. "What do you see?"

He wiped away the blood, revealing a tattoo of a full moon nearly obscured by a cloud. Beneath it, a rangy mutt trotted along, tail in the air.

The Dark Moon Dogs.

"What is it?" Lilah asked again, more determined this time.

He schooled his face into an emotionless mask. "He's werewolf. I hope you killed them all."

A chill snaked down Lilah's spine. To hear Roarke sound so casual about killing made her wonder if she'd guessed wrong about him. Where had the Boy Scout, the man who did only good deeds go? At one time, she'd called him the Dudley Do Right of the werewolf pack, and at one time she would have been right in doing so. Not now, not with his cold, hard expressionless face. Deep in his eyes, she saw the glint of bloodlust.

The corpse lay at her feet like so much carrion. "One got away." She didn't add she wanted to kill him, that the only thing that had held her back was some kind of loyalty to Adrian. He hadn't proved himself strong enough to lead her, and yet, she'd followed his directions. Her capitulation would lead to another attack on her life.

Questions filled Roarke's gaze. He knew she was uninjured, had seen most of her bare skin. If he wondered why, how, the man escaped, he said nothing. "They're part of a pack, the Dark Moon Dogs. They've been encroaching on Northwoods territory and even took a couple of my pack members away from me. I've heard from others that they're doing the same in other places. They're a threat to the werewolves, one the Luna Guard hasn't been able to thwart."

"Let me see that." Lilah knelt beside him. His warm, spicy scent filled her nose, almost obliterating the scent of rotting carrion that emanated from the dead wolf. She'd thought her attackers were only after her. She didn't realize they posed a bigger threat, until now. The Immortal Council. The Luna Guards. How many more groups did she have hunting her? She examined the tattoo and realized she'd seen it other places.

"He'll have a matching one on his calf."

Roarke nodded and started to peel back the man's blood and excrement soaked jeans. "You've seen them before."

"Yeah." From the other room she heard Adrian start to emerge, felt him pause as he took in the length of the sunbeams reaching across the floor.

"You might want to be careful," Roarke said, gesturing to the shaft of light perilously close to her.

Lilah nodded, not alluding to the fact her werewolf blood gave her the powers to walk in the light. She glanced at Adrian. "We've got it covered out here. Why don't you rest?"

He shrugged, cast a disgusted glance at Roarke, then back at her, before turning and going into the bedroom.

"You always order him around?"

Lilah heard the threat in his words, the belief that Roarke thought Adrian beneath her, not fitting to be her alpha. Not like him. The men were itching for a testosterone pissing match. She only hoped they were somewhere safe before they succumbed to their male need to show dominance over her. She could take care of herself.

She didn't answer, instead, turning her attention to the matching tattoo on the man's calf. In her mind, she flashed back to an alley. Newly turned, newly changed, she'd only wanted to get away, to find somewhere she could be left alone. Two men rushed her in the sultry summer night. A flash of fang, fur and claw filled her mind as if someone pulled a curtain over the memory, and then she'd been the only one to emerge from the alley.

She pressed her lips closed, not wanting to divulge that one of these bastards had been the one to make her into a lycanthrope. Another reason to stay alive, if for no other reason than that she could kill them all. "Tell me about them. You called them the Dark Moon Dogs. Sounds like they're making trouble for your pack. If that's the case, why are you here instead of protecting your territory?"

"They're making trouble for everybody." Roarke rose to his feet and turned toward the kitchen. "You have any black plastic sacks?"

She nodded. "What kind of trouble?"

He disappeared into the kitchen, returning with several plastic bags. "I'll be right back." He dropped the bags on the ground next to the corpse, and Lilah knew what he intended. How Roarke knew how to handle corpses, she didn't know. It seemed so unlike the pack leader she'd left behind. Leading a pack also made for messy cleanup sometimes, and she knew imagining Roarke handling dead bodies would ruin her Boy Scout image of him. Besides, if she let him reveal his secrets, he'd have to know hers.

She split open the plastic and wrapped several layers around the body. Roarke returned with a roll of duct tape, using it to secure the plastic to the body. "I've got some chain and cement blocks in my truck. We can use it to submerge the body in the river. It's not the best way of getting rid of it, but it's the quickest. You probably aren't going to be here long enough for it to matter."

"My prints and saliva are all over him, and his friend escaped. I doubt he'd bring pack business to the authorities, but it's there. I think we have a bit more to worry about than just dumping a body." She rose to her feet and stepped away from the bundle. "Besides, this is home. Yeah, it looks like shit, and it was better until someone decided to pepper the wall with bullet holes, but we had it secured for Adrian and had our plans, our routines. I'm not letting some weak pup drive me away." She raised her gaze, including him in her slur.

Roarke stepped forward. "I'm not a weak pup. Before you went off to college, I was your alpha. You might have been human, but I was still your alpha, and I'm your alpha now. I want to keep you alive."

"Why?" Lilah crossed her arms over her chest. Since the rising of her dual beasts, she'd been alone, hunted. Now, not one man, but two wanted to keep her safe. She still hadn't figured out the power dynamics with one, and sure as hell refused to be rolled by a second. "Why do you want to keep me alive?"

"Maybe because I have my own reasons."

"And what are those reasons, wolf boy?" Adrian stood in the doorway, leaning nonchalantly against the frame. He wore only his jeans, the top button undone. Legs crossed in a casually male pose, feet bare, Lilah fought the wave of arousal that rolled through her. "You think I'm not doing a good job?"

"Come out here into the sunlight and say that." Roarke stepped forward and held up his hands in a "come and get me" gesture.

A snarl crossed Adrian's features. Lilah stepped back as Adrian's pupils bled away the color of his irises and his eyes turned dark. His fangs extended. *Oh shit.* He'd invoked the bloodlust, she realized belatedly.

With an angry growl, Adrian charged.

Chapter Four

Adrian bowled into Roarke. His right shoulder hit the werewolf in the solar plexus, sending him scrambling backwards. Roarke hit the floor with a thud. Wooden boards vibrated beneath the impact, and Lilah felt the tremors beneath her feet. Hovering over the werewolf, Adrian stood a hairsbreadth from a shaft of sunlight, seemingly oblivious to the danger in which he placed himself. A snarl crossed his face. "Get up." He raised his fists.

"Adrian!" Lilah bolted forward. If the men thought arguing would keep her safe, they had better wise up damn fast. Shit, with all this noise, ten packs of werewolves and twenty gangs of vampires could come roaring through the door and no one would hear their arrival. They'd be dead. Shot, stabbed, beaten or poisoned, the method didn't matter, only the fact that this stupid foolishness did absolutely nothing to keep her safe. And staying safe remained her top priority.

Her vampire rose, fangs pressing against her gums. Grabbing Adrian's shoulder, she hauled him off of Roarke and then stepped in front of the scrambling werewolf. "Stop it!"

Adrian snarled. "Get out of the way, Lilah. This is between the mutt and me."

Crossing her arms over her chest, she glared at the vampire she'd let into her home, her body, and possibly her heart. "So he's a mutt?" Her icy question filled the room.

"You're not—"

"That's right, I'm not a mutt, and neither is Roarke." She stepped slowly forward, a deliberate movement to send him back into the dark safety of the bedroom. "We don't need this. Not here. Not now." Her hands shook, and she curled them into fists to keep her weakness from showing. This pissing match of testosterone would get them nowhere but dead. "C'mon, Adrian."

Standing statue still, Adrian met her determined gaze with his own. He glanced over his shoulder at Roarke, who worked himself into a seated position.

Lilah thrust her hand behind her. "Roary, stay down." Her low voice stilled his actions. The werewolf inhaled audibly, two sniffs, and Lilah clenched her lips closed hoping he wouldn't smell her dual nature. Let him think he came after her because of the werewolf attack and her being a vampire. If he knew she harbored a wolf inside her skin...He simply couldn't know. Not until she had time to figure out what his appearance meant. Dreams long thought dead hovered just beneath the surface.

"I don't answer to you," Roarke said as he stood.

Adrian's lip curled into a snarl and revealed an extended fang. "And you don't tell me what to do." He sprung into action.

Buffeted from both sides, Lilah thrust one arm in front and one behind in an attempt to keep the two men from clawing at each other's throats. She reached for Adrian, her fingers curling around his arm. For a moment, she thought she had him. Then, he yanked his arm away, nearly pulling her off her feet. She stumbled, and he met Roarke with a savage growl.

Lilah whirled to stare at the two men. The thud of fists against flesh marked Roarke's first punch, a jab to the solar plexus. Not needing to breathe, Adrian grinned savagely, and let his fangs fully extend. They pressed against his lower lip, white against the blood red of his mouth. A shiver of desire wound down her back and clamped on her pussy. Raw male strength filled her living room, and the scent of hot male had her bitch wagging her tail in invitation.

Adrian curled his fingers into claws and raked across Roarke's chest. Quick reflexes saved him from the worst of the damages, though blood welled along the shallow cuts. Nostrils flared, Adrian pressed his advantage.

A beam of sunlight fell across his arm. He hissed with pain, yanking into the scant shadows, and lost the advantage. Roarke swept his feet out from underneath him, dropping the vampire to the floor. Teeth bared, Roarke drew down on the vamp, and Lilah's gut twisted as she realized he intended to tear out Adrian's throat. Blood loss killed vamps.

"Roarke." Lilah yelled. She pulled away from the haze of desire and launched herself at the two men. Grabbing his shoulders, she fought to pull him off of Adrian. "Roary. No! Not like this."

Roarke stilled.

Adrian looked over Roarke's shoulder at her, and her eyes met his. The dark knowledge that he hated being her blood-drinking lap dog shone.

"I'm sorry," she mouthed, not quite ready to admit to either one of them that she needed—wanted—his protection. Not when this alpha male enticed her wolf almost beyond rational thought.

Roarke focused on Adrian. Nostrils flared, pupils dilated, Lilah recognized the signs of an imminent attack. Right now, he took the vamp's measure determining how much trouble he was worth.

The flat of her hand connected with Roarke's cheek. Her palm stung, fingers lingering against his stubbled chin.

Roarke snagged her wrist. He pulled her against him, one hand wrapping around her waist to flatten against her ass. Every inch of her body collided with his hard, muscled one, and from her breasts crushed against his chest to the ridge of his erection pressing into her stomach, he proved more than enough wolf to be her alpha.

Her breath whooshed from her lungs. His scent filled her, penetrated her pores surrounding her and she wanted to roll in it like a dog with new snow.

A disgusted sound tore itself from Roarke's throat. He sniffed audibly. "You smell like him. You've fucked him, and he's all over you."

Lilah lifted her chin, hoping like hell Adrian stayed on the ground. This was her battle, a battle between an alpha male and his bitch, except she hadn't let him take her yet. On one hand the young fantasies she harbored flared to life with the knowledge she gained with maturity, the knowledge of how a woman uses her body to pleasure her partner and herself. To feel the steel length of his cock filling her, thrusting long and deep had her pussy creaming and her nipples hardening against his chest. God, she wanted him.

"I can fuck whoever I want to fuck." She threw the syllables at him, daring him with her gaze and the rise and fall of her breasts to try and overpower her.

"Not anymore."

"The days you could tell me what to do are long over, Roarke Connelly. It's been years since I've been in the Northwoods, and you never followed my scent." There, let him chew on that for a while. She pitched her voice low enough to remind him not only of the men she killed and the danger she faced, but also of the sex he could have had with her. If only he'd followed her. If only their lives had been different.

"It disgusts me that you smell like him."

"Did I ask your permission?"

Roarke's fingers loosened their hold on her wrist. He kept his hand clamped over her ass, her pelvis in close contact with him.

"Let go of me. I'm not a child."

"No," he said with a squeeze of her buttock, "you're not." His hands fell to his sides, and yet, she remained pressed against him. Lips parted, she willed her body to move away to put some space between them. Her tongue brushed against her lower lip, and Roarke groaned.

"Roarke, we can't do this." Finally, as if weights held her limbs down she stepped back. It might have been one step, but it was enough to put space between them. She glanced down his chest, to the jeans cupping his lean hips and the impressive bulge of his cock against his fly. Her mouth watered, and she pulled her attention to Adrian.

She bent over and offered him her arm. The vampire scowled and shook it off. In a fluid motion he stood, then backed away into the encroaching darkness from the bedroom. The snarl he gave her spoke eloquently about his thoughts on the situation.

"We can't do this. Not like this and not right now. I think you should leave, Roarke." Lilah shook her head and started to circle Roarke.

Adrian stopped at her words. He turned and looked at her, the inquiring gaze making her wonder if he half expected her to leave with the werewolf.

Lilah swallowed hard. She'd have to deal with that later. Right now, she needed to get Roarke away from her. He can take the Dark Moon Dogs, his newfound skills in hiding bodies, and his sexy as sin body and leave. "Now, Roarke. I need you to leave now."

"No." He crossed his arms over his chest and stepped forward.

"Yes." Lilah pointed to the door. "Get out. I don't want you here. I don't need you here. So go back to the Northwoods and leave me the hell alone." She trembled in her boots and hated herself for the weakness. Things had been fine for a vampire and a werewolf-vampire freak. Which in reality wasn't that fine at all, but at least she knew where she stood. Roarke lent too much ambiguity to the situation, though certainly not to her hormones.

Lilah focused on Adrian, who saw himself as her personal protector. Watching him, noticing the way his gaze flicked between her and Roarke, and then back again, made her wonder how she had screwed things up so badly with him. Trust. It all came down to trust. And right now, she trusted Adrian who'd stood by her side a lot more than a sexy man whom she had harbored fantasies about since becoming a teenager. Lilah expelled a pent-up breath.

"I'm not going anywhere," Roarke said.

"Yes, Roarke, you are. I want you out of here. Go home, Roarke. Just...go home." Lilah turned away.

"You're not human anymore, Lilah."

Her eyes widened. Her wolf. Her vampire. She struggled to keep them both hidden from him, though how with his lupine sense of scent she thought she'd manage, she didn't know. "No," she admitted. "I'm not."

"You're a bitch. My bitch."

Adrian stepped forward.

"No, I'm not." She held out her hand to stop him. "I'm a wolf, but I'm a hell of a lot more, too. I think you'd better leave." Her fangs ached to descend. Parting her lips, she let them flex, just a little, enough so she felt the press of sharp tips against her lip, before they retracted.

"You don't know what you're fighting. The Dark Moon Dogs have nearly torn up the Northwoods pack. And they've done it other places. Not satisfied with the Luna Guard or the way pack hierarchy works, they're dismantling our world, pack by pack, and they've decided to start in on the Northwoods. If you have them after you, then they won't stop until you're dead. Because you can't kill them all. No one can." Roarke breathed deeply, and Lilah suspected he tried to get a good lungful of her scent.

Not backing down, she remained rooted in place. "So why show up now? I've been hunted for months...years. Hell, I've kind of lost count. The calendar doesn't mean much when you don't have a place to hang it."

"I'm here because it's time I did what I should have done a long time ago."

Lilah laughed. The sound burst from her throat with the sound of a gunshot, startling them all. Nearly bent in double, she tried to still the guffaws rising inside her and failed. "Damn, that sounds like a horrible line from a movie. What should you have done a long time ago? Because if it's to protect me, you missed your chance. And if it's to fuck me, well no one asked if I wanted you to. Don't you have plenty of Northwoods bitches lining up to be your mate?"

"The pack doesn't know I'm here. This isn't pack business. And why is the vampire still listening in on the conversation?" He glanced over his shoulder.

"Because whatever affects me affects him. You don't have anything to hide do you?" With one hand she reached up and rubbed the back of her neck. Tension knotted her muscles. Her bones ached. Her head pounded from the fight, Roarke's arrival, then keeping the men from tearing out each other's throats. Even now, she saw the way Roarke's glance slipped to Adrian, and the away Adrian kept his weight balanced, as if he expected to attack at any moment.

Suddenly, Adrian stood behind her. His big hands curled into her shoulders. Working his thumbs into her muscles, he eased her stiff muscles. He stepped closer to her, so close the thick rod of his cock pressed against her, and she licked her lips. Sex, violence, it all twined in the werewolf-vampire world in which she lived.

~* * *~

Lilah's strength drew him to her like a magnet. Beneath her cool exterior, he smelled her wolf's need to mate with Roarke. And he supposed he understood it. After all, protecting her from Mikhail's mistake had brought them closer, and her lust for blood called to his. Still, watching this newcomer come in with no understanding of their situation, fighting for his own needs, it rankled.

"I think you should go back into the room where we can talk." Adrian pitched his voice low, restraining the need to invoke the bloodlust and take out his fury on anyone who dared touch his woman. He closed his hands around her shoulders, felt Lilah lean into him, and his dick throbbed. "I don't think you understand what we're doing here."

"And I don't think you understand why I'm here," Roarke snapped.

Lilah remained silent. He appreciated her belief in his powers to force the alpha wolf to submission. Perhaps he should. Perhaps he should unleash the side of him he'd kept hidden for too long. Lilah wanted an alpha. She'd get it, and her wolf would just have to deal.

"Go!" Adrian ordered.

Roarke moved back a step.

Adrian snarled, revealing a hint of fang. "Keep going." Standing square, staring down the wolf in a show of dominance, he watched as Roarke moved back, step by step, until he passed beyond the doorway. A squeeze of Lilah's shoulders had her following with him pressed close behind. The FitzReal family hadn't survived centuries because they were weak. Just because he'd been around only for a few decades didn't mean he didn't know how to wield power.

He pointed to a chair and directed Roarke into it. A gentle shove sent Lilah back into her chair, and he remained standing. "I think it's time you listened to us," Adrian said. Though he spoke softly, his voice carried authority behind it, and he watched Lilah turn and look at him as if she'd never seen him before. And in reality, she hadn't. He'd let her lead, let her think she had the say in things, because he wanted to see how far she'd really go. But now, with this mutt invading their territory, it was time to take charge.

"You don't know—" Roarke started to speak.

"And you fucking don't know either. You barge in here as if you own the place, as if you were solely responsible for Lilah and everything that happens to her. Well, I've got a news flash for you, mutt. You don't know jack. You have no idea what we've been through, or why we've been through it. So before you start pissing on another man's turf, you ought to sit down, shut up, and listen. All right?" As Adrian spoke, fury built inside him. Fear for Lilah's safety, for the fact that Adrian might jeopardize it, exploded. He aimed the wrath directly at the werewolf. "Hell, for all we know, you brought the Dark Moon Dogs down on Lilah so you could claim savior."

"But I wouldn't."

Adrian shook his head. "And how in the hell are we supposed to know that?" He stared at Roarke, daring him to speak. "That's right. We wouldn't." For once, Lilah remained quiet, too. His fingers curled with the need to touch her, to see what she thought about his stepping up and taking charge. He had no doubt she liked it. The smell of wet pussy filled the air, and a glance down showed her nipples hardened into tiny points.

Roarke swallowed hard. "So why are you here? What do you know that I don't?"

Adrian laughed. It bubbled up from deep inside him, a joyous stream of mirth that finally, he had something on the mutt. "A whole hell of a lot, wolf boy." Adrian replied when his chuckles subsided.

Lilah frowned. He loved her like that, the full, pouty lower lip he longed to nip and suck on until she curled her fingers into his shoulders and wrapped her thighs around his hips. With her nipples poking at him like twin headlights, and the smell of her arousal in the air, to all five senses, she was the most beautiful woman he'd ever seen.

"So, are you going to tell him or shall I?" Adrian asked her.

Lilah licked her lips. She glanced from Roarke to Adrian and back again. "I don't know if we should. What right does he have to know?"

Adrian shrugged. "Well, if you want him to hang around, he has to know. If it were up to me, I'd kick his furry ass to the door and not look back. But something tells me that isn't going to work. Not with your beasts."

"Beasts?" Roarke leaned forward. "Lilah, what is it?"

Adrian waited. Telling Roarke about her werewolf side, and how she acquired it, belonged to her. If she didn't want to tell him, then he had to leave. But once he knew, as the alpha of the Northwoods pack, he'd have to stay, because in truth she'd be a Northwoods bitch and subject to his rule. He doubted Lilah wanted that, even as sexual tension sparked between them. He'd let her make the decision.

"You're right. I'm not human. I'm a vampire and a werewolf." Lilah spoke softly. She rested her hands between her spread knees, gripping the edge of the chair so hard he though she might dig splinters under her nails.

"How in the hell did that happen? And where did it happen? Shit. That complicates things doesn't it?" Roarke exhaled.

Lilah glanced up at Adrian, and he nodded just enough to let her know that it was her tale to tell. "Which one? The werewolf or the vampire? Because the vampire came first," she said.

Roarke hissed and lunged off the chair.

Lilah and Adrian reached for him at the same time. With his longer reach, Adrian caught Roarke, shoving him back down in his seat.

"I didn't do it. My brother did and that's why I'm here. To protect her. My younger brother, Mikhail, turned Lilah."

"And the bastard's dead, I hope."

Lilah shook her head. "No, I wouldn't let Adrian kill him. I was young and stupid. I didn't know what I was getting into. He turned me yes, but it wasn't completely against my will." She closed her eyes and breathed deeply.

Pain radiated from her, a pain Adrian's family helped to cause, and it twisted a knife in his gut every time he saw it.

Roarke's eyes widened. He shook his head. "You had to know what that would do to your relationship with the wolves. Why, Lilah? Why?"

She glared at him like one wolf staring down another. "Because I wasn't getting what I needed from the Northwoods pack." After a long, tense silent moment, she looked away.

Pride filled Adrian. His woman, his vampire, standing up to this alpha wolf. He smiled, though his gut twisted to think of what his brother had done to her.

"And the wolf? How'd you become a werewolf?" Roarke asked softly.

"I was attacked. I'd gone back to Northwoods territory. The Dark Moon Dogs attacked me and bit me. They knew I was a vampire. They smelled it on me, and I guess it convinced me I wasn't welcome there anymore. Especially when you didn't show up." She said the last quietly, as if she'd been afraid to admit it out loud.

Adrian rested his hands on her shoulders, the only comforting presence he could give in front of Roarke. He refused to give up his higher position by kneeling, but oh, how he ached to pull Lilah to her feet, wrap his arms around her, and hold her. He'd known in the back of his mind how much it'd hurt her. He'd felt her anger and her rage, yet until she admitted it out loud, he never guessed how much being forced from her home territory ached. And he despised his brother even more for making her face this alone.

"Fuck," Roarke snapped. "I didn't know." He moved to kneel before her, reaching for her.

Lilah flinched away.

His hands tightened, and she leaned ever so slightly into his strength. A beginning, one on which he hoped to build. "I think she's said enough," Adrian said, his gaze pushing Roarke back into his chair. "Now you know. The question is, what are you going to do about it?"

"Whatever Lilah wants me to do." Roarke dragged his fingers through his hair. He rose to his feet and paced in front of the chairs. Turning, he looked at Lilah, then to Adrian. "Look, the Dark Moon Dogs are ripping up not just my territory, but also that of other packs. I came here because I found out about Lilah and I tracked them here. I want to stay. It's not good for the Northwoods, and it's probably not sane for me, but I want to step up and do what I should have done before. If Lilah will have me."

Adrian held his breath, waiting for her response. He opened his mouth to order Roarke to leave. They'd lasted this long without the werewolf's interference. But the answer lay with Lilah. Roarke belonged to her past. Thinking of her lusting after another man, and a mutt at that, had his lip curling to reveal his fang. To think she wanted him, longed to feel his cock buried deep inside her had fury filling him. His cock hardened, hands threatening to squeeze on her shoulders. She belonged to him. Even now, he smelled their mingled scents on her skin, smelled the heat of her wet cunt, and knew she screamed for him. Only for him.

"If you want to stay, I won't stop you," Lilah answered. "But you sure as hell didn't pick a good time to show up."

Roarke stopped pacing. "Thank you. I'll go work on the door. I can work around sunshine better than he can." He stopped in front of Lilah with a long, lingering look at her, turned and left the room.

Adrian watched him go. He released his hold on Lilah long enough to walk around her. Then kneeling beside her, he pulled her into his arms. She went willingly, folding her lush curves against him. His dick hardened, his hands lingering on her back, sliding down to cup her ass. "You went back home for him."

Against his chest, she nodded. "I did, and now he came here for me." She sighed heavily and burrowed into his warmth. Her hands wrapped around his waist, fingers caressing a trail along his lower back. "I didn't ask him to come here. I didn't ask for this."

Adrian nuzzled her hair, wishing he could simply enfold her in his arms and make her confusion go away. "But you asked him to stay." Slowly, he stepped back, his hands still cupping her waist. "Why, Lilah? Why did you ask him to stay?"

Her eyelids fluttered closed, obscuring her violet eyes. Her lips parted, and he focused on the plump, lower one thinking what it would be like to capture in his mouth and suckle. "Because my wolf needs him."

She shook her head and wrenched away from his grasp. Wrapping her arms around herself, she went to the doorway and peered into the living room. Beyond her, he heard the sounds of booted feet against the wooden floor, the rustle of denim and the muttered curses of a pissed off wolf.

Drawn to her, Adrian walked up behind her. He reached out to touch her and hesitated. Deep inside, a possessive instinct had him curling his fingers against her shoulder and pulling her back against his body. He wrapped his other arm around her stomach, hauling her to him so the throbbing ridge of his cock nestled against her soft flesh.

"What is he to you? Do you love him?" He snarled out the words, half-afraid to think of Lilah loving someone else, anyone else but him.

"I thought I did at one time," she whispered.

"And now?" he pressed, needing to know the truth. "Do you love him now?"

"I don't know."

Her words cut him like a knife. "If you think I'm going to turn you over to the wolf, then you're mistaken." He pressed his lips to her neck and scraped her with his fangs.

She shuddered against him.

He thrust his hips into her, letting her feel his thick cock. "I'm not going to let you go that easily." He nipped her again, and then laved the red marks with his tongue.

She moaned, and he watched as Roarke stopped and looked back at them, the man's face darkening like a thundercloud.

Chapter Five

A different kind of hunger rode Lilah as she stood in the kitchen. With Adrian resting in the bedroom in preparation for taking a night watch, and Roarke working in the living room, she had the kitchen to herself. She stifled a yawn. Curling up beside Adrian and sleeping the early evening away sounded heavenly, except she wouldn't leave Roarke alone. Not until she fully discerned why he was here. Childhood adoration and young adult crushes hoped he'd returned for her. The practical adult part of her, the part that helped her to stay alive knew he hadn't. And it stung.

His talk of the Dark Moon Dogs resurfaced memories she'd thought long dead and buried. The dark alley, shadows where she swore there were none, the hiss of pain as fang and claw bit into her leg, falling to the ground, and then nothing but fire as the lycanthrope virus spread through her veins. She reached for the counter. The smell of bacon rising from the pan became the scent of charred, burnt flesh. Instead of the hiss of spattering grease, she heard the swiftly indrawn breaths of her attackers. Her fingers curled around the counter, nails biting into Formica.

On the stove, the pot of water boiled. The rolling bubbles churned like the blood in her veins, the vampire and lycanthrope viruses battling one another. Her fangs dropped from her gums, nails lengthened into claws. Fight. Survive.

"Lilah!" Adrian's voice cut through the memories and brought her back to the here and now.

Whirling around, she faced him standing in the doorway, his arms crossed over his chest, his jeans low on his hips. The indolent male pose sent a flash of heat to her pussy.

"You okay?" Adrian asked.

Lilah nodded. "Yeah. Dinner is almost ready." She dropped one of the plastic containers taken from a local butcher shop into the pan, a makeshift double boiler, and then added a second one for her. Expertly, she flipped the bacon and cracked open a couple of eggs.

"Feeding the wolf?"

"He has a name. And yes, I am. Figured it was the least I could do for his work in the living room. Besides, I'm hungry." Lilah insisted.

"And it's nice to cook for two." Adrian strolled forward. He grabbed a chipped mug from the cupboard over her head and stood by the stove, waiting for the blood to heat through.

Usually she hated it when he did that, but tonight his presence calmed her. He reached over her and handed her two plates. She quickly dished up the food, then grabbed a glass and half filled it with lemon-lime soda. Grabbing her container of blood from the pan, she poured it into the glass, wrinkling her nose as it mingled with the soda.

"Still watering it down?"

She nodded and turned away, but not before she caught the flash of sadness in his eyes. "Would you mind telling Roarke—"

The thump of boots against the wooden floor stopped her train of thought. She looked up to see him standing in the doorway, a tool belt that he'd gotten on a quick run to the hardware store, slung low on his hips. Her heart stuttered, and she looked from Adrian to him, then back again.

"Dinner's ready," she said, grabbing her plate and hurrying away from the stove. Adrian stepped back, and Roarke grabbed his meal, looking askance at Lilah's carbonated cup of blood.

"You drink it like that?" Roarke looked dubious.

Adrian chuckled. "That's exactly what I keep asking her."

For a second, the two men shared a moment of companionable humor. Lilah watched them, not quite comfortable with the idea of Adrian and Roarke being friendly. Her fork clattered on her plate, and she realized her hands shook. Without a table, she had nowhere to set her plate except the counter. She gripped it with both hand.

"The way I take my blood is none of your business." She exhaled and watched as Adrian backed away from the stove.

Roarke looked around as if searching for a dining room table.

"Pull up some floor. We usually eat in the living room." She wondered if the bare room in the front of the house could even be called a living room. Returning there brought up memories of her in Adrian's lap, begging him to lick her, to fuck her. Heat flushed her body. Her cheeks reddened. Leaving the glass on the counter, she turned and walked away.

Behind her, Roarke chuckled. "She always has been a feisty little thing." His words followed her out of the kitchen. Some gratitude she received for cooking for him.

Heavy footsteps followed her. Compared to them, her heart beat double time, her breath caught in her throat. Two men under one roof—her roof. Her pussy danced with the thought. Clenched and released, her juices dampening her panties. She smelled her arousal and knew with their sensitive vampire and lycanthrope senses of smell, the men could too. Tonight it'd be just her and them. She sank to the floor, crossed her legs and balanced her plate on them. One thing at a time, and first, she needed to eat. She'd figure out the rest as it came. Though she feared before the night was over, she'd be the one coming over and over again. She didn't know whether to rejoice or worry.

She gulped down one egg before realizing the men stared at her as if she were a strange creature. Resting her fork on the edge of her plate, she noticed Adrian's untouched mug of congealing blood and Adrian's still full plate.

"What is it?" She asked, making a show of picking up her fork and cutting off a piece of egg. She brought it to her mouth. Slowly wrapping her lips around the morsel, she pulled it from the fork and chewed thoughtfully.

Both men watched her, lips parted, eyes fixed on her mouth.

Oh hell. She swallowed past the sudden lump in her throat. "This is about me. More specifically sex with me, isn't it?" She set her plate on the floor and laid her fork on it. "Well if neither one of you are going to eat until we get this figured out, then speak."

Adrian looked at Roarke, then to her. "He's not sleeping in our bedroom."

"I didn't ask to. Though you will be awake during night watch." Roarke snapped. He grabbed a piece of bacon and chewed it.

Lilah watched his jaw work, the up and down, back and forth motion she'd never paid any thought to until this evening. Now, she wondered how his lips would feel at her cunt, his tongue circling her clit or spearing her channel. Her nipples hardened with the mental image of his head at her breast, his blonde highlights against her pale skin.

Adrian wrapped his fist around the mug of blood and brought it to his lips, drinking it down in several long swallows. He wiped his bloody lips with the back of his hand and slammed the mug on the floor.

“He’s not sleeping in *our* bed,” he repeated. “In fact, I think you should take watch with me.” Adrian’s angry words pulled her attention away from Roarke as he picked up a second piece of bacon.

Lilah quirked her lips at Adrian’s emphasis on calling it their bed. “Did I ask him to?”

Adrian snarled at her question.

“Look, I know this isn’t easy for any of us, including me. But if we could tone down the macho grunting for a moment and have a real conversation about sleeping arrangements, watches, whatever, I think it’ll work out much better.” Aware her eggs cooled, she ate another piece, thankful at least that the men weren’t staring at her like a plump, juicy hare. She finished off the last egg and nibbled on a piece of bacon. “Let’s look at the facts. There’s one bed and three of us. If we can be adults for a moment, I think we can work something out. We have to take watches, even if they’re cursory. Adrian can’t be out in the sunlight. Roarke, you can.” She neglected to mention one of the benefits of her lycanthropy was that she, too, could be out in sunlight. She paused to watch both men.

Adrian stared at Roarke, contempt in his gaze.

Roarke stared at her with a predatory glint in his eyes.

Her wolf leapt up in challenge, the vamp edging toward Adrian. “And I will be on watch tonight. Roarke, you can have the bed,” she said after long moments.

“But it’s our bed!”

Lilah bolted to her feet. “It’s a bed, Adrian. Yeah, it’s ours, since we scavenged the frame and bought the mattress and bedding. But being nice and offering the man who fixed our door somewhere to sleep besides the floor, doesn’t mean I’m offering to fuck him.” As soon as the words left her mouth, she realized she’d said the wrong thing.

Adrian’s eyes darkened, his fangs exposed. He sidled closer to her, his gaze never leaving Roarke.

The wolf stepped forward. “You haven’t offered yet,” he growled.

Lilah shivered. Heat coursed through her veins. The promise in his husky words had her rethinking her acceptance of night watch tonight with Adrian. Licking her lips, she looked from the wolf to the vampire and back again.

“I haven’t offered,” she said, though every cell in her body screamed for him to take her.

Adrian stiffened, but made no further move toward Roarke. "Let him sleep in our bed. I hear a werewolf's sense of smell is keener than a vamp's. Let him smell us there, smell the fact that we had sex, and know that he can't have you."

Lilah stepped forward, her palm flattened on Adrian's chest. "Look, buddy, I will say who can and cannot have me." The idea of two men fighting over her turned her panties wet and made her revel in their masculine show of power. Her inner bitch wriggled and wagged her tail, daring the men to chase her, to see who became alpha. "And if need be, I'll sleep in the bed with no one, okay?" She stepped back, then bent and picked up her plate.

Roarke exhaled. "I'll behave myself if the vamp will."

Adrian nodded, though didn't give ground. "As long as you don't touch her, I'll be a perfect gentleman." He turned on his heel and strode away, his booted feet thudding against the floor.

Lilah watched him go and then turned to Roarke. "Thank you. I guess I never realized how possessive he really was." She smiled, took Roarke's empty plate, and picked up Adrian's mug on her way to the kitchen.

The domestic chores soothed her jangled nerves as she filled the chipped sink with water and scrubbed the dishes. Fatigue pulled at her. She needed at least a couple of hours sleep before watch tonight, in case there was a battle. Roarke's words echoed in her mind, and she couldn't help thinking what it would be like to have sex with him. *Or with him and Adrian.* Of course, the two men would rip out each other's throats before agreeing to share her, but for a moment, hands buried in the sudsy water, she allowed herself to dream. She had a feeling she'd have few enough of these idyllic moments in the coming days, and she knew she should grasp on to every one of them and never let go. And if the men didn't know what went on in her mind, so much the better.

~* * *~

The image of Lilah naked beneath the werewolf slammed into him with primal force. Her skin, so pale it was nearly translucent next to his tanned flesh. Her dark hair along his body. His cock plunging deep into Lilah's wet and clenching pussy. The mental picture tormented him with the fact that his woman was attracted to the mutt. He snarled.

She stood at the sink, the clink of dishes and the slosh of water the only sounds. Eyes half-closed, she moved as if on automatic pilot. A soft smile curved her lips. A deep inhalation brought with it the fragrance of her cream. She was hot, though for which one, or for both of them, Adrian couldn't tell. He strode forward and wrapped her in the steel vice of his arms. His incisors brushed along the vein in her neck, and she shuddered.

"You're mine. I took you in after my brother turned you. I taught you everything you needed to know. I saved you," he growled. He pinned her between his body and the counter. His erection nestled between her jeans-covered buttocks, and he rocked his hips against her, silently telling her the extent of his need.

"I know. This isn't easy for me." Her breathy whisper made his cock twitch with the need to be inside her.

"Well, it's hard for me." He slid his right hand around her hip to flatten it against her stomach. A flick of his wrist opened the button on her jeans, and the zipper slid down like a knife through butter. He caressed the satin of her panties, feeling her heat and her cream through the flimsy fabric. With his left hand, he tugged her jeans down and they swished to the floor, pooling around her legs. He pushed aside the thin barrier of material and stroked her labia.

"Do I do this to you? Or is it the mutt? Does the thought of both of us taking you, fucking you, turn you on this much?" Adrian asked.

"Yes," Lilah moaned. She relaxed against him. Her panting breaths filled the air.

Adrian glanced toward the empty doorway and saw no one. Thinking about Roarke out there in the house, listening to them, smelling them, had him ripping her panties away. Cloth tore, and he let them flutter to the floor. She spread her legs, and he gathered her cream on his fingers. Behind the fly of his jeans, his cock pounded.

He leaned forward, tucking her into the curve of his body. His arm tightened around her waist. Deep in his soul, fear raised its ugly head. Losing Lilah to the mutt would be like losing a part of his body. Yet, he doubted she knew that, doubted she fathomed the depth of his need for her. When his brother had told him what he'd done and he'd gone to the rundown basement apartment where he'd found her...Adrian squeezed his eyes closed. He buried his face in Lilah's lustrous mane of dark hair and inhaled her scent into his lungs. His fingers parted her slick labia and he caressed the swollen bud of her clit.

She whimpered and shuddered in his arms. He made her cream. He made her hot. And he'd make her come. And when she did, he wanted it to be with his name on her lips and his cock in her body. Rotating his hand, he pressed his palm against her clit and toyed with the entrance to her channel with two fingers.

"Yeah, baby, that's it," he whispered in her ear. He thrust his hand beneath her shirt and cupped the globe of one breast. Though her bra, her diamond-hard nipple pressed into his hand. Her tiny mewling cries, stifled so as not to let Roarke hear, only challenged him to make her scream.

He slid his hands away to unbutton his jeans and shove them from his hips. He lifted her, sliding his cock along her slick nether lips. Now wasn't the time for finesse, for making love or extended foreplay. His need to dominate her burned like the sun. And if he was going to lose her to the mutt, he wanted her to know exactly what she walked away from.

His cockhead nestled against her entrance, the promise of her walls slick and tight. A single pump of his hips sheathed him balls-deep inside her. Damn, she was so hot, so tight around him he thought he'd blow right there. A groan of pleasure rumbled through his chest. He listened, in the living room, heard the rustling of someone laying out a bedroll and thought of Roarke out there, hard and horny and knowing he wasn't going to get any of this. Adrian grinned savagely.

He pulled out and teased her opening with the head of his cock. Pinching her nipples, he scraped his incisors across her neck, until she titled her head and offered herself to him. Her gasps and cries filled his ear, a passionate tempest that could only grow louder. This was the woman he'd saved, strong, vulnerable, and sexy as hell. He plunged his cock into her again and her cries grew louder.

Each thrust brought both of them closer to the brink. She tilted her hips, legs spread, letting him support her against the counter. The jeans tangled around their legs made deep penetration difficult, but he tried. He wanted to crawl inside her and never leave. Her muscles tightened around him, and he toyed with her clit.

He thrust into her, balls swinging against her, with a triumphant growl.

"Oh God, Adrian! Harder!" Lilah said, all pretenses at trying to be quiet lost.

Yeah. He didn't voice the words, instead focused on the wet slap of flesh against flesh, the way her cunt fluttered along his length, and the way his dick twitched to get inside her. His head hit deep inside her, and from the way she ground against him, he knew she was close.

He pulled back the hood of her clitoris and rubbed his finger against the engorged bud.

Lilah erupted. Her cream flooded the length of his cock. Around his shaft, her muscles fluttered, convulsed, and she shuddered in his arms. Head thrown back, her tender, pale skin against his incisors, he did the only thing he could. He bit her.

His fangs slid effortlessly through her skin, sinking into the vein beneath. Blood, hot and rich with adrenaline and endorphins, flooded his mouth. He swallowed the coppery stream, then pulled his lips away and licked the wound. On the counter, dishes and pans rattled as he fucked her against the unyielding surface. And then, Lilah screamed again as she came, and he saw nothing but red haze of passion and blood. Over and over again he plunged into her body as if he couldn't get enough, and as his seed burst forth from his sacs, he knew he probably never would.

~* * *~

Roarke shifted on his bedroll, his cock harder than the floor beneath him as he listened to Adrian and Lilah fuck in the kitchen. The big bed sat next to him, empty and unused, redolent with the scent of sex. It permeated the air, seeped into his pores, and he groaned. Not for the first time, he regretted seeking out Lilah. Yet, with the pressure to his pack from the Dark Moon Dogs and the rumors he'd heard regarding her, he knew he had to. She wrapped herself around his soul and refused to let go.

He closed his fingers around his turgid length and stroked base to tip, imagining the wet heat of Lilah's cunt.

The tang of blood filled the air.

Roarke snarled. Damn vamps, always going around biting everyone. And that fucker had bit Lilah. From the sounds she made, she enjoyed it, sounded as if she writhed against Adrian with the need to get him inside her any way she could. His lips twisted into a frown, not quite able to reconcile the sweet young girl he'd known with the sexual creature in the other room. He squeezed and rubbed his thumb over his head, using his pre-cum to lubricate his strokes.

Oh yeah, instead of the vamp, it'd be him behind her. He'd have her on all fours, his cock buried deep inside her, his chest covering her, protecting her. She'd offer herself to him like a bitch in heat, and like the alpha male he was, he'd take her.

He imagined the weight of her breasts filling his palms, the generous globes swinging with each thrust of his hips. He'd look over her body, and yeah, the vamp would be watching, eyes dark with passion, a tent in his pants, and knowing he could do nothing but watch. He imagined covering her with his seed, his scent, marking her like his own personal sexual territory.

His back bowed off the sleeping bag. In the kitchen, Lilah's moans and whimpers grew louder and more demanding. Adrian's groans and heavy breathing punctuated her vocalizations, and it took all his willpower not to switch and howl out his frustration at the moon. Instead, he tightened his fingers around the base of his penis, holding back the release that had his balls tightening and a tingling starting in his lower back.

When Adrian came, he'd come too, and then, in his world, it'd be his cock pumping seed into Lilah, not the vamp's. A snarl curled his lips. Lilah's cunt had to be a hot vice of pleasure, and from the sounds of flesh against flesh, she liked it rough. The fingers of his left hand curled into the floor, the change starting. Nails lengthened. He scored the floor with a swipe of his hand. Slivers dug into his flesh and reminded him that'd be another thing he'd have to fix.

And then, her voice a high pitched wail, Lilah came again. Adrian followed, his triumphant shout grating against Roarke's nerves.

Roarke released his tight grip on his cock and stroked once, twice more. His pleasured groan echoed in the living room as his cock twitched and seed pumped over his fingers. The slick evidence of Lilah's affect on him covered his hand, his stomach, even dripped onto the bag next to him. Good, let them smell him in their bedroom. Let Adrian remember that Roarke wanted the woman he fucked.

Roarke rolled onto his side, facing the door and tucked his cock inside his boxers. He zipped, but didn't button his jeans. He slept on top of the sleeping bag, too hot to crawl inside. Shuffling and muted voices sounded, sleepy with sexual satisfaction. Footsteps echoed, and belatedly, Roarke realized they entered the bedroom.

Every muscle in his body went rigid. Did the vamp think to flaunt his possession of Lilah in front of him? They stood in the doorway, Adrian holding her. Lilah's legs wrapped around his waist, her wet pussy pressed intimately against him, her breasts crushed against his chest. She had her arms around his shoulder, her head resting against his cool skin, and the thought of Lilah letting herself that close to a dead man turned his stomach.

Adrian didn't stop. Instead, he strode to the bed and laid Lilah down. Moments later, he settled himself between her thighs, and Roarke forced himself not to look. Not when he heard the wet sucking of lips against nipple, not when Lilah moaned, "more." He thought about clearing his throat, reminding them of his presence. Werewolves treated nudity and sex as natural, part of the beast living inside them. He knew nothing of vampires, but from the way Adrian rutted with him in the room, Roarke suspected that to be true of them as well. He frowned.

"I want to bite you," Lilah moaned.

"Do it." Adrian's rough growl filled the air.

The coppery aroma of blood burst into the room. Roarke's stomach dropped. Bile filled his throat. On the bed lay a woman he didn't know, and the thought scared him. What had Lilah become? What had the vampire done to her? And why did he still want her?

Chapter Six

Lilah arched into Adrian. Curling her fingers around his buttocks, she dug half-moon furrows into his skin. His cock slid against her labia, teasing her, tormenting her. She buried her face against his chest and her fangs ached to sink into his skin as he sank into her body. Adrian's rough permission for her to bite him had her pressing the tips of her incisors against his skin. And then slowly, she bit him.

His hot blood filled her mouth, bursting across her taste buds and tightening her channel around his cock. Drawing air into her lungs, she smelled Roarke's unique essence. She breathed deeply, wanting him in her body as much as Adrian. The thought shocked her into releasing Adrian's chest with a mewled cry. Belatedly she remembered to lick the wound and then turned to stare at the man lying on the floor.

His back was to her. In the dim light—her vampire soared as she felt the sun slip beneath the horizon—she stared at the wolf's bare back. Muscles and sinew bronzed from hard work in the sun, a sun Adrian could never see, caught her gaze. Her breath caught in her throat. She closed her eyes in an attempt to focus on the man on top of her, the man whose teeth and lips grazed her neck and shoulder.

Adrian changed his angle, the head of his cock brushing against her G-spot with each thrust. Her body trembled on the edge of orgasm. Thinking of Roarke on the floor, listening to her, watching her have sex with Adrian, had her putting on a show. The idea that she was on display turned her on. Arching her back, she rubbed the tips of her nipples against Adrian's chest.

"Yes! Harder! Deeper!" she cried out, not caring if she sounded like the female lead in a porn flick.

Adrian cupped her ass and hauled her against him. "Yeah, baby," he growled. Flesh slapped against flesh with wet sounds.

She felt trapped in her mind, watching herself fuck Adrian, but not taking a part in it. Detached in her mind, she went through the motions, her body already spent. What interested her more than the man on top of her was the one on the floor. Did he lay there, his fist wrapped around his cock, pumping in time with the rhythmic bouncing of the bedsprings? What did he think? Did he imagine himself there inside her? Questions swirled in her mind.

"Lilah," Adrian's moan cut straight to her core. It brought her back to the pleasure, reminded her of the vampire on top of her, all he'd done for her, and all he continued to do for her. Squeezing her eyes closed against the sting of tears, she wrapped her arms around him and pulled him even closer.

"Yes," she breathed. "Yes." Lilah lost herself to the sensations. She pressed her lips to Adrian's throat, his cheek, his chin. She tasted the salt on his skin, his scent surrounding her pushed her closer to the edge. She pushed Roarke from her mind, never able to forget about him completely. Taking Adrian inside her body meant something to her. Not just the meaningless fucking, yet, she didn't know what it was. And frankly, right now, she didn't care.

Deep inside, her muscles contracted, holding him tight. She cried out, her release washing over her. It roared through her veins, crashed against her like the tidal waves across the shore, and let it wash her clean. Tears leaked from her close eyelids. Above her, Adrian stiffened. His fingers dug into her buttocks, his cock pounded deep inside her. He roared as he came. Hot jets of seed bathed her insides, and she clenched her muscles to hold him deep. Adrian slumped onto her.

Lilah strained to hear anything above her own panting breaths. No sound came from the floor.

Adrian rolled to the side, taking her with him. His leg slung across hers, holding her to the bed. He buried her face against his chest, where she hoped her tears wound mingle with his sweat.

Tears? She never cried during or after sex. That was for emotional saps that had far more to give than she ever had. She dashed them away under the guise of caressing his skin and swallowed hard. Still no noise from the floor.

Lilah drew a shaky breath. She snuggled closer, masking her churning thoughts with forced intimacy. Damn it, she couldn't deal with this right now. Not with her life in danger. Not when she struggled to just stay alive and deal day by day. The vampire next to her worked to keep her alive. And Roarke's arrival brought out something primal in him, something she'd never seen before, and frankly she liked it. A lot.

Adrian's hand flattened on her back. He stroked, shoulder blades to waist, then back again, long soothing, sweeping strokes of his hand. Sleep tugged at her, brought by the hypnotic movement of his hand against her skin. She battled it. Staying awake pounded at her, a need she couldn't deny. And yet, in Adrian's arms, she drifted off, slowly, until he gently tucked her beneath the blankets and brushed his lips across her forehead as he slid out of the bed and dressed for watch. Sated from her sexual exertions and tired of constantly worrying about the two men in her life, Lilah drifted into sleep. With Adrian on watch, she'd be physically safe.

She feared more for the werewolf sleeping on the floor and what he'd do to her heart.

~* * *~

Like a swimmer reaching for the surface, Lilah struggled to wakefulness. She opened her eyes and rubbed the gritty feeling away. From the living room, light filtered into the bedroom. Next to her in the bed, Adrian's cold, near-dead form lay by her side, and she shivered. She hated waking up with a corpse, though usually she was long out of bed. Her body twinged, reminding her of her sexual gymnastics.

Steady footfalls pulled her from bed. In the living room, someone paced across the room, stopped, turned, and then paced through the same space. She tossed back the covers and sat up. Heedless of her nudity, or the fact she might be seen by the wolf in the living room, she swung her legs to the edge of the bed and stood. The dresser gave up a black bra, tank top, jeans, underwear, and her socks. She dressed in the monochromatic wardrobe and bent to lace up her boots.

She stepped to the threshold of the bedroom door and looked.

Roarke paced in the living room, the tool belt slung low around his hips. A t-shirt stretched across his broad chest, defining the muscles beneath. His jeans looked painted on, and his boots only made her more aware of his masculinity. He dragged his fingers through his hair and turned.

Roarke stopped. "Lilah, you're awake."

She nodded, then pulled the door closed. Though there wasn't any danger of sunlight hitting Adrian sleeping in the bed, and she knew he literally slept like the dead. Still, she didn't want to disturb him. "Yeah, I am."

"Sleep well?"

She listened for sarcasm and heard none. "Yeah," she answered with a grin, "I did." She stepped into the living room, noticing that more of the bullet holes looked freshly repaired. The scent of sawdust filled the air, and she realized he'd been sawing some pieces of lumber to fix the window.

"I've started repairs. There's some structural things I want to discuss with you. Some options on how to make your house more defensible, but nothing too major." Roarke motioned to the work he'd already made. "What do you think?" He focused his attention on her.

Lilah stared at the new light-colored wood replacing the broken pieces. A pile of used lumber sat in the corner. She glanced back at him and saw he hadn't moved.

"It's nice. Where'd you get all this stuff? And don't say your truck." She expelled a puff of air.

"I woke up before Adrian went to sleep and made a quick run to the lumberyard. Look, I know it's your house, but I think if a few changes are made it'll make things better. Bars on the window would prevent entry. A small foyer, walls to maybe break up the space."

Lilah shook her head. "Corners to hide behind. I don't like it. And I refuse to live in a jail. Bars on the window are out of the question."

"So you're going to keep repairing what's there, even as it's broken over and over again." Roarke drew his eyebrows together and frowned.

"If I have to." It's been broken before. I'm sure it'll be broken again." Lilah pressed her lips together aware that they probably weren't talking about the house anymore.

"That's kind of a fatalistic way to look at things."

"It's practical, Roarke. I'm fighting for my life. You're acting like you're fixing up the house so I can run a home and garden show. It needs to be fixed easily, and I like the open plan." She clenched her fingers into a fist and stared at him.

Roarke focused his attention on her. Lips parted his gaze touched her from head to toe, lingering on her breasts and hips. "Open, huh?" Heat filled his gaze.

"Yeah, open." Warmth rose in her cheeks, and she felt the telling flush creep over her skin. "So did you like lying by my bed last night? Did you like listening to me fuck Adrian, because I really want to know."

Roarke fisted his hand, opened it again, spreading his fingers, before drawing them into a fist once more. "Maybe. Did you like putting on a show? 'I want to bite you, Adrian. Harder! Deeper!'" His falsetto reminded her of her own words, and her flush deepened.

"Damn it," she growled. "It wasn't like that." Except it was, and she knew it. She'd arched her back, showing of her body like some busty blonde on an adult film. Hell, she was surprised she hadn't drawn Adrian down to the floor so she could have sex right next to him and knew that he couldn't touch her.

"Really?" Roarke stepped forward. He stopped inches from her.

His strength, his masculinity overwhelmed her. Lilah gulped. "You don't have to believe me. You can repair the house, but I want you to keep it the same as it was. I don't want anything changed."

"Sometimes things change, baby. Whether you want them to or not." He reached up and fondled a strand of her hair, drawing it through his fingers.

Lilah shook her head, yanking her hair from his grasp. "No! I need things to stay the same." She stepped back and wrapped her arms around herself, tried not to think about dreams she'd once had that he'd shattered so many years ago.

"Stay the same with Adrian. What is your relationship with him? Is he just your fuck buddy?" Roarke frowned. He glanced to the closed bedroom door, then back at Lilah.

Lilah bristled at Roarke's insinuation. "You mean am I using him just for sex?" She chortled. "Look at me Roarke. When have I ever used anyone?" If he thought so little of her, then he could just turn around and walk his sexy ass out her door.

"You haven't. I just don't get it. I don't think Adrian can protect you, and he's a vampire. A bloodsucker! So what's with your relationship with him? You can't tell me you love him."

"Our relationship is complicated, and not something I wish to discuss with you. And even if I did, it's none of your business," Lilah replied, aware she'd just answered Roarke's unspoken question.

"If I'm to keep you safe, I need to know everything." Roarke strode forward and grabbed her arm.

Heat flashed through her from his touch. She inhaled, drawing his scent into her lungs. Deep inside, her bitch wagged her tail playfully. The urge to run and see if he would follow had her tensing her muscles, ready to spring. Her breath caught in her throat. Erotic need filled his gaze as it dropped to the rise and fall of her breasts with each breath.

"I can keep myself safe, thank you very much," Lilah answered. She stepped back and yanked her arm from his tight grip. She'd been keeping herself alive before Adrian arrived, and she could do the same without Roarke as well. But oh how her wolf yearned for the strong alpha male to dominate her. She imagined them entwined, both in wolf form, his teeth tight on her shoulder, his cock hard and knotted inside her as they came. Adrian couldn't give her that. Hell, Adrian didn't even like her wolf. She licked her lips.

"So what is your relationship with Adrian? You don't love him. You are fucking him. And he's trying to be an alpha male to you, though I could be so much better. Tell me Lilah. You never used to consort with vampires. But you used to smell human, too."

That was before I became a vampire. She ran her tongue over her fangs, careful to keep her mouth closed. That he hadn't been able to tell exactly what she was buoyed her. She could deal with one preternatural community at the time. She shook her head.

"Things have changed," she said, aware of the irony in her words.

"But you don't want anything to change," Roarke whispered. He tracked her across the floor, his long strides following her until she backed against the wall. She reached for it, curling her fingers into the plaster and drywall so hard they gouged holes. Roarke stared at her fingers and the tiny rain of plaster dust her grip caused.

"Not any more than they already have," Lilah whispered. She followed his gaze to her fingers and snarled. Pulling them from the plaster, she stared at the dust under her fingernails.

"What did that bastard do to you? You told me that you were both vamp and were, but that's not possible. What did he do?" Roarke yelled. He leaned in, sniffing along the curve of her neck with an audible inhalation. Roarke punched the wall next to her head.

Lilah stared at his eyes, a direct challenge to his dominance. Her upper lip curled into a snarl. "Nothing. He did nothing."

"He damn well did something. Look at what you did. No human could have done that. I want the truth and I want it now!" Roarke bellowed.

"No!" Lilah screamed back. She pushed his chest.

Roarke stumbled backward. With a snarl, he lunged at her. Grabbing her shoulder, he forced her to the ground with a thump. Her knee hit the floor, rattling the boards. Roarke pushed her onto her side. He pinned her down, his grip firm enough to hold her in place, yet light enough that it wouldn't leave any bruises. He buried his face in the curve of her neck and nipped her.

Lilah shivered. Cream flooded her pussy and she gave a tiny whine of submission. Her bitch arched into the strong male above her, drawing his essence into her lungs. Her muscles clenched, channel slick and ready for his penetration. Feed and fuck, that's all it was with her wolf and her vampire, and she lived firmly entrenched in both worlds.

"Tell me! Tell me what that blood sucking asshole did to you. Things have changed, and they're never going back to the way they were," Roarke growled

That's exactly what she feared. "He didn't do anything. I was like this before I met Adrian. Let me up." She closed her eyes.

Roarke released her with his hand, his presence keeping her pinned to the floor like one of his subordinate wolves. "If I find out that the vampire did anything, I will kill him."

Roarke's words bust the dam that held her emotions back. Lilah shoved him off of her, surprise giving her the edge. Not caring if she revealed her preternatural abilities. This posturing was going to stop and it would stop now. She straddled him, dropping to her knees and holding his shoulders to the ground.

"You'll do nothing of the sort. Leave Adrian out of this," Lilah growled. She leaned forward and bit Roarke's neck. Her fangs lengthened, scraped his flesh, and beneath her, he shuddered.

He arched his hips, the thick ridge of his erection brushing against her cunt. Lilah bit back a moan. This wolf made her so hot she feared she'd combust. Her fingers curled into his pecs, his hand going to her hips. He brought her down onto him, thrusting against her denim-clad flesh.

Lilah stared at Roarke. With his eyes closed, pleasure filled his face. She'd never seen him like this, never seen him lost in ecstasy, and she wanted to see it again. She nipped his skin.

"Lilah!" Adrian's voice barked across the living room. "What the hell are you doing?"

She looked up, startled to hear his voice. Her hair tumbled to one side, and she imagined the kind of picture she must present to him, her body straddling his, Roarke looking as if he wanted to bury his cock deep inside her. She narrowed her eyes. Adrian shouldn't be awake. She didn't move, instead, she challenged Adrian with her gaze. "Trying to explain things to Roarke. He seems to think that this is all your fault."

She watched Adrian's eyes glow red and his fangs grow longer, she realized baiting him like that, especially with the sunlight slanting across the living room floor making it difficult for him to reach her, probably wasn't the smartest thing to do. She rolled off of Roarke and rose to her feet.

"The wolf can crawl back to whatever hole he came from. This is not my fault. If it's anyone's fault, it's the wolves. Hell, it's probably his fault for not protecting you." Adrian stepped forward and eyed the beams of light.

Lilah crossed the room to him. "Adrian, no." She turned to face Roarke who stared at them both. "Roarke, don't. It's not your fault, but it isn't Adrian's either."

"Lilah, get out of the way," Adrian ordered. He pointed to the bedroom behind him. "This is between me and the mutt."

"He's not a mutt. He's the alpha of the Northwoods Pack and I demand you treat him with some respect. Damn it, Adrian, you might be old vampire, but you know better than to antagonize a werewolf. Just because you guys don't get along, it doesn't make it right."

"Vampires and werewolves have never gotten along. And it is his fault that you're the way you are," Adrian sneered.

"And what is that, Adrian? Can you even say it? Can you even say what I am?" Lilah pressed her hands to her hips.

"What are you, Lilah?" Roarke's voice cut through the air.

She whirled to face him. "I already told you all you need to know."

"You can't tell me this vamp has nothing to do with it." Roarke bounded across the space separating them and stared from her to Adrian.

"No!" Adrian and Lilah spoke at the same time.

"Then how is this all my fault?" Roarke addressed his question to Adrian.

Lilah stepped to the side, out of the way between them, but close enough that she could intervene if things got out of hand.

Adrian glanced at her, and in his eyes, she saw he sought her permission before speaking. She shook her head, hoping he realized that she didn't want all her secrets told. Not yet, anyway. She expelled a harsh breath and waited.

"Whatever happened to Lilah happened in your territory and you didn't protect her. But then again, the werewolves have been doing whatever the hell they want for centuries. Most of the time that includes terrorizing innocent people and killing vampires." Adrian shook his head.

"Those are lies and you know it. We've tried to maintain relations with the vampires, but it's the cold bloodsuckers who want nothing to do with us." Roarke remained where he stood, though if looks could kill, Adrian would be dead a thousand times over.

"And both of your prejudices are doing nothing to help the cause. Adrian, go back to bed. I can handle Roarke," Lilah said.

"I'm sure you can." The innuendo in his words made it clear exactly how Adrian thought she'd be "handling" the werewolf.

Lilah shook her head. Damn males and their overabundance of testosterone. "You can't order me around, Adrian. I thought you'd figured that out by now." Disgust made her words harsher than she intended.

"I'll do whatever it takes to keep you safe." His voice rumbled across her senses, reminding her of how he'd fucked her last night, and all the times he'd dove into danger to keep her safe. Her feelings for him churned with confusion, and Roarke's presence provided little clarity.

"Then go back to bed," Lilah said. She stepped forward and cupped his cheek, hoping the intimate gesture soothed his fragile male ego. Brushing her thumb across his lips, she struggled to ignore the sizzle of sexual awareness flaring through her. Nipples hard, she stood on tiptoe and brushed a kiss across his cool lips.

"Go," she whispered. "I won't do anything."

Adrian wrapped his arm around her waist and hauled her against his body. He slanted his lips across hers, kissing her long and deep. His tongue plunged into her mouth, fingers threading through her hair to hold her in place.

Lilah melted against his body. In the back of her mind, she wondered if he put on this show for Roarke's benefit, a way to brand her as his. As he swallowed her moan of pleasure, Lilah realized she didn't care. Her tongue caressed the length of his, drawing him deeper inside her mouth. She felt his fangs on her tongue, against her lower lip, and a part of her wanted him to bite her.

He pulled away. "I trust you," he whispered, his voice husky with need.

Lilah blinked at him, her body still reeling from his sensual onslaught. His words penetrated the fog. He trusted her. She grinned, thankful at least to have one male who thought she was capable of handling this on her own.

"I won't." Again, she marveled at this new and improved Adrian.

"Good." Adrian pressed another quick, hard kiss to her lips. He looked over her shoulder at Roarke. "This isn't finished, not by a long shot." Releasing Lilah, he turned and went back into the bedroom. He slammed the door so hard it rattled in its frame.

Lilah stared at the closed door, knowing the daylight hours must be pulling on him. They'd do the same to her, except for her lycanthropy kept her awake and safe in the sunlight.

"So, you going to tell me what that was about? Seems to me he's doing an awful lot of marking his territory. Might make a wolf think your vamp is a bit insecure." Roarke asked. He crossed his arms over his chest.

Lilah winced at the truth in his words. At one time, she'd thought the same thing. Now, she didn't know what to think.

Chapter Seven

Adrian woke not feeling any better about the situation. In the living room, he heard the pounding of hammers and the sawing of wood. Lilah and Roarke spoke in soft tones. The smell of sawdust permeated the air, masking any other scents. He bolted to his feet, half afraid of what he'd find when he opened the bedroom door. He shook his head. Lilah promised him she'd behave. He had to trust her word.

He closed his eyes and willed his fangs to stay hidden. A glance in the mirror showed his eyes their usual amber color instead of red with bloodlust. Promising himself that he'd stay calm, no matter what he found, he opened the door.

The living room looked almost as good as new. Light colored wood marked the places where the damage had been repaired, and the door once again hung whole on its hinges, the windows were shuttered, the siding repaired. Lilah sat in the corner, smoothing plaster on the walls. Roarke stood in the other corner, replacing the last of the shutters. Harsh electric lighting illuminated the room.

They'd been busy in a good way. He squared his shoulders, knowing Lilah wouldn't like what he was about to say, but knowing he had to say it anyway. He stepped into the room, his long strides carrying him to her.

Roarke turned and looked over his shoulder. "You're awake."

Adrian nodded. "Yeah."

Lilah wiped the last of the plaster with the trowel and then turned. She had dust across her nose and a smudge of dirt on her cheek. He thought she'd never looked more adorable. He swallowed hard, preparing himself for the battle about to come.

"Lilah, I think we should leave," he said.

"What? What do you mean leave?" She set the trowel on a paper plate beside her.

"I think we should leave. You're not safe here. The work, it's good. But that gang found you here. Roarke found you here." He jabbed his thumb in the werewolf's direction. "That means others are going to be able to find you too."

Lilah expelled a sigh. She glanced to Roarke, who stood out of the way and silent.

"He has a point. I wouldn't want my woman in any more danger than she had to be," Roarke said.

Adrian appreciated the support. "So it's settled. We're leaving tonight."

"We haven't settled anything. And we didn't do these repairs just to have you announce that we're leaving. This is my house, Adrian. Yeah, it's nothing special, but we deliberately chose it that way, remember? A place where I could have a home, something I haven't had since—" She bit back her words, though Adrian knew exactly what she'd been about to say. Since his brother had turned her.

Damn Mikhail! His impulsive actions had ruined everything and now Lilah had to pay the price. "I know. And if there were any way to make this different, I would. I'm sorry, Lilah," he said, and he hoped she understood that he spoke about more than just the house.

She must have for she nodded. "Thank you. But I'm still not going anywhere. This is *my* home, Adrian. You can't drive me away, even if it's to keep me safe. I simply won't go." She crossed her arms over her breasts and lifted her chin. Determination flashed in her eyes.

"If you stay here, you'll be a sitting duck waiting for more attacks. I don't think that's wise."

"I don't think I've ever done the wise thing as long as you've known me. I am not going anywhere." She picked up the trowel and turned back to the wall.

Adrian growled with frustration. Her name wasn't the only one on the title. However bringing that up at the moment might get him more than he bargained for. "They know where you are. They're going to be back," he said.

Lilah snarled and flung the trowel onto the floor. Plaster splattered everywhere. She ignored it and stomped in Adrian's direction. "Then tell them to fucking bring it on. Do you hear me, Adrian? Bring. It. On! I am so damn tired of running, so tired of trying to stay alive. I didn't ask for any of this. I didn't want it, but now that I have it, I'm stuck with it. So they can bring it on. I'm ready to rumble." She folded her hands back in her direction.

Roarke grinned.

"I'm just trying to keep you alive. We can pack and be out of here in two hours." Adrian tried to explain some sense into her. He knew the wolf wouldn't.

"Do you have any idea where we'd go? And what about the effort Roarke spent to help fix this place up. I don't agree with all his ideas, but

I think we can make this place safer than it is. A fixed position is so much more defensible."

He hated to admit it, but she made sense. "Fine. I'll start patrols, widen our sweeps. And I want a serious strategy talk between the three of us. I'm assuming the wolf stays."

Roarke shrugged and looked as if it would be her decision.

"He stays. Do your rounds, then come back and we'll talk," Lilah said.

"Fine. And I want the wolf to get some sleep. He's no use to us if he's dead on his feet." With those words, Adrian turned on his heel and went back to the bedroom. He emerged moments later fully dressed in head-to-toe black, a gun tucked into the waistband of his jeans at the small of his back. He strode through the living room and out the door, determined to check the perimeter and then return and try to convince Lilah to see reason.

~* * *~

Roarke stood at the stove dressed in a t-shirt, jeans, and boots. The smell of bacon permeated the air. As far as he was concerned, it was the perfect way to start the day. Not for the first time did he wonder what the hell he was doing here in the middle of this mess. After Adrian's attempt to get Lilah to leave last night, she'd become defiant, doing everything she could to piss the vampire off. At least that meant no rowdy sex, and as he listened to her deep, even breathing as she slept, and inhaled her not-human scent, he wished the thought of her being mad at the vamp didn't make him so happy.

He listened to her footfalls as Lilah made her way into the kitchen. She'd been doing some blend of what looked like yoga crossed with martial arts in the living room, and standing there, watching her lithe form did nothing but give him a hard on. She stopped in the doorway. His sense of smell detected her perspiration and the smell of her sex. He grinned. Feed or fuck, it was the werewolf mantra. His body stiffened, and he willed his cock to behave.

"Smells good." She stopped beside him and eyed the skillet. Her stomach grumbled audibly.

"Thanks. Should be ready in a few moments."

"Anything I can do to help?" She opened the cupboard door and pulled out two mismatched plates.

A home. She'd called this place her home, yet with the scarred counters, the hodgepodge of thrift store dishes, he wondered what kind of home it really was. Thoughts of his sprawling two-story house with the workout room in the basement and the hot tub in the backyard made this place seem like a squatter's shanty. And that's exactly what it was, he realized. A transient home. The kind of place she could pick up and leave at a moment's notice, except now, she didn't want to leave. He frowned, thinking of how much more defensible his house would be.

"I'm sorry, what did you say?" He realized while he'd been thinking she'd been speaking and he hadn't heard a word.

"I said it's still dark. Why are you awake?" She arranged a fork on each plate, then tore off two paper towels and folded them like napkins.

Roarke shrugged. "Couldn't sleep."

"Yeah, me neither," she admitted.

Adrian stepped into the kitchen. He plopped a bag of blood into the microwave and heated it. When the appliance dinged, he poured half the bag of blood into a mug and took a long swallow.

"You're up early," he said to no one in particular.

Lilah shrugged. "Couldn't sleep. I didn't think you liked your blood microwaved. Said it made it taste funny." She grabbed another mug, and poured the rest of the still-warm bag into it, then poured lemon-lime soda on top of it. Roarke scowled as she drank several swallows.

Adrian shrugged. "Looks like the wolf is using the stove. I'll manage." He drowned the rest of his mug, and then washed it in the sink, turning it upside down in the drainer to dry.

Roarke worked not to bristle at the vamp's tone. He quickly shoveled several slices of bacon onto one plate, and the rest onto another. Adding two eggs to each plate, he handed one to Lilah.

"Breakfast is ready," he said. He opened the fridge, noticing that the vamp hadn't said anything about the new supply of groceries filling the appliance.

He leaned against the counter and started eating. Adrian stared at him. His gaze flickered to Lilah, then back again. "So what are your plans today? New carpeting and wallpaper?"

Lilah frowned.

"I thought I'd trim some of the hedges and overgrowth in the yard to give a clearer line of sight." Roarke polished off the bacon.

Next to him, Lilah's stomach rumbled, and he wondered what she'd been subsisting on before he arrived. With the limited supplies in the house, it sure didn't look like anyone had been feeding her. When her shirt had ridden up during her exercises, he'd seen her ribs, not liking her gaunt appearance. She needed someone to care from her, and obviously, Adrian wasn't up to the job.

"Anything that helps our line of sight will also help theirs," Adrian commented. "Just so you know that."

"I do, but we can't have any surprises. I've already discussed my ideas with Lilah," he lied, hoping she'd keep her mouth shut.

She looked at him, arched an eyebrow, but said nothing.

"And she approved them? Without asking me?"

"She will." Roarke spoke with a finality that had Lilah setting her plate down and whirling to face him.

"Don't talk about me like I'm not in the room. You know damn well you didn't approve anything by me. Whatever argument you're trying to start? Don't. In fact, if you can't be civil to Adrian then get the hell out!" She whirled to face the vampire. "And the same goes for you. I'm not a pawn. I'm not a toy. I'm a woman. And I'm strong enough to make my own decisions." She threw her hands into the air and stormed out of the room.

Roarke watched her go, half of his attention on her heart-shaped ass, the other half on the vampire. He scowled at Roarke, and then turned and stormed after her. Moments later, the bedroom door slammed.

Thinking about Adrian and Lilah in the bedroom together brought his beast close to the surface. Snarling, he stared at the remnants of his dinner, his stomach churning. He pushed himself away from the counter, and went in search of Lilah.

~* * *~

Lilah looked up from the scrap wood she sorted into what looked reusable and what was scrap. She figured she could carry the remainder out back and burn it, though the thought of fire made her inner vampire cringe in fear. Roarke stood less than ten feet from her, his hands hanging loosely at his side. She closed her eyes and breathed deeply, the motion inadvertently pulling his scent into her lungs. She so didn't need this right now

"Yes?" she asked, trying not to sound bitchy, tired, and bored all the same time. Frankly at this point, she was more than ready to ditch the men and try this on her own. Except, without Adrian's connections and Roarke's fighting skills, she figured her plan would get her real dead real quick.

"Look I didn't mean to piss you off back there. I should have asked you first," he said.

"You never have before. I don't expect you to start now." She rubbed the bridge of her nose, thinking back to when she was ten and broke her leg. No matter how many times she told Roarke it wasn't his fault, he blamed himself. And she could count many other times as well. No, he never did listen to her. She was just the human girl child who liked to tag along with the lycanthropes.

Roarke squatted down in front of her and rested his arms on his legs. For a moment, Lilah wished he'd shift, get territorial, something to make her hate him. Because right now, he reminded her too much of the gallant young man she'd had a crush on, and the one person how had dominated her happily ever after fantasies.

"You're right." He smiled, and his sheer, wholesome good looks sent warmth tingling through her.

Lilah hated her body's response. Anger radiated from the bedroom, and she didn't need to be an empath to feel the hatred Adrian emitted. He downright despised Roarke, and frankly, she didn't blame him. But caught between a rock—her gaze dropped to the tight fit of Roarke's jeans—and a hard place, she had no where to turn. It was reminiscent of when Mikhail had turned her and Adrian had come to the rescue. Lilah dragged her fingers through her hair, tired of being someone else's damsel in distress.

"Lilah?" Roarke questioned.

She shook her head and pulled herself from the hypnotic trance of her thoughts. Directing her gaze towards his face, she drank in the sight of him. The weight of her situation, of being forced to constantly look over her shoulder pressed down on her. Had she been just a normal girl, well, okay a normal vampire, then maybe this wouldn't have happened at all. Mikhail would have turned her, left her, and she could delude herself into thinking Adrian was her blood-sucking knight in shining armor. Except now, she couldn't. And in her heart, Roarke had always been her hero.

"I should..." Her voice trailed off as she realized that there were so many things she should do. Checking on Adrian, though with dawn so close, she figured he'd be in bed right now, ranked high on her list. And if he were in bed, her body screamed that there were so much more enticing ways to make up than an apology. She swallowed hard.

"I know." Roarke rested his knee on the ground and reached for her. He cupped her cheek, threading his fingers through her hair.

Closing her eyes, she leaned into his touch. The beat of his heart, a steady and hypnotic rhythm she'd not known how much she'd missed until now, thrummed through his veins. Her vampire longed to sink her fangs into his neck and drink from him. Her wolf wanted to howl at the moon. So many wants. So many desires. And not enough time or words for all of them.

"This has to be hard on you," he said.

"Yeah," she breathed. "It is."

"Tell me, Lilah, what do you want?" He moved closer, his breath a warm breeze across her lips.

She leaned forward, flattening her palm against his chest. For a moment she knelt there, the pungent aroma of pine smelling so right tinged with Roarke's musky scent. She swallowed hard.

"To be safe, but not wrapped in cotton. I can take care of myself. I just need you and Adrian to see that. I'm a big girl. I'm..." She cringed at the thought that once again she'd nearly let the reality of her life slip to him. She pulled away.

Three steps took her to the wall. Her heels thudded against the baseboard.

Roarke stood and crossed the space between them. He leaned against her, one hand pressed flat next to her head, the other cupping her hip to haul her against him.

"That's the second time you said you were something and stopped." He leaned forward and inhaled audibly. "Cut the crap, Lilah. You're weren't shitting me, were you?"

She bit back a groan as the hard ridge of his cock pressed against her. With him so close, her breasts brushed against his chest with each breath, her nipples hardened. Warmth pooled low in her stomach. She forced herself to stare over his shoulder at the closed bedroom door.

"No. I'm not, but then you didn't have to smell me to know that. I smell like a wolf...and something else. I smell like a vampire, except something's not right. I didn't lie to you. You saw me drinking blood," she admitted.

"You're a vampire?" he leaned forward. "Do you want to bite me?"

"Any red-blooded woman would want to bite you, and you know it."

The bedroom door opened. Adrian stood there, his face a thundercloud. "I turn my back for one minute, wolf," he snarled. His footfalls echoed as he stomped across the living room.

Lilah regretted that there wasn't enough room for her to push beneath Roarke's arm. She shoved at his chest, sending him stepping away from her. "I don't belong to you," she growled at Adrian. The hair on the back of her neck rose. She curled her fingers against the need to shift, to show him exactly what she was and why he hated her lupine side.

"No, you don't. But a wolf shows up and now you're all bitch in heat, aren't you?" Adrian taunted her.

"So that's what this is about?" Lilah rushed him, getting into his face. She snorted with frustration. "You don't like my furry side. You never could handle the fact that I walk in your world and I walk in his." She jerked her thumb at Roarke. "Well you have to handle it. If you want to be in my life, if you want to try and "protect" me, then you need to deal with the fact that I'm a vampire and I'm a werewolf."

Adrian snarled.

Roarke gasped.

Lilah shook her head and thrust out her hand, keeping him from coming any closer. "I already explained this part, remember? Now is not the time." She whirled back to face Adrian. "I know you don't like to see me shift. When I did and when I let my long tongue wrap around your cock, it disgusted you. I knew it, and yet, I did it anyway. You have to deal with my inner bitch, because right now she wants an alpha wolf a lot more than the vampire wants another bloodsucker. But, that doesn't mean I'm going to let her win." Lilah paused, drawing in a deep breath.

Adrian's eyes darkened. Hints of red showed in his amber irises, and between them, the bloodlust rose. His fangs protruded over his lower lip, hands balled into fists to keep from reaching out and touching her. "I thought you had the bitch under control."

Lilah barked mocking laughter. "So did I. But one smell of him, and she's got her tail in the air begging to be mounted. You're going to have to deal. Hell, I'm going to have to deal. You took me in, Adrian. I can't ever forget what you did for me." She licked her lips, watching as his gaze followed the moment and wondered if she could turn this into the advantage. Just because vampires didn't live on the fuck and feed mantra didn't mean they didn't still have the same impulses.

She trailed her fingers over his chest, aware of Roarke's gaze burning holes into her back. She pushed him from her mind. Right now, focusing on Adrian remained her top priority.

"I need you," she whispered.

Saying the words aloud twisted her up inside. Her stomach churned, lurched, and she tasted the remnants of breakfast and blood. Swallowing it down, she kept her gaze locked to Adrian's amber-red eyes.

"I really do. You keep the vamp in check." Her breath whooshed from her lungs.

"Is that all you need me for?" Pain filled Adrian's eyes, the stark soul-deep pain of someone who thought himself in love.

Shit! Lilah suspected, yet had always ignored that little fact. His brother might have turned her, but Adrian had always been in love with her. She closed her eyes and drew in a deep breath trying to steady herself. She felt the need for blood churning in her veins, knew her own eyes probably held hints of red.

"I don't know. It's not like we really got to know each other before the threats on my life began." She answered as honestly as she could.

"When did they begin, Lilah?" Roarke's question cut through the tension surrounding her and Adrian.

"Not long after I was turned." She thought back to it, barely a fledging when the first attacks came. They seemed to know exactly where she was, who she was with, and Adrian had lost two house servants that day.

"You know I can protect you better than the wolf can," Adrian said, pulling her attention back to him.

"Maybe you can. Maybe you can't. But you hate my wolf. If you can't get over the fact that I can turn furry, then you're useless to me. I'm sorry." Lilah shrugged and turned away.

"Wait!" Adrian grabbed her shoulder and spun her around. His fingers closed around her skin, gripping hard enough to leave bruises.

Lilah drew the pain deep inside, relishing it, enjoying the fact that he cared enough to mark her. Her fangs tingled. Her nipples hardened, and she wondered whether the vampire or the bitch thought pain was sexy, because as a human, she sure as hell didn't. *It means you're alive*, the wolf whispered in her mind. The vampire echoed the sentiments. Lilah closed her eyes, her two natures more in tune than they ever had been, all over the rough touch of a vampire.

"I don't hate your wolf," he whispered. His head dipped toward hers.

Lilah closed her eyes and swayed towards him. Her traitorous body yearned for the caress of his lips across hers, his arms like a steel band around her body crushing her breasts to his chest. Even before Mikhail had turned her, she'd wanted his sexy older brother. Swallowing hard, she wished, oh how she wished, she could believe his words.

"I'll change right here. And then we'll see if you really accept my wolf." She stepped back from his embrace. She focused on the change, calling her inner bitch. The wolf responded, tail flagging in the air, tongue lolling out of its mouth. She removed her clothing, aware of both men's gaze locked onto her form. As she bared her breasts, she thought she heard Roarke's harsh intake of breath. Adrian's eyes darkened, the amber irises turning red. She peeled her jeans and panties down her legs, kicked off her boots, then stood there naked for one heartbeat, two. And then she shifted.

One moment a woman stood there, the next a wolf on all fours. She grinned, tongue dangling from her mouth, and padded over to Adrian.

She stopped. The scent of an intruder filled the air. Whirling towards the door, she growled, enough warning for the men. The door slammed open, and when she saw who stood in the doorway, the hackles on the back of her neck rose.

Mikhail! She lunged at her sire.

Chapter Eight

Lilah ran low to the ground, hitting Mikhail in the legs. He somersaulted over her, the flash of metal in his hand barely visible. A knife! She whirled to bark a warning to Adrian and saw he'd already kicked the blade out of his brother's hands. Behind Mikhail, four men, all muscled and smelling of vampire, rushed into the house. They all used knives, and Lilah had a fleeting thought that perhaps her and Roarke's repairs wouldn't be for naught, before the wolf took over. Her jaws snapped. A growl rose from her throat.

An answering rumble filled her ears. Roarke! Her ears perked up, a large, dark grey blur herding two of the men away. She bit at the closest man, his steps dodging away in time. He swiped the knife at her. She ducked, then lunged up and grabbed a mouthful of his leather jacket. A shake of her broad head tore the material, and she spat it out to bite again. This time, she grabbed the tail of his shirt, before he yanked it out of her mouth.

The other man went to backup Mikhail in his fight with Adrian. Lilah regretted only having one man to take down, but as she jumped at his throat, her paws shoved against his chest, and sent him sprawling half-in, half-out of the front door. Streaks of orange crossed the sky. Lilah growled, and the vampire scrambled backwards. She slammed against his legs, and he stumbled down the front stairs.

Let the sun finish him if she couldn't. She pounced on him, using all of her weight to pin him to the ground. Saliva dripped from her mouth as she lowered her nose and breathed deeply of his fetid stench. She drew his scent into her nostrils, and inhaled nothing but pure vamp. The thought that her sire had come back to claim her or some such bullshit, lowered her muzzle to his throat. She grabbed on with her teeth and tore.

Hot blood gushed from the wound. Lilah lapped at it, her vampire rejoicing in the spray of crimson liquid.

The man whimpered. Not one to give pity, she snapped his spine with a second bite of her teeth. The man lay on the sidewalk, nothing but a corpse, and as soon as the sun topped the horizon, he'd be nothing but ash.

She bounded back into the living room. Adrian and Roarke both fought two men. A long, angry gash along Roarke's side had her running to him and biting into the ankle of one of his attackers. Tendon tore, bringing him down. Lilah pounced.

Roarke yipped and nudged her off the fallen man.

Lilah growled. Yet again, another male told her she couldn't kill, and she bared her blood-stained fangs hoping he'd gotten the message. She'd killed once. She'd kill again. She swung her muzzle at the vampire, telling him in no uncertain terms to tend to his battle. She'd take care of her own.

The man lunged with his knife, catching Roarke along the shoulder. Blood welled from the cut, and he yipped in pain. He focused his attention back on his attacker, leaving her with the wounded man.

Lilah nipped the back of his knees. Maybe Roarke wanted him alive for questioning, and Lilah itched to know who sent them. She bit into the flesh at the back of his thigh and swung her head, tearing muscle. The man screamed with pain. His wounded noises only goaded her into severing his other Achilles tendon. He might be able to crawl, so she grabbed his wrist and twisted his arm as far back as it could go. Then, she pulled. His shoulder dislocated with an audible pop.

The wounded vampire whimpered with pain. He tried to curl into the fetal position, tried to wield his knife, but Lilah bit his wrist and crunched bone in her powerful jaws. She batted the knife away with her paw and then went to help Roarke. The scent of his blood called to her, made her wonder what it would taste like sliding down her throat. She lunged into the fray right next to Roarke.

Side-by-side she fought with him. They moved in sync, as if they'd battled together before. Where she lunged at the vampire's leg, Roarke went for his arm, his side. His teeth found purchase along the vamp's ribs, and Lilah swept the attacker's legs out from beneath him, bringing him to the floor. She kept her jaws in his leg, feeling muscles and tendons beneath her teeth. The urge to snap into them, to rip into the bloody flesh had her battling the need to shift and drink. Watered down blood paled when faced with the coppery taste of a vampire in his prime. Her nostrils pulled the scent into her lungs. She growled around the flesh in her mouth, not wanting to release the attacker.

She willed Roarke to go for the vamp's throat and put him out of his misery. Already they had one, if he didn't die of blood loss, lying on the floor, unable to get away. The thrashing prey beneath her invoked her need to bite, to kill. If Roarke didn't, she would defy his orders.

Roarke glared at her, his eyes glowing with the same need to hunt and kill that raced through Lilah's veins. He growled, ordering her away from the body. Lilah stood firm. The hair rose on the back of her neck, her fur making her look puffed out and menacing. She shook her head and tightened her teeth in the vamp's leg. She'd be damned before she let another man order her away from a kill that was rightfully hers.

~* * *~

Of all the times to throw her weight around, Lilah had to choose now. He supposed it shouldn't have surprised him, not when the vampire she'd taken outside didn't return, and the sun crested the horizon. On the floor, another vamp lay, his limbs all but useless, and Roarke had seen the gleeful way she'd nearly torn the attacker from limb to limb. He never remembered her being this bloodthirsty. Obviously, the vamp changed her. The wolf hunted to defend life, territory. The thrill of the chase might be considered sport, but when it killed, it had a damn good reason.

Blood stained the fur around her muzzle. Her hackles raised, eyes glowing feral, she never looked more beautiful to him. He took a step toward her, warning her away. She had enough death on her conscience. She didn't need another, not when he and Adrian could take care of things. Behind him, the vamp fought like a fiend possessed, and all the blood Roarke scented belonged to the attackers. After being in the same room while Lilah and Adrian fucked, he knew he'd recognize the vamp's scent.

Lilah refused to budge. Oh hell, they were in the middle of a battle. They didn't have time for childish pissing contests, though frankly, that's all the three of them had been doing since his arrival. He stepped forward and with a bite of his jaws ripped out the vamp's throat. The prone figure gurgled, muscles twitching, and then its undead life bled onto the floor. Absently, Roarke realized they'd have to sand the blood out if they decided to stay.

His side stung. The wound along his shoulder burned. He drew air into his lungs, not liking the way blood matted his fur. Changing would stop the bleeding, but he fought far more effectively in wolf form. He whirled toward the two men on Adrian.

Lilah blocked his path. She pointed her muzzle in the direction of his wounds, stepping forward and licking them with her tongue. The long, sure strokes soothed the burn. He growled and clacked his teeth together, warning her away. Before she could try and force him from the battle, he scrambled toward Adrian and his attackers. The motion drew one man's attention and he whirled to face the wolf.

Lilah followed. She tried to get ahead of Roarke. Growling low in his throat, he used his greater size and speed to push her back. He herded the man away from Adrian and toward the still-open door. Sunlight slanted across the floor in streams, and the vampire worked to stay out of their deadly rays. Seeing what Roarke was doing, Lilah worked on the other side to keep the vampire from going far. At least she wasn't attacking, and in her wolf form, he doubted the light would hurt her. He hated to take the chance, though.

She rammed her body into the vampire. He stumbled and sprawled, his hand reaching out to catch himself as he fell. Light slanted across the floor, directly over his skin. It blistered, smoked, and with a yelp, he yanked his hand away and rolled to the side. The smell of charred flesh filled the air.

Lilah pounced after him. Light gleamed off her fur, and Roarke realized he'd been waiting to see what would happen when she encountered the sun. Thankfully, nothing, and ignoring his wounds, he bounded into the fray. He pounced on the vampire, keeping him from sliding farther away. Hoping Lilah stayed in wolf form, Roarke shifted. He needed his voice for this.

"Who sent you?" he snarled. Blood dripped along his shoulder and his side. He ignored the pain, the burn that told him the knife had cut deep into flesh and muscle. "What group are you with?" He glanced at Lilah, and she remained in wolf form. Perhaps in her human shape sunlight could harm her. That would be a complication he didn't need.

The vampire lifted his chin, inadvertently baring his throat. "I'm not telling you." Behind them, the sounds of scuffle filtered to his ears. He couldn't risk a glance and hoped Adrian still held his own. Frankly, it was more than he expected from the vamp.

Roarke closed his fingers around the vampire's neck. Lilah stood ready, her teeth bared, her muzzle just inches from his neck. Leaning forward, he applied pressure on the vampire's carotid artery. They might not need to breathe, but they still needed to have blood in their veins.

"Do it," the vamp snarled. "Kill me and a hundred more will come."

"Shut up!" The other attacker yelled behind him.

The vamp grinned, his incisors visible. "I've heard wolf tastes good." He glanced at Lilah. "And bitch tastes even better."

Lilah spun. She trotted in the direction of the fallen knife, picked it up with her teeth, and carried it to him. She dropped it on the man's chest, and Roarke swooped it into his hand before the vamp had a chance to try and get the weapon. He pressed the blade at the vamp's throat. A thin trickle of blood welled along the shallow cut.

Lilah whined. She licked her lips, and Roarke understood the need inside her. Even in her wolf form, her vamp still held sway. He forced his attention from her, knowing he didn't understand how she became both, what it meant, and frankly, it freaked him the hell out. He pressed the knife a little deeper, tiring of this game. His wound hurt. His woman was in danger. And he had questions that they needed answered. A quick, clean stroke slit the man's throat. Lilah stepped back and changed. She donned clothing, watching the fight between the two men avidly.

Roarke grabbed his jeans and yanked them on. He hissed in pain as his wound bled anew. Holding his hand to it, he looked from Lilah toward the two men fighting and back to her again.

Lilah darted down the hall. Thankful she moved out of the line of fire, he watched the two men. Though the attacker was half a head shorter than Adrian, the two men looked enough alike as to be brothers. Both had the same light blond hair, though the attacker's was longer and shaggier in back. Their eyes flashed red. With their similar fighting styles, they looked evenly matched.

She returned, her arms full of first aid supplies. "Sit," she pointed to the floor.

He remained standing, not ready to relinquish his defensible position by sitting down and making himself vulnerable. With a snarl, Adrian punched the man in the jaw, sending him stumbling back toward the door. Lilah watched, her lips parted, her breathing ragged. Her chest rose and fell, drawing his gaze to her pert breasts with their hard nipples. Like twin diamonds, they pressed against her tank top, and he realized she hadn't replaced her bra. It still lay on the floor behind him where she'd removed it to change. His mouth went dry, and a new kind of pain filled his body.

"Sit," she ordered again. "If you're worried about them, don't be. This has been a long time in coming." She sounded resigned to that fact.

"You know him?" Roarke sat.

Lilah knelt beside him and opened a bottle of peroxide. She doused a handful of cotton with it, and started wiping his wounds. The antiseptic bubbled and hissed along his wounds. He winced.

"Yeah," she admitted, removing the last traces of blood from his skin.

He glanced down at her slender fingers so close to him, the nails blunt and unpainted. She moved quickly, efficiently, as if she'd had experience in bandaging wounds. "So who is he?" Roarke asked as she pressed several four-by-four squares of sterile gauze to the wounds.

She ripped off a piece of tape and slapped it across his bandages. "You don't need to know right now. It'd only piss you off." She secured the gauze with another piece of tape.

He turned to keep an eye on the action.

"Hold still," Lilah hissed. "Damn it, you're going to pull the wound open again."

He obeyed, the feel of her fingers against his skin too tantalizing to ignore. Though he was wounded and a fight happened in the same room as he, the image of her touching him in a far more intimate manner filled his mind. He imagined her sliding her fingers over his pecs, tracing each ridge of his abs, then down to the waistband of his jeans. A flick of her wrist would open the buttons and his cock would emerge as hard and thick as it was now. He shifted, trying to ease the sudden tightness in his pants.

She snarled at him and turned her attention to the wound on his shoulder. It ran from the top of his bicep, over the joint and down to cross his shoulder blade. She sucked in a harsh breath when she saw the extent of the injury.

Her concern pulled his attention from the fight in front of him. The two men circled each other warily, and were he still in wolf form, he would have leapt at the attacker's legs, bringing him down for Adrian to finish him off. "That bad?" He asked.

She murmured something noncommittal and continued to doctor his wounds. He let his chin fall to his chest and exhaled a long, deep breath. His eyelids fluttered closed, and he struggled to stay aware. The fight moved to the far corner of the room, well away from the open door and half-shuttered windows and their deadly sunlight.

"I think this will need stitches," Lilah said with a frown in her voice.

"Stitches?" He bit back a chuckle. "You, um, haven't been around full werewolves have you? I'll be just fine in the morning."

"And if so, then we can pull out the stitches. This goes down to the muscle. I don't like the way it looks." She pressed the pad to the wound.

He winced with pain. Damn, maybe she was right.

"Hang on." Before he could say anything, she rose to her feet and hurried into the kitchen.

She returned momentarily holding a needle, thread, candle, and a book of matches. She quickly lit the birthday cake-sized candle, ran the needle through the flame, then blew it out. She threaded the needle, and he yelped as the point slid into his skin.

"What are you doing?" Roarke snarled.

In the corner, Adrian growled, fangs showing, and wrapped his fingers around his attacker's throat. Bending his head, he bit and drank deeply.

"Stitching you up." She worked quickly, and he was reminded of her sitting on the floor at her father's feet working on some craft project. She liked to do something with colored floss and a wooden hoop. Her home had been filled with the items, and he frowned, thinking yet another piece of domesticity had been torn away from her.

She finished, tied a quick knot, and then bolted to her feet. "Adrian, no!" She yelled and rushed the two men.

Damn it, did she want to protect every one of them, including her attacker? He surged to his feet, his wounds protesting the sudden movement. Stumbling, he hurried forward, but not in time to stop her from grabbing the man's shoulder and pulled him away from Adrian.

"He's your brother," she said, spinning the attacker away. "You can't kill your brother." Reaching behind her, she closed her fingers around the handle of a knife he saw she'd stuck through one of her belt loops. Pulling it free, she pointed it at the man. "I can, however, kill my sire." She lunged.

The man skittered away, darting into a rectangle of shade between the light streaming in the partially open shudder and the door. Wide-eyed, he looked around the room.

"Lilah, don't do this," Adrian said. He hurried to stand on the other side of her, well away from the light streaming in.

"I have to. Do you know what his foolish actions caused me?" She stepped forward. The knife in her hand shook.

Roarke watched, his gaze darting from Lilah to Adrian, to his brother and back again.

When no one made a move, Mikhail stepped into the sunlight next to his brother. "Whatever you want, Lilah," he said.

"No!" Adrian's brother said. He leapt.

"Mikhail!" Adrian yelled. He lunged forward, Lilah's hand on his arm keeping him from stepping into the deadly sunlight.

Roarke stood there. He stared at the man who had sentenced Lilah to a blood-drinker's life. Hate poured through his veins. He forced himself to stay lose, stay ready for anything. The pain from his wounds ceased to bother him. Dying would be too good for the likes of the vampire standing between light and them. Any step he took meant death, and Roarke hoped like hell the vamp chose him.

"There will be more. Search his pockets and you will find the address. Come alone, and we may call off the blood hunt." His flesh bubbled and burned, turning red and blistering within the blink of an eye. "The bounty on her has increased. Few will be able to resist the temptation." With a soul-wrenching cry, he disappeared into a pile of ash.

"Mikhail, no!" Adrian stared at the pile of debris that had once been his brother.

Roarke glared at the remains

"Adrian, step away from the sunlight." Lilah walked him backwards, step by step, until he backed into the hallway. Roarke watched them go and turned to the fallen man.

He stumbled, his mind whirling with what he'd just seen and heard. A bounty on Lilah's head. He shook his head. Her wolf would make the vampires want her dead. And her vampire made the werewolves want to kill her. Oh hell, now he knew why she was so damned determined to do this herself. Just like a ten year old who climbed the tallest tree, then fell on the way down. The drive to prove herself against others her age, no matter that they were lycanthropes and she was human, had sent her ten feet up in the tree. She'd clung there, terrified. He'd talked her down when she refused to have him follow her. And when her foot slipped and she fell the last four feet, she'd broken her leg. She was damned lucky she didn't crack her head open.

Roarke rubbed the palm of his hand over his eyes. And now, he'd been unable to catch her again. The attack in his territory, it had to be what had made her a werewolf. But who had attacked her, and for what reason? It didn't serve any political purpose, none that he saw anyway.

He questioned the fallen man ruthlessly. Though his rib ached, he kicked and punched the fallen vampire, taking out his anger on the pitiful bloodsucker's prone form. Then, when he could say no more, Roarke dragged him into the sunlight and watched him burn.

Adrian and Lilah returned. Adrian glanced at the ashes on the floor and frowned. Loss covered the vampire's face, and Lilah's arm around his shoulder made him appear as if that were the only thing holding him up. Not that Roarke blamed him. The idea of killing his own brother, not that he had one, turned his stomach. He didn't envy Adrian that fact, especially when his brother had committed suicide right before his eyes. When it came down to it, suicide or murder, it was all the same, and his brother was still dead.

"What did he say?" Adrian growled. He stepped away from Lilah, though he staggered away from the sunlight and the pile of ashes. His amber eyes looked pale, washed out, as light as his skin.

"Same as your brother. Others will come. They're paying big bucks to have Lilah killed. Apparently they're part of a gang." He held out a piece of paper with a symbol on it to Adrian. "I found this in his wallet. Maybe you can make out what it is?"

Adrian unfolded the paper. He swallowed hard and handed it to Lilah. "It's The Party." He pinched the bridge of his nose. "We did not need this right now, Lilah. I can find out where their headquarters are in town. If my brother was mixed up with them..." His words trailed off.

Lilah rested her hand on his shoulder and squeezed. "Tell me about The Party. They sound like big trouble."

"The Dead Man's Party. It's a radical group of vampires. They separated from the Immortal Council probably a century ago, not liking the Council's "do no harm" policy toward humans. You can dislike the Council all you want, but they've made it hard to humans to know we even exist. The Party would like to change that. My brother, Mikhail, he thought they made a lot more sense than the Council. I tried to dissuade him from having anything to do with them, but he wouldn't listen. He turned you, and frankly, if he hadn't left, I'd have destroyed him myself. I have to go after them."

Lilah nodded, moving slowly like one would around a predator. "I want to go with you."

Adrian shook his head. "You have to stay here. Roarke's wounded. I'm sure he'll want to be watched over as much as you do. I'm going to rest. I'll head out tonight."

"You'll share your plan with me. And I want to know everything." Lilah said.

Adrian nodded, though said nothing. He turned and disappeared into the bedroom, closing the door behind him.

Roarke stared at the closed door. The vampire had hidden depths, and from the startled look in Lilah's eyes, she saw them too. He motioned for her to join him on the floor. She sank to her knees and then sat next to him.

"So do you think he'll tell you his plan?" Roarke asked, wondering if he'd have a half-cocked vampire stirring up a hornet's nest.

Lilah shrugged. "I wish I knew."

Wounded and needing to keep her safe, Roarke wished he knew too.

Chapter Nine

"So do you want to tell me what happened?" Roarke leaned against the wall and stretched his legs out in front of him.

Lilah stared at him. Her hands shook, and she handed his bottle of soda to him before she could shake it too much. Her own bottle of water remained in her tight grip. She stood there and pressed the fingers of her free hand to the fluttering pulse at the base of her neck and closed her eyes. "If I do, will you promise not to hate me," she whispered. She remained standing.

"Sit." Roarke patted the floor next to him. "Look, it's been nothing but fight and argue since I got here. The little stunt you did, fucking him in front of me, it was a territory thing. I get it. Hell, I've done it myself."

Lilah frowned, not wanting to think of Roarke with any other woman, of his having sex with her, especially in front of other people. She pulled her gaze from his bare, muscled chest and breathed through clenched teeth.

"What I'm saying is things have been a little intense. And I never did tell you why I'm here. I'm here for you, Lilah. The Dark Moon Dogs have split my pack, turning longtime members against each other. They've eroded my power base, and if you're not by my side, I don't give a flying fucking damn about that. I came back to get you."

Lilah sucked in a breath at the heat in his words. "But I'm human. I used to be, anyway. If they've done what you've said, you need a hereditary werewolf of high standing in the greater pack. I'm a mutt." She grimaced.

"No, you're not." The vehemence in his voice rocked Lilah back on her heels, and she was thankful she sat.

"I used to be human. I used to be a lot of things."

"Yeah. Sweet, innocent." He closed his eyes and shook his head. "I remember you in pigtails missing your front teeth. I remember the way you chased after us lycanthropes, even though you hadn't a snowball's chance of keeping up with us. You did though. Ran yourself so ragged you used to fall asleep and I'd carry you home, but you kept up with us. No one in the Northwoods would call you a mutt. Not while I'm the alpha."

Tears stung Lilah's eyes. She blinked them away. It'd been a long time since she'd seen this tender side of Roarke, and she'd forgotten its effect on her. "That's sweet of you to say, Roary, but we both know they'll still call me a mutt behind my back. And I'm a vampire too. The bloodlust rules me as strong as it does Adrian. I'm a mutt and a bloodsucker. That makes me part of two worlds and unable to be fully in either one of them." She shook her head, reverting to the use of her childhood nickname for him.

"Ah, Lilah. What happened to make you so jaded? You always used to see the best in things. The glass never was half-empty to you. What happened?" He looked at her, really studied her.

Lilah feared he could see to the black depths of her soul. Telling him the truth would change everything between them, and yet, he already knew. "Adrian's brother, Mikhail, turned me. I was in college, young, naive, all those things you knew I used to be and now can't believe I'm not now. He wowed me, Mikhail FitzReal with his family's name and fortune. He was as far from Northwoods and rural Michigan as I could get, and I loved him for it. He turned me. Nearly left me for dead. Luckily, Adrian found out what his brother had done and came to my apartment. He found me, carried me back to his estate, and nursed me through the change. When I woke up, I was a vampire, and Mikhail was no where to be found."

"Bastard," Roarke growled. "If he weren't dead, I'll kill him myself."

"Well, he knew Adrian would too, because until tonight we never saw him." She yawned, the day completely light and her mental and physical exertions catching up with her.

Roarke wrapped his right arm around her and pulled her against his body. She snuggled against him, inhaling his scent. It reminded her of home, a home to which she could never return. She'd made her home here, in this run-down house she hoped to rebuild when the threats on her life were over. The Northwoods would never be her home again. She dashed away tears with the back of her hand.

"Hey, don't cry." Roarke brushed a tear away with his thumb.

"I don't cry," Lilah sniffed. "When I found out I was a vampire, I didn't cry. When I was transformed into a werewolf, I didn't cry. I can't believe I'm doing it now."

"You have to let that out sometime. You can't bottle it all up." His hand stroked up and down her arm. The gentle sweep of his fingers against his skin soothed her.

Lilah let her eyelids flutter closed. "The Dark Moon Dogs attacked me. I'd come back to the Northwoods. It was foolish, but I wanted to see—" She looked at him, and in the broad daylight, she saw the longing in his gaze. His words taunted her with her childhood dreams of what should have been. The human and the prince of the Northwoods living happily ever after like some fairy tale. "I wanted to see you," she said.

"You didn't. And you should have. If I'd known what had happened, I would have gone after them and made them pay. You shouldn't have to deal with this." He feathered his fingers through her hair.

Unable to stop herself, Lilah snuggled closer to him. "Well, I am. And I didn't want to jeopardize your standing as the pack leader. I was vampire then, and we both know what werewolves do to the vampires who enter their territory."

"Yeah," he admitted. "But I didn't think vampires could be given lycanthropy. Gods, if they can, then there's hundreds, thousands of vampires who have been bitten by werewolves. There could be a whole population of vampires out there who also are werewolves."

"But I'm a mutt either way. The vampires were content to let me go, but I wasn't a sanctioned turning. So I'm not allowed in the vampire world. Adrian risked everything to take me in and protect me, and as the head of the household, he could, knowing I'd never be a legitimate turning. This political stuff just makes my head spin."

"Mine too." Roarke grinned. "At least with the wolves it's all dominance. If I can kick your ass, I can rule you. Works well."

Lilah laughed. "Works for me." She kissed him on his stubbled cheek. A quick peck, just the barest hint of her lips touching his skin. Electricity zinged through her body with a sexual heat that had her lamenting the early morning hour. She thought of Adrian, sleeping the sleep of the undead, curling up next to his cold corpse-like body held little appeal. Not when Roarke was out here. So warm. So alive.

She stood too fast. The room spun on its axis, and she pressed a hand to the wall to steady it. "I'll go get your sleeping bag." Before he could answer, she bolted form the living room. She stepped behind the closed bedroom door, the cool dark room helping her to regain her equilibrium. Drawing air into her lungs, she stared at the mussed bedding on the floor, bedding that smelled like Roarke.

It'd be easy, too easy really, after what they'd just shared, for her to bring the bedding to him. He'd open up the sleeping bag and they'd lay on it, just talking, or maybe doing nothing at all, but simply lying there. Holding each other. And maybe, if she were really lucky, have sex.

Her cunt tightened. Wetness flooded her pussy. Sex with Roary would be everything she imagined it to be and more. From his words out there, he'd be tender, caring, see to her pleasure first, and then he'd take his own. She cleared her throat in a feeble attempt to banish the image of her lying on her back, knees wide open, Roary above her, his cock plunging into her slick opening. She gathered the bedding, knowing even after the fabric was gone the scent would linger, and carried it back to him.

"The sunlight doesn't bother you, does it?" He asked when she arranged the sleeping bag partially in the light.

Lilah shook her head. "No. I think it's my wolf. She keeps me from burning." She stepped back from the bedding, afraid if she were too close to it, she'd give into her urges. "I'm going to sleep now. If you need anything, you know where stuff is."

"Thanks," Roarke said. He rose to his feet and stretched out on the sleeping bag. "This will be perfect."

"You're welcome." Before she could say or do anything foolish, like kiss him, she turned and went back into the bedroom. Even with his sleeping bag gone, she still smelled him on the air. Stripping her clothes, she crawled into bed next to Adrian. She propped herself up on her elbow and stared at his sleeping form. She brushed a strand of white-blond hair from his forehead. He'd done so much for her, and yet, he wasn't Roarke. The thought of turning away from him twisted her gut. The alpha in the living room drew her, always had, and she suspected, always will. There were things she didn't know about her life, like would she live as long as a vampire, or would the werewolf's lifespan, albeit still longer than a human's, dominate. She wanted to find out with Roarke, and with Adrian. Breathing a frustrated sigh, she settled into the bed. She wouldn't be able to find the answers tonight anyway.

She woke to Adrian packing a bag. Dressed in head-to-toe black, a cap over his luminous hair, he looked like a different vampire than the one she knew. "You're going," Lilah said as she rubbed sleep from her eyes. She sat up, the blankets slid to the floor. Her nudity didn't bother her, though Adrian turned. His nostrils flared as he gave a long, leisurely perusal of her naked body.

"I'm going," he said. "I'll be back before sunup. If I'm not, I want you and Roarke to get the hell out of here. Go back to his pack, go anywhere, just don't stay here. If I'm not back, then things have gone horribly wrong." He slid his bag over his shoulder, checked a gun and slipped it into its holster.

Lilah watched him. She refused to believe this would be the last time she saw him. He palmed a knife, putting it in a sheath at the base of his neck. A small gun went into an ankle holster, the other in a shoulder holster. A long dagger hung from his belt, and she knew he had other weapons concealed on him. This Adrian was mad, bad, and dangerous to know. She shivered and wrapped her arms around herself. "Stay safe," she said.

He nodded, then opened the bedroom door and stepped out. "Keep her safe," he barked to Roarke. The front door slammed, and he was gone.

Lilah rocked back and forth on the edge of the bed. A keening sound emerged from her lips, and belatedly, she realized it came from her. Grief welled up. The flood had started earlier this morning with the tears she'd shed while talking to Roary. Everything she kept bottled inside collided, breaking open the barriers she'd built. Her eyes stung. Wetness rolled down her cheeks, and she realized she was crying.

She pressed her fist to her mouth, biting it. Her fangs sank into flesh, blood welling in the puncture wounds. The coppery smell penetrated the fog surrounding her, and she lapped at the ruby drops on her skin.

"Lilah?" Roary called from the living room. "You okay?"

The flood doubled. Hell, she remained calm, cool, could keep it all inside until someone asked her if she were all right. The verbal reminder that someone cared, and if Adrian didn't return, she'd have someone on whose shoulders she could lean, turned on the waterworks like a broken faucet.

She heard a muffled curse and heard the stamp of booted feet on the floor. Then, he knelt before her. "Lilah, baby," he crooned. "It's going to be all right." He wrapped his arms around her and tucked her against his chest.

"No, it isn't," she wailed. The memory of Adrian standing there loaded with weapons filled her mind. He didn't look like the Adrian she'd known. Didn't look like the vampire she remembered, all rich and stuffy compared to Mikhail's free spirit ways. And now, Mikhail was little more than a pile of ashes on the floor, though if Roarke had cleaned while she'd been sleeping, he wasn't even that anymore. And Adrian went out to do a job she should have done. Breaking and entering was more her style. Not his.

"He'll be back." Roarke spoke with such determination, Lilah wondered how he knew.

"You don't understand. It's Adrian. He's not a fighter. He's not like me." She snuggled closer to his chest. His warm skin contrasted sharply with the cold form of Adrian in the bed less than an hour ago. The beat of his heart against her ear rendered him vital and alive next to her when she felt so very dead. She swallowed the bile rising in her throat.

"I've been so strong for so long, because I've had to be," she whispered.

"Have you ever thought Adrian was strong too?" Roarke asked. He tipped her head back and cupped her chin. "I don't think you're giving him enough credit. He knows about this group, and he knows what he's going in against. I may not like that he's a vampire or that you've been having sex with him, but one thing I will admit, the bloodsucker can fight."

Lilah grinned at Roarke's choice of words. She blinked away the tears, though sorrow still threatened to pull her down. "I guess you'd know, wouldn't you?" She squeezed her arms around him, trying hard not to feel how good her breasts felt crushed against his chest. "Maybe all that guy stuff was good for something after all?"

"Yeah, maybe." His hand slid down her back to the curve of her waist and pulled her harder against the body. He sent them tumbling backward onto the floor.

Lilah straddled him. Her pussy pressed against his crotch, and though his jeans, her folds intimately cradled his hard cock. She moaned and leaned forward. Her bare breasts brushed against his chest, her nipples tight.

"Roary," she breathed and closed the space between their lips.

Hot. The sensation of warm flesh against her lips flooded her pussy with juices. She sank into him, undulating her hips against his shaft.

Roarke cupped the back of her head. He crushed his mouth to her and parted her lips with his tongue. He plunged into her, fucking her with his mouth.

The wolf raised her head. Lilah stiffened in his arms. She tore her lips from his and drew a shaky breath.

"Roarke!" She ripped herself from his embrace, rolling onto all fours. When she came up, she shook her fur, raised her muzzle to the ceiling and howled. Long and loud, she howled, letting the bitch take over and release her frustrations to the world.

She glanced at the open door. Beyond laid the front door and the moonlit night. With a yip, she took off at a run. She rushed down the short hall, into the living room. The front door hadn't been closed, and without even looking back, she raced outside.

"Lilah!" Roarke yelled.

Lilah shook her head and darted for the backyard. She yipped, howled, flopped over onto her back and rolled like a puppy in the grass. A large wolf appeared in her peripheral vision.

Roarke.

The high fence of the backyard shielded them from view. She jumped to her feet. Whirling to face him, she bared her teeth.

Roarke nipped her shoulder.

She flipped over, baring her belly and wriggling on the ground. Spreading her legs, she offered her neck, her stomach, anything in submission to him. The bitch reveled in the presence of the alpha wolf. Roarke stood, watching her. She watched him as she rolled to her feet, her head still lowered in a submissive posture. Turning, she presented her hindquarters to him and flipped her tail over her back.

Grass rustled as Roarke approached. Raising his muzzle, he sniffed the air. His breaths chuffed from his lungs. He touched his nose to the back of her legs.

Lilah shivered, but remained still.

His twitching nose found the sensitive skin beneath her tail. He sniffed her rear, her vulva, and then with his tongue licked her.

Lilah squatted down. She didn't need to look behind her to see Roarke's arousal. She smelled the pheromones on the air, and here, beneath the moon in her wolf form, she wanted him.

His front paw rested against her hip. She jumped away and with a wolfish grin spun around to face him. Jerking her muzzle toward the back of the yard, she took off at a run. He might think he could take her, but she'd make him work first.

He yipped his approval and took off after her. The fenced-in back yard provided little room to run, but Lilah made the most of it. She spun, twirled, made serpentines, and doubled back until Roarke ran beside her. His tongue lolled out of his mouth, and she barked her happiness at having him there. Tired of the chase, she flopped down on her stomach and laid her head between her paws.

Roarke stood over her, his attention focused on the house and beyond. The wolf threatened to overtake the woman, keeping her from becoming mired in her human thoughts. Instead, she thought of only one thing. He was her alpha. She rose to her feet and nipped at his shoulder in a playful attempt to draw his attention back to her. Then, she turned, presented her hindquarters to him, and looked over her shoulder invitingly.

A low rumble radiated from his chest. Lilah watched. With all her senses on alert, she smelled the exhaust from cars a few streets over, the decay of greenery they hadn't had time yet to fix, the wood from the repairs, and most of all, she smelled Roarke. She wagged her tail and waited.

He stepped forward and rested his muzzle against the base of her tail. Inhaling deeply, he sniffed her. She knew he had to smell how hot, how ready she was for his possession. Primal need settled deep in her core, and had she been in her human form she would have been slick and ready, her clit a throbbing, swollen knot of pleasure. He licked her fur, long, loving strokes that made her think of caressing hands. Roarke accepted her wolf. He knew intimately what it was like to live with a wild creature beneath the skin. Something Adrian probably never could do. She whined, thinking of her vampire lover hunting down the rogue gang.

Roarke stopped. She turned and looked at him, encouraging him to continue. His long licks made her wonder what his tongue would feel like on her clit and labia. She spread her legs, squatting down in preparation for his mounting. She'd never been taken in her wolf form before. Tonight would be the first. Their first. She let her eyelids flutter close to better concentrate on the sensation of his tongue against her fur, her vulva, and the musky, male wolf scent of him behind her.

She curled her toes into the ground, and suddenly, she touched dirt. Like electricity, the change washed over her, twisting bone and muscle until the woman replaced the wolf. She knelt on all fours, her ass in the air. Though the sensations were different, this was Roary and she'd wanted him for a very long time. She had to show him that she accepted his beast, just as she yearned to have Adrian accept hers. She saw not the wolf, but the man. Her man. And still, Roarke licked her.

Lilah moaned. She thrust her buttocks at him. The long sweeps of his tongue drove her wild. Her cream dripped down her thighs. Her breasts swung free, nipples hard and aching, and all she could think about was Roarke behind her, his chest pressed against her back, his cock buried deep inside her pussy. His big hands covering her breasts, stroking, kneading them until she feared she would explode.

"Roarke, please," she begged. Teasing swipes of his tongue brought her closer and closer to the edge. He pressed his broad forehead to the underside of her buttocks, his nose damn neared buried in her folds, and plunged his tongue inside her. Quick in and out, a tease and a swipe, he licked along the length of her channel.

Lilah's panting breaths filled the air. She lifted her hand with the need to reach between her legs and stroke herself, but Roarke's growl kept her palms planted on the ground. He licked, faster and faster, his tongue swiping over her clit with each stroke. She pumped her hips against his muzzle. His fur provided a different texture against her legs, his tongue long and nubile. Gods, she never imagined it could be this good.

Then as her climax burst through her, she couldn't imagine anything. Eyes closed, she keened her release into the wind. Spasms ran the length of her channel, her body shuddering so hard she nearly collapsed on the ground.

Suddenly, strong hands where at her hips, the muzzle and fur replaced by the man. He knelt behind her, his thighs strong against the back of her legs, and he leaned forward. He pressed his lips to the dimples at the base of her spine, working his way upwards until he'd kissed every vertebra, every inch of skin. He licked the sweat off the back of her neck, and she shuddered.

"More," she whimpered.

His big hands closed around her breasts. Her hard nipples pressed into his palm, and she arched her back to fill his hands to overflowing with her flesh. Squeezing and kneading, he whispered words to her, words she didn't know for they were in the old lupine language. The velvety accent slid over her skin, inflaming her already aroused nerve endings. She ground her hips against him and was rewarded with the feel of his hard cock between her cheeks.

She raised her face to the sky, her eyes focused on the partial moon showing in the inky dark sky. In the city, streetlights drowned out some of the splendor of the stars, but she caught sight of a few bright ones and thought of nights spent in Northwoods Territory stargazing with Roarke. Oh, she remembered.

The blunt head of his cock pressed against her labia. The promise of the thick intrusion made her moan. She dropped her head, arching her back as if she were still in wolf form, and thrust against him. His head slipped inside.

"Fuck, Lilah. You're so tight," Roarke growled.

"And you're so big. Take me, Roary! Take me!" Lilah pleaded.

He did, a pump of his hips seating him balls-deep inside her. Lilah savored his cock filling her, stretching her more than Adrian did. Closing her eyes, she groaned and struggled to catch her breath. Her muscles fluttered along his length, and for a moment she wondered, now that she'd had Roary, how could she go back to Adrian?

Chapter Ten

Roary had never experienced anything as indescribable as being buried to the hilt in Lilah's tight cunt. Her muscles fluttered around him, drawing him deeper. The hard knob of her cervix brushed against his head, and he thought of filling her womb with his seed. Cubs. Their cubs. He clenched his fingers on her hips to still the urge to pound into her right there and make it a reality. She didn't smell in heat, though with her vampire state, he wondered if she'd smell the same as a werewolf female in estrus. She might not even be able to conceive at all. He'd better stick around long enough to find out.

Slowly, oh so slowly, he had her whimpering in front of him, Roarke pulled out. In the moonlight, his cock glistened with her juices, and he looked down at it, the head just disappearing between her labia. What a beautiful sight. He thrust home again, her heat welcoming him. He'd damn well make sure she was taken care of and safe. She'd never have to worry about anything again as long as he was around.

All the protective instincts he'd tried to keep under wraps roared to the surface. His woman. His mate. His bitch. *His*. Roarke pinched her nipples and felt her shudder from her head to her toes. Her breathy cries filled the air, and the thought of her coming around his cock had his balls drawing tight up against his body. The slap of flesh against flesh echoed in his ears, mingling with the wet sounds of sex.

He smelled her on his skin. Her juices created an ambrosial bouquet of scents meant for him alone. He inhaled deeply. His heart hammered in his chest and he knew, with just one more thrust, he'd come. He willed his body to wait and trailed a hand over her stomach.

She spread her legs wider, taking him even deeper as his fingers brushed against her mons. He stroked her outer lips, a back and forth teasing motion in counterpoint to their thrusts. His fingers brushed his shaft, and he groaned at the slick touch. He made a wide circle around her clit. The plumpness begged to be touched. Swollen free of its hood, it rolled against his fingers like an overripe berry. God, she was so hot, so wet, and he wanted to wrap his lips around that nub and suck it until she screamed.

"Touch my clit," Lilah panted.

He rolled his fingers over it in feather-light touches that left her panting and begging for more. He liked her like that, her sheath tight around his cock, his name on her lips. To know that he was the one who brought her this kind of pleasure—not the vampire, but him—filled his chest with an emotion he dared not name.

Lilah. His Lilah. With a groan, he thrust harder with the need to be buried as deep inside her as possible. He wanted to possess her, claim her, mark her as his for all times, and damn if he wasn't doing it right now. He moved both hands to her hips, his fingers tightening hard enough to leave bruises, but she was a lycanthrope, which made her difficult to damage for long.

"Fuck yeah," he moaned as the first tremors of her climax started. With her cervix brushing hard against the top of his cock with each thrust, he worked to get deeper inside of her, and she welcomed it all. Her whimpers grew shriller, higher, until she screamed his name and her body convulsed around his. Her cunt gripped his cock so tight he thought she'd squeeze the come from him. Only the force of his hands at her hips held her upright.

He plunged into her body one more time and felt the seed shooting up from his balls. It burst from him in a rush. His triumphant shout hung in the air, a verbal declaration of his possession. Wave after wave of his release rolled through him, and he clenched his eyes closed as he swayed forward onto her. He caught himself with his palm flat on the ground, not wanting to crush her. His cock twitched inside her, and then was still.

Roarke gulped air. Never before had his release been so powerful. He rested his head against her sweaty back, and slowly, torturously slid his half-erect shaft from her body. He pulled her backwards with him until she sprawled on his lap. She wrapped an arm around his neck and rested her face against his chest. Reaching up, she stroked his stubbled chin.

"Roarke," she breathed his given name.

Sadness filled him when it wasn't the nickname she'd given him. He'd become half-used to being Roary to her, though as a teenager he'd hated the derivative of his given name. At one time, he'd thought it made him sound weak. Now, he welcomed it as a measure of the closeness between them.

"Lilah." He stroked her hair, and rose to his feet, still holding her in his arms. With both of them naked, he carried her around the front of the house and through the door, closing it with a kick of his foot. Not bothering with his sleeping bag, he strode into the bedroom and laid her down on the bed. Then, he stretched out beside her.

Having her here amid the sheets that smelled like Adrian hardened him again because he knew she'd chosen him. He slid his hands down her arms and captured her wrists. She gasped as he pulled them over his head, the motion thrusting her breasts at him. Leaning forward, he took the closest nipple into his mouth and rolled it around his tongue.

Lilah moaned.

Her sweaty skin was as enticing as a delicate pastry to him. He buried his face against her breast, toying with her nipple. Sucking hard enough to hollow out his cheeks, he squeezed her wrists in his left hand while he brought his right to her other breast. Yeah, now this was what he was talking about, having her spread out beneath him, constrained, her body his for the tasting. He grinned against her skin.

Her breasts, so round and perfect, tormented him. Though he could count each one of her ribs, the plump flesh against his mouth and hands pronounced her all woman. As if he could ever forget. He released her nipple with a pop, then turned his attention to her other breast.

Lilah writhed beneath his attentions. He stroked his hand over her ribs, not liking their prominence. Running for her life meant Lilah failed to take adequate care of herself. He wondered if dousing her blood with lemon lime soda had anything to do with it. His fingers found her hipbone and he swept his fingers over it, down to her mound. Against her leg, his cock throbbed to life once more.

He stroked her labia, loving the way she arched her hips to meet his touch. His fingers slid easily between her folds, and he swirled two digits around her opening. Even now, she mewled for deeper penetration and damn if he didn't want to give it to her. But not yet. He yearned to hear her whimpering and begging. Sliding his fingers away, he rolled between her thighs, and felt her legs wrap around his hips. Her heels dug into his buttocks.

Her slick pussy rubbed against his shaft, sliding it along her labia. He groaned, her wet heat surrounding him with the memory of what it felt like to be buried deep in her pussy. He flexed his hips, pressing the head of his cock against her clit. Her cry rewarded his efforts.

He buried his face between her breasts. He licked the valley, up one slope to circle her nipple with his tongue, and then he descended again and turned his attention to the other breast. He pressed her to the mattress, her arms stretched above her head like an offering. She stretched languidly beneath him, and he forced himself to savor each and every lick and nibble.

He kissed a trail downward, stretching his arms as far as they could go. Swirling his tongue around her navel, he nipped her skin. Lilah moaned. To have hours to explore this woman, the thought made his cock jerk against her leg. They didn't have hours, at least not as many as he would have liked. Still, he cherished this time with her, time without

Adrian around to distract her, or to argue with him. He closed his eyes and inhaled deeply, imprinting her smell in his mind.

Then, slowly, he kissed his way back over her stomach, between her breasts, to her collarbone where he laved the hollow with his tongue. He nibbled her chin, swiped his tongue across her lips, and kissed her. He made love to her mouth, thrusting his tongue inside and stroking it along her own. He tasted her, suckled her lower lip in his mouth.

She whimpered into his mouth, and greedily, he swallowed her cries. Roarke thrust his hips against her. His cock slid into her channel, and with a groan, he sank home. Her heels pressed against his buttocks, and he released her hands so he could brace his palms on the bed and fuck her harder.

He groaned as he filled her, his balls slapping against the tender flesh of her ass. The hard points of her nipples pressed into his chest, and her fingers curled around his shoulder blades. Her nails dug tiny half-moon furrows into his skin. Eyes closed, her head tilted back, lips parted, as ecstasy crossed her features. He'd never thought he'd seen a more beautiful woman.

She belonged to him. The first ripples of her orgasm fluttered around the head of his cock.

"More," she moaned. "Deeper."

He obliged. A pump of his hips sent her over the edge into a screaming orgasm. Her body trembled around him, her release so pure and total it stole the breath from his lungs. He plunged into her, over and over again, his skin burning with the need to be closer to her. Deep inside, his wolf raised his head to the moon and howled at the claiming of his mate.

He rode the waves of her orgasm. Moving deep inside her, he pushed her to the brink, dipping his head to bite her shoulder. He laved the red marks with his tongue. A tilt of her hips pulled him even farther inside her, and then, he saw nothing except the lights flashing behind his closed eyelids. His balls tightened, his sacs filled to near bursting. Another thrust sent him over the edge.

He cried out, a hoarse yell as he spilled himself into her. Her panting breaths mingled with his, their sweaty flesh sliding as they sought a more intimate connection. He slumped against her, then aware of his weight, rolled to the side and gathered her in his arms. He inhaled and grinned. There, now the bed smelled like him and Lilah. And Adrian. He licked a drop of sweat from her shoulder.

The front door banged against the wall.

Lilah whimpered and stiffened in his arms. They lay on top of the covers. He reached for the blanket, then closed his hand and let it fall to rest against her side. His leg covered hers, his cock still half inside her channel. He reached down to cup her ass, though whether to protect her bare body from Adrian's gaze or simply claim his possession, he couldn't say.

Adrian's heavy footfalls echoed in the living room.

"Roarke, he's back," Lilah whispered.

"I know," he answered, pressing his face into her hair. Frankly, it couldn't be much past two in the morning, and he didn't expect the vampire to return to soon. A part of him, the selfish part of him that wanted Lilah all to himself, hoped he'd never return at all. He tucked Lilah closer to his body and looked over her shoulder at the doorway to the bedroom.

Suddenly, Adrian stood there. Hands balled into fists, eyes glowing red, he glared at the bed. A scratch covered his forehead and slid down his temple. His lip looked split, and his shirt had a knife slash across the stomach. Apparently, he'd gone out looking for a rumble and found it.

"I see you've made your choice. I smell you all over each other. You wasted no time in fucking her once I was gone. Like a couple of beasts in heat," he growled.

Anger roared to life inside Roarke. "How dare you talk to her like that!" He untangled his legs from hers and tried to shove her away.

Lilah shook her head. She rolled, her breasts bobbing with the movement, her thigh tipped back giving him a partial view of her wet cunt.

"It wasn't like that," she said.

"The hell it wasn't." Adrian punched his hand through the wall. Plaster cracked, the dust pluming around him in a cloud. He yanked his hand back, bringing with it another shower of plaster dust.

"Adrian!" Lilah rose to her feet.

Adrian glared at her nude form. His nostrils flared, his erection straining the seams of his jeans. Anguish filled his gaze, and Roarke realized in spite of everything, Adrian still wanted Lilah. The vampire wiped his dusty hand on his black jeans, leaving behind white streaks.

~* * *~

After everything they'd gone through, Lilah couldn't believe Adrian's response. She never imagined he'd possess a jealous streak, not when he understood the need for blood and sex that ran through her veins. She couldn't help it. Her wolf yearned to be with her alpha, and her vampire required Adrian's domination. And yet, he'd barely given her that, so was it any wonder she turned to where she could? Aware of Roarke's come on her legs and smelling him with every step she took, she strode across the bedroom to Adrian.

"You're back. Thank Gods." Emotion welled inside her, a relief so profound she feared it'd push tears from her eyes. She wrapped her arms around him and hugged him to her naked body. The thrust of his cock pressed against her stomach. It'd only take a flick of her wrist to undo the button on his jeans and lower the zipper, and then she could drop to her knees and show him how very happy she was to have him back.

Adrian shoved her away from him. "We're finished. You have your wolf now." He spun toward the closet, grabbed a duffel bag and started stuffing clothes into it.

She stumbled away, nearly falling to her knees. Roarke rose to his feet, and she shook her head, sending him back to the bed.

"Adrian, no!" She cried. She curled her fingers around his shoulder and squeezed with all her preternatural strength.

He stilled, but didn't turn around.

She breathed deeply, wishing like hell tears didn't sting her eyes. "I worried about you. I'm glad you've returned."

"Obviously not glad enough if you've spread your legs for the wolf." He shoved shirts and two pairs of jeans into the bag.

"Don't leave me," she said. Her heart wrenched. She swallowed hard and willed the pain to go away. Imagining her life without Adrian, she couldn't. When she had wakened from her turning, his face had been the first she'd seen. Not his brother, her sire.

"I need you." It killed her to say those words and admit her weakness.

Roarke remained behind her. She prayed he'd stay still, that she'd have time to explain how whole, how vibrant she felt now that she had both a vampire and a wolf in her life. Almost as if the dual sides of her nature were suddenly balanced.

"You don't need me. You have him." Adrian repeated the words. He whirled away from her and stormed toward the door.

She hurried to follow him, her bare feet slapping on the floor. Her breasts jiggled, and she sensed Roarke following their movement. "He's not a vampire. He can't satisfy my vampire. You can."

Adrian stopped. He jerked as if he'd been shot, and slowly, so slowly she swore time halted, he turned and looked for her. "Your vampire," he said, eyes narrowing. "Is this what this is about? Because I thought you preferred your wolf."

She shook her head. "I understand the wolf. I grew up with them. The vampire scares me, but you—" Her voice broke. Her breath shuddered in and out of her lungs, and she battled the fear rising inside her. The red haze of bloodlust tinged her vision. Her incisors lengthened, itched to sink into flesh, and when she peered deep inside, she found her wolf huddled into the corner, tail tucked between its legs. "You don't scare me. And you make it all better."

Adrian's eyes widened. "How? My brother turned you against your will. You're an unauthorized turning and will never be accepted in the world of vampires, and then I let you go back home and you became a wolf. How have I made it all better? Obviously, Roarke has come for you, and you accept him. Perhaps you'd be better off with him."

"Do you really think that?" Lilah asked. Roarke's earlier words about Adrian rang in her mind.

"No, but it's tearing me up to know you lay in our bed and fucked him," he admitted.

Behind her, she heard the slide of skin across sheets and the pad of bare feet against the floor as Roarke stood. "I think we should all sit down and talk. And I think I should go put on some jeans. Lilah, you might want to dress too. I'm sure your naked body distracts us both." He turned to his bag and pulled out a pair of jeans.

Lilah watched him pull them on, concealing the taut globes of his ass and his half-erect cock. He buttoned his pants, then leaned against the wall and crossed his arms over his bare chest. Lilah stared at him for a moment, drinking in the sight of his hair-dusted pectorals and the abs she knew she'd trace with her tongue as soon as she had a chance. The bloodlust rose, matched by her inner bitch as the two struggled for supremacy. With the vampire and the wolf right in front of her, she felt like a sweet-a-holic at an all you can eat ice cream bar. Roarke jerked his chin toward her clothes.

She pulled on a pair of jeans, not bothering with underwear, and aware of the men's gazes on her, pulled a tank top on and left it untucked from her jeans. "Maybe we shouldn't talk in the bedroom," she said, all too aware of the smell of sex, old and new, surrounding her.

"Good idea." Adrian's gruff response startled her. He turned and went to the living room, where he sank onto the floor with a weary sigh.

Watching him wince from pain, Lilah frowned and shook her head. She darted into the bathroom, returning with the first aid supplies and sat down next to him.

"Take your shirt off," she ordered and opened up the bottle of peroxide.

"I'm fine." He waved her attempts away, but this close, she saw blood welling from his scratches.

"The hell you are. Now let me take a look." She tugged his shirt free of his jeans, and he quickly pulled it over his head.

"There's no use fighting with her. She badgered me into getting patched up." Roarke said. "Speaking of which, you should probably pull out the stitches since I'm healed."

"When I'm done with Adrian," she said to him as she rose onto her knees. She dabbed the peroxide soaked cotton ball on his wound and watched the antiseptic bubble against the injury. When she was certain it was clean, she leaned forward and drew her tongue along the length of the wound, knowing the coagulant in her saliva would speed the healing on the wound. She didn't do it to Roarke, but then again, being so close to him had set her nerves on edge. And if she licked his bleeding wounds, she knew she wouldn't have stopped. Then, he'd gone all tender and disarmed her.

"There. I'm not going to put any bandages on it. I'll just do the same to the one on your stomach." She sat back on her heels.

"I'll be fine," Adrian said, gently pushing her away when she bent to study his abs.

"I'm sure you will." Her gaze flicked to his erection, and she knew at the moment, he probably felt no pain. Not with her warm breath against his flesh. She dabbed the cotton ball over the wound, then dipped her head.

She drew her tongue along the length of the wound, moving slowly, savoring him as if this might be the last time she would taste his skin. His muscles fluttered beneath her touch. His hand curled against the back of her neck, massaging there, holding her face against his skin.

Lilah groaned as she sealed the last of the wound. Her womb heavy with need, she pulled back to find herself captured by Adrian's red-tinged amber gaze. Her mouth opened, her tongue sliding forward to draw the taste of his blood along her lower lip. The bloodlust rose, her fangs aching to plunge into him. Her body reminded her it'd been too long since she'd fed, really fed, not the watered down approximation of feeding on which she'd become accustomed to living.

Roarke cleared his throat.

Lilah blinked as if she emerged from a trance and scooted farther away from Adrian. She held out her hand, the gesture awkward, but when Adrian's cool fingers curled around hers and squeezed, she took a deep breath and found herself grounded. She reached for Roarke, and he clasped her other hand. She doubted the two guys would hold hands and complete the chain. It felt good though to have both sides of her nature in harmony. And now that she had it, she'd be damned if she'd give it away.

"I told Roarke everything," Lilah said to Adrian.

He nodded, his expression grim. "And he's still here."

"Yes, I'm still here. I'm not going anywhere. I think Lilah needs us both. From what I understand, she's under attack from both the vampire and werewolf communities. You know the vamps, and I know the wolves. Together, we can protect her. And obviously, she's attracted to both of us."

Lilah glared at him, daring him to keep quiet about her feelings, whatever they might be at the moment, for either man. "Roarke's right," she said, cutting off his words. "And there's something else Roarke and I discussed. I can't be the only vampire bitten by a werewolf. And I'm sure there've been werewolves bitten by vampires. That means there might be others out there like me, and if that's the case, it's something the Immortal Council and the Luna Council have to know. My first goal is neutralizing the threats to my life. My second is going to be to find these hybrids, these werepyres and find out more about them. I have so many questions. I think they can answer them."

"Fuck," Adrian cursed. He shook his head. "What if they don't want you to find them? What if they're behind the attack on your life?"

"What?" Lilah blinked. "Why would they do that?"

"Because you're a threat to them, Lilah. We all are."

Chapter Eleven

Lilah had looked so happy, so sure that she could make things turn out all right. And maybe she believed that. She'd grown up in Michigan, probably had little girl fantasies of a prince and a white knight in shining armor. Well, Adrian knew he sure as hell wasn't a white knight. That seemed more like Roarke's style. And now, he'd just dashed her hopes about the werepyres, which indeed was the correct term. The Immortal Council had known about them for ages, and they'd turned a blind eye to the fact that their war with the werewolves had created such abominations.

Abominations like Lilah. Adrian shook his head and wished he couldn't think that way about a woman he genuinely cared for. Decades of training as a descendent from vampire aristocracy was hard to break. What he learned tonight proved his brother hadn't changed and that they had bigger problems than he'd originally thought. He frowned.

"What did Mikhail get himself involved with this time?" Lilah asked. "You know your brother always had some scheme or another. He told me how he wanted to punish you for something, though he never told me what. What did he want to punish you for?"

"For not turning him when he wanted to be turned. I knew he was impulsive, rash, and certainly not a good candidate to be a vampire. But, he took the decision out of my hands. He sliced his wrists open and nearly bled to death before I found him. I did what I had to do to keep my brother alive, though the transformation brought out his worst qualities, as I feared it might. However, I couldn't let him die. I'd watched my parents die. I couldn't lose my brother, too." He slid his fingers from Lilah's hand and balled his hand into a fist. "I'm sorry. But tonight I learned Mikhail wasn't a part of The Party. He recruited from them, but he wanted something different and he'd died for it. The Party had nothing to do with my brother."

"I can't believe Mikhail worked alone." Lilah voiced his own inner disbelief.

"No, he was working with another group. I'm not sure who they are, but we have to bring this to the attention of the Immortal Council."

Lilah curled her fingers into his arm. Fear radiated from her in waves. His incisors lengthened, and out of the corner of his eye, he saw Roarke struggling against the predator response her fear evoked in the wolf. Surely, she had to sense it. She carried two predators inside her.

"They want to kill me," she whispered. Her wide eyes reminded him of the terrified young woman Mikhail had turned and he reaffirmed his vow to make sure no one ever hurt her again.

"Don't you think the Immortal Council has an intelligence network? Don't you think they know what's going on? If they're after Lilah, I don't want her anywhere near them." Roarke stated.

"I don't either, but no, I don't trust that they have this information."

"What information?" Lilah asked.

"The fact that when Mikhail couldn't recruit any more support from the Party, he went looking beyond them. Some say when he discovered what Lilah was, he made contact with others like her. And using her as their rallying cry, he was going to force the Immortal Council to acknowledge them. I don't think he wanted to kill her. I think he wanted to kidnap her." Adrian felt as if he'd dropped a bomb.

Lilah's chin dropped to her chest. She closed her eyes and shook her head. Disbelief radiated through her, and the pain and horror in her eyes when she looked at him rocked him back on his heels.

"No. I won't be a pawn in his schemes any more. I thought when he was dead he wouldn't have this ability to manipulate me. We have to convince the Immortal Council that I mean them no harm. With Roarke here that job isn't going to be easy."

"I'll leave if it will make things easier. It'll hurt like hell, but I'll do it for Lilah."

Adrian's admiration for the wolf grew. "Your leaving would hurt Lilah. I think if we need to go to the Immortal Council we should go with her balanced and secure with the both of us. I think that will make a greater impression than if we ran half strength and scared. The Immortal Council despises weakness."

"They'll see Roarke as a weakness. They'll believe I've turned to my wolf side, let it rule the vampire. And they'd be right. This is my fault. I never fully embraced what I'd become. When Mikhail turned me, I thought only of dealing, and you, well you did the best you could. We've got to go to the Council and we've got to do it as soon as possible."

"There's one more thing," Adrian said. After all he'd said, he hated revealing this last piece of information, but it was the most important. "The Party sees you as a threat. They're planning on attacking you. We've got to get out of here before the moon turns full."

"We can go to my place," Roarke offered.

"You'd bring her right into the heart of werewolf territory? That's not what I'd call keeping her safe," Adrian said.

"I won't bring my trouble to Northwoods. We'll find somewhere else or we'll stay right here." Lilah insisted with a squeeze of his hand.

"You can't stay here with a large group of Party members coming to attack. We simply can't defend against those odds." Adrian turned to Roarke. Not liking heading into werewolf territory was putting it mildly, but at the moment, it seemed they had no other choice. "Do you think you can keep her safe?" He cared little about his own safety. Against a bunch of mutts, he could hold his own.

"Do you think you could keep *us* safe?" Lilah asked. She squeezed both men's hands and pulled them toward her. "I'm not going anywhere without both of you being safe. Somehow, I think you're both tied into this somehow. I need my vampire and my wolf to be happy. Both of you want to make me happy, don't you?" She grinned and looked like someone about to open the biggest box on Christmas morning.

He couldn't deny her. With Lilah radiating such happiness, Adrian knew he'd walk over flaming hot coals if it meant keeping her that way. He waited for Roarke's response. The wolf thought too long, in Adrian's opinion, for the answer to be good.

"Yeah, I think I could. I'm the alpha. My pack members have to obey me. Comes in handy sometimes." Roarke admitted with a grin.

"I bet it does. So when do we leave?"

"How many hours do we have before sunrise?"

Adrian shrugged. "Three, maybe four."

"And you can hide under a blanket or something, right?" Roarke asked.

"What are you thinking?" Lilah countered.

"Pack your bags fast and light, sweetheart, because we're leaving tonight." He slid his fingers from hers and rose to his feet. He turned to the bedroom where his bag was and disappeared.

Lilah looked at him. "I'm sorry to put you through this. I know the pack where I grew up is probably the last place you'd ever want to go. But I'll make sure they don't hurt you. I promise." She released his hand and stood.

"And I'll make sure they don't hurt you. The higher stakes belong to you. Not only is your life in jeopardy, but now you're going home. I hardly think it'd be easy. But I'll deal. It's you I'm worried about."

"I'll be fine." She held her chin up, her eyes defiant. Yeah, that was the vampire he loved.

Wait. *Loved*?

Adrian stepped back and glanced toward the bedroom where Roarke packed his back. The room smelled of them, the kind of hot, sweaty sex he liked to have with her. They'd fucked in his bed. How in the hell could he be thinking of love at a time like this? He brushed his fingers through his hair.

"I'm sure you'll be fine, baby. And I'll make sure of it." He turned and followed Roarke into the bedroom. They had a long drive ahead of them, and most of it would be made under the cover of a blanket. Sometimes he envied Lilah's ability to go out in the sun.

~* * *~

Roarke tossed his bag into the back of the truck and double-checked the three blankets in the back seat. Thank goodness he'd purchased a four-door truck for pack business. It might be hell on gas mileage, but at least it'd hold the three of them comfortably and safely. It also was four-wheel drive. He watched Lilah toss her bag into the back of the truck. She opened the passenger door and stepped inside, situating herself on the seat and buckling the seatbelt.

Roarke stared at her as he opened the door, the stern set of her jaw, the way she clenched and released her hands in her lap. Lilah acted like she was tough and could handle this, but he knew her. When it came to returning to the Northwoods, he suspected she ranked that right up with multiple root canals in the same day. Except, he wondered if vampires even needed root canals. He chuckled to himself and stepped into the truck.

"What's so funny?" Lilah asked. She frowned and looked over her shoulder at Adrian as he arranged himself on the bench seat in the back.

"Just thinking about root canals."

"What?" She chuckled as he put the key into the ignition and started the truck.

The vehicle roared to life. "Nothing," Roarke muttered. He backed out into the empty street, and within ten minutes, her house had been left behind. The ritual weighed heavily on his mind. For all his talk about coming clean, speaking honestly, he held back the biggest secret of them all: the way to ensure Lilah's safety.

He waited until they were on the interstate, though far from being outside the garish lights of the city. "There's a way to ensure your safety in Northwoods." Roarke spoke slowly, carefully, afraid if he blurted everything out he'd have Lilah and Adrian bailing out of a 70 mph truck before he could stop them.

"What are you talking about? I'm with you. What more safety do I need? Unless you've lost that much control over your pack," Lilah said.

"There's a ritual. I've read of it in the pack histories, though it's not practiced much anymore. When there is a threat to the pack, the alpha bitch has sex with the pack members to bind them all together. In this case, Lilah, you're the alpha bitch, and you will have to have sex with Adrian and me at the same time." He turned and glanced at her, before returning his attention to the road.

"The vampires have something similar," Adrian commented.

Lilah stared straight ahead, her eyes unblinking. "You're kidding, right?"

He flinched, his ego wounded by her stark question. "No, I'm not. I'm sure you don't want to hear this any more than Adrian, but we're your pack. Not the Northwoods, though I rule them. I don't know who infected you, and I doubt you know either. I consider you part of the pack, but in reality, you're your own pack. Adrian and I are just along for the ride."

Lilah drew a sharp breath. Her mouth went dry with the images racing through her mind. After a long moment, she nodded. "Tonight. We're going to stop at a hotel soon, right? Because you haven't slept yet, and frankly, I'm tired. Before dawn, let's pull into a hotel, and then we can perform the ritual there."

"You're sure about this?" Her quick acceptance of his words startled him, though he had no doubts she probably had fantasies. He knew the romp in her yard had fulfilled one of his.

"Yeah, I'm sure." She swiveled in the seat to look at Adrian. "I feel like I have to do this. My wolf and my vampire, they need something to bind them together. I think the ritual is it."

Roarke released the breath he held with a whoosh of air. He glanced in the rearview mirror at Adrian. The vampire stared ahead, his face a stony mask. Distrust and fear warred in his gaze. "I don't know what this will do in the vampire community, Adrian. Will this cause more problems?"

Adrian shrugged. "I don't think anything like it has been done before. And you know how vampires feel about werewolves. But if Lilah wants to go through with it, I won't stop her."

"Will you participate?" Lilah wriggled in her seat so she could stare back at him. "I feel like I have to do this, but if you're just going to go through the motions, then I might as well not do it. Are you with me?"

Adrian nodded slowly. "I'm with you. Just don't expect me to do anything to the wolf."

Roarke laughed. "I was going to say the same thing. This is for us to focus our attention on Lilah. No offense, but I'd rather not have sex with you, Adrian." He grinned at Adrian's answering smile.

"Deal." Adrian said.

Lilah unbuckled her seatbelt. She leaned over the back of the seat and kissed Adrian on the cheek. "Thank you," she said. Before she sat back down, she leaned over and kissed Roarke on the cheek as well. "And thank you for the idea. I, for one, think it sounds perfect." She refastened her seatbelt and stared at the flashing streetlights and billboards. "There has to be something out there. I don't know how the others handle it, but sometimes I feel like I'm being torn up inside. It's like the vampire and the wolf want to fight, but when you think about it, their natures are more similar than they are different. Both appreciate a good hunt and a good fuck. There's a circle of life the wolves live, and although vampires are damn neared immortal, they have the circle too. Blood, life, death, birth, sex, feeding, it's all intertwined. And the need to balance it all is overwhelming sometimes." She fell silent, as if she feared she might have said too much.

Listening to her, Roarke realized she knew far more about the life of the wolf than he had ever imagined. "That was eloquent. You said it perfectly." He reached across the space separating them and squeezed her knee. If it weren't for her vampire, he could bring her home to his pack. He had no doubt the core members, the ones who knew her growing up, and had known her father, would welcome her back with open arms. Her vampire cooled any welcome she might receive, and with the Dark Moon Dogs making trouble, some might call him weak for going to her. He focused on the white line in the center of the highway, his thoughts zooming through his mind as fast as the dashes painted on the road flashed by. The Dark Moon Dogs. The Party. It all came down to the fucked up politics of the preternatural world. He grinned. At least such stupidity was universal. Human, vampire, werewolf, all politics were screwy as far as he was concerned.

Adrian lay down on the back seat and pulled the blanket over him. Lilah curled up, her neck bent, her legs tucked beneath her. From behind her, Adrian handed her another blanket, and she pulled it over her. Soon, her deep, even breathing filled the truck's cab. The steady sound soothed him, and with Adrian disinclined to talk, Roarke found himself left alone with his thoughts.

About thirty minutes before sunrise, Roarke found a small hotel. Nothing fancy, the discount chain boasted a clean bed, a place to crash, and so long as he paid in cash and used a fake name, some anonymity for Lilah. He pulled into the parking lot.

"Lilah? Adrian? We're at the hotel. I'm going to go register."

In the back, Adrian stirred. Lilah murmured, but remained sleeping. With a parting glance at the tumble of mahogany hair around her face, he opened the truck door and stepped out. Ten minutes later, he returned with two room keys. Silently, he passed one to Adrian, then drove the truck around the back of the hotel. Lilah still hadn't woken.

"I'll get the bags, if you want to bring her inside," Roarke said. His fingers itched to hold Lilah in his arms, but letting Adrian take care of her would only smooth the way for the ritual tonight. He locked the doors on his side, and then grabbed the three duffel bags and the cooler of food and blood bags. He doubled checked the doors once Adrian gathered Lilah into his arms. Roarke's heart clenched at the sight.

"Are we there?" She murmured against the vampire's shoulder.

"We're here, honey," Adrian said, his lips brushing her hair. He pressed a kiss to the top of her head, and carried her inside.

Roarke led the way, holding open the doors. As soon as they stepped into their simple king room, he closed the door, locked it and fastened the chain. He made sure the curtains were closed. He watched as Adrian set Lilah down on the bed. She kicked off her shoes and socks. Yawning, she stretched, arching her back and pushing her breasts against the fabric. He dropped the duffel bags next to the low table that held the television.

"So, what do we do?" Adrian turned to face him. He stood stiff, hands clenched in half-fists, his lips a thin, tense line.

We fuck. Mentioning it like that wouldn't get him any brownie points. "Well, there are a few ritual words to say, but this isn't an official pack function. Pretty much Lilah tells us she's taking us as her pack, and then she has sex with us...at the same time." Oh yeah, he'd forgotten to mention that part.

"At the same time?" Lilah sat up on the bed, her gaze darting from Adrian to Roarke, then back again. A big grin covered her face as she pulled off her tank top. "When do we begin?"

Roarke stared at her naked breasts and prayed his mouth wasn't hanging open like a teenager's. Then, at the excited look in her eyes, he laughed. "Anytime you want, honey."

~* * *~

Lilah watched both men stare at her naked chest. A power like she'd never felt before surrounded her, filled her, and reminded her that while she may bow to the dictates of her wolf and her vampire, she was very much a woman. And right now, the woman held firm control over the other two aspects of her personality. She slid from on top of the covers. She stood next to the large king-size bed and unbuttoned her jeans.

"I don't know the ritual words, but I can tell you what I feel. Adrian, you protected and sheltered me when I was my most vulnerable. You taught me about my vampire and myself. I want you in my pack, because in my pack, you're both alpha males to me." She unzipped her jeans and pushed them over her hips. She stood naked, letting both men visually drink their fill of her body. "I take you both as my pack."

Adrian's throat worked as he swallowed. She let her gaze roam his chest. His t-shirt stretched across pectorals and biceps, and where it was tucked into the waistband of his jeans, she saw the outline his lean, flat abs. She stepped forward and fisted her hands in the fabric and tugged it free of his jeans. He shivered as she flattened her hands against his skin. She caressed him from waist to collarbone, then circled him with her arms and stroked his back.

"You're mine." She curled her fingers into his flesh, scoring him with her nails. Releasing him, she walked around him, tore his shirt from his body, and leaned forward. She licked his wounds, moaning as the coppery taste of his blood filled her mouth.

She licked them closed. Cupping his ass, she squeezed. "You're mine," she repeated.

Turning on her heel, she faced Roarke. Lilah swallowed hard as she faced him. The depth of emotion in his gaze rocked her back on her heels. Raw lust filled his eyes, tempered with something possessive, something more. She dared not name it, not wanting the answering emotion in her own heart. Tonight was a sexual ritual. She headed into the Northwoods Territory and dared not think of anything else.

"Roary, my childhood friend, I welcome you into my pack. You watched out for me, cared for me, and I loved you for it. My bitch calls to your wolf. She howls her pleasure at finally finding a mate." Lilah padded barefoot across the carpet. She unbuttoned the top button of his shirt. With a grin, she ripped open the placket of his shirt, sending buttons flying.

"And I think you'll find I'm a completely different than I was back then." She dropped to her knees and unfastened his jeans.

Roarke groaned. He cupped the back of her head, his fingers clenching and releasing against her scalp as she lowered his zipper and freed his cock. Thick and hard, she inhaled his musky scent and brought her lips to it. Wrapping her fingers around him, she stroked him, base to head, then her grip tightened, and she worked him, sliding the foreskin back and forth over his sensitive crown. His breathing hitched, and the woman and the wolf knew they held the power.

She glanced over her shoulder. "Come to me, Adrian." She wiggled her buttocks. "My ass is all yours tonight."

Adrian said something in his native tongue as he advanced toward her, tearing off his jeans as he went. He knelt behind her, his big hands on her hips. He bent his lips to the nape of her neck.

Lilah leaned forward and wrapped her lips around Roarke's shaft. She drew him deep into her mouth, the taste of him mingling with Adrian's blood. Roarke's salty essence made her hunger to feel his broad shaft penetrating her. He cupped her face, a hand on each cheek, and held her to him. She nibbled along his length, sucking and swirling her tongue along the veins that roped his shaft. Each groan urged her on.

Adrian cupped her breasts. A pinch of her nipples sent a spasm of heat straight to her pussy, her channel contracting, growing wet in anticipation of a sexual invasion. Adrian palmed her flesh, his lips raining kisses along the back of her neck, her shoulders, and her back. Each swipe of his tongue against her skin sent a sensual message to her nerves. Her nipples hardened, and around Roarke's cock, she moaned.

She pulled back, his shaft slipping from her lips with a heavy weight. She wanted to be sandwiched between the two men, her breasts pressed against Roarke's chest, his cock along her stomach, Adrian's shaft parting the cheeks of her ass. She licked and kissed a trail along the arrow of hair bisecting Roarke's abs, pausing to swirl her tongue in his navel. She nipped near the indentation, tasted his sweat, his skin, and there, just beneath her lips, his heart pounded.

Blood. Her fangs tingled, made her long to sink them into his flesh. He must have known, sensed it somehow for he dropped his hands to her waist and whispered, “Bite me.”

Lilah moaned. Adrian’s fingers slid along her labia, his thick digit toyed with her swollen clit. Caressing the hood, he urged the bud to expand more, and the touch of a calloused fingertip made her bite down in pleasure. Her fangs penetrated Roarke’s skin, and hot blood flowed into her mouth.

Pleasure radiated along her nerves. He tasted so real, so primal, the wolf in her rising with the vampire at the smell, and taste, of blood. She wanted to drink him down, have him in her body in every way possible.

Another finger thrust into her channel. Her muscles contracted and a heavy weight at the top of her womb told her she was about to come and come hard. She whimpered, still drinking of Roarke.

“Lilah,” Adrian’s rough growl pulled her attention from the blood pouring into her body, and she pulled back.

She’d drunk a lot, and had he been human, he probably would have collapsed. Her blood sang with vitality. Licking the wound, she pressed an open-mouth kiss to the skin. She sucked, wanting to leave a large hickey branding him as hers. She nipped and pulled at the skin, Roarke’s groans and erection telling her how much he liked the rough treatment. When he had a bruise marred by two little pin points, she stopped and looked up at the werewolf.

A second finger joined the first thrusting into her slick core, and she realized Adrian finger fucked her. In front of her, Roarke stroked and rubbed her clit, and then his finger made a foray into her channel. Lilah moaned. The two men filled her, stretched her, and she thought perhaps she’d take both of them in her pussy. She sought and found Roarke’s mouth, pulling him down to her. She kissed him, letting him taste his blood on her lips. Her tongue stroked the length of his and the fingers at her pussy grew more insistent.

“Let us hold you between us,” Adrian said. He bit her shoulder, his fangs sinking deep as he drank from her.

Pleasure tore her lips from Roarke’s, and she moaned as Adrian drew her juices back to circle the tight ring. One finger, then two, pressed against her back entrance. She relaxed, allowing the digits to slip inside.

Roarke added a third finger to her pussy. Fore and aft, the men filled her, their fingertips touching through a thin barrier. They stroked in counterpoint, Adrian filling her ass as Roarke retreated from her cunt. Back and forth until she hung suspended between them and could do nothing but ride the waves of pleasure as they crested through her body.

Lilah whimpered. Her wolf howled deep inside, the need for release overpowering. Sated by Adrian's blood, her vampire welcomed Adrian's gentle attentions, and the woman simply enjoyed it all. Her muscles tightened, her nipples diamond-hard where they brushed against Roarke's chest. She rocked, her hips moving with each thrust and retreat. And then she could do nothing but hold on as her release crested. She screamed, her body vibrating with the force of her climax. Waves of pleasure crested through her, slammed into her with all the force of an out of control freight train. Her nails dug into Roarke's skin, and he growled as he pressed the palm of his hand against her clit to prolong her pleasure.

Too much. So sensitive, her pussy nearly hurt to be stroked, she whimpered and cried as the waves subsided. She wanted more, so much more.

"Are you ready?" Adrian asked, his voice husky with need.

"Yes," she moaned spreading her legs and wrapping them around Adrian's hips to draw his cock into her body. She felt his crown bumping against her clit, and she thrust against it.

The broad head of Adrian's penis pressed against her sphincter. Lilah relaxed, willing him to fill her completely. And then, with a push, her muscles stretching around him, he did. He rested just inside, a low, erotic groan issuing from his throat. Lilah closed her eyes. She pressed her forehead against Roarke's chest, the sheer act of holding her head upright almost too much. Her orgasm left her limp, ready for the men's passion. Adrian thrust his hips and filled her fully.

"Oh yes! Your turn, Roary," she whispered. She couldn't wait to be filled by both of them, to finally, at last, have her wolf and her vampire sated.

"You ready?" He asked, positioning his cock at her entrance.

"Please," she breathed.

At her soft word, he thrust into her. More delicious than before, with Adrian filling her from behind, Roarke filled her from the front. Inch by inch, he worked his way into her tight sheath until both men were seated balls-deep inside her. She imagined their flesh touching between her legs, their balls hanging together, their thighs on either side of her. Two sets of hands held her upright, one on her hips and one on her waist. And then, Roarke leaned forward and kissed her. His tongue filled her mouth as his cock filled her cunt. With a moan, he started to move.

Lilah shuddered. She never imagined it could feel like this, all sweat and sex. Her juices dripped down her legs, the men's husky sighs and groans surrounding her in a sensual cocoon. As Roarke thrust into her, Adrian retreated, the counterpoint keeping her on edge. She whimpered and thrust her hips back and forth between them.

Each thrust pushed her higher. She drowned in pleasure, the men anchoring her to the world. She leaned back against Adrian. His strength buoyed her, reminded her of when she'd woken up from the turning and he was there. His name was a mantra on her lips; Roarke's name a chant, and together, the two men pushed her farther than she ever thought she'd be able to go.

Chapter Twelve

With his cock tight in Lilah's ass, Adrian looked over her shoulder at the werewolf. His head thrown back, mouth open, the heartbeat in his neck pulsing like a beacon as he pumped into Lilah's cunt. She hung between them, suspended, and had he been thinking he might have called it an apt description of her life. As it was, he could do nothing but thrust into her, feeling the werewolf's cock slide along the length of his, separated by only a thin membrane, and it was the most erotic thing he'd ever experienced.

Lilah's whimpering cries escalated. If there were anyone in the adjoining rooms, no doubt they heard. Adrian didn't care. Let them listen. Let them know he possessed this woman, body and soul. He grinned, baring his fangs and thrust again.

"Oh God. Adrian! Roarke! I'm coming!" Lilah exclaimed. She shattered between them, her cunt and ass milking them for all they had. Her body shuddered, her breath pounded in and out of her lungs, and her pulse, oh hell, it fluttered and jumped, daring him to lean forward and take a bite.

He couldn't resist. He slipped his fangs into her, the pleasure of her blood filling his mouth as he filled her body pushing him over the edge. Against her skin, he groaned. He pumped once more, then stiffened, as he spilled his seed inside her. His world narrowed down to tight muscles around his cock and the rush of his orgasm. Balls tight, lights flashing behind his closed eyelids, he gave everything he had to the woman in his arms.

Roarke growled. The feral sound raised the hair on the back of Adrian's neck, and had he any strength, he might have pulled Lilah behind him for protection. He stiffened and came, triggering another round of cries from Lilah. Spent, the three stumbled to the bed. His cock slipped from her, and he noticed Roarke's had done the same. Then, he knew nothing but the sweet weight of Lilah's body draped over his, and the heavy weight of the werewolf on the bed beside him.

"Damn," she whispered. "Damn."

"Yeah," Adrian groaned. He threw his arm over his forehead. For long moments, neither said anything.

Lilah flipped over on her stomach. She curled her arms around both men, a sleepy, contented smile on her face. "So, since you're my pack now, does that mean you guys get to do what I say?" She grinned mischievously.

"Only if you do what I say," Adrian said. He leaned forward and kissed the tip of her nose.

"And that goes double for me," Roarke said. He snuggled next to Lilah, his hand curving protectively around her stomach.

Adrian watched Lilah and the wolf, realizing that at this moment it didn't bother him that the wolf had his hands all over her body. He curled against them, loving the feel of Lilah's lush, warm curves next to him.

"So what happens when we get to your territory?" Adrian looked over Lilah's head and asked Roarke.

Roarke shrugged. "I need to make sure I have control of my pack and ensure Lilah isn't harmed. Then, I'll go after the Dark Moon Dogs." He stroked Lilah's hair. Her soft, even breaths and tiny snores told Adrian she'd fallen asleep.

"Let's get her under the covers," Adrian suggested. Outside, he sensed the rising sun. The light weighed on him, pulling him down with the promise of sleep.

Roarke nodded, and together, they eased the covers down and Lilah between them. Adrian laid on one side of her, as far away from the window as he could get, and Roarke laid on the other. Tucking the covers to his chin, Adrian closed his eyes. Lilah's scent surrounded him, and the presence of the wolf reminded him of what they'd just done. He'd liked it. He really did, and that, more so than the fact that he might love Lilah, scared him.

~* * *~

Coming back to the Northwoods twisted like a knife in her gut. Lilah stared out the truck window at the familiar houses and yards she'd known while growing up. The houses had changed, some had new paint, others had fencing and new cars in the driveway, but the small Michigan town never knew about the lycanthropes who lived in their midst. Or maybe they did and they simply didn't care. Lilah had never been able to tell which.

She breathed deeply, pulling Adrian and Roarke's scents into her lungs. The two men steadied her, kept her from spiraling down in her thoughts. They passed the bar, the alley behind the place where she'd been infected. Stiffening in her seat, she struggled to look away, and knew if she went there, the dark stain of her blood would still show against the old brick building and the mocking laughter of her attackers would ring in her ears.

"We're almost there," Roarke said.

Lilah nodded, hoping he took her jumpiness as a sign of nerves caused by returning home. The small bungalow where she had lived with her father sat on the corner, the big oak tree still boasting the rope and board swing her father had made for her. She smiled and when she glanced at Roarke, he looked at her, old memories haunting his eyes.

"It's been a while," she said in an attempt to ease his worries. Then, he pulled into the driveway of his home, only two blocks down from hers. The two-story house looked small on the outside, but Lilah remembered the spacious rooms and the full-sized basement.

"We're here," Roarke announced. He glanced at the stars shining outside the window. "It's safe, Adrian."

The rustle of blankets announced Adrian's waking. He sat up, his hair mussed from sleep. Lilah grinned and resisted the urge to pull him to her for a kiss. "You still have that hot tub?" Lilah asked. "Because I'd love a good long soak." She watched as the mental image of her naked and surrounded by frothy bubbles filled the guys' minds. They grinned, eyes wide and dark with hunger.

"I do. And the last one there has to scrub everybody's backs." He opened the door and bounded out.

Lilah sauntered after him after winking at Adrian. She watched as in record time, he hurried everything into the house. He dropped the bags inside the door and carried the cooler to the refrigerator.

"The hot tub is still on the back porch. I don't mind being the loser." He set the cooler on the floor, and then grabbed Lilah around the waist. Hauling her against him, he captured her mouth with his. His long, lingering kiss and the hard ridge of his erection left no doubt what he planned to do with her once he got her in the hot tub.

Although she had minor aches from early this morning, her pussy creamed at the thought. "I'll hold you to it." She turned to Adrian. "Follow me."

"With pleasure." The rumble of his voice swirled through her veins, and she paused, reaching back to tangle her fingers with his. Right now, she ignored her fears about being back in the Northwoods and simply desired to savor every moment she had. Something in the back of her mind told her if she didn't, she might loose this time forever.

Twenty minutes later, Lilah sank chin-deep in churning water. One of the jets pulsated against her lower back. She closed her eyes and sighed with pleasure. Adrian sat next to her, his arm resting along the back of the tub. And Roarke sat on the other side of her, his hand against her thigh.

The back door banged open. Three men dressed in jeans and work shirts with the sleeves rolled up stormed onto the back porch. The leader boasted a scar running from the corner of his mouth over his chin, as if his lip had been torn open. Thick curly black hair erupted from the opening of his shirt. His jeans stretched taut over muscled thighs. He looked like a scarred, pissed off bulldog.

The other two men were just as muscular, but much younger. Henchmen, Lilah decided, and focused her attention on the scarred man.

Roarke sat up, his gaze narrowing. "Haven't you heard of knocking?" He glanced at Lilah making sure the bubbles covered her chest. "Get out. I'll see you when I'm ready."

Bulldog, as Lilah decided to call him, stepped forward. He sniffed the air, glaring at her. Derision filled his gaze, not lust, and Lilah didn't know whether to be relieved or worried Roarke might rip of his head. His smell identified him as a wolf. A stinky, nasty, sweaty wolf, but a wolf just like the two standing behind him.

"What the hell are you doing with two vamps?" He strode forward and slammed his fists on the edge of the tub hard enough to rattle it.

Roarke lunged at him. Water sprayed as Roarke rose out of the water, his hands gripping the wolf's throat. He hurled him backward, then reached for a towel and wrapped it around his waist. He stepped forward, pushing the three men back on the porch.

"What the fuck are you doing barging in uninvited and questioning my actions?" Fury radiated from him. "Go back to your junkyard, dog." His voice growled, a low, menacing threat.

"I heard you were back. Nice of you to run off when the Dogs are trying to take over this place."

Energy crackled along Lilah's skin. Her wolf howled, the need to shift and stand beside its mate over riding everything. She gripped Adrian's arm, trying to bring the vamp to life and haul the wolf back from the brink. She whined, the soft sound drawing the men's attentions.

"She's a bitch?" Bulldog roared.

"Leave her out of this." Roarke shielded her from their sight with his body. He pointed at the door. "I shouldn't have to tell you twice. Get out.

I'll call a pack meeting tomorrow tonight." He crossed his arms in front of his chest.

Lilah sucked in gulps of air. She watched Bulldog's gaze flicker back from her to Roarke, to the vampire again. He glanced at the two men behind him and jerked his finger toward the door.

"Now," Roarke roared. "They stay. You all go." He grabbed his jeans and yanked them on, giving Lilah a flash of his pale ass.

Pack business. She'd seen it before, knew how bloody it could get. The fact that Roarke dressed told her he didn't intend to shift and simply tear the men's throats out. They challenged him. They had come uninvited into his den. By pack law, he could have them killed and no one would be any wiser. The fact that he didn't spoke volumes.

Roarke stepped forward. He grabbed Bulldog around the throat and lifted him so the hefty man dangled an inch off the ground. Squeezing his hand until the man's face turned red, he leaned forward and growled. "You're my second. When I give an order, you take it. If I tell you to stick your dick in a light socket you say, 'Yes, sir. How far, sir?' I'm tired of your fucking little power games. You will return to your fuck buddies and you'll tell them that the alpha has spoken. There will be a pack meeting tomorrow and they will all be there. You will be there, do you understand?" Roarke flung the man away from him.

Bulldog stumbled, his arms cart wheeling as he landed on his ass. He gasped for air, his wheezing breaths filling the night. The two men behind him, to give them credit, stood still. They didn't tremble and they didn't piss themselves.

"Show me your throat," Roarke ordered.

Bulldog glared.

Roarke kicked him. "Show me your fucking throat!"

Bulldog lifted his chin a fraction of an inch.

"Not good enough." Swooping to Bulldog's side, Roarke grabbed his hair and cranked his neck back so hard Lilah heard it pop.

She gasped.

Clenching Bulldog's hair, Roarke lowered his face next to the man's neck. He growled. "You're too pathetic to bite." He said after long moments and shoved Bulldog away. The man scrambled out of arm's reach.

Roarke stood and turned to face the two henchmen. "You two, on your knees."

Both men dropped to their knees, chins raised, throats bared to Roarke. He strode around them, his deliberate footfalls echoing on the deck. Bulldog didn't stand, but moved to his knees, his chin lifted in a mocking of the two other men's obedient postures. Roarke kicked him. Bulldog grunted.

"Tony. Marcus. Your bitches expect better of you. I am your alpha. You will do what I say, and I order you away from my second. He's poison. And like poison, he'll have to be leeched out of the system. If I see you within so much as ten feet of my second, I'll kill you all. Spread the word. Anyone caught near him shall suffer the consequences. He is shunned. His name shall not be spoken by the pack."

Bulldog whimpered.

"Go home boys. Let's pray you don't make a mistake as stupid as this one again."

"Yes, sir. Thank you, sir." Marcus and Tony rose to their feet and hurried away, leaving Bulldog on the deck.

"You can't shun me," he said.

"Yes I can, Eugene. I just did. You're still my second until you're replaced, but you're dead to us. No one shall speak to you, including your bitch and cubs. I'll call them myself." When Eugene didn't move, Roarke snarled. "Get out of here," he barked.

Eugene rose to his feet, keeping his eyes averted. He hurried after the brothers. A moment later, the front door slammed, and the sound of tires squealing on the pavement filled the air. Once they were gone, Roarke turned back to the tub. The jets had stilled during the confrontation, and Lilah wrapped her arms around herself. Roarke's actions chilled her to the bone. If he'd lost that much control over the pack, she shuddered to think how she would be welcomed. She wouldn't. She'd be killed where she stood and there was nothing Roarke or Adrian could do about it.

He strode back to the tub and sat down on the edge. "I'm sorry you had to see that. Eugene has been trying to take me out for a while. I have to make a phone call. When I get back, I'll explain."

Lilah nodded. She vaguely remembered Eugene, now that his name had been mentioned, as Roarke's uncle's enforcer. He must have stepped up when Roarke's uncle had passed away, leaving the ownership of the pack to Roarke. A dangerous man, she remembered being afraid of him as a child. Now, she wasn't. In the social pack of the wolves, shunning was tantamount to death, and with his phone call, Roarke would sentence and execute him. She nodded.

She watched Roarke step into the house for what was understandably a difficult job. When the door closed, she turned to Adrian.

"What was that all about?" he asked. "I don't like that we've brought you here." He brushed a strand of hair away from her eyes.

"I'm glad he did since it's pack business. Roarke's in a precarious position right now. The pack isn't going to like you or me. No matter what they say or do, we cannot start a fight here. We need to help Roarke get the Dark Moon Dogs out of his territory and seal up his power base. With him strong, we won't have to worry about attacks on my life. Do you really think The Party is going to come after me, if I'm surrounded by werewolves?" Deep in her heart, her feelings or possible feelings for Roarke aside, she felt being here was the best thing to do.

"You have a point." Adrian glanced at the house, and then back at her. "But I'm a hundred percent vampire. How do you think they're going to act towards me?"

"It's going to be rough. You can handle it. Just don't start anything and always let them make the first move. You're with me, and you're with Roarke." She chuckled when Adrian frowned and shook his head. "And no, not that way either."

"You don't have to protect me. It's not your job. I'm supposed to be protecting you. I just wish there were some better way to do that than to bring you here." He stroked the back of her neck, the gentle back and forth moving erasing the chill of Roarke's confrontation with his pack.

Lilah nodded as she watched him step out onto the back porch.

He scanned the area, and when he saw they still sat in the hot tub, he grinned. Shedding his jeans on the way, he stepped naked into the water and activated the jets once more. "I made the phone calls. It's done. There will be a pack meeting tomorrow, an hour after sunset. I want you there, Adrian. And you too, Lilah."

"I'll be there," she said, and heard Adrian rumble his assent. "Have things really gotten that bad? I never saw a challenge like that when I was here before."

"Because most of it was hidden from you. Eugene's been causing trouble since my uncle ruled the pack. I think Eugene thinks since dad went AWOL that he should have taken over the pack since my uncle and his second both were killed in that car accident." He eased next to Lilah and stretched out his arm along the back of the tub. When he encountered Adrian, he pulled back.

"That's okay," Adrian said.

Gently, Roarke cupped the back of Lilah's neck, his hand above Adrian's. He massaged gently, and Lilah sat there in silence. The two men in her life on either side of her and thoughts of pissed off werewolves running through her mind. She hoped the rest of the pack fell in line, otherwise she would have been better off taking her chances back at her house. And she knew neither Adrian or Roarke would want her returning there any time soon.

~* * *~

Adrian thought seeing a werewolf pack meeting from a vampire's point of view proved interesting. He leaned against the front wall of a large rec room in Roarke's basement, arms crossed over his chest. As alpha, Roarke stood in front of him with Lilah next to him, and a step behind him, in the traditional submissive role of the alpha's bitch. The murmur in the room grew to a deafening roar and Roarke raised his hands for silence.

Adrian had to hand it to the wolf. Faced with pissed off people, a member of a hated species in the room, and a woman who everybody wanted to kill, he handled himself well. In fact, Adrian compared him to some of the members of the Immortal Council he'd known throughout the ages, and Roarke bested even the smooth, ancient vampires. That was quite the feat.

"Where were you?" a scruffy looking young man asked from the back of the room. Beside him, his companions looked down at the ground and tried not to be noticed.

"Handling business," Roarke said.

"What kind of business? With the vampire bitch?" The speaker sat in the front row, his black hair molded into a mohawk with three inch spikes. More metal than flesh hung from his ears, and he had a stud in his nose and his lip pierced. He wore all black, though Adrian suspected it was a fashion statement more than for fighting.

Roarke bounded forward. He shoved up the man's right sleeve, revealing a tattoo the same as the dead wolf had. "What the fuck you doing with the Dogs, Charlie? Why don't you just drink too much and drive too fast like other boys your age?" He tore the sleeve as he shoved it down. "Yes, I had business with Lilah. But she's not the 'vampire' or the 'Vampire bitch' to any of you. She's my mate, bonded by pack law and ancient ritual. You'll treat her with respect or you'll have me to deal with." Roarke leaned into the man's face until he nodded. The stench of fear rolled from him.

Keeping law by the fist held some definite advantages. Of course, when the masses got tired of oppression they fought back, but Adrian didn't see that here. Those he saw causing trouble were in the minority. The rest looked submissive, fearful even. Eugene stood in the corner. No one looked at him. No one spoke to him.

"We're not here to discuss Lilah. We're here to discuss the Dogs. Charlie, get your ass out of here, and take any other mutts with you." Roarke glared at him.

Charlie rose shakily to his feet, he nodded to two other youths trying to be toughs and they followed him out. Adrian looked at the remaining ones closely in an attempt to see if they really were Dogs and simply not acknowledging it. Roarke must have had the same idea, because he forced each pack member to meet his gaze. When they all did, he took his seat. Lilah and he sat as well.

"I've heard about the attacks while I was gone. Apparently, my second did not defend you properly. For that and his subsequent actions on my return, I've shunned him." Roarke focused his attention on a wolf with his arm in a sling. "James, I'm sorry they hurt you. I'll have extra wolves patrolling your property. In fact, I call for extra patrols. My new second, Adrian, will assign them after our discussions tonight."

Adrian straightened up. Surely, another wolf had to be called Adrian.

Cries of disbelief and outrange rang in the basement room, and frankly, Adrian understood why. He was a vampire from the aristocracy. He couldn't be a second in command and an Enforcer, if Roarke were to be believed, to a bunch of werewolves. He glanced at Lilah, saw her sitting there, her expression schooled, though her glance flickered between him and Roarke.

"Silence!" Roarke roared. "I am your alpha and I appointed the best person for the job. He might not be a wolf, but he can fight and keep you safe. You will honor my decisions or be packless."

That was a hell of an "or else" Roarke tacked onto that statement, and though the mutterings continued, eventually the room grew silent.

Adrian rose to his feet and went to stand behind Roarke. He laid his hand on the wolf's shoulder, surprised when he didn't flinch from his touch.

"I am honored to be your Second, pack leader." He hoped he sounded deferential enough. His kind had always been at war with the wolves. To be subservient to one chafed. He'd do it for the woman sitting behind them. Lilah. Even now, he smelled the hint of her on Roarke's skin.

"You kept my mate safe. You will keep her pack, our pack, safe as well," Roarke said.

Adrian suspected it was some sort of ritual closure. Damn these wolves and their rituals. With each word, Adrian felt himself being bound deeper into the pack. But then again, so was Lilah, and from the wary look in her eyes, she didn't like it any more than he did. In front of the pack, he doubted he could give her an encouraging grin, so he settled for standing behind Roarke and offering his support the only way he knew how.

Chapter Thirteen

Roarke expected his pack's outraged reaction to his announcement that he replaced Eugene with Adrian. Having a vampire as his Second certainly was unprecedented. But after seeing the way Adrian had kept Lilah safe, Roarke knew he wanted no one else at his back. Not only would Adrian keep vigil over Lilah, he'd also do the same for Roarke. Adrian was all about Lilah's happiness, so he'd do it for no other reason than her. Right now, that was enough.

Roarke sensed her disbelief and anger radiating at the back of his head. He ignored it. Adrian stood behind him like a rock, and that strong presence would make the pack think twice about messing with any of them. He expected Lilah to shift and knew once the pack saw he ran with a wolf bitch at his side, well, provided pups came along soon, he figured people would quit minding. As far as he knew, she could be with pup. They hadn't used protection. He'd seen no condoms in her house. She hadn't taken any pills. For a moment, his control slipped, and he frowned. If she were in this much danger and pregnant, well, he doubted Adrian would live to be his second for long.

He dismissed the last of his pack, the news about the Dog attacks not sitting well. Eugene's actions left the pack in a hell of a mess, and frankly, Roarke debated killing him and keeping the miserable scum from breathing any more air inside pack territory. He suspected Eugene conspired with the Dogs, and surely, by now, the rogue group had heard of Roarke's return and his ultimatums. He closed his eyes and pinched the bridge of his nose. With just Adrian and Lilah in the room, he could afford to be concerned.

Roarke stood, swiveled his chair around, and faced them.

"What do you think you're doing making Adrian second? He's a vampire." Lilah asked. She kept her voice down in case any pack members were still nearby.

"Like I don't know that," Roarke said. He'd dealt with pissed-off wolves, now he had to deal with his bitch. He bit back a frustrated growl. "But he kept you safe. And should something happen to me, he'll continue to do so."

"Nothing's going to happen to you, right?" Fear filled her eyes. When he didn't answer, she glanced at Adrian who remained impassive.

She knelt beside Roarke and rested her arms on his knees. "Tell me you're not in danger because of this. If you are, I'll leave."

Roarke snagged her arm and pressed his cheek into her palm. "I'm an alpha male of a large and established pack. I'd be in danger even if we didn't have to deal with the Dark Moon Dogs. I'm a werewolf. Danger comes with the territory." He turned his face and kissed her skin.

Lilah sighed and leaned against him.

Adrian stood next to them, an almost comforting presence, and Roarke appreciated his being there. "Now, let's go into the workout room. I want to spar with you." Roarke raised his head. "And with you, Adrian. We'll have to set up regular training schedules. I don't want either one of you training with any pack members but me."

Lilah stood. Her brow furrowed and she screwed up her mouth in the cute way she did when she was thinking about working up a good mad. "You said the ritual would make me part of the pack. I'm not pack now?"

"Not like that at all. The ritual made us a pack. You, me, and Adrian. We balance your wolf and your vampire. We're your own, personal pack. The Northwoods Wolves, I don't trust at the moment. And neither should you. Either of you." He reached for her, and she pushed him away.

"So you brought me up here, into a pack of wolves that you don't trust? You lead them! How can you not trust the wolves you lead?" Lilah spun away, moving toward the door.

Roarke bolted after her with Adrian hot on his heels. "Lilah, wait!"

"No!" She yelled. She left the room, rounded the corner and hurried down to the workout room. Good. At least there he could corner her and get her to explain. He would have thought she'd be ecstatic that he appointed Adrian his second.

Steady thumps told him she'd found the heavy weight bag and pounded on it. He watched the bag swing, realizing she easily had the strength of most of his male wolves. The vampire must give her additional strength. He filed the information away. Moving to the outside of the bag, he held it for her, and if anything, she pounded harder.

He held the bag, understanding her need to vent her frustration and kept silent.

She pushed the bag away, nearly knocking him over with the force of the blow. Whirling, she growled under her breath, and he sensed her bitch growing dominant. "If you didn't think the pack was safe, you shouldn't have brought me here," she snarled. "And if you didn't think it was safe, you shouldn't have let him bring me." She included Adrian in her temper. "What'd you think that ritual would do? Let you fuck me again!"

"No. It wasn't like that." He closed his eyes against the wash of pain that her words evoked. He'd never do anything to hurt her. Didn't she know that already? Apparently not because she was mad as hell at him.

"Then why did you bring me here?" She spat the words at him. Her accusation stung. An alpha never put his bitch in harm's way.

"Because I love you!" The words left his mouth in a rush of air. He stared at her, watched her absorb his words. Stop. Her eyes went wide. Her hands flew to her mouth.

"You what?" Adrian growled.

"Fuck you, Roarke. Go to hell," Lilah whispered. She sank to the mat, her fist pressed to her lips and her eyes welled with tears.

"Only if you go with me." Roarke stumbled to her and dropped to his knees in front of Lilah. He tilted her chin to look into her eyes, and the anguish he found there ripped his soul in two.

"Lilah, please." Roarke had never begged for anything in his life, but if it meant having Lilah in his life, he'd beg her for everything. The strong alpha knew his mate, his bitch, brought him to his knees, and it left him shaky as a newborn pup.

Lilah swallowed hard. She glanced at Adrian and he dared not follow her attention. The fact that the vampire remained in the room even after he'd confessed his love to her told Roarke all he needed to know. When it came to Lilah, she'd never fully be his. Not in the way he'd wanted, an alpha and his bitch, cubs and the pack. Adrian's brother had seen to that. Gently, he turned her face to focus on him, and her dead eyes stared back at him.

"You can't love me. I'm a vampire," she whispered after long moments. Lilah balled her hands into her fists and pounded them on the blue mats beneath them. "Do you know how long I've waited to hear you say those words? And now, when you do, I'm a bloodsucker. I have no place in the pack, in the Northwoods. Just let Adrian and I go."

"I can't." Roarke's hoarse admission brought Adrian to stand beside them. "Do you think I want this to happen this way? I know how you grew up. Your father worked with my uncle, the pack leader. All those happy cubs and mated households that we used to have in the Northwoods, that's what I wish I could have with you. But you never would have let me, Lilah. You and I both know that." He extended his hand, offering it to her. "I'm not asking for anything. Yeah, I'd love it if you told me you love me too, but I'll wait. I've waited a long time. What's a little longer?"

"You always were a white knight, Roarke." Lilah rose to her feet and stepped back. At least she didn't go to the vampire. If she'd wrapped her arms around Adrian, Roarke didn't know what he'd do and he suspected Lilah knew.

"If you want to punch me, I'll give you a free shot." Roarke turned to Adrian. "Both of you." He grinned and held out his arms.

"You make that sound far too tempting, wolf. However I'll leave that decision up to Lilah."

"Don't hit him. There's been too much fighting already." Lilah's defeated sigh echoed in the workout room. "I don't want any one else to be hurt because of me."

"Anyone else? I don't understand. What do you mean?" Out of the corner of his eye, Roarke saw Adrian's expression held the same confusion as his own.

"Roarke and I are here because we want to keep you safe. If we get hurt, it's our choice. No one else has gotten hurt because of you." Adrian said. He strode across the mat, most likely because of Roarke's admission and stopped next to Lilah. Opening his arms, he pulled her into an embrace.

Jealousy stabbed through Roarke. His hackles rose, his wolf growling with the need to claim his mate from the interloper. Stepping forward, he glared at Adrian. Then, he stopped. Expelling a harsh breath, he focused on Adrian and Lilah. She might be in his arms, but she looked at him. The eye contact reassured his wolf, reminded him that Lilah held two beasts within her, and right now Adrian did what he could to soothe her vampire. Considering how hard she punched the workout bag, it was probably for the best.

He willed his possessive streak under control. "Adrian's right." It galled him to say the words. Right now Lilah needed to hear them, and frankly, at least this time they were true. "I'm here because I want to be here. I know pack business looks rough right now, but you're really safer here than if you'd stayed at your house."

"What about when this is all said and done? What if I want to go home?"

He started to tell her they'd cross that bridge when they came to it. The idea of her leaving Northwoods territory burned. "If you want to go home, I'll honor your decision."

"But you won't come with me."

Roarke shook his head. "I'm the alpha of the pack. I can't leave again. I shouldn't have left to find you, but I had to."

Lilah sagged against Adrian. The vampire cupped the back of her head. The tender, protective gesture made Roarke wish she'd trusted him. He went to her, and after silently checking with Adrian, stood behind her, his hand on her shoulder.

"So if I want you in my life, I have to stay here. Damn it, Roarke, you always came in, tried to do the right thing and ended up fucking it up worse. And how do you know the Dark Moon Dog attacks aren't related to me? They were the ones who infected me, after all." She flung the words at him like an angry accusation.

"We don't know that. We are, however, in a position to find out. It's been a long night. Why don't we go to bed? I bet we can make you forget all about your worries, and if it makes you feel any better you can forget all about the fact I told you I loved you."

She barked harsh, mocking laughter. "As if I could forget that."

"You've been through a lot and we need to make plans. Roarke, I'll want to talk to you about the pack and see what kind of training we can get setup. Lilah, you need to rest. The pack needs a strong alpha bitch. You're the strongest of them all. It's up to you, and us, to make the pack believe." Adrian gently turned her, and Roarke wrapped his arm around her waist.

The two men cradled her between them. Glancing at Lilah and Adrian, Roarke admitted if he couldn't have her all to himself, then at least he shared her with his second. In the world of the pack, that made all the difference. He led the way upstairs to his bedroom. The heavy shades would block the sunlight from Adrian, and perhaps, in the tangle of limbs and sweaty skin they could pretend, just for a little while, that the pack didn't hinge on Lilah being a successful alpha bitch and Adrian being a successful second.

~* * *~

Roarke's warmth washed over her, bathing her in a spicy heat that curled her toes and settled in her pussy. She breathed deeply, drawing his scent into her lungs. He loved her. The revelation shocked her, though she wondered why it did. Roarke had been looking out for her for a long time. He just hadn't seen her until now.

She leaned against Adrian, his cool skin a contrast to Roarke. He smelled of the coppery tang of blood, the warmth of life, and the pulsing heart beat of a living creature. Her hand slid over his ribs to cup his hips, and she thought of turning to him, pressing him against the wall, and taking him there. She struggled to read his expression. He'd supported Roarke, stepped back when the wolf had spoken of love. Yet, surely he had some feelings, some thought about what transpired. He might be Roarke's second, but pack law failed to bind the vampire. And Adrian was known for making his own rules.

Roarke led them down the hall, his scent growing stronger with each step. Here, in his inner sanctum, was his bedroom. It took up one end of the second floor, the vaulted ceiling with its exposed beams giving the room a lodge-like feel. From the pine wood to the deep red and blue plaid blanket on the king size bed, the room felt masculine. A large dresser, big enough for more than one person's clothing, dominated one wall. A huge mirror hung above it.

Lilah frowned. She imagined another woman, another werewolf, a pure werewolf, sharing this room with him. Her clothes sitting in the drawers alongside Roarke's clothing, her naked body revealed in the mirror as Roarke made love to her. Jealousy reared its ugly head. Her inner bitch growled, wanting to mark the room, the dresser, the man as belonging to her. Her vampire drew strength from Adrian standing next to her, and Lilah knew in that moment that she needed both men. And until Roarke figured out how to give her what he wanted, with Adrian by her side, she knew she'd be unable to tell him she loved him.

Lilah turned to Adrian. She flattened her palm on his chest, feeling his steely muscles beneath her touch. Slowly, she stroked his pectorals. His nipples hardened, and through his shirt, she circled one with her finger. If Roarke really loved her, he had to accept her relationship with Adrian, and that meant she fucked the vampire first. She leaned forward, pressing her cheek against his chest and breathed deeply. Her hand tugged at his shirt, freeing it from his jeans, and then she slipped her hand beneath.

The drive to show Roarke how she felt about Adrian, even if she couldn't formulate the words, had her caressing his skin. She moaned back in her throat as he stepped closer to her. The promise of his erection pressed against her stomach, and she undulated against the thick bulge. Her ass pleasantly ached with the memory of him filling her, and for a moment, she thought about turning around and letting him take her backdoor again. She dipped her fingertips beneath the waistband of his jeans and decided against it. Her clit ached. Her pussy readied itself for sex, and this time, it'd be with Adrian.

He let her pull his shirt over his head and drop it to the floor. She unbuttoned his jeans and pulled down the zipper. His cock surged through the opening, and she trailed her fingers along the length of his shaft. The bed creaked, and she saw Roarke stripping off his clothes and crawling on top of the mattress. His erection made her mouth water, and she drank in the sight of his dusky, tanned skin, the brown curls surrounding his staff. An alpha male indeed, she thought, turning her attention back to Adrian's exquisite paleness.

He kicked off his shoes and removed his socks and his jeans, until he stood as naked as Roarke. Lilah stepped back and simply looked at him. From his bare feet, up his lightly furred legs and powerful thighs, to the erection standing at attention, up over his washboard abs and flat pectorals, to his neck and chiseled jaw. Hunger blazed in his amber eyes, his white blond hair making him look like a Nordic God. Her vampire shoved the wolf out of the way. *Mine.*

Lilah let her vampire take full reign, her fangs growing large, lust for blood mingling with the lust for sex in her veins. She grinned, revealing those white incisors, and Adrian's eyes darkened. She went to him, wrapping her arms around him and stroking his muscled back. The taut globes of his buttocks called to her, and she lowered her hands to them and squeezed. He groaned and bent his head.

She kissed him, lips and tongue drinking from him, sliding along his incisors until he pricked her tongue, and she let him suck the blood into her mouth. The coppery taste fueled her, made her cunt went, and she thrust against him. The thick rod of his cock pulsed against her stomach.

Roarke's heavy breathing spurred her on. She spread her legs, leaning forward just a bit to give him a view of her ass. Let him imagine he took her there. Let him imagine the hot walls of her channel wrapping around his cock. Lilah dropped to her knees. "I'm going to suck your dick now, and then you get to fuck me," she whispered.

Adrian moaned as she fondled his balls, her breath warm against his shaft. Spreading her legs, she knew she gave Roarke a show and indulged her inner exhibitionist. She nibbled along the side of Adrian's cock, delighting in the way it jerked and twitched under her ministrations. His balls begged for her touch, and she rolled them in the palm of her hand.

She could kneel here for hours. The wooden floor pressed against her knees, yet she didn't mind. The musky smell of him called to something deep inside, and she ran her tongue along his length. She moaned, the vibration of his skin against her lips making her wet and needy. She looked up at him, saw his eyes dark with hunger. His fangs protruded, and she almost offered him her wrist.

Almost.

Lilah took her time. The underside of his shaft called to her with the sensitive bundle of nerves beneath his head. She sucked on it, tongued it like he did her clit, and her bud throbbed in response. Then, she wrapped her lips around his cock head.

The bed creaked.

Adrian cupped her head, thrusting into her mouth until his curls rested against her lips, and she had all of him. She moaned, her hand sliding from the base of his shaft to plunge between her legs and tease her clit. She wriggled her hips, rocking against her searching fingers, and she knew both men wished they could be there doing the same. She dipped a finger inside her channel and the walls fluttered around her digit.

Roarke groaned.

Lilah sucked harder. Her cheeks hollowed out. Eyes closed, she enjoyed the thick cock in her mouth, his smell, his taste, and she grazed him with her incisors.

Adrian shouted.

A trickle of blood filled her mouth. She lapped at his essence, the salty taste of his pre-cum mingling with his blood. Roarke would never allow her to bite him. Adrian craved it. He thrust past her lips, the head of his cock slipping past the tight ring of muscles at the base of her throat. She rubbed her clit harder with the need to come while he pumped into her mouth. Harder and faster, the sound of their breaths and Roarke's mingling in the air.

She smashed her finger against her clit and clamped her lips around Adrian's cock. His shaft stifled her scream, the sound vibrating along the length of him. With a groan, he stiffened, and his hot seed splashed against her throat. She swallowed, licking him whole, and then slipped his rod from her mouth. She crawled up his body and wrapped her arms around her neck. "You wanna bite me?"

"Oh yeah," Adrian groaned. He wrapped his hands around her waist and carried her to the bed.

She clenched her legs around his hips, and as he tossed her on the mattress, he followed, settling his weight between her spread thighs. His cock, once more hard and ready, pressed against her slick labia. She rubbed against him, and his big hands clamped onto her hips to hold her steady.

"This is my show now." His voice rumbled along her skin.

Suddenly, Roarke's warmth pressed against her left side. Lilah waited for Adrian to push him away. He didn't.

Adrian remained firmly in place between her thighs, his lips raining tiny kisses on her neck, her collarbone, her shoulders. He trailed his mouth over the slope of her right breast, his fangs scraping against the skin. He moved his torso, though his cock remained firmly pressed against her slick labia. And then he closed his lips around her nipple. He sucked, the pull going straight to her clit. She curled her fingers into his hair and held him against her breast.

A twin mouth joined Adrian's as Roarke fastened onto her left breast. Nipping and sucking, he toyed with the hard nipple with his tongue.

Lilah arched off the bed and cried out. Her cream ran freely between her legs. Having the two men worshipping her body, each caress, each lick taking her higher, left her gasping for air. Her body vibrated with her bitch ready to be mounted and her vampire sated on the blood of her lover.

Adrian sank his fangs into the pale skin of her breast. He sucked deeply, drinking from her. Shivers of pleasure arched through her veins, her clit and her nipples tied together in a three-way circuit of need. Her channel tightened, her orgasm so close she could reach out and touch it. Then, he swiped his tongue across the punctures, and slid lower. Roarke's hand covered her other breast.

Lilah parted her legs even more. To feel Adrian's face buried in her cunt, her juices over his lips and chin so she could lick her essence from his face, she canted her hips in silent invitation. "Taste me," she whimpered. She slid one hand down Roarke's back, the other cupping his head to hold him to her.

Adrian breathed a puff of warm air across her swollen labia. Lilah moaned. His tongue fluttered along her labia barely tasting her, teasing her.

Roarke nipped her.

She cried out, the pleasure too much to bear. Her release pounded through her, leaving her a screaming, writhing mass of ecstasy. Fingers curling into Roarke's skin, she held him to her, and then Adrian speared her with his tongue. She bucked off the bed, and strong hands clamped around her hips to hold her still. Roarke's or Adrian's, she didn't know. She relished being pinned down, these strong males doing whatever they wanted to her body. Letting the bliss overtake her, she simply rode on a wave of feelings. The pack, her home, she'd worry about it all tomorrow. Adrian wrapped his lips around her clit, and wrung another orgasm from her. Oh yeah, it was going to be a long night.

Chapter Fourteen

Somewhere between the time when Adrian went down on her and Roarke started sucking her breasts, Lilah ceased to care about anything other than the two men in her life. Adrian crawled over her body. The head of his cock probed her entrance. A single thrust buried him balls-deep inside her, and her legs wrapped around his waist. Her heels pressed into his buttocks, holding him deep inside her.

Roarke remained by her side. His fingers slid over her stomach, down over her drenched curls, to circle her throbbing clit. The way he pleasured her, worked with Adrian's thrusts, made her wonder, just for a moment before lucid thought fled, if the men worked this out between themselves. She met Adrian thrust for thrust, his cock filling her so full and deep. The hard, deep strokes pushed her closer and closer to the edge. She released Roarke and clenched onto Adrian's shoulders, using his height as leverage against him.

She pressed her face against his chest and bit him. He shuddered, his shaft lengthening inside her. The taste of hot blood, the smell of their sex, Roarke's fingers on her clit, and Adrian's cock in her cunt, it combined to envelop her in a haze of sensual pleasure. She loved them for giving her this, for understanding the needs of her vampire and her werewolf. Her bitch threw back her head and howled, and her vampire drank.

She came again, the utter completeness of the moment driving tears to her eyes. Above her, Adrian strove toward his own release. Roarke's fingers slipped from her clit, caressing her sides, stroking the length of her flank and over the curve of her buttock. And then, with a hoarse shout, Adrian came. His hot seed filled her, reminded her of the cycle of life, of blood and death and sex. She clung to him, his body the anchor she needed as her body shattered apart once more. A salty tear ran over her cheek, and then Roarke was there, licking it away.

She turned her head and he captured her mouth. He kissed her, plunging his tongue past her lips to make love to her the only way he could. Adrian's cock still filled her, though it softened, sated from their sex. Against her leg, Roarke's dick throbbed, and she yearned to take it inside her.

Adrian rolled to the side. For a moment, Lilah felt bereft. She whimpered, and then Roarke's heat replaced the chillness of Adrian's skin. With a single thrust, he plunged into her. Adrian lay on the side, this time his fingers skimming over her flesh, his cold digits stroking her clit.

She whimpered, and then Roarke was there, kissing her, claiming her. Each thrust buried his cock deep inside her, and again her legs wrapped around him and held him tight. She should be sated. She should be curled up between them sleeping the sleep of the dead. Yet, her bitch craved Roarke's possession, his mouth against hers, his shaft inside her body. She thrust harder, deeper, and knew, after tasting the heights to which only he could bring her, she'd never voluntarily go without them.

His husky groans and sighs fueled her desire. She loved him. Damn her to hell, she did, never had stopped, and with her body she told him what she couldn't with words. Pleasure so intense it bowed her back and stole the breath from her lungs worked through her. Her hands roamed over his skin, clenched his ass and brought him even tighter to her. Next to her, Adrian flicked his fingers over her clit, sliding the hood back and forth over the hardened bit of flesh.

She crested one more time and then shattered, her world sundering her into a place of light and darkness and sound. Her keening screams echoed in the room, the men's husky groans a delicious counterpoint. Rapture brought every nerve to life, every inch of her skin so sensitive she doubted she could stand the slightest touch. And yet, she could.

Roarke plunged into her once more. He stiffened and with a hoarse shout, he came. He buried his face in the curve of her neck, his panting breaths warm against her skin. His come filled her, dripped down her legs, and he collapsed on top of her. His arms wound around her in a vice-like grip and held her to his chest.

Moments later, he rolled to the side, taking her with him, and Adrian snuggled against her back. Hot and cold. Life and death. Wolf and Vampire. The two men spooned her, their arms surrounding her. And sated, she could do nothing but lay there and feel, her walls broken into shards around her.

"I love you," Roarke whispered. His lips brushed against her temple, and this time, she didn't flinch and didn't turn away. She simply snuggled closer to him and felt Adrian press along her back. She released a contented sigh and felt sleep pull at her.

Downstairs the sound of a slamming door echoed through the house. Instantly, Roarke sat up. He threw a blanket over Lilah and Adrian. "Who's there?" he yelled.

"Your Second and I've brought some friends." Eugene's voice barreled up the stairs ahead of him. He burst into the bedroom and stopped. Audibly, he sniffed the air. "You've fucked the bitch," he growled and strode forward.

Roarke remained where he was, lounged against the headboard, the blanket over his hips. "So what if I did. I'm the alpha here and you're shunned." He glanced at the three men behind Eugene and shook his head. "Charlie, James, Todd, I thought you guys knew better than to associate with someone who was shunned. Eugene's caused trouble for our pack for a long time. And Charlie, you're a member of the Dogs." He didn't move, and Lilah knew if he came to them, it'd show weakness.

Still, she didn't like the men standing in front of their bed. No doubt the intruders could smell what she and Adrian were and what they'd just done. The hackles on the back of her neck rose. Inside, her bitch growled and revealed her teeth.

"Ooh, look at that. The bitch is upset. You just spread your legs for vamps or do you want a real lover?" Eugene swaggered forward.

Lilah lunged.

Adrian's hand on her arm held her back. He turned to Roarke, and the wolf slid one foot to the floor.

"You don't want to make me get out of this bed, Eugene. I suggest you take your boys and turn around and get the hell out of here." Roarke kept his voice level and calm.

Lilah struggled to keep her emotions churning deep inside her. She wished she had a tenth the deadly quiet that Roarke held, though she knew that came with being the alpha's territory. Don't let them see you sweat. His voice rumbled along her nerve endings, everything female inside of her humming to the beat of his heart.

"I suggest you think twice about ordering us around. We're going to bring this up with the pack at the next meeting. I guarantee they're not going to want to be ruled by a vampire-fucker," Charlie said.

Lilah smelled his fear. It radiated from him like the stench from a rotting corpse. She bared a hint of fang, knowing next to her Adrian looked menacing. His eyes widened, and he took a step back. He didn't bare his throat, and for that transgression, Lilah knew he'd die.

"What'd you call me?" Roarke asked. He leaned forward, fingers curling as if to shift into his wolf form. If he did that, no one but the three of them would leave the room alive.

Lilah willed him not to shift. If keeping the peace in his pack required he kill any dissenters, she shuddered to think what kind of leader he would be. She'd heard horror stories of packs ruled by dictators. Her stomach churned with the thought that Northwoods could become one, and all because of her presence. Still, she dared not show weakness. She focused her gaze on the intruders, her fang revealed. The bloodlust rose within her and she knew her eyes glowed. Just another reminder she wasn't wholly wolf, but one she suspected these bastards needed.

"I called you a vampire fucker because that's what you are," Charlie said.

"I am your alpha." Roarke leapt off the bed, changing mid-air. He hit the floor in his wolf form and lunged for Charlie. His jaws snapped around the man's neck, brining him down.

Eugene stepped back from the struggle, as did James and Todd.

Inhuman growls emerged from Roarke's throat. He twisted his head. A sickening crack filled the air. Charlie twitched and then lay dead.

Underneath the covers, Lilah sought Adrian's hand. She clenched her fingers around his, her grip so tight she knew she'd leave bruises on a mortal. Adrian simply accepted it, a squeeze of his fingers letting her know he was there for her.

Roarke backed away from Charlie's body. He gaped at the other men, jaws open to reveal bloodied lips and teeth. When no one made any moves, he straightened and shifted back to his human form. He didn't grab his jeans, his nudity telling them he'd shift again in a heartbeat.

"Anyone else want to question their alpha?" Roarke asked.

"You killed Charlie," Todd said. He stepped in front of James, as if to shield the injured man from Roarke's wrath.

"He's a Dog and he insulted his alpha. I hardly think that gives him a reason to live." Roarke stepped forward. "You got a problem with that?"

Todd shook his head. "N-no." He bared his neck. Behind him, James did likewise.

"Good." Roarke fixed his gaze on Eugene. "I've shunned you. I've removed you as my Second. You know what my next step is. Don't make me do it."

Eugene held his gaze for a moment longer, and then stared at the floor. "You won't get away with this," Eugene muttered.

Roarke flew forward. Hands around Eugene's throat, he slammed him against the wall hard enough to rattle the large picture of a wolf hanging on the opposite wall. "Say that a little louder. I want my Second to hear you."

Eugene tried to swallow, a thin line of spittle dangling from the corner of his mouth. His eyes bulged. His face turned purple and still Roarke increased the pressure on his windpipe. He bobbed his head, a frantic nodding that had him looking like a puppet with seizures. At last, Roarke released him and he sank to the floor with a heavy thud. He scrambled to his feet and with a jerk of his thumb, ordered James and Todd to follow him. Todd grabbed Charlie's body and darted away. James stayed standing in the bedroom.

"Yes?" Roarke asked as he turned toward the injured man.

James dropped to his knees, his eyes sad. He looked up, baring his neck. "Kill me. It's your right," he said.

Roarke strode forward. Lilah wished she could see his face, to know whether his eyes held grim determination or forgiveness. He grabbed his jeans and pulled them on, then went to James. Gently, as if one might comfort a child, he rested his hand on James' shoulder. "I'm not going to kill you, James. I don't know what these men have over you, but if you tell me, I'll take care of it."

James hung his head and said nothing.

"You've got two choices for protection, James. You have Eugene and the Dogs or you have me. I'm going to be around a lot longer than those losers. So if you're keeping silent, know it's going to be time to pick sides real damn soon. If you don't pick the right one, you might not know until it's too late." Roarke squeezed James' shoulder reassuringly, and then stepped back. He sat on the edge of the bed, his arms across over his chest and watched as James rose shakily to his feet and left the room. Moments later, the front door closed behind him.

Roarke bent his head and released a pent up breath. He rubbed his eyes. Turning, he looked back at Lilah and Adrian. "I'm sorry you had to see that. Running a pack is a messy business, especially one as messed up as this one. I should have done more when my uncle died. I should have weeded out the dissenters and showed my strength. I didn't, and now I'm paying the price."

Lilah crawled out from beneath the covers and over to Roarke. She knelt behind him, her knees on either side of his hips. Wrapping her arms around him, she rested her chin against his shoulder. "It's okay. I'm here. You've done what you thought you had to do. It's all in the past. You shouldn't beat yourself up about it."

Roarke cupped his hand over hers. Turning his head, he brushed a kiss across her cheek. "But now you're paying the price."

"Don't worry about me. Ever since Mikhail had his tantrum and turned me, I haven't exactly been carefree. Now, let's talk about something we can fix, the Dark Moon Dogs." She sat back on the bed and crossed her legs, heedless of her own nudity.

Adrian slipped from the bed. He grabbed his t-shirt and tossed it to her.

She caught it, grinned at his nudity, and pulled the shirt over her head. It hung on her like a tent. Being surrounded by Adrian's shirt, his scent, sent shivers down her spine. Roarke frowned, but didn't move. Adrian pulled on pants and zipped them, but didn't button them. Watching the men, Lilah wondered if they expected more sex. Her pussy ached deliciously.

"Why don't we go down to my office? It's where I usually receive people and there's a map of the Northwoods." Roarke stood.

Lilah scooted off the bed, struggling not to grin like a maniac at the tiny twitches in her muscles. Adrian followed, sandwiching her between them as they walked. Her nerves hummed with awareness of the two guys. Inside, her wolf trotted with its tongue lolling out of its mouth, tail wagging in the air. The vampire shared the wolf's contentment.

Roarke opened a heavy wooden door to a large room on the first floor. An oak desk sat at one end with chairs at the other. A large map of the Northwoods, with homes and markers hung on one wall, and Lilah went to it, drawn by the familiar street names and landmarks among which she'd grown up. She saw red pins scattered among blue pins marking pack member's houses, and as she glanced at the alley were she'd gotten attacked, she saw that must be where the Dark Moon Dogs were. A large cluster of red pins marked some sort of encampment or base.

Adrian stood behind her, and Roarke moved to the other side.

"We need to find out more information. What kind of reconnaissance do you have on that spot?" She pointed to the cluster of red pins.

"It's a series of old tenement buildings where the Dogs have their base. We've sent a few squads against it, but they just regroup and come back stronger. I don't know what drives these guys. It's like they all have death wishes or something." Roarke shook his head, and Lilah knew what the admission cost him.

"So what do you want us to do?" Adrian asked.

"One final push. A surgical removal. We're going to torch the buildings, eradicate the Dogs and any supporters from the pack and from the area. We're going to take back the Northwoods." Roarke said. "And this is how." He pointed to the map showing where some of the more commonly used attack sites were. With four squads of men, they'd go in, draw the Dogs to a specific site and kill them. He laid out his plans, and the more Lilah listened to him, the more she realized this problem really had been brewing since before her attack. Her gut told her there was some deep-seated anger, some problem there.

"Do you know who they are?" she asked. "I mean, this sounds cold. I know you can't talk to other pack leaders. If you do, it would be like admitting weakness, but I think these guys have it out for you and for Northwoods." Lilah pressed her lips together, half-afraid she'd said too much.

Adrian looked at her and nodded, silently backing up her hypothesis.

Roarke frowned. He stepped away from the map and turned toward the credenza along the other wall. On top sat a series of photos, some Lilah recognized as belonging to his uncle. He picked up one of the pictures, and then set it down again. "I don't like what you're saying, Lilah. It fits. It makes sense, but I don't have to like it." He turned to face her. "We're going to take them down and take them down hard! I need to pay a visit first." Without waiting for an answer, he jogged out of the room. Muffled footsteps sounded on the stairs as he hurried back to his bedroom.

Lilah leaned against the bookshelf beneath the map and stared at Adrian. He glared at the map as if it were something abhorrent to him. With a scowl, he went to the credenza and the pictures.

Roarke's footfalls thumped on the stairs again, and without saying a word, the front door slammed and he was gone.

Adrian turned to face her. Stony determination filled his eyes, as he looked from her to the map, then back again. "So where do I fit in? You grew up here. You've known these people all your life. Hell, Roarke was probably your first crush, wasn't he?"

Lilah's cheeks reddened and she looked down at the floor.

"He was, wasn't he?" Adrian asked. He chuckled and shook his head. "So why do you need me? You have the wolf of your dreams waiting for you to join him. Who apparently appointed me his Second, but why? You know the pack won't accept me. He can't rule with Machiavellian tendencies. They don't work. People want their say, whether their leaders want to give it to them or not." He shoved his hands into his jeans pockets and rocked back on his heels.

Lilah shook her head. "That's stupid." She frowned and when Adrian glared at her, she bit back laughter.

"What do you mean that's stupid?" He stared at her, his words a direct challenge.

Lilah snarled. "I'm your alpha bitch. You don't question me any more than you question Roarke. Look, he appointed you to be his Second. If he didn't think you'd do the job and do it well, he wouldn't have done it. He can't afford to look weak, not with the Dogs and not with me around. Your place is as his Second. You do what he tells you to do."

Adrian's scowl deepened.

Lilah resisted the urge to sigh and roll her eyes. Great, they were in dangerous territory and Adrian wanted to start a testosterone pissing match again. The fact that both men had shared her body, that he'd fucked her and gotten to do so first had to mean something. If it didn't... Lilah bottled up the fear and worry threatening to erupt. She was making her way through uncharted waters as much as the men were. As the alpha bitch, she had to keep the women of the pack in line. She doubted either one of them had fully understood the depth of her responsibilities now that Roarke had named her as his.

"I'm his pet vampire, then?" Adrian asked. He shook his head. "I can't live like that."

"If you're his pet vampire, then what am I?" Lilah asked, determined to shock him out of whatever funk or craziness seemed to have gotten into him. She didn't understand it, and right now, she didn't want to deal with it either. "I'm his alpha bitch and I'm also a vampire. If anyone is his pet vampire, it's me. You're a Second. That's important."

"So what does a Second do?"

Lilah opened and closed her mouth, gaping like a fish out of water. Damned if she knew. Growing up, she'd been human and kept as far away from werewolf politics as she could get. "You take over the pack if something happens to Roarke. You enforce his rules and the Enforcer reports to you to learn how to do that." She wished she knew more, but she gave him all the information she had.

"So why haven't I met the Enforcer yet?"

"Maybe because we just got back into town, his current Second is acting like an idiot, and there hasn't been time to introduce you?" Lilah strode forward and curled her fingers around his arms. "Look, I know even less about this than you do, because obviously you guys talked about something while I slept. But it's my job to keep the pack's bitches in line. The last time I saw a lot of them, I had missing front teeth and pigtails. Do you really think they're going to take me seriously? First I'm human, now I come back like some freak?"

"You're not a freak," Adrian asserted.

"Try telling that to a bunch of tradition bound werewolves," Lilah replied. "There's a place for you here. It might be just because I'm here. I can't imagine you and Roarke being friends under other circumstances. That's tough. It really is, but if he didn't think you could do whatever will be asked of you, he wouldn't have appointed you to the position. And that's the cold, hard facts." She eased her grip, aware she held on a little too tightly. Then again, she had a tendency to do that in every aspect of her life, so it shouldn't be any different with Adrian. And, it wasn't. She stood on tiptoe and brushed her lips across his.

With a groan, Adrian wrapped the steel bands of his arms around her and deepened the kiss. His tongue plunged into her mouth, drinking from her. His hands slid down her back to cup her buttocks, and he pulled her against him so she felt the length of his erection.

"You're an amazing woman, Lilah." Desire filled his voice, deepening it so it caressed along her nerve endings.

Her stomach fluttered. Her breath caught in her throat, and she clenched her fingers at his waist. "Why do you say that?"

"Because you're here, and you're trying to talk a vampire into doing a werewolf's job. Faced with what you're facing, I think most people would be justified to turn and run. Roarke brought you to an unsafe place. Get the hell out and go find somewhere where you can be safe. I don't think your house is it, but it certainly isn't smack dab in the middle of a wolf pack. Faced with these two choices, I would have chosen as you did: the house. We chose to follow Roarke and come to the Northwoods. I hope we don't regret that choice."

"We better not," she whispered. "Because if we do, I'll kick his furry ass from one end of this territory to the other. The alpha bitch isn't without her powers." Standing on tiptoe, she sealed her promise with a kiss.

Chapter Fifteen

Roarke sat behind his desk, his booted feet propped on the edge, his arms crossed over his chest. In front of him sat his Enforcer, Jason Veranos. Having been out of town for the last few days, Jason knew nothing of his alpha's return or the events that had transpired since then. Roarke stared at the wolf and wondered if he could even trust him anymore.

"So the Luna Guard wants to come in and take care of things themselves," Roarke said with a frown. Of all the things he needed, the werewolf's elite fighting force coming in and taking over would do nothing except signal to the werewolf community at large that he couldn't control his own pack. A weak alpha. It never could be said the Northwoods pack had a weak alpha at the helm, and frankly, he'd seen what happened when an alpha stayed long past his prime. Roarke shook his head. In the basement, Adrian and Lilah trained. He tried not to think about her dressed in workout clothing, sweat on her skin, her body honed into a fighting machine.

"The Dark Moon Dogs have spread. They're not just in the Northwoods, though the majority of the activity is centered here. The Guard thinks that if they come in, clear things out, it'll keep them quiet and ensure the humans don't need to know. They know about your bitch." Jason wore his brown hair in a single braid that hung to the middle of his back, and the chiseled planes of his face were set in stony acceptance.

"Lilah. They know?" Roarke knew he'd been deluding himself by thinking that they didn't know, not when her life was in danger. He'd hoped...Hell, he didn't know what he'd hoped except that somehow, he could bring her into the pack, and they'd forget all about her being a vampire. Yeah, fat chance of that. The werewolf-vampire wars had been over a century ago. He wished they could simply get on with their lives.

Jason nodded. He tapped the screen of his PDA. "There's a bounty of ten thousand dollars for someone to bring her into the Luna Council, dead or alive. I think you should turn her in and let the Council deal with her. We don't need her kind of trouble right now. We've got enough of our own. I don't know what possessed you to go after her. It was damn stupid."

Roarke's scowl deepened. Only his Enforcer was allowed to speak to him like that. "No. I'm not turning her in."

"You're letting your feelings for her overrule your common sense about what's good for the pack. As your Enforcer, I have to advise you that isn't a good move. You don't want to appear weak. Eugene's saying she's cuckolded you." Jason uncrossed his legs and leaned forward. Bracing his elbows on his knees, he fixed his startlingly blue gaze on Roarke.

For a moment, Roarke felt as if his Enforcer sucked him into a web, as if he were drowning, and not for the first time he wondered whether his Enforcer had some preternatural abilities beyond being a werewolf. With a shake of his head, he pulled himself out of the trance. "No."

"Ten thousand dollars is a lot of money. I'm just asking you to think about it." Jason leaned back as if nothing had ever happened.

Roarke picked up a pencil and rolled it between his fingers. He watched the slender yellow stick twist and turn, all at his whim. He knew how the pencil felt. "Ten thousand dollars to turn in Lilah? The Luna Council must be kidding if they think I'm going to just hand her over."

"They authorized me to up the figure if needed. Fifty thousand dollars."

Roarke expelled a harsh breath. He sniffed, scenting Adrian just beyond the door. A moment later, the scent disappeared, and Roarke cursed under his breath. "No. I'm not turning Lilah in and if you want to remain my Enforcer, you won't speak of this to me again. Your job is to enforce my rules. I say no one hurts Lilah. She's under my protection. No one is to so much as look in her direction without asking first. You got it? I'm glad you're back. I'll introduce you to Adrian, my Second."

"The vampire." Jason's lips twisted into a grimace. "I don't know what kind of game you're playing here, but you're fucking with fire."

"Maybe I am," Roarke admitted. "But I guarantee you I'm not going to get burned."

"I hope so. I really do." Jason stood.

Roarke walked around the desk and the two men embraced in a hug. "It's good to have you back. Things aren't as bad as they seem, I promise."

"Thanks. It's good to be back. Dealing with the Council is always a pain. I'm just glad I'm back among real wolves." Jason released Roarke and stepped back. He followed his alpha out the door.

Roarke led them downstairs to the training room. The sound of rhythmic punching, and the unique, heady aroma of Lilah's sweat filled the room. In the corner, Adrian jumped rope, the thin cord a blur as he whipped it around his body. His feet moved, alternating, one after the other like a boxer, and Roarke nodded to him. It was time to introduce his Second to his Enforcer and pray they didn't kill each other. If Adrian only overheard part of the conversation then they were in a heap of trouble.

~* * *~

Lilah lifted her face to the setting sun, letting the warmth bathe her skin. After so many days of operating only under the cover of darkness, she relished actually being outside.

Lilah kept her senses alert as she walked. Just because she was alpha female didn't mean people still didn't want to kill her. She'd had a hell of a time convincing Adrian and Roarke she could go alone. She needed to. Pack business dictated that she meet the Matriarch of the pack alone, and it was only five blocks to Rosemary's house. As the oldest living female werewolf in the pack, the Matriarch held a status that few wolves could ever reach.

Be strong. Be powerful. Lilah held her head high, her bearing telling the world that she was there and she wouldn't be messed with. An old abandoned rail line cut the street in two, the division between this side and the far side of the tracks obvious. Lilah grimaced at the clichéd response. Where she walked, nice ranch or split-level homes with spacious yards occupied the tree-lined street. A cross street went right in front of the tracks, and once she passed it, the homes turned into run-down apartment buildings. She frowned, the map on Roarke's wall filling her mind. The Matriarch lived not far from where the Dark Moon Dogs had appeared to setup their base.

And Lilah had come alone. She'd frowned, and then smoothed out the expression. For the next forty minutes, she'd have daylight, and if she didn't feel safe, she'd just call Roarke to come and get her. As the alpha, it'd do him good to be seen there, his presence sanctioning her visit to the Matriarch of the pack.

Something rustled to her left. She turned, seeing nothing but a few blowing leaves. She stopped and glanced around. No one trailed her. She saw nothing. "Just make the visit. You're jumping at shadows," she muttered under her breath. She stepped forward, the scent of rank, unwashed wolf strong in her nostrils.

Lilah tensed, readying for a fight. Her hand closed around the blade tucked into the waistband of her jeans, and suddenly they were there, three young toughs dressed in black leather jackets, t-shirts and jeans. They all wore steel-toed boots. One held a short bat, the other two had fingerless leather gloves on their hands. Unable to strip and change, she let the vampire lose with a snarl.

Lilah lunged for the tough directly in front of her. A punch to his jaw, a kick to his comrade's chest, sent them both sprawling backwards. She followed through with the blade, slicing across leather and cotton.

The one with the bat swung. Three inches of solid wood connected with her ribs. Bones cracked.

Her breath whooshed from her lungs, pain blossoming from the impact. She snarled. Shoving the pain from her awareness, she punched and kicked again. Her world narrowed down to her attackers. She sliced with the knife, adding in a roundhouse kick or a punch when she could. Taking weapons to a visit with the Matriarch broke every pack law, otherwise she'd have had a gun and the battle would have been over long ago.

A punch to her lip landed. She spat blood and felt a tooth wiggle lose. Someone grabbed her hair, wrenching her neck, baring it to the men.

"Stop fighting us," he growled. "We come with a message."

Lilah sniffed. "You're Dogs. What kind of a message could you possibly have?" She struck out with her legs, bending backwards to kick the nearest one in the chin. Pulling herself forward, she ripped herself from his hold, a hunk of her hair coming free. The pain brought tears to her eyes, and she blinked them away. The three wolves circled her, warier now.

"You could have had a position in the Dogs. You know that, don't you? But you had to run back to your bloodsucker and now you dragged the pack into it," the one of the bat, obviously the leader, said.

"So that's why you attacked me in an alley and left me for dead. You guys have a nice way of asking." She spit blood and gingerly touched her lip with her fingers. "So what's the message?"

"Tell Roarke if he gives back what belongs to us, we'll leave his people alone. And when we ask for a meeting, he attends, alone." He gestured the other Dogs to step back. They did. "No harm. No foul, okay?"

"So you thought to rough up his woman a bit, right? Make sure the message hits home. I'll tell you what Roarke would say to your message. He'd tell you that he's your alpha, and you're all dead Dogs." She turned to resume her walk down the sidewalk. The sun looked as if it'd barely moved. The whole altercation probably took less than five minutes, though it had felt as if hours had passed.

"Think about the message. Roarke's got himself a mess. This is one way to get out of it."

Lilah whirled to face him. "And the other?"

"Die." The wolf shrugged. "And you can choose for him." He flashed a grin and with a hand signal sent the men scurrying back.

Lilah watched them go, wishing for a long, hot drink of blood to help speed the healing along. Arriving at the Matriarch's with wounds would only reinforce the fact that the alpha and his bitch weren't strong enough to hold the pack. She cursed under her breath. The Dogs knew exactly what they were doing. Not meeting with the Matriarch would have far worse implications, so squaring her shoulders, she jogged the remaining three blocks to the wolf's house. She'd give Roarke the message, and then she'd find a way to take out the Dogs on her own. The things they'd given her, a second beast and a chance to be with Roarke, paled when it came to their actions. They hurt the pack; therefore, they must die.

~* * *~

Slouched in a phone booth at a rest area, Adrian watched the headlights of the passing cars on the interstate. Overhead clouds obscured the stars and moon, the darkness complete and total except for the vehicle and rest stop lights. He clenched the black receiver, every cell in his body telling him to return to Roarke's house and be with Lilah when she returned. A phone call shortly after dark reassured him she was still at the Matriarch's house and would come back when they were done. Apparently, in spite of her bruises the two had hit it off well. The Matriarch knew her father and shared stories about Lilah's childhood.

He breathed a sigh of relief that something was going right for them. On the other end of the line, he waited to be patched through to his contact at the Immortal Council. It'd been a while since the FitzReal name had been used, and Adrian decided to invoke what power it still held. His foster parents had been in good standing with the Council, so much so that his foster father had turned down a chance to serve on that prestigious body.

"Adrian," the voice on the other end of the phone was aged, old when even his foster father had been young. "It's been a long time."

Over three decades, Adrian thought, but who was counting? "It has, thanks for taking my call. I need to know what actions the Council has sanctioned against Lilah St. James and other werepyres." Adrian stiffened as two mortal women walked out of the rest area, laughing and joking among each other. Their staggering walk and too-shrill humor announced their inebriated state, and as he breathed deeply, he smelled their mortal blood. His stomach rumbled.

"No pleasantries first? I'm shocked, Adrian FitzReal. I thought your father had taught you better manners than that." On the other end of the line, the vampire Adrian knew only as the Reverend, gave a long suffering sigh. "Very well. I know you youngsters have no patience anymore. No appreciation for the ways of their Elders. I'll tell you the Immortal Council has their hands full with the Party. It seems some within that organization think its time that werepyres were brought into the fold as it were. They're seeking out Lilah. With your connections, some think she can be their new queen. But you want to know about the attacks on her life. They're going to continue. The Council thinks she's a threat, and you know what happens to those who threaten the Council."

Adrian knew. He clenched his jaw, sick determination settling in his gut. As he feared, his brother had stirred up more than a hornet's nest with his half-assed plans. "Any word about me?" As Mikhail's older brother and guardian, Adrian bore full responsibility for Mikhail's actions.

"You're keeping the abomination alive. I think your actions speak for themselves," the Reverend said.

Adrian stiffened. "Lilah is not an abomination. And if she survived being turned and infected, then others have too. I'm not asking we search them out and welcome them with open arms, but I'd like to know what happened to them."

"There are some roads that if you take them, not even I will be able to protect you. I'm using all the influence I have to keep the Council's eyes turned elsewhere. Your brother is dead. Let his mistakes die with him." On the other end of the line, a murmured conversation and the clink of crystal told Adrian that the Reverend enjoyed a meal while he talked with Adrian.

"I can't do that," Adrian admitted. He looked at the mortals, all lost in their short, fleeting lives. They knew nothing of the worlds that transpired just beneath their noses. He had a sinking feeling if this went bad, and it could go no way but, then they'd learn a lot more than they ever thought possible. He shook his head, not wanting it to come to that.

"Then such support as you've enjoyed in the past may come to an end, young FitzReal. I'm sorry, but even for immortals, the Council only has so much patience. Go back to your wolves. Take your place among them, a place you can never truly hold because you long for their blood, and think about how the Council would have dealt with such matters. Squabbling and biting are for the lesser races. You're a vampire. Once upon a time that meant something." The phone line clicked.

Adrian stared at the dead receiver. "Once upon a time only belongs in fairy tales," he muttered as he hung up the phone. Someone waited outside to make a call, and he stepped aside, making sure the man was mortal. A quick thought fogged his mind, in case he'd overheard something he shouldn't, and then Adrian slipped behind the wheel of Roarke's truck. He drove back to the Northwoods with the Reverend's words ringing in his mind. Once the problems with the Dogs settled down, and he had half a mind to make them go away on his own, he was going to take Lilah and go to the Council. Without their approval, the threats on her life would never cease. Maybe it was time for immortal dogs to learn new tricks. Chuckling at his analogy, he sped back into town. Perhaps he wouldn't miss the entire pack meeting after all.

~* * *~

Returning from her meeting with the Matriarch, Lilah followed the instructions to the bar where Roarke met with a few key wolves. Jason, the Enforcer she'd met earlier, would be there, as would other high-ranking pack members. He said little about what they would discuss; though it didn't take much to figure out they'd be discussing her. And Adrian.

She jogged the last few feet, the pounding music and lights from the bar spilling out into the street. An alley between the bar and the Chinese restaurant next door had her stomach churning, and not from warring food smells. Inside, wolves and humans mingled. The pulse of so many heartbeats had her mouth watering and reminded her it'd been too long since she'd fed.

She opened the door and stepped inside.

The throbbing music kept its loud volume, emphasizing the loss of conversation. She strode to the bar, her boots thumping against the hardwood floor. Murmured speculation and appraising glances followed her progress.

"Looks like you got into a little trouble, honey. What'll you have?" the bartender asked as she approached.

She leaned on the bar, cocking her hip to give the table behind her a good view of her ass. She grinned and let a little of her vampire glamour loose, knowing the human behind the bar wouldn't know what hit him.

"Something good on tap." She reached into her pocket and pushed a five-dollar bill across the bar.

The human swept it beneath the bar and passed over a frothy glass of beer. "No trouble all right."

Lilah grinned. "Would I cause trouble?" She found an empty bar stool and sat, wanting the patrons to get a good, long look at her. The alpha female, unescorted, raised some eyebrows. She knew the wolves in the room smelled her. Her wolf reveled in the attention, the surety of being the strongest member of the pack next to her mate, making her want to play. Her vampire sulked, not liking the canine company.

Lilah finished the beer, the false courage not nearly enough. She set the empty glass on the bar, caught the bartender's eye, and then slipped from the stool. She walked toward the back of the bar where steps led to rooms upstairs.

"You can't go up there," the bartender said.

Lilah flashed him a grin. "Watch me." Then, aware every eye was trained on her, strode up the stairs with a wiggle of her hips.

Conversation resumed behind her. The stairs led her around a corner, and she breathed a sigh of relief once she was out of sight. Upstairs, she smelled her mate and the other wolves. Closing her eyes, she drew his scent into her lungs. It steadied her, reminded her of her position, and that she had a message to deliver.

Upstairs opened into a hallway with several doors. The lingering odor of sex testified to what the rooms were used for. Roarke's scent came from the door at the end of the hallway. She strode closer to it, certain she smelled only males in that room. Muffled conversation stopped.

Closing her hand around the doorknob, she turned it and opened the door. She stepped inside, the door slamming behind her. "Good evening, gentleman." Lilah said, noticing there were only two others besides Jason and Roarke. She recognized none of them.

Roarke burst to his feet. "What are you doing here? This is a closed meeting, bitch." His eyes narrowed, warning her that the meeting might not have gone in their favor.

"Before you turn me in for the Luna Council's reward, you might want to know the Dogs jumped me on my way to my meeting with the Matriarch. They have a message for you, mate." She emphasized his title, reminding everyone in the room she was the alpha bitch and not to be crossed.

His eyes widened. A sweeping glance took in her split lip, a bruise on her cheek, and the other bruises and aches not visible by clothing. "Are you all right?"

Lilah nodded. "I held my own."

"What's the message?" Roarke asked.

"They want you to give back what belongs to them. And they're going to call for a meeting. They want you to come alone," she deadpanned. Telling Roarke about their demand that she die would escalate the tension more than anyone was ready to handle. No, she'd take care of that part of the message herself.

"There's more," he said. "Tell me everything, Lilah." His gaze bored into hers. Power radiated from him, the strength of an alpha male in his prime.

Her nipples pebbled. Her pussy clenched and wept thinking about the wolf to which she belonged. She licked her lips, wincing as her tongue brushed over her injury. "They seem to believe you're in trouble and giving me to them will fix it. Otherwise, they've said you will die." She glanced around the room, noticing for the first time, Jason the Enforcer, looked quite unhappy.

"Get rid of her. She's a liability. Maybe if she's gone, the Dogs will leave," Jason snarled.

"Sure. The alpha's just going to give away his bitch because you said so." She swaggered forward and planted her palms on the table. "Look I know you guys don't like me. None of you do. But I'm here to stay. I don't think Roarke's going to send me away, reward or no reward." She turned to face him. "So when do we get to kick some Dogs?"

"The Enforcer's right. She needs to go." One of the strangers surged to his feet. Lunging for her, he grabbed her arm and yanked her to his side. "As a member of the Luna Guard, I take her for the Council. They'll be most pleased your arranged this." He nodded to the other man in the room.

"I do what I can for the Council." He bowed his head and rested his hands, palms down, on the table.

Lilah twisted in his grip. She yanked free, her cracked ribs protesting. Fangs unsheathed she whirled on the man, her punch smacking his head up with a crack. Grabbing her knife, she brought it to his throat. "The Luna Guard? You brought the Guard here without asking me?" She snarled at Roarke.

"I didn't know he was Guard." Roarke glared at Jason. "You betrayed me."

"I did what I had to for the pack." Jason rose to his feet and went to stand next to the betrayer. "This one betrayed you." Placing his hands on either side of the man's neck, he twisted. The man's neck snapped and he slumped forward, dead.

Chapter Sixteen

Lilah whirled on Jason.

Roarke lunged for the Guard officer.

Lilah trusted her alpha to bring him down. Her knife flashed in the fluorescent lighting in the room, and her fangs itched to rip open his throat and bathe in the Enforcer's blood. "You bastard," she snarled.

Jason ducked her slice, his hand coming up to grab her wrist. She yanked free of his grasp and tried to swipe his feet out from beneath him. He smacked her wrist, the blow hard enough to send her knife sprawling, and grappling, she tumbled to the floor with a loud thud.

Snarls and growls filled the air. Out of the corner of her eye, she saw the Guard officer and Roarke fighting, their blows landing with hollow smacks of flesh against flesh. She wriggled from beneath Jason, flipping him over and straddling him. Her hands went to his neck. She closed her grip around his windpipe.

"You're not an Enforcer if you want to hurt the alpha's bitch," she whispered, her grip tightening.

Jason's hands came around her throat, his big-fingered grip hurting. She kneed him, and he turned so the blow landed on his hip rather than his groin. Fangs lengthened, and she pressed against him. A knee to the ribs had him releasing her, and she lowered her mouth to his throat.

His smell, a prime werewolf, filled her nostrils, and she closed her eyes to savor the elixir. Beneath his skin his pulse pounded, the carotid artery her own personal highway to heaven. She grazed his skin with her teeth and she smiled when he shuddered beneath her. He slapped his palms on the floor.

"Do it. Prove you're nothing but a bloodsucker." Jason lifted his chin.

A muffled groan from across the room caught her attention. With his knee planted in the guard member's chest, Roarke pinned the man to the ground. "Lilah, hold him," he snarled at her.

She pouted, wanting to play with her food. Instead, she hauled Jason into a seated position and wrenched his hands behind his back. She stood there, with him on his knees before her, his head tilted in a submissive pose.

"Why, Jason? Why?" She asked as Roarke secured the guard member. The scuffle had been quick and decisive.

"If you're out of the way then Roarke can do his job as the alpha. He should have brought down the Dogs a long time ago. You distracted him. You make the pack weak," Jason said.

Lilah shoved him to the ground and planted her knee in the center of his back. Yanking his arms even farther back, she debated about dislocating his shoulder just to send a message. She waited on Roarke's orders.

"Your disobedience makes us look weak. If you want to prove your loyalty, dispose of the corpse and this guard. Make sure there are no others in our midst," Roarke ordered. He eased off his captive, hauling him to his feet. He shoved him into a chair and sat across from him.

"You trust him to do that?" Lilah scowled. "He betrayed you. The punishment is death." She pulled his shoulder just far enough out of the joint that Jason's breath hissed between his clenched teeth.

"I trust Jason will do his job. He knows what will happen." Roarke rose to his feet and went to her. He extended his hand, a silent order that she take it and ease off of the Enforcer.

Lilah shook her head, but did as Roarke bade. She clasped her hand in his and stepped back. "He'd better have a damn good explanation for what he did. At least let me drink." She glared at Jason, daring him to do something to give her cause to wound him. She bared her fangs and snarled.

Roarke nodded.

With a grin, Lilah bent over the Enforcer. She cranked his neck back and lowered her lips to his skin. He tasted of salt and fear, and as she sank her fangs into his neck, he stiffened. She drew his blood into her mouth, the rush of hemoglobin making her close her eyes in ecstasy. Throat working, she gulped down his lifeblood, the adrenaline sweetening the crimson liquid. After several swallows, she pulled her head back and licked the wound.

Jason looked at her. He tried to move away. The bloodlust hummed in her veins, and fangs descended, eyes glowing red, she looked nothing like an alpha bitch. She smiled and turned to Roarke. Slowly, forcing the vampire to wait for now, her eyes lost their red color and her fangs receded. Once again, she looked like the alpha bitch, and only her scent gave her away as something else.

"Remember that she stopped of her own free will," Roarke said. "Take care of things, and you'll have no cause to worry." Turning Lilah away, he escorted her to the door. Once they were outside the room, he pinned her against the wall. His hips held her trapped, the hand clasping hers, bringing it up above her head, his other hand braced against the wall beside her head. "What the hell did you think you were doing?" he snarled.

"Delivering a message and possibly saving your life." Deliberately, she licked her lips, removing the vestigial taste of Jason's blood from her mouth. "I'd think you would thank me."

"You barged into private pack business."

"And you left a note where you were on the desk. If you didn't want me to come, you shouldn't have said anything."

"I trusted you to be a good little wolf." His voice deepened and he bent his head closer to her and inhaled deeply. "God, sucking his blood made you wet, didn't it?"

Lilah arched into him, letting her hips thrusting against his answer for her.

Roarke stepped away and hauled her away from the wall with a jerk of his arm. "Come on. We don't have time for that now." He pulled her behind him as he stormed down the hall and back to the bar. As they rounded the corner, he stopped, and they descended looking like a happy couple. Stares and murmured conversation followed them out, and she had no doubt as soon as the door closed behind them that they'd be the talk of the bar.

"At least I'm here to walk you home," he grumbled. "I can't believe you came here on your own. Adrian should have accompanied you."

"He's out. Vamp business." She frowned. She should have been involved in whatever he was doing. After all, she was a vampire too. The men's possessive natures made her seem all one or the other, never a mixture of both. The rare display in the room served a purpose, and she knew, if Roarke had his way he'd keep her blood sucking side under wraps.

"What kind of vamp business?" Roarke scowled.

Lilah shrugged. "I don't know. He didn't tell me, and I learned a long time ago I wasn't his keeper, though he seems to think he's mine."

Roarke stopped. He moved them against the building and listened.

Lilah sniffed the air.

The Dogs.

At least one of the scents was familiar, and she recognized it as the leader of the little gang that had attacked her. They'd been busy, and perhaps they decided not to give Roarke a chance to make a decision. Or maybe her bravado had made the decision already. Either way, they were about to rumble—again.

Roarke ducked into the alley, and she followed. He hastily removed his clothes, stashed them in a wooden box she suspected might have been put there exactly for that purpose and changed. She followed suit, the brief flash of air against her bare skin replaced by the comforting pelt of fur. In her lupine form, her sense of smell heightened, and she indeed recognized the scents of two of the men. Silently, he urged her back into the alley, ducking into a basement doorway. Descending the stairs, he pushed her toward the end with his body, and Lilah followed.

Roarke stood like a statue, ears perked, nostrils wide to catch any hint of a scent. From her position at the bottom of the stairs all Lilah could smell was Roarke, and his masculine scent invaded every pore of her body. She struggled to keep the bitch under control, the female wolf wanting nothing more than to be mounted right there in the alley. The edge of danger heightened her desire, and Roarke looked back at her and shook his head.

The men stopped at the head of the alley. Lilah waited. She strained to hear anything, and aside from Roarke and the hint of garbage from the Chinese restaurant, she smelled little else. She hoped the garbage sitting between them and the street would stifle their scent. More muffled conversation filtered to her ears and then the wolves left.

Roarke inched down the stairs. He turned and licked her muzzle, her shoulder, his panting breaths ruffling her fur. She lifted her muzzle, letting him groom her chin and throat. His teeth lightly bit down, a warning that he was still her alpha, and then released.

She lifted her tail. The bitch took over, the need to reaffirm life and that Roarke was her mate forcing her to squat and beg him to mount her. A soft whine emerged from her throat. Roarke nipped her.

She whirled to nip him back. He shouldered her out of the way. She stumbled, bumping into the door and rattling it on its hinges. He growled, and she presented her hindquarters to him. He thrust his muzzle between her legs, inhaling audibly. A swipe of his tongue across her vulva had her trembling, and then he hooked a front leg over her back and pushed her on her side.

She landed against the edge of the bottom stair. Concrete bit into her back, certain to leave a bruise when she shifted. Her cracked ribs protested, and she whined with pain.

Roarke glared at her. He sniffed her side, his tongue licking along each rib until she winced at the slight pressure. Stepping back, he shook his head. She stared at him, his penis distended, lust rolling off of him in waves. If he thought to spare her because she was hurt, she'd quickly change his mind. Bounding to her feet, she let her flagging tail signal her interest, and she licked his muzzle. He submitted to it, his ears twitching as she worked along his chin, his throat, to the nape of his neck.

Take me. She willed him to couple with her, her rump wriggling with anticipation. Still, Roarke hesitated. She growled, her need growing. The wolf lunged for its mate, pushing him back. He whined as her teeth made contact with his shoulder, and she bit down hard. She licked the bruise, bending her head to nudge between his legs. The pink head of his penis called to her, and she swirled her tongue around it. Roarke stood rigid, all four legs braced against the concrete as she licked and sniffed his erect cock.

She stepped back and lowered her head, her front paws following so that she thrust her ass into the air. Standing and nodding her head, making sure he knew exactly how it was supposed to be, she turned, lowered her front and waited.

His warmth surrounded her, his weight coming down on her like a welcome blanket. She wiggled beneath him, the head of his penis bumping against her opening. His teeth clamped into her ruff and with a single thrust, buried himself inside her. Lilah sighed and closed her eyes with contentment.

Growls and yips filled the alley, obvious sounds of canines coupling. Lilah let his weight sink into her, his teeth firmly grasping the extra skin on the back of her neck. He plowed into her channel, even in wolf form, his cock stretching and filling her. She worked against him, her hips moving in tandem with his.

With her eyes half-closed, she gave herself over to the pleasure. His growls rumbled in her ears. His fur against her back generated heat, enough to burn her alive. The vampire cringed, hiding away from the canine and its animalistic desires. Lilah grinned. Had she been human, she might have whispered his name, begged him to take her harder, faster, but she wasn't. The wolf could only pant and beg for more in the only way she knew, with her body.

The force of Roarke's thrusts had her pressed against the building. Her nose pressed against the cool, damp bricks. A drop of condensation tricked over clay and mortar to land on her nose. The chill surface contrasted with Roarke's heat. Like a generator, he warmed her, wrapped her in his essence, and she breathed past the mildewed reek of the building to drag his scent into her lungs.

Fur shifted into skin. "Lilah," Roarke groaned, his body no longer canine.

She whined as his cock grew as he shifted, changing into the broad head of his human one. She hung there, suspected with her back legs and hips against his, and then with a mental twist, she shifted. Fingers dug into the crumbling mortar to find purchase amid slippery bricks. Her cheek pressed against the side of the building, lips squished together to make speaking impossible. She wiggled her ass, the chill air against her superheated skin a welcome respite.

His fingers dug into her hips. Close, so close to her mound, and she spread her legs to invite his touch deeper, farther down. Her clit throbbed. His hot breath rushed against the back of her neck.

Lilah closed her eyes and whimpered. Roarke's spicy scent surrounded her, his wolf the mate to her own. Adrian wouldn't have done that, taken her in wolf form and then watched her shift so he could take her as a man. Roarke did. She felt his thrusts grow more frantic, imagined if they were still in wolf form his penis would be forming a hard knot to bind them together. Her muscles fluttered around him.

She slid her hand down the wall and reached between her legs. Her fingers danced across her clit, the ripe bud slick and swollen beneath her fingers. She rubbed, her whimpers escalating as her orgasm neared. And then she was there, flying apart, Roarke's hand against her lips stifling her cries. She bit into the fleshy pad, needed to hold onto something, anything. The building provided little support and only Roarke's body behind hers kept her standing.

His big hand covered hers. Pushing her fingers out of the way, he strummed her clit. His thrusts grew harder, more frantic as he growled raw, carnal demands in her ear. An alpha male, Roarke knew exactly what he wanted, and Lilah knew she'd let him have it.

"Yes," she whimpered as he made tiny adjustments in the angle of each stroke. The head of his penis brushed against her womb, the pleasure-pain of his ramming thrusts bringing her back up to the edge once more.

So good. And all for her. Emotion choked her throat. He said he loved her. In his canine form and in human, he acted on those words. Oh, she might have angered him, and Lilah had no doubt that her barging into his meeting did exactly that, but he cared for her more than words could ever express. She widened her stance, baring herself to him. His fingers slid down to her channel, his fingertips touching his shaft with each stroke. Rubbing his palm over her clit, he did nothing to enhance his own pleasure, only hers.

Her wolf titled back her head and howled. Muscles fluttering, she hovered on the edge, so close yet so far from that elusive precipice. What would Adrian think if he saw them rutting in the alley, the Dogs already having made one appearance tonight? She didn't know, and right now, she didn't care. A tear leaked from the corner of her eyes.

"Now," Roarke growled. He stiffened inside her, the hot jets of his seed triggering another climax. She whimpered, biting her lip with the need to scream her release to the world. Muscles convulsing, she let one, final stroke of Roarke's fingers against her clit send her spiraling out of control. He held her, his hands strong on her waist, his body sturdy behind hers, while she sought the stars and then some.

Eyes closed, she reveled in the intense pleasure pouring through her. Over and over again, the waves of her orgasm never seemed to stop. It took a man, a wolf, like Roarke to do this to her, to make her feel as if she were coming and coming and it would never end. Finally, she drew a ragged breath and forced her eyes open. Roarke still held her. The cool brick façade pressed against her breasts, his thighs like corded steel behind hers. Trapped between hot and cold, living and unloving, her position mirrored her life, and she couldn't help but find some irony in it.

"Let's get dressed," he said. "We need to find Adrian and take care of the Dogs." He stepped away, his fingers not quite leaving her skin.

She nodded and stumbled sideways on shaky legs. Tangling his fingers with hers, Roarke led her up the stairs. He checked the alley. She sniffed, though the scent of their sex filled her nostrils and blocked out most everything. He took her back to the box. She dressed quickly, the smell of Roarke on her skin making her smile.

They hurried back to Roarke's house. He'd walked to the bar, he'd explained, having lent his truck to Adrian for his "vampire business." From the tone of his voice, Roarke didn't quite trust Adrian, and Lilah frowned. She reached up and brushed her fingers along his cheek and jaw, wanting so very much to try and have the men in her life get along.

After their encounter in the alley, Lilah knew, deep in her soul, she couldn't go back to her house.

She debated telling him. After all, he'd dragged her here against her better judgment. She'd cursed him, railed against him for taking her away from her home. But what was a home really other than brick and mortar, wood and insulation. A shelter, nothing more. A cardboard box would do, as would a mansion, and either place would be sterile without Roarke's warming presence.

He glanced at her. For a moment, she wondered if he'd read her thoughts. Then with a soft smile, he clasped his fingers with hers and walked just a little bit faster. She snuck a discreet glance, saw he still had an erection, and wondered what else they'd do once they got home. Perhaps if Adrian wasn't there they could sneak upstairs for more sex. The thought had her grinning like a fool, and even though she wiped the expression away, from Roarke's wink, he'd seen it.

Roarke's truck sat in the driveway, a silent announcement that Adrian had returned. Lilah tamped down her disappointment. She followed him inside, scenting the vampire in Roarke's office. Following her mate, she waited while he opened the door and stepped inside.

Adrian sat behind the desk, arms folded across his chest, a pad of paper and a pen lying on the blotter in front of him. He looked up when they entered. His nostrils flared and he scowled.

"What'd you find out?" Roarke asked, releasing her hand to take a seat in one of the chairs in front of his desk. If it bothered him to have his Second, a vampire, occupying the place he usually did, he said nothing.

Adrian's scowl deepened. "The Council warns me to be careful with whom I associate and not dig into things too deeply. Whatever hornet's nest my brother stirred up will have to remain so, because I'll get no help there."

"You went to the Immortal Council? Why?" Lilah asked. She ignored the chairs and perched on the edge of the desk.

"Because you're a vampire, Lilah." He sighed and shook his head as if he'd had this conversation a thousand times before. "And as such, it's their right to protect you."

"But they want me dead."

"Exactly. And the Council members are old. They seek to distance themselves from their squabbly children, and wolves seem to be testier than most." A smile quirked his lips, quickly extinguished. "So we are on our own. Did your meeting go well?"

Roarke shook his head. "A traitor tried to turn Lilah over to the Luna Guard. He's dead, and my Enforcer is taking care of the guard member."

Lilah watched his expression for signs that he distrusted Jason's actions or motives. She saw none and wondered why that didn't reassure her.

Adrian steepled his fingers. "I see. So we go after the Dogs ourselves."

"There's something else," she blurted. "I was attacked, detained really," she added when Adrian opened his mouth to interrupt. "The Dogs have a message for Roarke. Turn over what is theirs and they'll go away. If he doesn't, he chooses death. I'm pretty sure they meant me. They said something about infecting me and wondering why I didn't join them."

"That's it. We go to them and we take them down." Adrian stood.

Lilah looked up at him, seeing once again the stalwart vampire who had protected her through so much. She looked back at Roarke, the wolf she loved, then to Adrian, and she realized she loved them both. Oh sure, she doubted herself, tried to talk herself out of it, but she really did love both of them. And with Roarke leading the pack, and Adrian as a Second, she wouldn't have to choose. She fought to keep a silly grin off her face and nodded sternly. "So we go."

Adrian looked to Roarke, the Second taking his job seriously. Lilah waited, certain they'd tell her she couldn't go, that she'd have to stay behind like a good little woman. Except the Dogs wanted her. And what they wanted, they'd get. Just not in the way they planned.

"If you follow orders, you can go," Roarke said to her. "I'm sure you won't stay here unless we bound and gag you. And while that has its appeal..." His words trailed off, and the mental image of her lying on the bed, arms and legs tied, a gag in her mouth while Adrian and Roarke ravished her filled her mind. Her lips parted. Her breath came in husky pants.

"That won't fight the Dogs," Adrian finished.

"No. No it won't." Roarke sounded disappointed. He stood and went to the map. Circling the area of red pins with his fingers, he drew their attention to that area. "I don't want Jason involved in this. We should go, hit hard, and get the hell out. Understand."

Both Lilah and Adrian nodded.

"Good. Then let's load up. It's time some Dogs learned their place," Roarke announced.

Lilah followed him out of the office, Adrian close behind her. Roarke led them downstairs to a room she hadn't been in yet, and when he opened it up, she saw he had a veritable arsenal. Handing each of them guns and extra knifes, they armed in silence. The Dogs. The very creatures who had infected her. She planned to take them all down, every single last one of them. No one messed with this alpha bitch and lived. Even if they had been the ones to unwittingly give her the position. She looked at Roarke's stern profile and wondered if he thought the same thing.

Chapter Seventeen

Arriving at the area where the red pins had clustered on the map brought them no closer to finding the Dogs. A series of abandoned buildings, some apartments, some old storefronts, all empty. In one of the upstairs apartments, Lilah had caught a faint trail, enough to track them out the door and down the street until the scent dissipated.

"They must have gotten into a car here," she said and pointed to the nearly abandoned street. She shook her head, tamping down her rising frustration. The need to rend the Dogs from limb to limb, to make them pay for harming her, her pack, and her mate, made her curl her fingers into tight fists.

Roarke nodded. "So we hunt."

Adrian glanced at the sky, a silent reminder dawn would be there in a few hours, and nodded.

Lilah stopped. A scent teased her olfactory senses from downwind. She sniffed. It smelled like Roarke, though he stood next to her. She tried to get a good whiff of the air. The elusive scent teased her, like someone just out of the line of vision. She turned and tried again.

"Lilah, what is it?" Roarke asked.

She held up her hand, concentrating on the scent. "It's you, but it isn't you."

Roarke inhaled audibly. Adrian did as well, rumbling his agreement with Lilah's statement. She stepped forward, letting her nose guide her. For a moment, she debated on shifting where the sense of smell would be so much stronger, she couldn't though, not and still retain her clothes and her ability to use weapons. As a wolf she had her own, but she also knew the two men couldn't be seen in public in the company of a wolf. It'd spark too many questions and threaten the existence of the pack. She suspected the humans in town simply turned a blind eye to the internal pack squabbles, but a wolf...that, they couldn't ignore.

Lilah felt as if someone slipped a leash around her neck and tugged, leading her slowly to the scent that drifted just out of reach. Before she knew it, she'd opened the door to an empty apartment building they'd already searched. Above her, she heard the creaking sounds of footsteps. She stopped.

It had all the hallmarks of a trap. Someone had drawn them into an abandoned area and she got the feeling that at any moment the doors would slam shut. She tensed, waiting for the trap to spring. When it didn't, she glanced at the men. They looked as unhappy as she.

She backed toward the door. Her wolf cried for open spaces, the stars above her, and the room to run.

"Adrian, go with her. I'm going to investigate a little more," Roarke whispered.

"No, we should stick together," she said. Her stomach churned at the thought of leaving Roarke alone in the abandoned building. The scent teased her with its familiarity, almost as if it were a family member. But other than his uncle, he had no known family members in the pack. His father had been gone ever since Roarke was a baby. Yet, the scent tormented her.

"Adrian, go with her." Roarke ordered again. Turning his back on them, he stepped forward.

Above them, boots thumped against the floor.

Adrian grabbed her arm. "Come on."

Lilah tried to dig in her heels, but his superior strength simply dragged her out the door. "We have to do what he says. He's your alpha."

He's yours too, Lilah thought, though kept quiet. Instead, a lifetime spent living among the wolves had her nodding her head and backing out the door. They went to the side of the building and pressed against the brick wall. Lilah scented the air again. The familiar odor had all but disappeared, reaffirming that this was a trap, one they were meant to spring. She inched along the wall, hoping Adrian followed her lead. Heading to the back where she hoped, like most of the apartment buildings on this block, a fire escape or some means of getting to the upper floor waited.

She made it along the wall with Adrian at her heels. Ducking around the corner, she looked up.

An opened window.

The scent hit her stronger now, so strong she nearly doubled over. Like Roarke, but not like him. She had a bad feeling about this.

She found the fire escape and leapt up, grabbing the lower rungs with her hands. Silently, she swung onto the platform, and then crouched, waiting. Inch by inch, she scaled the steps to the second floor. Sensing Adrian followed, she crouched beneath the window on the landing, and moved to the third floor. She glanced inside a grime-covered window. Empty. Good.

She returned to the second floor where Adrian waited.

She peered inside. A man, tall and broad shouldered, with his salt and pepper hair sat next to a camp stove. The small flame emitted little light, or heat, but her vampire sight gave her the ability to see clearly. He was wolf. She smelled the beast inside him, the familiar spices of her lover mingling with the scent.

He raised his head.

Lilah stiffened, afraid she'd been spotted.

The man rose to his feet and went to the door. He grinned and opened it, revealing Roarke standing there, ready to rush inside. "Roarke, how good of you to drop by. And alone. It's nice to know that you follow orders."

Lilah grabbed the sill, ready to swing into the room. Adrian grabbed her arm. He shook his head as Roarke entered the room. "Wait," he mouthed, and Lilah snarled, but did as he bade.

~* * *~

The man standing before him looked like a slightly younger version of his uncle. Roarke fought the urge to take a step back and clenched his jaw to make sure it wasn't gaping open. *His father.* He'd seen only pictures, and those decades old, yet looking at the man standing in front of him, he knew, if his uncle had lived, they'd look nearly identical. Vivid blue eyes nearly the same color as his stared back at him with a hint of amusement. A large tattoo of a howling wolf against a moon crossed the man's bare biceps. He wore a white tank top and jeans, his boots scuffed and worn. He stepped back.

"Why don't you come inside?"

Every muscle in Roarke's body went taut. Behind his father, for he truly believed that was who this man was, he saw Adrian and Lilah flanking the open window. He shook his head, hoping the imperceptible movement would be taken as a denial by his father, as well as telling his lover and Second to hold their positions.

"Why?" Roarke asked. The question grated from his throat, his voice raw with pent-up emotion. According to the uncle who had raised him, this man had betrayed the pack and his family. He'd left, good riddance to bad rubbish and all of that, and Roarke had known no different. Now, his father was involved with the Dogs. His stomach clenched. Bile rose in his throat, and Roarke feared he might puke. "Why?" he asked again.

"To take what is mine."

Lilah's hand curled around the window frame.

"And what is yours?" Roarke asked, keeping his voice calm. To hear his father publicly claim his love for the Dogs would damn him forever, but at least it would give him a reason to kill him. He shuddered with the thought of killing the man who had sired him. His own father. He hoped his Uncle had told the truth, though Roarke knew there were always two sides to every story.

"The pack." The man's words had a hollow, final ring.

"Why do you think Northwoods belongs to you?" Roarke stepped in the room, deciding it did him no good to loiter in the hallway. He closed the door behind him, trapping his father in the room with him.

The man's eyes flickered to the closed door and back. "Because when my brother died, it should have gone to me."

"You bastard," Roarke snarled. Memories of taking over the pack, forcing everyone to accept his uncle's decisions, even when a closer blood member existed, assailed him. Roarke steeled himself against the memory of fighting Eugene and the other pack members for his birthright.

"The pack is mine. You left before I even thought about taking over. You didn't even want me, so don't talk to me about *your* pack." Roarke threw the words at the man standing across from him.

"You don't know the whole truth," his father said. "And it's too late to fix the past."

"Then why the hell come back? The Northwoods Pack is mine and you know it. So let's fight right now, wolf against wolf. And when it's over and done with, we'll see who takes over the Northwoods."

"No!" Roarke roared. He leapt at his father, hands wrapping around his neck and sending him barreling to the ground. He hit hard enough to vibrate the floor. "You forced yourself on a member of the pack, and when she whelped your pup, you left. You fucking left. If you couldn't even raise your son, there's no way you could rule the Northwoods." Rage boiled inside him. After simmering for nearly thirty years, the hot boil of anger burst. He squeezed his hands, dropping to his knees to straddle his father's body.

His father gripped his arms, surprisingly strong, and tried to pry his hands free.

Two more Dogs burst into the room. Lilah vaulted through the window, engaging the one on her right, and Adrian followed shortly after, taking the one on the left. Out of the corner of his eye, he saw flying fists and the glint of metal. His father brought the side of his hand down on Roarke's elbow, hard.

Pain shot through his arm, weakening his grip enough for his father to thrust his hands aside. He bucked Roarke off, sending his son tumbling backwards. Roarke's father punched, kicked, the moves instinctive against someone whose fighting style was so like his own. For a moment, Roarke felt as if he battled an older twin, and he wondered what it would be like if he'd known his father, grown up with him. His wandering thoughts cost him a blow to the jaw.

His head snapped back, the tang of blood filling his mouth from where he's bit his cheek. He snarled. His father didn't deserve the consideration. In fact, calling him father in anything but a biological sense rankled. Roarke lunged. He heard a Dog cry out and the smell of blood filled the airs. Not Lilah's. Not Adrian's. That was all that mattered.

He saw Lilah straddling a prone body. A pool of blood seeped out from beneath him and she cleaned her knife on the man's shirt. She'd killed. His bitch had killed, and it was his father's fault. Roarke dodged a blow. It was his father's fault that he even had a bitch, that Lilah was anything other than a human, as she should have been. He redoubled the efforts, determined not to be thankful that through the Dogs' action Lilah's wolf had been created.

Dropping low, he tried to swipe his father's legs out from underneath him. A quick one-two blow to the stomach had him doubled over, an uppercut splitting his lip and breaking his nose. Blood gushed over Roarke's hands and he punched his father in the windpipe.

The man gasped. He looked up, his eyes full of hatred and defiance. No defeat, not submission as one should to his alpha. Father or not, he still belonged to the Northwoods pack, and that made Roarke his alpha.

Adrian's opponent went down. Lilah left Roarke's line of sight, but he felt her at his back, by the door. Good girl, keeping watch and out of the fight.

"Submit," Roarke ordered. "Submit and you'll keep your life." A mistake to be sure, but there'd been enough killing, enough bloodshed over something he didn't even know. It was time to end it.

His father laughed a hoarse, mocking chuckle that raised the hair on the back of his neck. "You think I'm going to submit to you, whelp?" He shook his head and glanced at his dead and downed Dogs. "You killed those who belong to me. Maybe I should kill someone who belongs to you." His gaze fell just past Roarke's shoulder where Lilah stood by the door.

Muscles tensing, weight balanced on the balls of his feet, Roarke moved to pounce.

"Roarke, no! He's baiting you." Lilah called from behind him.

A crack announced Adrian's breaking the downed wolf's neck. He stood up. "You should have thought of that before you came to attack our own." The vampire moved to stand beside him, a show of solidarity he expected from his Second.

"Tell me what happened, father. Tell me why you left the pack. I want—" Roarke shook his head. "I *need* to understand." He waved Adrian back several steps and held his hands loose at his sides. "I don't want to fight you. I don't even know you." Roarke's gut twisted. For a moment, all the pain and loss of not having a father rushed through him. Growing up without a dad had hurt. The taunts he'd endured, even though he was the pack leader's nephew, had been cruel. The little boy inside him wondered if it were true, if his father left because of him.

He breathed deeply, inhaling the man's scent, so similar to his own. Matching blue eyes, salt and pepper hair, Roarke knew this was exactly what he'd look like in thirty years. "Father." He tested the unused name on his lips, not liking the bitter taste.

"Don't call me that! My brother was more of a father to you than I ever could be, and that was exactly how he wanted it. You don't want to know what happened. It would ruin your illusions of my larger-than-life perfect brother. Peter needed only one thing to make his rule of the Northwoods perfect. A son. You were that son. I had everything and he stole it from me."

"I want to know the truth." Roarke stepped forward. "I want to make things right Fath—*David*." Behind him, Adrian and Lilah's presence shown like a beacon of light. A chance to reclaim his pack, without bloodshed, and remove the Dogs as a problem. His own father led the Dogs. The betrayal slammed him in the gut. His stomach twisted, and he struggled to keep from appearing week in front of David. So long as his father denied the relationship, then Roarke would too. It didn't bode well for a peaceful resolution.

David shook his head. His glance flickered to the two waiting by the door, then back to Roarke. "It's too late for that." He grinned, and the tell-tale sounds of people running down the hall filled the air. The scent of wolves, at least three, testified to the fact that they weren't alone.

"Adrian, Lilah, watch the doorway." Roarke advanced on David. "Then we'll end this." One more death, his father's, would secure the pack. He pushed the patricidal thoughts from his mind. This man contributed genetic data. Nothing more. When it came to running the Northwoods his uncle, Peter, had done everything, and then passed it onto Roarke.

David snarled. He circled Roarke, both men wary of making the first move. Being older did nothing to slow David down, the few quick jabs he threw as fast and hard as any Roarke had ever faced before. Deep in his gut, he feared he might not win. He shoved the defeatist thoughts aside. No, he had to win, for Northwoods and for Lilah. Tired of the game, he punched.

The edge of his knuckles caught David along the jaw. David's head snapped back and he countered with a quick uppercut. He missed by a millimeter, and Roarke committed himself to the fight. With a snarl, he punched again, and as his knuckles hit the solid flesh of David's torso, the fight erupted in earnest.

Snarls and growls filled the hallway, the scent of rank wolves on the air. In her human form, Lilah would be at a disadvantage against the wolves. David landed a punch to his side, momentarily forcing the air of his lungs. Lilah was a big girl. She could take care of herself, and he'd better focus on his own fight.

A sting ran along Roarke's ribs. He touched it, his hand coming back sticky with blood. Fur sprouted from the back's of David's hands, his fingers turned into the pads of his paws with long claws. A partial shift. Face lengthened into a grotesque parody of a cross between a man and wolf's muzzle, teeth elongating past David's lower lip. His muscles pressed against the seams of his clothing, the rip of cloth filling the air.

Roarke ducked. He countered with a one-two punch that had David's head snapping back. Blood dripped from a cut on his lip, the tangy scent filling the air. Outside, he felt Adrian and Lilah take notice.

Stay there, he mentally willed. He shifted his own hands into paws, and caught David along the shoulder. Blood welled from the gash, soaking into his white tank-top. He stumbled. Roarke forced David to the ground, swiping his feet out from underneath him. Boots connected with ribs, the crack of bone audible in the room. Using his weight, Roarke pinned David beneath him, his hands once more fists as he pummeled his father in the ribs. He punched his face, breaking David's nose. Blood gushed over his lips, and he spat it away.

He looked down at his father, unable to separate the threat to his pack from the fact that this man sired him. He hadn't seen his father in decades. Had no memory of the man, and yet, here he was, looking exactly the way Roarke expected. "I don't want to kill you," Roarke growled. "Don't make me do this." Emotion choked his throat. If he killed his father, he'd never know the truth behind why he left, perhaps never even know the truth about the schism growing in the pack.

"If you want to be alpha, then you do what you have to do. An alpha can't afford to have emotions," David said.

"I know. But that doesn't make this any easier," Roarke whispered.

David lifted his chin and bared the bleeding side of his throat. "Do it," he said. "Show me you're worthy."

~* * *~

Worry for Roarke kept Lilah's attention split between the activities in the room and the three wolves facing them down. Adrian took on two, his torso bleeding from multiple bite wounds, and a slash across his upper thigh. One of the wolves lay dead against the wall, the other staggering on its feet in front of Adrian.

Lilah snarled at the wolf before her. A mangy coated mutt, dried blood caked along its muzzle, stared at her. His teeth snapped together and claws clicked on the hallway floor. Warily, Lilah watched it. From inside the room came the snarls and growls of a struggle, the smell of blood. She tried to block the image of a bruised and bloody Roarke from her mind.

The wolf leapt. Lilah let the bloodlust surge through her veins. The wolf blinked, tried to halt its flight, but it was too late. The creature slammed into her, sending them both stumbling backwards. Grabbing the beast around the neck, Lilah sank her fangs into flesh, blood flowing hot and welcome into her mouth. She tasted the tang of an illegal substance and spat out the mouthful of blood. She jabbed her knife into its soft belly.

The squish of blood and organs being sliced open sent a flood of blood and liquids over her hand. The smell of offal filled the air; she'd pierced the large intestine. Slicing downward, she opened a gash from sternum to pelvis.

The creature lay on its side, organs spilling onto the floor. A quick, merciful swipe of the blade across its throat killed it, and she turned to watch Adrian finish off the other wolf just as efficiently before she raced down the hall to assess Roarke's situation.

Blood smeared the floor around them, creating a sticky surface on which to fight. Blood ran down his father's neck and shoulder, his right arm hanging limply at its side. She could see through to the muscles beneath and knew tendons had been cut. Roarke boasted a cut along his side, a black eye and a split cheek. He straddled his father and reached for his neck.

Lilah stifled a squeak. While there was layers of meaning and subterfuge behind his father's appearance, she couldn't watch Roarke take the man's life. She turned away and found Adrian there. She buried her face in his chest.

Suddenly, the sounds of a scuffle intensified, and Lilah turned back to find Roarke's father had toppled Roarke, and stood over his fallen son. He kicked Roarke in his injured side, and Roarke cried out.

Lilah stepped forward. Adrian's hand closed around her arm. "No, this is his fight," Adrian said.

Lilah nodded, her eyes never leaving the sight in the room. Roarke managed to regain his footing, and the battle moved across the floor, away from the smears of blood toward the window. Fear rooted her to the spot. Fear of what would happen if Roarke succeeded in killing the leader of the Dogs. Fear of what would happen if he didn't.

Roarke managed to get his hands around his father's throat. Slamming him against the wall, Roarke held him there, pinned. The man's face turned red. He gasped for air.

Finish it! Just a little more pressure, a squeeze of the fingers, and then one way or another, this could be all over.

His father jabbed a blade into Roarke's side. Pain loosened his grip, and his father shoved him back. Blood flowed from an angry cut, and Roarke gasped for air. Lilah feared the blade had perforated a lung, and this time, Adrian released her, following on her heels as she ran into the room.

She caught Roarke as he stumbled backwards, gently holding him in her arms. She lowered him to the ground. His father bolted out the window.

Adrian followed. The clang of footsteps on the fire escape sounded ominously loud, fading away as both men dropped to the ground. Lilah smoothed a lock of hair away from Roarke's forehead and tried to assess his injuries.

"I've got to go after them," he said. He struggled to free himself from her arms, but a moment later, he gasped in pain and laid back.

"We've got to get you home. That blade might have hit your lung." Lilah willed Adrian to return. Between them, they could get the alpha back to his house and start patching him up. Alone, she could do it, but she might jostle his injuries more if Roarke couldn't stand. His ashy skin, and lips tight with pain told her he probably couldn't make it five feet, let alone all the way back to his house.

"I'll be okay," he said and struggled to stand.

Against her better judgment, Lilah allowed him. Adrian was needed to chase after Roarke's father, and if she could return Roarke to his house alone, all the better. Wrapping her arm around his waist, she took most of his weight and led him toward the door.

Chapter Eighteen

Lilah thanked the wolf's fast healing metabolism as she walked Roarke, step by painful step, down the hall and down the stairs to the old abandoned apartment building's first floor. She saw no other Dogs, no signs that this place would have been anything but a place to trap the unwary. Certainly not their headquarters and she scowled thinking that they were once again back to ground zero when it came to the interlopers.

Darkness protected them from prying eyes. Roarke's reputation as their alpha was damaged enough without him being seen bloody and limping being led back to his house. Once outside she sniffed the air, though the tang of Roarke's blood overrode all of the obvious scents. "Let's go," she said, turning him down the sidewalk toward home.

"Wait, we have to go after David." Roarke stopped. He grabbed her hand. "Don't let him get away."

It took her a moment to figure out he spoke about his father. She'd never known his father's name. He trusted her with his body, his pack, yet his father's name had never been mentioned to her. She suspected she should have heard it one time or another, though as a child he'd kept very close-lipped about his absent parents. "You're in no shape to go anywhere but home," Lilah insisted a little sharper than she intended. She dragged him forward several steps.

The pounding of footsteps and the scent of a vampire forced Lilah to stop. She watched Adrian jog back to her. He halted beside them, adding his arm around Roarke and taking most of the werewolf's weight from her. "I lost him."

Roarke cursed. "We have to go after him."

Adrian's grip tightened. "We can't. You can hardly stand. Do you think you'd win a fight?" He dragged Roarke back the way they had come. "You're going home."

"What about you?" Lilah asked. "You're not going after him are you?"

"I'm his Second. It's my duty. And we can call the Enforcer." Adrian said. He glared determinedly ahead, and Lilah knew she wouldn't get, and keep, both men home with her without a fight.

"What if he comes back? He's Roarke's father," Lilah said.

Between them, Roarke flinched.

"He knows where Roarke lives. What if he comes after us at Roarke's house? Send Jason after him. We need you there to help keep your alpha safe. He's wounded, and I'm not exactly one hundred percent after the fight." She hated telling him that, knew the vampire would coddle her more than Roarke, and frankly, his wounds were far worse than hers. "So you need to be a Second and guard the alpha and his bitch."

If Adrian thought she had a point, he didn't say anything. Instead, he nodded, took a little more of Roarke's weight.

"How far did you trace him?" Roarke asked as they turned the corner.

"Several blocks. He shifted into full wolf form and took off. I tracked him until his scent dissipated. I think he had someone waiting." Adrian said.

"A car." Roarke nodded. "Eugene, I bet. I should have killed that mutt when I had the chance."

"How do you know?" Lilah asked. She bit her lip, wanting to demand that there'd been enough killing. In her name and in the name of the pack, and none of it made any sense. Instead, she kept quiet.

Roarke shook his head. "I should have guessed when Eugene was causing all those problems in the pack. He knew my father, or at least he's old enough to know him." Roarke stopped and wiped his hand over his face. "What a fucking mess! I know nothing about why my father left. I need more information before I'm forced to kill him."

"Or, he gets what he wants, which is you gone from the pack," Adrian said in a dry voice.

"My father left. My uncle passed the pack to me. It's mine by right of inheritance and I'm alpha enough to keep it."

They walked in silence until they reached Roarke's front door. He unlocked it, and gingerly Lilah and Adrian helped him inside. "I need more information, and there's none to be had. I've gone through all my uncle's records. There's nothing about my father, or why he left. It's like he didn't even exist."

"Just a little farther," Lilah encouraged. They led him upstairs to the master bedroom, and sat him on the bed. "There, now let's take a look at the wound. Adrian, will you get first aid supplies from the bathroom?" She helped pull Roarke's bloody, sticky shirt over his head and gasped at the wound. Already it had clotted and begun to heal.

Adrian returned moments later with disinfectant and bandages. "I'm going to go clean up. Let me know if you need anything." He left, and she heard water running.

Lilah dabbed a cotton ball along Roarke's wound, painfully aware she'd done this before. "You shouldn't have come for me," she whispered when his breath hissed with pain. "You should have stayed here and solidified your pack."

Roarke brushed his thumb across her cheek, leaving behind a smear of blood. "Do you really mean that?" Sliding the pad down over her lower lip, he gave her vampire a taste of his coppery essence. He brushed his thumb back and forth, a feather-light caress that hardened her nipples and sent heat flooding to her pussy. "Do you regret that I came for you?"

Lilah sensed Adrian hovering at the connecting door between the bathroom and the bedroom. Her emotions churned like a storm-tossed sea inside her. "No. Never," she whispered. "I just think it might be too much. The attacks on my life seem to have stopped, but for how long? Adrian and I aren't welcome in the pack, and even if you resolved the issues with the Dogs, I don't think we'd ever be welcome here." She closed her eyes, the home she thought she'd regained slipping through her fingers like the drops of Roarke's blood. Blinking away the sting of tears, she finished bandaging the wound on his side, then turned to his other, smaller injuries.

Roarke reminded quiet.

Adrian stepped from the bathroom. He halted in front of the bed and rested his hand on her shoulder. "The pack is the best place for both of us," he said.

His words startled Lilah. Eyes wide, she stared at him. Looking from him to Roarke, then back to the vampire, she saw the alpha was just as shocked as she at the turn of the conversation. "I'd like to think it was," she said, a soft smile curving her lips. "I kind of like it here. But Roarke took on more than his share of trouble when he came and got me."

Roarke grabbed her wrist, stilling her absent cleaning motions against his wound. "And don't you think I knew that? I'm an alpha wolf. I know exactly what I was getting into when I sought you out, and I don't regret a moment of it. You're trying to protect us again, Lilah, and as much as I love you, I don't need your protection."

She closed her eyes and nodded. Once again, he'd spoken of love, a love she couldn't return until some issues that lay between them were solved. "Adrian, you better call Jason. We've lost enough time as it is."

Amusement danced in Roarke's eyes.

Adrian nodded, and then went to the phone on the bedside table. He punched in the number, and moments later relayed a terse, edited version of what had happened to the Enforcer. He hung up. "He's on it."

"Good." Roarke said. He turned to Lilah. "Now you need to believe that I'm here because I want to be. What can I do to convince you of that fact?"

Lilah stared at him. Her stomach dropped. His question caught her completely unprepared. "I don't know. I've been on my own for so long, I guess it's hard to trust anyone." She looked at Adrian. Grim understanding filled his eyes.

"You're not alone anymore," Roarke said. He cupped her cheek with the palm of his hand and leaned forward. Brushing his lips across hers, he kissed her.

Lilah stiffened, afraid he might tear his wounds open again.

"Trust me," he whispered against her lips.

Behind her, Adrian's weight settled onto the bed. The mattress dipped, sending her tottering back against him. His hands tugged at her shirt, his lips finding the curve of her neck. "You're not alone," he said.

"You seem okay with this," Lilah said as the need for air parted her from Roarke's mouth. Big hands circled her bare waist, thumbs caressing the soft skin of her stomach. She curled her hands into Roarke's shoulders, the cloth and bandages forgotten on the comforter beside them.

"I am okay with this," Roarke said.

"And so am I," replied Adrian.

"Why?" Lilah swiveled so she faced the vampire. "Look, not that I don't like making love to both of you at the same time, because I do." A heated flush crept over her cheeks. She ducked her head, half-shocked after all the things she'd done that she could still even blush. "But Adrian you don't like werewolves, and Roarke, you hate vampires, yet you made him your Second and me your bitch? It seems like both of you are altering your lives quite a bit just for me."

Adrian cupped her chin, turning her so she faced him. "Lilah, you think too much. We're here because we want to be. Just let it go at that."

"But what happens when you don't want to be here anymore and all this vampire-werewolf politics shit becomes too much?" Lilah shook. She hated her vulnerability, the fact that tears stung her eyes. Breathing deeply, she struggled to calm her nerves.

"Do you really believe that would be the case? If I'd wanted to leave, I would have done so before now. Trust, Lilah. You have to trust." He breathed the last sentence onto her lips, before claiming them in a soul-stealing kiss. Adrian's tongue slipped into her mouth, stroking along her incisors as if willing them to extend.

Behind her, Roarke cupped his hands over her breasts. Her nipples pressed into his palms, the heavy weight of her in his hands making her ache for more. His injuries worried her. Adrian's words echoed in her mind. *Trust*. She had to trust both Roarke and him, not only as her lovers, but as her alpha and his Second. She moaned, and Adrian swallowed it. Roarke squeezed her nipples, as if he sensed her capitulation, and hot cream flooded her pussy.

Trust. Somehow, that simple five-letter word was a stronger aphrodisiac than both men's hands on her at the same time. Roarke played with her breasts, palming them and rubbing the nipples between his fingers. Adrian simply held her while his mouth ravished hers. The plunge and retreat of his tongue reminded her of the thrust of his cock inside her cunt. She sat on the bed, her entire being suspended between the two men.

Closing her eyes, she gave herself over to the men. Somewhere she'd lost her shirt and bra, and the button of her jeans had come undone. Adrian did nothing but hold her and kiss her, the gentleness in his lips slanting across hers driving her to arch against Roarke's fingers. She felt claimed, taken, and the only thought running through her mind was how fast she could surrender to these preternatural men.

Lilah fisted her hand in Adrian's shirt. She tugged it free of his jeans, the cool skin of his bare chest calling to her fingers with a siren's song. She traced each ridge of his abdomen, up over his flat pectorals, then down over his obliques. The power inherent in his body humbled her. His fangs deliberately pricked the end of her tongue, and he drew it into his mouth to suckle. The sensation shot straight to her core. She thought about grabbing Roarke's wrist and sending his hand down to her clit, but couldn't release Adrian long enough to do so. She flicked her fingers over Adrian's nipples. He shuddered, and against his lips, she grinned.

Lilah licked his lower lip and drew it into her mouth. Sucking gently, she unfastened his pants, and then pushed him back. Straddling him, she rained kisses on his mouth, his chin, his neck. She pulled off his shirt, and he let her shove down his pants.

"My boots." Adrian's voice rasped with desire.

They separated long enough for boots to thud against the floor. The rustle of fabric and the creaking of the bed settled down, and when the three of them returned to the bed Lilah found their positions shifted. She straddled Roarke with Adrian's hands on her hips. She moaned as he thrust against her, the thick ridge of his cock brushing her slick folds.

Lilah leaned forward and buried her face in the hollow of his clavicle. His rich, male musk washed over her senses. She licked him, nipping and tasting his nipple. She drew the bead into her mouth and sucked just as she wanted the men to suck on her breasts. Undulating her hips against Roarke, she worked her labia along his hard length. Behind her, Adrian covered her, his cock brushing against the crease of her buttocks, tormenting her with the promise of double penetration.

Trust. Oh yeah, she trusted them with her body and her life. Nipping, she slid down Roarke's body, his abdomen a terrain to be explored with teeth and tongue. The swirl of his navel fascinated her, as did the arrow of hair leading down to his shaft. She licked his wounds, knowing her vampiric saliva would help him heal. His cock bumped against her chin and made her mouth water. She buried her face in the hair and inhaled. Nothing smelled better than a fully aroused wolf.

Adrian nipped between her shoulder blades and Lilah grinned. Except for maybe a fully aroused vampire. Circling Roarke with her hands, she drew his cock to her lips. She circled the crown with her tongue, pausing to torment the bundle of nerves just beneath the head. Behind her, she wiggled her ass at Adrian, and he palmed her buttocks. Gathering her moisture, he smeared it along her crease and circled the puckered ring of her anus. The pressure of one finger had her whimpering against Roarke's cock.

She wrapped her lips around him and sucked. Inch by inch, she worked him deeper into her mouth until she stroked him from base to tip with her tongue. Her hands reached between his legs to fondle his balls.

Roarke groaned.

She set a steady suction, a pull and retreat that had his hips bucking off the bed. Lilah's channel clenched and released with the knowledge of how his rod felt plunging into her over and over again. And then, Adrian's fingers filled her entrance, his thumb reaching back to circle her anus. The dual stimulation stole her breath, made her whimper against Roarke's cock. Her cream flooded his hand, and she felt his teeth scrape against one muscled buttock.

Lilah released Roarke's cock with a low moan. "Bite me," she whimpered. She tongued the werewolf's shaft, sliding down the underside to take one of his balls in her mouth. She rolled it with her tongue, alternating her sucking between one and the other.

Roarke speared his hands in her hair. He held her to him, the trust implicit in his actions sending a fresh rush of cream to her slit.

Lilah released his balls with a soft pop and then took the head of his cock in her mouth once more. She made love to his shaft, using lips and tongue and just the barest scrape of her teeth to keep him on edge.

Behind her, Adrian slid his thumb into her back entrance. He stretched her, his light thrusts pumping in and out. His hand caressed her flank with long strokes. She thrust back against him, needing, wanting more. Yet, Adrian held her on the edge.

She whimpered with frustration, the thick pole in her mouth keeping her from making much noise. Determined to make Roarke come, she redoubled her efforts, tonguing his slit until she tasted the salty essence of his precum. She curled her fingers against his thighs.

Lilah stole a glimpse at Roarke's expression and found him staring over her head at Adrian. No malice or jealousy filled his gaze, just acceptance.

Adrian's digits slid away from her and her whimper filled the room.

"I want to watch him fuck you," Roarke growled.

Lilah shuddered at his words. Her heart swelled at the raw emotion in Roarke's gaze. She drew a deep breath as Roarke shifted just enough to better watch. Then, Adrian's crown pressed against her pussy, and she was so wet, so ready that he slid inside. A long, sure stroke had him buried balls deep. The things three people could do to one another, and Lilah clenched her fingers just thinking about. She couldn't gasp, couldn't do anything but feel his cock plow into her body. Stroke after stroke, so hard, so deep he brushed the mouth of her womb. Lilah's cheeks hollowed out, her fingers finding the sensitive skin behind Adrian's balls, as she transferred the pleasure she was feeling onto him.

Trust. It all came down to that simple word. Between these two men, both from different worlds, yet each bound into the pack. Roarke claimed his spot from heredity, and Adrian stood as Roarke's Second because of her. It humbled her. It stole the breath from her lungs, and made her feel like the most cherished person on the face of the Earth.

A tear splashed from her cheek to trail into the curls surrounding Roarke's staff. She blinked them away, the sting of emotion too much to bear as Adrian's thrusts grew harder, bolder.

Lilah's muscles clenched. So close, so ready, and then as if he sensed what she needed, Adrian reached around her body to brush his finger against her clit.

Lilah reared back. Roarke's cock slid from her mouth. She screamed, her body convulsing around Adrian's shaft. One more plunge had him coming home, a hoarse shout announcing his climax. Lilah struggled to hold on, her orgasm tearing through her with a primal intensity. Over and over her muscles clenched, released, the pulses radiating through her body. Beneath her, Roarke growled, his hand tangling in her hair to bring her lips back to his cock, and she could do nothing but wrap her lips around his shaft and suck. Adrian's hot seed filled her cunt. She pulled Roarke's cock deep into her throat until his head slipped past the tight ring of muscles. She fucked him with her mouth.

Adrian pulled out, and she lowered her buttocks down to rest on Roarke's legs, effectively pinning him beneath her. She breathed deeply as her heart rate slowed. She came back into her body with the feel of Roarke's shaft filling her mouth. She tasted his salty essence. His wolf's musk surrounded her, penetrated her more thoroughly than Adrian had.

With a guttural cry, Roarke came. He pumped his seed into her mouth, and Lilah swallowed every drop, every ounce until she licked him clean. She slid him from her mouth with a pop, her hand cradled around the base of his shaft. She slumped over, her head resting on his chest. Beneath her ear, his heart pounded. Roarke wrapped his arm around her.

Adrian cradled her back, his hand cupping her breast, his legs tangled against hers. The three of them lay there, sweaty and panting. Lilah closed her eyes and breathed their combined scents. It felt so good, so right; she wondered how she'd ever questioned Roarke for coming after her. Maybe he knew best. Northwoods belonged to him as much as any pack, and surely he'd do nothing to harm it.

Trust.

Adrian toyed with her nipples, and she wriggled closer to the vampire's cool skin. He needed to feed soon. Their blood supply in the fridge was running low, though theoretically as a Second, he could use any member of the pack for sustenance. A stab of jealousy clenched her gut. No, he'd drink from no one but her...or Roarke. Otherwise, he'd have to use bagged blood, just as she. A pact between the three of them, something she knew though it had never been spoken.

Lilah lay cocooned between the two men, her thoughts finally grasping the fact that the phone had yet to ring. Their lovemaking had been a distraction but they waited for the news of Jason's hunt.

Roarke's father had spent enough of his time trying to ruin the pack. It was time for the bastard to leave once and for all. Lilah bit her lip, not wanting to voice her thoughts. Roarke's deep, steady breathing told her she didn't have to, that he'd fallen into a healing sleep. She grinned and snuggled closer to him, wishing her will and the arm wrapped around his chest were all she needed to keep him safe.

Adrian nuzzled her neck. She relaxed into his embrace, the men's earlier words haunting her. Yeah, she thought too much. Always had, always would. Slowly, she pulled her arm away from Roarke and turned to face Adrian. She buried her head against his chest, and with a contented sigh, both his arms wrapped around her. He held her tight.

"You need to feed," she whispered.

He nodded, his chin bumping the top of her head. "Later. There are a couple of bags left in the fridge."

Lilah shivered, the sweat cooling on her skin.

"Here, let's get you and Roarke under the blankets." Adrian slid to the edge of the bed, peeled back the comforter and sheet, and then helped her slide beneath it. Together, they helped Roarke get under the blankets. Adrian crawled into bed, sandwiching her between them.

Lilah flattened her palm on Roarke's chest, the steady beating of his heart reassuring her.

Adrian kissed the curve of her shoulder. "We did the right thing," he said. "I hated Roarke when he first showed up. Damn, I hated him like my worst enemy, but only because I knew you. He'd gotten to you and you wanted that. I think I was jealous of that. An immortal vampire, all the wealth and the world at my disposal, and I thought you hated me."

"Never," Lilah breathed.

"Shhh, let me finish." His cock nudged the cleft of her buttocks, momentarily distracting her from his words. "I love you, Lilah. You're a part of me, and I know I'd do anything, even becoming a werewolf's Second." He bit back a bark of laughter. "Hell, I'd become alpha, if that's what it took to call you my own. We've got our issues to deal with, but one thing that's for sure, is us. You know that don't you?"

Lilah nodded, Adrian's unexpected words sending her head spinning. "Thank you," she said. Words choked her throat, and she simply lay there, letting Adrian's presence comfort her. "Jason should be checking in soon, shouldn't he?"

Adrian sighed, and Lilah wondered if he expected a similar response from her. Some undying declaration of love, no doubt, and she wrinkled her nose. She'd made her choice, knew unless things were settled between the pack and the Immortal Council, how she couldn't tell either man she loved them. Because love made people do stupid things. In the middle of a fight, stupid things got people killed.

"I'm sure he'll check in soon. He knows this area as well as Roarke." Adrian sounded distant.

Lilah doubted he wanted to talk about Roarke's father. She fell silent.

"It'll be all right. I'm sure things will work out. Just give Roarke time to get his pack under control and then we'll go to the Immortal Council." Adrian gave her a comforting squeeze.

Lilah nodded. She kept her mouth shut for once, not wanting to counter Adrian's words. He had faith things would work out, but she suspected finding out Roarke's father ran the Dogs was only the beginning of their problems.

Chapter Nineteen

The sound of rustling woke Lilah. She blinked, the heat from Roarke baking her front and Adrian's body chilling her back. Downstairs the somewhat-familiar smell of another werewolf drifted to her. She sat up, pulling the sheet to her bare breasts. Outside, the sun pounded against the drawn drapes, and from Adrian's cold, lifeless body, he slept his daytime rest. She lifted her hand to wake Roarke and stilled it. He needed his rest.

The smell grew closer. Lilah glanced at the tangle of clothes at the foot of the bed. To sort out her own and go downstairs would waste valuable time. Roarke was the pack alpha, and the sounds certainly didn't sound menacing.

"Roarke," Lilah whispered, not wanting to alert whoever was in the house.

He snorted, but didn't wake.

She nudged his shoulder. "Roarke." Damn, she hated to wake him, but if it were an intruder she wanted at least one of her men at her back.

He remained still.

Lilah lifted the covers.

Footfalls sounded on the stairs. Several quick thumps, and then Jason stood in the doorway.

"Jason, you scared me," Lilah said. She breathed a sigh of relief and checked to be sure she clutched the blanket over her breasts. A discreet glance reassured her both men were adequately covered.

"I need to speak with Roarke," Jason growled.

Lilah's bitch went on alert. Hackles raised, she stomped to the forefront of Lilah's mind. Her pulse hitched. Raising her chin, she glared at Jason. "He's sleeping. I suggest you come back later when you're invited. This is our den." Only the thought that if she bared herself long enough to get her clothing she'd have the wrath of both Adrian and Roarke on her kept her from getting out of bed, getting dressed, and personally showing the Enforcer the door.

He sniffed the air. "You've fucked each other." A growl vibrated beneath the words.

"That's none of your business, Enforcer. If you won't leave at least tell me what news you have of the Dogs' leader." Deliberately, she kept quiet about his identity. Somehow, she knew, if Jason figured out the

Dogs were lead by Roarke's father, he'd have more ammunition to use against them.

Jason crossed his arms over his chest. "I don't have to tell you anything, vampire bitch."

"Suit yourself, but if Roarke rips out your throat for waking him, I warned you." She shook her lover again.

He stirred, groaning as he blinked his eyes open. "You nearly killed me woman. Can't you wait." He stretched and sat up. "Oh hey, Jason. What'd you find out?"

"That you're a vampire fucker! It's a good thing I didn't find the leader of the Dogs, because I think I'd have told him to challenge you for ownership of the pack. I don't think I like the way you run things." Jason stepped forward, his gaze dropping to Roarke's wounds.

Lilah stiffened. Her hand curled into Roarke's arm, her nails leaving tiny half-moon furrows.

Roarke tore off the bandages, revealing the half-healed gash along his ribs. He sucked in a breath of air, his wince of pain nearly imperceptible. He pried Lilah's fingers from his arm and swung his legs over the edge of the bed. With more strength, than she suspected he possessed, he stood without swaying and pulled on his jeans. As soon as he buttoned and zipped them, he glanced back to her and Adrian.

"Let's take this downstairs." He reached for Jason's arm to steer him back out the door.

Jason sidestepped.

Roarke jerked. His fingers slipped along Jason's arm. Pain bracketed his eyes.

Jason nodded and stood his ground. "Yeah, and if I challenged you for the pack right now, you'd lose. So, I don't think I'm going anywhere. The vampire isn't going anywhere. So how come your bitch isn't sleeping like the dead, too?"

"Because she's a wolf."

"With a fetish for blood." Jason crossed his legs at the ankles and leaned against the wall. "So you want to know what I found out about your old man?"

Roarke's eyes widened. He glanced at Lilah, and she shook her head. With each word Jason said, her gut clenched tighter and tighter. At least he stood by the door. Hate rolled off of him in waves, defiance that would lead to stupid things like trying to pull the covers back. She tucked the blanket closer around Adrian's chin, leaving just his eyes revealed.

"Sure, cover up the vamp. Afraid I might pull the shades," Jason taunted.

"Jason," Roarke grabbed his arm and yanked him away from the wall. "Downstairs, now." He shoved his Enforcer out the door.

Jason stumbled.

Roarke followed. He turned, and barked at Lilah, "Get dressed and meet us downstairs. I want you there."

"Relying on your bitch to guard your back?" Jason sneered.

"Get your ass downstairs," Roarke replied.

Lilah listened to him shove Jason downstairs. Half-afraid of what the wolf would do while she was absent, she flipped the covers over Adrian's head, scurried out of the bed, and dressed in record time. Taking the stairs two at a time, she stepped into the den and saw Roarke seated behind his desk, Jason in front of it. She went to Roarke and stood behind him. Now maybe the Enforcer would tell them what he saw. And if he didn't, Lilah swore she'd kill him herself.

~* * *~

Roarke glared at his Enforcer, a wolf he'd called friend before his trip to find Lilah. Since then something changed. Maybe Jason had become corrupted by the Dogs, or perhaps the Luna Council had gotten to him. Either way, his Enforcer's actions called his loyalty into question. "So, what did you find out? I want to know everything."

Jason shrugged. "I think we should bring this before the pack. Let them decide what to do with the information and with you." He leaned back and swung his booted feet onto the edge of Roarke's desk. Crossing them at the ankle, he stared at his alpha.

Roarke detested the challenge in Jason's eyes. He pointed at the Enforcer's feet, but he only settled more firmly into his chair. "I don't like your attitude," he said. "I'm your alpha. You will do what I say." If it came down to a fight, Roarke knew in his present condition he couldn't take the Enforcer. Adrian might, but sunset was a bit too far away to take chances.

"Only if you can make me." Jason shook his head. He rolled up his sleeves, revealing muscled arms without any tattoos. At least his Enforcer hadn't joined the Dogs, or if he did, he wore no outward symbols of his allegiance.

"Look, you called a member of the Guard here and damn neared got my bitch kidnapped. You obviously don't like the way things are being run around here. So why don't you either challenge me, or get it over with." Roarke stood and fisted his hands. He pounded them on the desk and leaned forward. His wound pulled. He ignored it, the illusion of strength meaning far more to him at the moment than reopening his injury

"I don't want to do this." Jason slid his feet to the floor. He shook his head and released a heavy sigh. "Look, I've known you since you were a pup. I don't want to do this. I'm the Enforcer. It's my job to think of the pack, and right now buddy you're thinking with your balls, not your brain." His glance flicked to Lilah standing against the wall.

"So why did you bring in the guard?" Roarke sat back down, trying to deescalate the tension between him and his Enforcer.

Sadness filled Jason's eyes. He glanced at the floor between his feet, shoulders slumped. An air of defeat circled around him like buzzards around a kill. Whatever reasons Jason might have had for disobeying his alpha, Roarke saw they were eating him alive.

"Why, Jason?" Roarke repeated his question.

"Because what you're doing is going to tear the pack apart. You know how we feel about vampires, and now you bring in a bitch who is one. Yeah, I know she's a wolf, but you know as well as I her infection wasn't sanctioned by the pack. She's a mutt in the truest sense of the word. And her vampire lover as your Second? What were you thinking? It's time you go in front of the pack. Let them decide whether you're worthy to be our alpha or not." Jason's words held a finality that sent shivers down Roarke's spine.

"You can't mean that. I've done nothing but work for the pack." Roarke rose to his feet. Circling his desk, he leaned against it, directly in front of Jason. If his body blocked the Enforcer's view of his lover, all the better.

"If you want me to leave, I can." Lilah's concerned voice slid between the two men.

Roarke looked to the Enforcer. He cared little whether Lilah stayed in the room. The matter of her staying in the pack was settled. She needed to hear this, but if he went before the pack as Jason wanted, then she'd hear it anyway. Only then, it'd be tinged with emotion and hatred.

Jason nodded. "Pack business."

Roarke gestured for Lilah to leave. He watched her go, his friend's betrayal a more fatal wound than the one in his side. Whatever happened, however the pack ruled, he sensed Jason wouldn't be his Enforcer when everything was said in done. In fact, he doubted Jason would even remain in the Northwoods. The thought saddened him.

Lilah closed the door behind her with a final-sounding click. He waited until he heard her footsteps go down the hall, before he turned his attention back to Jason.

"Okay, now you'll tell me what you know," Roarke said.

Jason nodded. "I trailed him to a rendezvous not too far out of town. He hooked up with several members of the Dogs. They headed down the interstate. I followed them as far as I could and then came back here to report."

Roarke frowned. "That doesn't tell me anything. Where did they go? Did you get plate numbers? We need more information. If I knew better, I'd say you didn't care because you already know what the pack will decide. I can't abide sloppy work."

"So you're going to shun me like you did Eugene, right?" Jason shook his head. "Bring it before the pack. If you're still the leader, then we'll see how things go, okay?"

"No, it's not okay." Roarke lunged forward. Grabbing Jason's shoulders he slammed him back so hard the chair tipped onto its back legs. The wound in his side stung. Starting a fight with his Enforcer was a damn fool idea. Roarke had no other choice. "Why didn't you follow them? You could have tracked them back to their den. Fixed them where they lay. But you didn't. Why?" Roarke snarled. He bared his fang.

"Because it doesn't matter. Damn it, the Dogs are going to claim the pack, and that's the only chance we have. Just get the hell out. You turned your back on the Northwoods when you went after the vampire bitch." Jason pushed Roarke back.

Pain shot through his torso. He hissed, stumbling backward. He slammed into the edge of the desk. His hands came down hard on the corner, curling around it. Nails dug into the wood, and fresh blood ran down his side.

"Hell, you can't even try to force me to do anything."

"You're a coward," Roarke snarled. "I might be injured but at least I'm out there fighting for my pack! You're sitting here telling me that the

Dogs are going to take over and there's not a fucking thing you can do. Get out of my sight, Jason. You're not worthy to be my Enforcer." The words roared from his chest, fury and anger propelling his voice to a shout. Stupid pups. Thought they should just turn to the strongest master. He shook his head as Jason rose to his feet.

"That's not what I'm saying at all," he said, his eyes cold and dead. "Tonight, the pack will decide."

Roarke released the edge of the desk. Steeling himself against the pain, he stood straight. Jason looked at him, then with a miniscule shake of his head, turned and left the room. He waited until he heard the front door slam, and then Roarke sank to the chair his Enforcer had vacated. Soft footfalls told him Lilah returned.

Roarke rubbed his palms over his eyes. All he wanted was to have a safe pack. A good pack like the one his uncle ran. Where had he gone wrong? He groaned and pressed his palm to his side. It came away sticky with blood. His father wanted the pack, and right now, with Jason's betrayal heavy on his heart, he wondered why the hell he didn't just give it away.

Lilah silently entered the den. She curled her fingers over his shoulders and squeezed gently. "Let's get you upstairs. If you have to go in front of the pack tonight, you need to be healed."

He nodded and let her help him to his feet. As he followed her up the stairs, he took it as a sign of his weakness, and wondered again, about Northwoods.

~* * *~

An hour after sunset, Roarke sat in front of his pack. Lilah sat next to him, between him and his Second. On his other side sat his Enforcer. The mood in the room ran the gamut from support to distrust and anger, most of it directed at his bitch and his Second. He looked at people he'd known all his life. Friends, acquaintances, and realized, none of them, not even his Enforcer had ever been as close to them as Lilah. He swallowed hard and faced the accusing glares.

Eugene sat in the front row, surrounded by a large contingent of Dogs. "You left your pack to seek out a vampire," he snarled.

A chorus of agreement rose around him.

"Why shouldn't we get rid of you?" Eugene bellowed.

"Because he's trying to hold this pack together." Jason insisted.

Roarke battled the urge to stare at his Enforcer. What kind of game was he playing? In the back row sat the Luna Guard member Roarke had specifically asked him to handle. Obviously, Jason believed letting the Luna Guard know about private pack business constituted handling things, and once again, he wondered whose side the wolf was on. He sat back in his chair and remained silent as procedure demanded. Neither Lilah or Adrian could speak on his behalf, and he couldn't speak on theirs.

James rose to his feet. He held his arm, still bound in a sling, before him like an accusation. "I'm sorry, Roarke. You've been a good alpha to us, and you tried. But you're facing things that your uncle never did, and frankly, I don't like that you've brought vampires into our midst. I don't trust them. No one trusts vampires. And you have to do something about the Dogs. They're taking over, and if it means peace, then so be it." He shook his head and shuffled from side to side. Next to him, his wife cupped his good arm and helped him to sit down again.

A chorus of agreement rose around James. Roarke struggled against the stab of utter loss the wolves' words sent through him. He'd done so much for them, and yet, they turned away as if he were a plague.

"You can't mean that!" Roarke rose to his feet, not caring about the protocols. They were his pack. He wasn't going to let them drum him out without a fight. The wound along his side had healed to an angry red scar. If it meant taking on the pack, he'd do that. No regrets. No worries. "The Dogs are attacking you. James, they broke your arm. Eugene, your affiliation with the Dogs caused you to be shunned. They're wounding, even killing, your pack members. How can you possibly think that you would be better off with them than with me?"

"They're not vampires," someone snarled in the back.

Out of the corner of his eye, he saw Lilah jerk as if shot. Tears shone in her eyes. He tried to see the pack through her eyes, the people she'd known as a child now turning against them. He knew she thought it was because of him.

Roarke shook his head. He pressed his lips together, the knowledge that he'd been losing his pack for a long time creating a hollow feeling in his gut. Lilah wanted an alpha male. She needed it. He'd seen the way his domination made her come, the way she loved to have the strong wolf remind her just how feminine and vulnerable she really was. His presence brought out those same alpha characteristics in Adrian. And the funny thing was, he hadn't been an alpha wolf for a long time. A bully, yes, but never an alpha.

"So you'd rather take the devil you don't know over the one you do. Lilah grew up in the Northwoods. She knows you, and you know her. She hasn't changed just because she's a vampire. She's still Lilah St. James." Roarke stepped forward on the small, raised stage. His folding chair clattered against the floor when he bumped it with his foot, the harsh sound echoing in the room. It silenced the murmurs beginning to rise again.

In the back of the room, he caught the Guard member's gaze. The man's expressionless face said nothing, his attention focused only on Roarke.

"A vote." The Luna Guardsman rose to his feet. "You can ill afford to have a fight for alpha amongst yourselves, not when you battle the Dogs. Call forth your candidates and vote."

"He's right," Jason said, as if he'd planned this all along.

"Who would you nominate?" Roarke asked. A muscle in his jaw twitched.

Eugene stood. "Me!"

Roarke snarled. Virulent hatred roared through him. After being shunned, the wolf had the audacity to vote.

The Luna Guardsman stood. "I nominate Jason."

Now they got to the heart of the matter. Roarke nodded with scarcely a glance at his Enforcer. "Anyone else?" He asked with an arched eyebrow.

"David Connelly." His father's voice rang out loud and clear over those assembled. "I asked the alpha to turn over what should have been mine. The former alpha was my brother. But when he didn't, when he denied my rights as a father, he threw away the Northwoods. I ask that you give back to me what is rightfully mine. If that means voting for me, then I ask for a vote." He finished his speech with a courtly bow and strode to the front of the room. He stopped in front of the dais.

"You would vote for one who leads the Dogs. If he loves the Northwoods and wants to help our pack, then why would he attack it?" Roarke roared. He stepped forward and to the side, not wanting his father to block him. The urge to curl his fingers around the man's neck and squeeze nearly overtook him. He glared at his father, the man he'd once wished would come back to claim him. No more, never more.

"Anyone else?" The Luna Guardsman asked.

Roarke glanced back at Jason. "You let him lead your rebellion? I expected better of you than to hide behind the Luna Guard."

Jason stood. "A vote! I call for a vote!"

"A show of hands," Roarke yelled. "There will be no reason to hide behind your choices now." In the audience, heads nodded, and he hoped he'd gotten through to them. Two Dogs and his Enforcer stood against him for pack rulership. In the old days, they'd simply all retire to a secluded place and start fighting. The man left standing would lead the pack. Today, they called for a democratic vote. It sickened him.

The Guardsman moved through the crowd. He stopped in front of the dais and motioned for Jason and Eugene to join him. "As a member of the Luna Guard and loyal only to the Luna Council, I shall be the impartial witness and official to this election. Are there any who wish to protest?"

Heads shook throughout the audience.

Roarke breathed deeply. He had to trust in his pack. They would make the right choice for the Northwoods, and as their alpha, no matter how much it hurt, he'd have to abide by that. Forcing himself on his pack made him worse than the Dogs in his estimation. He waited.

"If you would like Roarke to remain as your alpha, raise your hand." The Guardsman's voice rang over the crowd and sent it into a hush.

So quiet Roarke swore he heard each and every breath, everyone waited. Then, one by one, hands went up over the crowd. He breathed a sigh of relief, noticing as more hands were added to the mix, until at least fifty percent, maybe more, had their hands pointed toward the ceiling. Perhaps, just maybe, he'd come out of this unscathed, and maybe, the generated furor would help run the Dogs out of town.

"Keep your hands up until I touch them." The Guardsman stepped forward and one-by-one counted the hands. As he tapped them they fell, and Roarke noticed a few more hands falling as well.

The Guardsman returned. "Thank you. Now, if you favor Jason."

A scattered amount of hands, not nearly as many as Roarke figured his Enforcer had hoped rose. Once again, the Guardsman counted. Even fewer hands went up for Eugene, and those were counted as well. Finally, the Guardsman called out for Roarke's father. The name David Connelly ran through the crowd like a firecracker, igniting conversation and debate. Hands soared into the air, and from what Roarke could see, at least as many as for him.

His stomach fell. As Roarke watched the Guardsman walk among the members, he had to try and believe that the member of the Luna Guard simply did his duty. Yet, no one but his Enforcer had asked him here. And that meant his Enforcer had hoped to use him to gain legitimacy and the role as pack's alpha. Roarke frowned. At least from the way the votes fell, Jason wasn't going to be alpha. If he were ousted from office, it would be by his own father. His scowl grew.

He stared at the back of David's head. The wolf stood proud in front of his former pack members, shoulders square, head high. His uncle's lack of information made his position against his father suspect, but so, too, did David's return, and as the leader of the Dogs. Roarke waited for the Guardsman to return to stand in front of the crowd.

"Your votes have been counted. Thirty-five people voted to keep Roarke as your alpha. With thirty-seven votes, the pack has declared David Connelly the new alpha of the Northwoods pack." The Guardsman nodded his head and then slipped back to his chair in the back of the room.

Outbursts of rage and disbelief, along with cheers of agreement, erupted from the amassed crowd.

David turned. "You can move your things out of the house once you find a place of your own. For the peace of the pack, you, your bitch, and your Second will leave."

"You infected my bitch, you dirty mutt." Roarke stepped forward.

David held up a hand. "That wasn't my doing or that of my Dogs. Just leave, Roarke. The Northwood Pack doesn't want you around anymore."

"That's not what the votes said. You're going to drive my pack into civil war. I won't let that happen."

Jason rushed past Roarke. At the edge of the stage, he knelt and bared his throat. "I offer you my services."

"Not your loyalty?" Roarke growled.

"My loyalty is to the Northwoods pack. Those who hold the pack's interests in mind will have my loyalty as well." Jason nodded to Roarke, and then turned his attention back to David.

"Very good. Then ensure my *son* doesn't interfere in the process." David stepped away from the dais. A feral grin crossed his face. He raised his arm and gestured. "Dogs, to me!" He roared.

From the crowd, several men rushed the stage.

Chapter Twenty

Roarke whirled to face his bitch and Second. "Adrian, get her out of here," he yelled. He stepped back, a strong hand on his arm holding him still. Yanking his arm away, he rushed toward the Dogs.

Bodies flung themselves in his way. He kicked and elbowed, bending forward to shove a known member of the Dogs out of his path. Someone punched. The blow glanced off his shoulder, and his wounded side ached. Ahead of him, he saw Adrian's broad-shouldered form herding Lilah toward the door. *Get her out of here!* A hand reached from the crowd and yanked on Lilah's hair. She screamed and stumbled to the side.

Adrian lunged for her. He grabbed her arm, holding her against him while he waded through the crowd. Someone threw a punch. Adrian ducked, the blow glancing off his shoulder, and then a fist caught him in the jaw. His head snapped around, his arm releasing Lilah. Hands reached for her and she was yanked from his grasp.

A roar of anger ripped from Roarke's throat and echoed in the room. He plunged through the crowd, ignoring the hands reaching for him, the screams of rage and cries of pain. His world narrowed down to the need to get Lilah out the door and safe. He threw punches, the need to protect his mate paramount in his mind. He snarled.

The room erupted into a bloodbath. The smell of too many wolves in too small a place and the tang of spilled blood fill the air. His father's fault. Roarke could blame no one else other than David Connelly, the new alpha, for the chaos in this room. The Luna Guardsman was nowhere in sight. Probably for the best, because right now, Roarke desired to sink his teeth into the man's throat and rip it raw. He saw a wave of mahogany hair close to the door. Adrian turned to look at him, his eyes glowing eerily red. Fangs extended past his lower lip. His strength sent wolves flying, and finally, he grabbed onto Lilah's arm and pulled her outside. Now, to find the same escape for himself.

A fist caught him beneath the jaw. His teeth clacked together. Whirling to face his attacker, he jabbed, a quick, hard, one-two blow that sent the man stumbling into the crowd. He rushed for the door. A foot hit his calf, tripping him. He stumbled into a bunch of toughs, led by Eugene. The wolves circled him and pushed him back into the crowd.

The wolf roared to life inside him. Howling with the need to be free, his inner beast flared to life. Shifting, changing, his clothes tore and suddenly, his eyes were level with the men's waists, not over their head. Snarling, he leapt into the air.

All four paws hit the man square in the chest. He fell to the ground with a thump, clearing the path behind him. Roarke darted through the crowd. Using his smaller size to an advantage, he wove through the people, ducking feet and hands, not caring that he left his clothes behind as tattered ruins. Let them think he lacked control. His muzzle ached, bruises already healing when he shifted, and undoubtedly would heal some more when he returned to human form.

A burst of fresh air called to him through the musk of the many pack members. Pouring on a burst of speed, he raced through the door. Just outside, more pack members in human form milled around. Darting around the building, Roarke stopped. He sniffed the air for Adrian and Lilah. Easily, he picked up their trail and followed it to the parking spot where he'd left his truck, and his truck was gone.

Closing his eyes, he panted his relief. Adrian had gotten Lilah out safely. He trotted away from the parking lot, choosing the alleys and backyards to roam like a stray dog. With an easy gait, he covered the distance to his own backyard. Soft lights shone through the windows. The domestic scene contrasted sharply with the horror of having his pack turn on him. Flopping down on his stomach, he let his tongue loll out of his mouth. The scent of night dew gathering on the grass filled his nostrils. Back at the community center, no doubt the very pack members who had cared for him as a child plotted his demise. He shook his head. Lilah was safe. Nothing else mattered.

The back door opened. "I think he's out here." Lilah's voice floated on the air like the song of an angel. She ran off the deck, her steps light and quick.

Roarke breathed in her scent. He rose to his feet, not wanting to appear defeated in her presence. Shaking himself, he shifted, and no sooner had he turned human than he pulled her into his arms. Instantly, his cock hardened. It throbbed between them, proof that both of them were alive. He breathed in her scent. Raising his head, he looked at Adrian. "Thank you for getting her out of there," he said.

"It's my job, and you're welcome," Adrian said. If the vamp had any second thoughts about Roarke bringing them here, he said nothing. "So what are we going to do now?"

Roarke kept his arm wrapped around Lilah. Her warmth burned into his skin; her scent tormented his nose. "We have to go back. With David as the new pack leader who knows what they're going to plan. We've got to take the Dogs out tonight." His lip curled into a snarl, his body's needs relenting beneath a fathomless well of anger and a driving need for revenge.

“Be serious. That place is a madhouse. You really think in that chaos you can get the Dogs and not take out some of your own pack members?” Adrian asked. He herded Roarke toward the door.

Roarke wished he were in wolf form to growl at the bloodsucker. “We’ve got to go and we’ve got to go now,” he growled. He strode toward the house, taking Lilah with him.

Adrian followed alongside. “I’m not saying we can’t, but you’ve got to think realistically here. Let’s get a bag packed and get out of town. We can regroup and then we can come back.” He halted in front of Roarke and stared at him. “You may have a crazy death wish, but your first duty is to keep Lilah safe.”

“Get out of my way.” Roarke reached for Adrian.

Adrian grabbed his wrist and pulled it back and across his body. His shoulder wrenched, muscles pulling, and with a pop, it slid from the joint.

Roarke howled. He curled his fingers into claws and swiped at Adrian’s neck. Pain tore through Roarke’s arm. It burned in his veins, his old injuries reopening. His right arm hung useless at his side. He shrugged, trying to pop the joint in, but pain flared along bone and cartilage, so strong it made stars appear behind his closed eyes. Damn it, he had no idea what Adrian was trying to prove, but right now, he wasn’t in the mood for any of it.

“Stop it!” Lilah’s shrill cry cut through the night and the haze of Roarke’s anger.

“He’s being a fool.” Derision dripped from Adrian’s voice.

“Well, so are you.”

Roarke closed his eyes as he listened to Lilah and Adrian bicker. Grabbing his arm he pushed it up and back into place with a satisfying pop. The pain remained, though lessened, and an experimental roll of his shoulder showed it ready to use once more. He barreled into Adrian, slamming the vamp against the siding. Fingers curled around his neck, mouth open in a parody of a wolf’s show of fang.

“What’d you call me?” He pressed his forearm to the vamp’s neck, though he knew Adrian didn’t need to breathe. He snagged a knife from Lilah’s waist and pressed the point between two of Adrian’s ribs. Feral snarls and growls emerged from his throat.

Lilah looked from him to Adrian, then back again. She stepped away slowly. "Roarke. Adrian. You guys really don't want to do this."

Adrian's throat worked. No sound emerged. For a moment, Roarke debated on releasing the pressure just to see what the bloodsucker would say. Instead, he jammed the blade a little farther against the skin. It split, blood trickling to surface around the cut. Fury pounded through him. His body heaved, breath billowing in and out of his lungs as if he'd run a hundred miles. Sweat beaded on his forehead. Inside, his wolf growled, readying for the kill. His pack deserted him. His Second questioned his motives. Even his bitch wanted him to stand down. Not tonight. Not after everything that had happened.

He clenched his jaw. "I'm tired of people fucking telling me what to do. Go after the Dogs. Leave the Northwoods. Let someone else take over. Give up. Give in. Well, fuck you!" Roarke roared. "You're either with me on this or against me. And if you're against me, then you better get out of here, because I'll drain your blood and let you fry in the sun."

Lilah choked back a gasp. Her hand flew to her mouth.

Roarke whirled to face her. His wolf looked out from his eyes, the drive for a kill overriding all human emotions. When he looked at her, he saw his bitch. She belonged to him. Nostrils flared, he drew her scent into his lungs. A possessive snarl rumbled through his chest. He sniffed, the scent of her creaming slit redolent in the air. His fingers curled on Adrian, and he rattled him against the wall.

"Roary," Lilah whispered his name. She stepped forward. She didn't touch him, but she stood close enough that her scent wrapped around him like a blanket. "Come back to me, baby."

A shiver ran down the length of his spine. He whipped his head away and stared at Adrian. The bloodsucker had taken his woman, had tried to claim her. He leaned forward, lips just inches from Adrian's neck.

"Roary, he kept me safe. He got me out of there." Lilah said. She spoke deliberately, as if she tried to calm a wild animal.

Roarke shook his head.

"That's it, honey. Breathe. Come back to me." Lilah reached for him. Her hand landed on his bare shoulder.

Roarke flinched.

Lilah stroked him from his biceps to his elbow. Her touch soothed the raging beast inside him. Another shiver ran through his body. He lowered his arms, though didn't step back. Keeping his focus on Adrian, he watched the vampire. The bloodsucker relaxed against the wall, his gaze never directly challenging Roarke.

Lilah stifled a sob. She jumped at Roarke, wrapping herself along his side. "Thank you." She pressed her cheek against the side of his arm, her breath tickling his bare skin. Every inch of her touched every inch of him, and he directed her back, away from Adrian.

"We still have to go after the Dogs," Roarke said.

"No. We've done enough. Let's just go." Dampness ran down his arm, and he realized Lilah cried.

Oh hell, his woman shed tears. He caressed her cheek with the back of his knuckles, catching her tears on his skin. He licked them away, and then tilted her chin to look at him. "We have to, honey. If we let them get away with stealing the pack, they won't stop."

"Shouldn't we take this inside?" Adrian asked.

Roarke nodded. Yeah, they should. Out here in the back yard, with pack members living all around them, who knew what might have been seen or overheard. Adrian opened the door, and Roarke followed him in to the living room. There, he sat on the couch, tucking Lilah into his arms. Adrian stepped out of the room. He returned moments later with a pair of jeans, and reluctantly, Roarke dressed.

"Going after the Dogs will be difficult right now. They're high on their win and ready for a fight. I don't think it's the Dogs you need to attack. It's your father." Adrian sat down in a chair across from the couch and crossed his legs at the ankles. He glanced from Lilah, once more curled in Roarke's arms, to the wolf, then back again.

Roarke glared at the bloodsucker. "I don't think you understand."

A smile quirked Adrian's mouth. "Oh, but I do. The politics of the vampires are not as different as wolf politics. The fights may be different, as are the methods of drawing blood, but in the end, whether it's a physical or verbal spar, it's still a battle, and one we must win." He settled himself more comfortably in the chair.

"What do you know of politics and squabbles?" Roarke asked.

Lilah turned away. Her leg pressed against the length of his, her arm touching his, but her attention shifted to the vampire. "I think there are a lot of things about Adrian we don't know," she said.

Adrian nodded to Lilah. "Yeah, there are. And now isn't the time to tell them. Let me just say that the FitzReal is an old and respected name.

You don't become old and respected in the vampire community unless you can play their games." He fell silent.

"So what do you propose we do?" Deferring to the vampire hurt in ways Roarke never anticipated. First, the bloodsucker keeps his woman safe. Then, he acts as his Second. Now, he plotted the way to bring down the Dogs. Those were all things Roarke should have been doing, and he hated how far he'd really fallen. Sleep tugged at him, a bone-deep exhaustion that came from fighting too many battles with too little resources.

"We go after David. He holds the keys."

"And how do we do that?" Roarke snapped. "Don't you think I've tried?" Anger propelled him off the couch. He stalked across the room, pacing, his footsteps echoing in the room, even against the plush carpet. "Damn it, all I've done is try. Try to keep the pack together. Try to keep the Dogs from taking cover. Try. Try. Fucking Try." He whirled on Adrian, letting the full force of his anger blaze in his eyes. The vampire didn't deserve it, not when he tried to help Roarke fight the Dogs, but right now, Roarke had no other place to turn it. He hoped the vampire understood.

"So tonight, we don't try. We do." Adrian stood. "We go back to the community center and we track David. You have his scent, and even if you didn't, he smells enough like you that we should be able to go pick it out. So go dress. Arm yourself." Adrian glanced at Lilah. "You too. We meet down here in fifteen minutes, and then we hunt."

Roarke breathed deeply. "Yeah, we hunt." For the first time that night, a sense of peace descended over him. Whether he attributed it to Roarke's words or maybe just the fact that finally, they had a plan, he didn't know. He went upstairs, listening to Lilah's footfalls as she followed him. He dressed, noticing she changed her clothes, and then left the bedroom without so much as a kiss or a grope. That was his girl. Had her mind on the business at hand. He followed her down to the workout room and the armory, slipping several knifes into sheathes at his ankle and his belt. He grabbed a Remington .45 pistol that ironically enough had belonged to his uncle. Checking the ammunition, he slipped it into a holster at his waist. Lilah grabbed a small .38 handgun. When he returned upstairs, he found Adrian already armed with pistol and blade. Without saying a word, the vamp led them to the truck.

"So what's our goal? Kill or information." Adrian asked as Roarke slid behind the steering wheel and started the vehicle.

"Information first, then we kill." Roarke answered. Adrian nodded, and in the back seat, Lilah fell silent. Roarke drove through the once-familiar streets to the community center feeling as if he were an outsider. His pack had ejected him. Peacefully yes, without the fighting and death that usually marked power changes within the pack. If he killed his father, by the number of votes alone, he would be alpha again. Did he even want to lead a bunch of wolves who thought so little of him?

Roarke shoved the disquieting thought from his mind. In his opinion, questioning what he wanted was a fruitless waste of time. His uncle had raised him to be alpha. He'd wanted Lilah. Once, he had them both, and he'd have them again. Except, now, a sense of freedom overwhelmed him. All those little problems, the day-to-day business of running a pack. It wasn't his problem. Someone fucked up? Not his problem. Someone try to reveal the existence of werewolves through their stupid actions? Not his problem. Damn, that felt good.

They arrived at the community center to find the parking lot still half full. Lights shone inside the building, the milling of wolves in the area obvious. He rolled down the window and sniffed the air. Yeah, his father had been here and left. He circled the parking lot and smelled. Gone all right, and as he turned out of the lot and down the road, he realized with a flash of clarity he knew exactly where his father had gone.

Memories, long suppressed, filled his mind. Of the woods, a place along the river, a clearing where he and his uncle used to go to fish. "Your father liked it here," his uncle had told him. "It was his favorite place for thinking."

"Just like us?" a childhood Roarke had asked.

"Yeah," his uncle replied. "Just like us."

Roarke remembered he'd just read *Tom Sawyer* in school and pretended that he could slip down there, build a raft and float away from the taunting boys who hated him for not having a father. Deep in his gut, he knew David would go there. If Adrian or Lilah questioned his directions, they kept it to themselves. He turned down the state highway, letting the lights of town recede behind him. The farther into the country he got, the more memories he had repressed flooded his mind.

"Why did my daddy leave?" Roarke asked his uncle.

"He believed the pack should be run differently. He doesn't appreciate the delicate balance we walk between the human world and our own." Those two sentences were all his uncle had ever said, but in them, the adult Roarke heard a wealth of loss, and sorrow. He closed his eyes as he turned into the familiar gravel driveway.

Down by the trees, a car waited. An old sedan, the fenders almost rusted out, the color a dark brown or maybe once a red. The driver side door sat open, and there, as if he were waiting, sat David.

Roarke parked the truck. He sucked in a breath of air as he unfastened his seat belt. "I want to go alone," he said to his companions. "Don't come out unless you think I'm in trouble." He didn't know what to expect, but the troubled man who looked very much old for his age wasn't it. He opened the truck door and rested one booted foot on the ground.

David looked up. "Roarke. I hoped you would remember." A sad smile crossed his face.

"Uncle Peter used to bring me here." Roarke closed the truck door behind him. He held out his hands, palm outward. "I don't want to fight. I want to talk. My uncle said you left because you and he didn't see eye to eye on the way the pack should be run. I'm tired of fighting. I want to know the truth." There, he'd said it. No time to take the words back now. Perhaps it was time to finally see of what his father was made. Roarke stopped.

"That's one way of putting it." David stood and closed the car door behind him. "Your uncle wanted me to infect your mother and bring her over. He felt you needed two wolf parents. And since you were human, he infected you."

Roarke stared at his father. "No," he said. Born human? It couldn't be, but yet, somehow it seemed right. The sad looks his uncle had given him, the way he was suddenly sick when he was four. Dear god, he'd been a child when his uncle had turned him lycanthrope. "No!"

"Yes." David nodded and stepped forward. "I'm sorry, son."

"No! You have no right to call me that." Roarke drew in a shaky breath. "You lie. I was born to be the alpha, that's what my uncle told me. You're the one who ran away. You're the one who turned away from your pack and family." He shook with the force of his anger. Deep inside a scared young boy realized the sum total of all his fears. The one man he thought had been his family, who he thought had loved him, had betrayed him. And the one he thought had betrayed him...Roarke trembled.

"I know this is hard for you to take. But it's the truth."

"So why didn't you take me with you? If you loved me, if you really were my father, you wouldn't have left me with my uncle."

"I did what I thought was best at the time. Look, I had no prospects, no job. How could I have cared for you and your mother?" David stepped forward. "Now that I'm the pack's alpha, I won't do anything to hurt the pack. I only want what's best for it."

"By forming the Dogs and attacking your very pack members you claim to want to protect. I don't think so," Roarke snarled. The more he looked at his father, the more he sickened him. Every word from his mouth was a lie. There was no way his uncle could have infected him, and his illness had other causes. Wolf pups got sick as much as human children.

"Think about what you're doing."

"I am thinking about it, and right now the best thing for the pack would be to gut you like the cur you are." Roarke curled his hands into claws. He had no need to shift, not when modern technology killed just as effectively as ancient battles. His palm hovered over the pistol grip. The cool metal called to him, the promise of having this over with once and for all. Curling his fingers around the gun, he drew and fired.

The shot echoed in the trees. David stumbled. His hand went to his chest, the wound high on his shoulder. He looked down at his bloody hand. Staggering against the car, he grabbed the door to keep himself upright. "Roarke, why?"

"To protect the pack." Roarke stood there, gun pointed straight at his father's heart. "Tell me the truth, and I'll let you live, if you're lucky." Behind him, the truck doors opened and he prayed Lilah and Adrian would stay out of his way and let him do what he had to do.

Chapter Twenty-One

The crunch of tires on gravel heralded another arrival. Roarke growled, but kept the gun trained on his father. What the hell? Had someone sold tickets and invited the entire pack. The door opened, and Jason's scent filled the air. His Enforcer. Roarke applied incrementally more pressure to the trigger.

"Roarke, wait!" Jason called. He stepped over, stopping when he reached the edge of the grass that marked the clearing. "Don't do it? There's something you need to see."

Roarke spun. He pointed the gun at his Enforcer.

Jason thrust a leather-bound book in front of him like a shield.

Behind him, Lilah gasped. "Don't shoot him!"

Adrian grabbed her arm, keeping her from rushing forward. "This is between them," he said, his low voice rumbling through the air.

"I've seen all I need to see," Roarke said.

David ducked. He darted along the fender of the car.

Reaching for his belt, Roarke grabbed a knife. He threw it, the blade sliding through the material of David's shirt to thunk into the side of the car. David stopped, looked at the blade just millimeters from his skin. He glanced at Jason and the book the Enforcer held. "Roarke, listen to Jason. He has the information you need."

"Stay there," Roarke growled. He strode to his father and yanked the knife out of the car. Resheathing it, he pressed the gun beneath his father's chin. "What's in the book?"

"The truth. Your grandfather chronicled the lives of the Northwoods Pack in that volume. It was his journal. When he stepped aside to appoint my brother as alpha, he still kept those records. I went to him, made sure he put the truth in that book. It's all there. Every word. Trust me."

Trust. Roarke paused as the word quickly circled through his mind. "Awfully convenient don't you think? Jason shows up with a book I never knew existed, supposedly written by a grandfather I barely remember. And it's going to tell me everything I need to know. I don't think so. And you still haven't answered about the Dogs." Roarke pressed the gun deeper into his father's flesh.

"The Dogs were my pack. I never meant for them to hurt anyone. There were those who thought your uncle should never have been alpha, and they were loyal to me." David's voice shook.

"He's right," Jason called. "That's why I didn't pursue him. I knew you'd find out the truth, and frankly, when you did, I didn't want your father's death on your conscience. I told you my loyalty lies with the Northwoods. It never has wavered, and neither has your father's."

"You were working in collusion with him. With this traitor." Roarke palmed his gun and debated shooting his father. A quick, clean shot and his problems would be over. He'd be the returning alpha of the Northwoods pack, and he'd never have to deal with this again. It's what his uncle would have done.

Roarke pulled the gun away from his father's throat and stepped away. "Go. Get the hell out of here." Trembling, he turned to Jason. "You'll tell the pack David's dead and that his final words were that the Dogs are no more." He flipped the safety on his gun and holstered it.

Jason nodded. "I'll do that." He handed the book to Lilah who stood next to him.

Ignoring his wounded shoulder, David darted into his car. He started it, and backed away, his tires spraying gravel as he left. Roarke watched him go, unable to stop the loss welling inside him. Once again, he'd lost his father. He hoped this time, perhaps when things were settled down, he could get him back.

"You have to call the pack together again," Roarke told Jason. "Give me a few moments to get things together, and then I'll speak with them. I was the second favorite from the votes. I'm the alpha again." He didn't stop to wonder why those words didn't fill him with the pride he'd felt before at leading the Northwoods Pack.

Jason nodded. "Don't you want to know about the book?"

Roarke stared at the damning thing that Lilah held in her hands. "Yeah, but let me take care of a few things first."

"Yes, alpha." Jason returned to his car, and Roarke watched him drive away.

Lilah and Adrian waited by the truck. Roarke stared at them, his lover and her vampire. Breathing deeply, he pulled their combined scents into his lungs, the ancient ritual they'd shared in the hotel room binding them together far deeper than his ties to the Northwoods Pack. As he looked at them, a plan formed in his mind. He released a sigh, the tension rolling from his muscles and strode toward the truck.

"We're going back to the community center," Roarke announced.

"Why?" Lilah asked.

Roarke pressed a hard, quick kiss to her lips. His cock hardened, the drive to take her, to brand her as his pumping through his veins. He nipped her lower lip. "Just wait," he said.

He turned from her, leaving her still holding the book, and opened the truck door. He swung behind the steering wheel and watched as once more, Adrian and Lilah joined him in the vehicle. She set the book on the bench seat beside her, and Roarke glanced at it. The smooth leather cover gave no hint as to what lay inside. The pages looked yellowed, brittle with age. The mystery of it swirled in his mind, told him there were far more things about his pack that he didn't know, than he did.

He rubbed the back of his hand across his eyes as he backed out of the parking area and turned onto the road. The silence in the truck deafened him. His entire world, crumbled down around him, and yet, his bitch said nothing. Had she known? As a human, did her father tell her things that he didn't know, and if so, why didn't she tell him? He shook his head, and knew whatever Lilah knew, she would have told him. No matter how much it hurt.

His thoughts coalesced, the truth of what he needed to do sitting solidly in his gut. He parked next to Jason's car and watched his Enforcer walk to meet him. Roarke jumped down from the truck, and met him halfway.

"I need to do something in there, and I need you to promise me you'll back my decisions one hundred percent," Roarke said before Jason could open his mouth.

Jason nodded. "Anything."

His quick acceptance caught Roarke off guard. "What do you mean 'anything'? Haven't I fucked stuff up enough for one night?"

Jason grinned, and in the smile, Roarke saw the boy he'd known. "Nah. You haven't even come close. Look I know you won't ask, but my father gave me the book. Told me to keep it from your uncle, and when the time was ready, give it to you. If that's betrayal, I'm sorry. And I wish like hell I would have given you the book sooner."

"Like when the Dogs showed up."

Jason's chuckle emerged more like a derisive snort, one Roarke knew the Enforcer aimed at himself. "Yeah, like when the Dogs showed up. Friends again?" Jason held out his hand.

Grabbing it, Roarke pulled the man into a bear hug. "Friends." He said, and thumping Jason on the back felt so good and right, Roarke wished he'd listened to his friend long ago. Instead, he'd been exactly the wolf his uncle had molded him as, ruthless, relentless, bordering on the edge of cruel as he ran his pack. Releasing Jason, he stepped back. "Let's do this."

Roarke entered the community center flanked by his Second, his bitch, and his Enforcer. No one held any visible wounds or scars. In the world of the pack, that was unheard of, and Roarke braced himself for the murmurs and speculation that rippled through the crowd.

The Luna Guardsman met them just inside the door. He nodded to Jason and turned his attention to Roarke. "I've made the announcement you requested. The pack seems to accept the decision without any problems. I'll leave things in your capable hands, Alpha." He disappeared back into the crowd.

Once again, Roarke ascended the dais in front of the assembled wolves. This time, pack members took their seat without any commotion. He breathed deeply and stood in front of one of the chairs. Adrian and Lilah seated themselves, as did Jason.

"Long live our alpha." The chant went up, growing steam until the walls vibrated with the force of the pack's words. "Alpha! Alpha! Alpha!"

Roarke stared at his wolves. After all that happened, he never expected such a thunderous response. He glanced back at Jason who only shrugged. In the back, the Luna Guardsman picked up the chant as well. The words degenerated into wordless cheers, cries of support and promises of loyalty. Eventually, the roar died into murmurs, then silence.

"Thank you. I am humbled and honored by your response. I stand before you, once again your alpha. As Jason, my Enforcer, has told you, David Connelly is no more. His last order to disband the Dogs stands. Anyone who disobeys that order disobeys not only the alpha, but the Luna Guard, and the Luna Council. Is that clear?"

Cries of "yes" went up through that crowd.

Roarke turned to Lilah. He held out his hand to her, a smile on his face. Now, while he had the favor of the crowd, was the time to implement his plan. He nodded to Adrian, and the vampire stood. Lilah rose to her feet and went to him. She clasped his hand. He gave her a reassuring squeeze, directing her to stand beside him. Adrian stood on the other side of her.

"This is Lilah St. James. She lived among the Northwoods as a human, and I know she's familiar to all of you. Through circumstances not of her control, she became a vampire, and then a member of our pack infected her without prior permission. But that matters not, because she's still the Lilah that I knew, and she is the pack's alpha bitch. She has met with the Matriarch, and she will be treated as befits her station," Roarke said. He let his words trail off, wanting those in the crowd to realize the full impact. He should have done this a long time ago, but hell, things happened, and he'd gotten pulled into plots and plans not of his own making. Hatred for his uncle stirred, and he tamped it down. He didn't need it here, not right now.

"But she's a vampire," someone called from the back of the room.

"That's right. She's a vampire. Our war was over a century ago. Don't you think we can forgive and move on with our lives? The vampires have done nothing to harm the Northwoods Pack, and with Lilah as my bitch, and Adrian as my Second, they won't. A strong pack with strong allies will be a lasting pack." Roarke looked at Adrian, uncertain of what the vampire would think of his words.

Adrian nodded sagely, as if he'd expected this, welcomed it even.

Roarke breathed a sigh of relief. He knew the vampire would have more to say once they were back at his house. "That is why I will be temporarily turning over the pack to my Enforcer." Roarke turned and nodded for Jason to come stand beside him. Throughout this entire time, Jason claimed he'd had nothing but the pack's interests at hand. His actions with the book showed that. In the back of the room, the Guardsman nodded as if he, too, agreed with the actions.

Jason stopped beside him. He looked from the assembled pack members to Roarke, and then back out again. "I can assure you, that I will take care of the pack in Roarke's absence. My first loyalty is to the pack. And I will act deserving of the post." He took a step back, but remained standing.

Roarke took a deep breath. "We will be going to the Immortal Council. My bitch still is not out of danger and I wish to ensure her safety."

From one of the doors in the back of the community center someone entered. Roarke stared at the stranger. He sniffed and smelled vampire. Biting back a growl, he looked at Adrian and saw the man stood still as a statute. Roarke clenched Lilah's hand so hard he feared he might leave marks. Eyes wide, his bitch looked at the new vampire.

"If they seek to harm your bitch, then they seek to hurt the entire pack," James said from the front row. He no longer wore his arm in a sling, and Roarke gladdened to see his healing.

"And that's why we go to the Council. I meant what I said. It's time we quit relying on the prejudice of our forefathers and cultivate new relationships. Much has come to light in just the last few hours to lead me to believe that we begin a new era for the Northwoods Pack, one which we will all benefit from. Let me speak to them. Should I find they still wish the wolves harm, then I will take action." Roarke finished his words, with a feeling of finality. He'd laid his thoughts on the line. The Pack wasn't democratic by any definition of the word, though such measures could be taken to avoid bloodshed. He trusted the pack members to believe his leadership sound.

"There will be no more discussion of this. Please go back to your homes. Any pack business you may bring to Jason and he will keep me informed." Roarke stepped back, then turned, and together with Adrian and Lilah left the building.

Behind him, the silence of the pack hung like a heavy weight in the air. He sensed it inside the building as he crossed the parking lot to his truck. Next to him, both Lilah and Adrian remained silent. Roarke longed to ask for their approval of things, but frankly, if they didn't approve, he didn't think he could take it. Not right now, when everything he did was to have Lilah next to him and safe.

~* * *~

Adrian closed the truck door behind him, with Roarke's words ringing in his ear. Go to the Immortal Council and plead for Lilah's life. It was a suicide mission, one he'd gladly undertake for her, if only she'd asked. Maybe he should have gone away. The mantle of Pack's Second, one that hadn't been removed when Roarke cavalierly passed over his role as Alpha to Jason, sat heavy on his shoulders. Behind him, Lilah sat staring at Roarke, as if she, too, struggled to fathom his motives. Pressing his lips together, he stared out of the truck's window and wondered, how or when, things had gotten so complicated.

It used to be Lilah and him. Keep her safe, try and make her feel as much for him as he felt for her. Then the wolf arrived, and suddenly, he saw pups and white picket fences in the sun, not the shadowy world of the vampires in her eyes. Roarke professed his love, and instead of rebuking him, Lilah only seemed to encourage him. And encouraged Adrian as well. If he breathed, he might release an exasperated sigh, but as it was, he listened to the emptiness of his chest, the heartbeat that hadn't been there for decades, and struggled to once again find his place within the pack, and Lilah's life.

The drive back to Roarke's house passed in silence. The vampire in the back of the community center looked familiar, and Adrian feared he belonged to The Party. If so, he'd tracked them all the way to the Northwoods, and even now, Lilah wasn't safe. Not when every wolf knew where the alpha lived, and with everyone at the community center someone could have sneaked to the house without them knowing. He struggled to keep his rising tension under wraps. Surreptitiously he glanced out the window, but aside from the palest shades of pink across the sky, he saw nothing threatening.

Roarke pulled into his driveway. Adrian bounded out of the truck, hurrying inside before the sun decided to peek over the horizon. They'd cut it close, damn close, but frankly, after all the excitement of the night, he doubted the time, or the approaching sunrise, was on anyone's mind except his. At least the sun kept The Party at bay.

He sniffed in the foyer, and not smelling anyone other than Roarke or Lilah, he motioned for them to enter. As soon as the door closed, he turned to Roarke. "So tell me what you have planned. That's quite the little shock you dropped on us there in the meeting."

"Yeah. What did you mean turning the pack over to Jason? Are you sure you can trust him?" Lilah asked. She held the book she carried out to him. "It's not like he immediately told you about this, now is it?"

"I know. But he had his reasons, and he's done nothing but support the pack. I can't say how or why, but I trust him. He'll be a good alpha until I return." Roarke went to the living room and after checking the curtains, sank to the couch.

"So when are you coming back?" Lilah asked. She glanced at the cushion beside him, and he looked like a hopeful puppy for a moment, but then she chose an armchair flanking the couch.

Adrian sank into the other chair, most definitely wanting to hear Roarke's answer.

"I don't know," the wolf said. "I'd thought I wanted this. My uncle told me I was born to be the alpha of the Northwoods. After what my father said, I just don't know. I want to ensure you're safe and take some time to figure things out. Then, I'll come back. Whether I take over as alpha or not is anyone's guess at the moment." He grinned and shook his head. "Never thought I'd be saying that."

"Bet not," Adrian replied. "But then I never thought I'd have taken in my brother's childe, killed my brother, and now watched as she became a werewolf and the alpha bitch of a pack." He shrugged, giving the outward appearance that it was all in a day's work. Taking things one step at a time worked well, helped him to keep his level-headedness. If he didn't, he might do something stupid like challenge Roarke for her, and he suspected the wolf had all the hassles he needed at the moment. Chalk it up to immortal kindness. If you lived damn neared forever, you didn't make enemies if you could avoid it.

"So you agree with my plan?" Roarke sounded surprised.

Adrian laughed. "I didn't say that."

"So what do you think we should do?" Lilah asked. She scooted to the edge of the chair. "I happen to think Roarke's got a good plan. I'm tired of running and hiding."

Roarke preened beneath her praise.

Fatigue pulled at Adrian, the sun outside an anchor dragging him into the oblivion of sleep. With a strength of will honed over the decades, he forced his body to remain alert and functional. "But what about the other vampire-werewolf hybrids, the werepyres. If the Immortal Council feels you're a threat, they'll see no reason in exterminating you like a cockroach."

Lilah shuddered.

"You think that will happen?" Roarke asked. "Damn it, why didn't you tell me!"

"Maybe because you were too busy running around fighting with the Dogs and getting your pack twisted all out of shape to listen. You stormed in here, made me your Second, made Lilah your bitch, as if you expected to still have the perfect werewolf family." A wave of jealousy rose with his bloodlust. He felt his eyes redden, his fangs lengthen, and just like Roarke battling his wolf, he couldn't stop. He shook his head and clenched the arm of the chair.

"Adrian!" Lilah's sharp yell pierced his emotional cloud.

"I'm sorry," Adrian said. The red receded from his eyes, his fangs drawing back into their normal position. "I just can't believe that we waltz up to the Immortal Council and ask them to stop the threats against Lilah's life. I do, however, have someone I can ask. Let me make a contact tomorrow night. I'll have more information on which way the Council might go as well as their present location."

Roarke nodded. "Thank you."

"We both want the same things, just our natures dictate we go about it the wrong way. If you'll excuse me." Adrian stood and with a nod from Roarke and Lilah, went upstairs to the bedroom. He nearly went to Lilah, pressed his lips across hers and buried his cock between her thighs. The need to take her, to prove he had some place in her life had his steps faltering. In the end, he went upstairs. If Lilah wanted him, she'd follow. When she didn't, well, he'd know what he needed to do.

~* * *~

Lilah watched Adrian leave wishing she could go to him. He looked tired, dead tired in fact, and he probably needed the sleep more than he needed a good fuck. Her body hummed. The emotions of the evening making her edgy. Roarke had put everything on the line for her, his actions telling her he had spoken truly. He did love her. As if she'd ever had any doubts. He watched Adrian leave.

Lilah crossed the space between them. She knelt on the couch, straddling him. Cupping his cheek, she turned his face to hers. "I appreciate everything you're doing," she whispered. She brushed her lips across his in a fleeting, gentle caress.

Roarke moaned. He tangled his fingers in her hair and hauled her against him. His tongue plundered her lips, prying them open and slipping inside. Warmth pooled low in her stomach, her pussy creaming for the feel of his cock. She'd almost lost him. Her heart shattered just thinking about what would have happened if he'd been injured more grievously. She curled her fingers into his hair, the sun-highlighted strands glowing against her pale skin. Outside, the sun rose over the horizon, and she bathed in the new day like a rejuvenating bubble bath. Her bitch trotted around, happy to be joining with her mate once more.

Roarke fisted his hands in her shirt. He tugged it free of her jeans. Material tore. Lilah moaned and arched into his touch. His hand splayed on her back, crushing her breasts against his chest as he pulled her against him. Heat radiated from his palm, the warmth sending her vampire into retreat. So different from Adrian's cold body and chill reserve.

He drew her lower lip into his mouth and suckled. Her clit throbbed. Her panting breaths filled the air along with the scent of their arousals. Musky male wolf mingled with her feminine fragrance creating a heady combination.

Roarke. Her wolf. Her alpha. Unable to deny the depth of her feelings, even if she didn't want to, she cupped his head as he released her lip to trail kisses over her neck, her shoulders. He finished ripping her shirt from her and released the front catch of her bra. He nipped the slope of her breast, and she sought the ridge of his cock.

"Yes," she breathed, as he took her nipple into his mouth and drew it deep.

He laved the tight bud with his tongue, then pulled back and looked into her eyes. Raw hunger blazed in his gaze, the look of an alpha about to claim his mate.

Lilah shuddered.

"Don't you think we should get Adrian?" he asked.

"No. I can't wait any longer." Lilah ordered, and as she commanded, he fastened his lips to her flesh once more. Distantly, she heard the tread of someone ascending the stairs, too lost in the haze of passion to decipher what it meant.

Chapter Twenty-Two

Lilah shrugged out of the remains of her shirt and her bra. She let them fall to the floor behind her. Bracing her hands on Roarke's shoulders, she arched into his seeking mouth. His sun-bleached hair and tanned skin contrasted sharply with her paleness. She loved looking at him, his head bent over her breast. Her nipples ached, pulled diamond hard by the force of her alpha's warm, wet mouth. An answering tug started between her legs.

His hands smoothed her ribs, down to the waistband of her jeans, then up until he cupped the undersides of her breast. He palmed her bare flesh, the appreciative noises in the back of his throat driving her to wriggle on his lap.

"Hold onto me," Roarke said as he drew in a long, shuddering breath. Wrapping his hands around her waist, he stood.

She clung to him, feeling the strength rippling through his muscles. He carried her into the dining room and laid her out on the table. Sunlight streamed in the curtainless patio doors, the blinds pulled back to reveal the yard surrounded by a privacy fence. She arched like a cat, the irony not lost on her, and a giddy chuckle bubbled up from her throat.

"What is it?" Roarke asked. He unbuttoned her pants, and she raised her buttocks to have him slip them, and her panties, off her legs. He unlaced her boots. They fell to the floor with a thud. A tug of his hands pulled her jeans to the floor with a whoosh. Roarke kicked them away and moved between her parted knees.

"Just thinking about a kitty arching in the sun," Lilah answered.

He stared at her sex, and she imagined her moisture gathering on her labia for him. "I can think of a kitty I'd like to pet."

Lilah shivered at his words.

He leaned forward, nuzzling the flesh between her breasts. "I love the way you smell," he groaned. He laved the valley with his tongue, turning his head to worship first one slope of her breast than the other. Lilah held him to her, marveling at the softness of his lips, the rasp of his stubble against her tender skin. She relished the contrasts, and for a moment, just a moment, she debated about asking Roarke to take her upstairs to Adrian.

His lips trailed down over her flat stomach and his tongue dipped into her navel. She arched off the table, the cool, polished wood beneath her an altar on which she offered herself. His lips, his breath, every molecule of him aroused her, and as he nuzzled the top of her mound, she cried out with the wonder of it all.

The alpha bitch of the pack. The title rang in her head, gave her power she never imagined she'd have. She curled her fingers into his hair and pushed him down toward her labia, plump and swollen for him. He murmured against her slick lips, his tongue darting out to capture a hint of her moisture. He licked her clit. Swirls of his tongue had her gasping for air, her hips canted to give him the best access to the swollen, nerve-rich nub. She clenched her fingers against his scalp, holding him to her.

"Yes. Fuck, yes." Lilah forced her eyes open, looking between her breasts and down her body at Roarke between her legs.

He sucked her labia into his mouth, drawing them hard and deep, and she screamed with the pleasure rolling through her veins. She imagined Adrian lying upstairs, his body cold as death, a hand wrapped around his cock listening to her get fucked. He'd stroke with long pulls of his hand, his foreskin flicking over his head. She'd sit there and watch as his hips arched off the bed, as he begged for more.

Roarke tongued the length of her slit. He drew her clit into his mouth, grazing it with his teeth. Pleasure-pain rocketed through her, and when he slid two fingers into her tight channel, she rocked against them. She craved him inside her. The penetration of his thick cock drove her to the edge of reason, and then beyond. Every nerve ending hummed. Her body tingled, waiting for the moment when he'd thrust balls-deep inside her and fuck them both. A sheen of sweat broke on her body, and she reached up to cup her breasts.

Roarke raised his head. "Fuck, baby. You're beautiful." He watched while she plucked her nipples, pinching them into tight, pink buds.

Lilah curled her ankles behind his buttocks and pulled him closer. "I want you inside me."

He deftly unbuttoned his jeans, the thick curls pointing to the tool still waiting to be revealed. The rasp of the zipper sounded like a heavenly chorus to her ears, and she watched as his cock emerged, free at last from the confines of his jeans. Her body sang like a soprano launching into an aria at the sight of his thick, vein-roped cock, so hard it nearly touched his stomach. Her mouth watered. She'd take it into her mouth and suck it long and deep...later. Right now, she wanted it in her. She scooted closer to the edge of the table.

Roarke grabbed his shaft and ran the head along her cream. She moaned at the slide of his skin along hers. The gentle touch promised the velvety steel of his shaft, and she whimpered. Her hips bucked in a futile attempt to slide the head into her body. Roarke controlled the movements, his fingers barely caressing her clit and bringing her closer to the edge.

He pulled back, evoking a whimper from her throat. His cock head slipped just inside her entrance. Lilah canted her hips and he slid easily inside. A long, slow thrust stroked all the right places as he buried himself so deep inside her she thought she could taste him. Now there was a thought. She tipped her head back, imagining Adrian's cock hovering above her lips. She'd wrap her mouth around him and suck him until she tasted the salty streams of his come.

Another stroke, another image, this time of her on hands and knees, with Roarke taking her pussy while she sucked Adrian's cock. Or maybe this time, Adrian could fuck her ass while she sucked Roarke to the edge, and then invited him inside her tight sheath. Yeah, that held possibilities, lots of them, and the fleshy slap of his balls against her ass made her moan aloud.

The sun rose, the golden beams slanting across her skin so bright she needed to close her eyes and simply enjoy the warmth creeping over her body. It felt decadent lying here like this, letting nature caress every inch of her bare skin. She lifted her breasts into the light, unable to stop and see the way the golden streams played across her tight nipples. Her gaze caught Roarke's, and he grinned.

"You look like a goddess, spread out for attention." His big fingers gripped her hips, hauled her even closer to him so the rounded curve of her buttocks dangled off the edge of the table. "Do you like that?" He slammed forward and pulled back again. "How about that?" This time, he rocked into her so hard it rattled the legs of the table against the floor.

Lilah closed her eyes, feeling as if his hands on her body pulled her beneath a tidal wave from which there was no escape. The back yard gate was unlatched. Anyone could probably walk in and see him fucking her on the table. She grinned, hoping someone did, wanting them to see what she had with the alpha. Vampire bitch she might be, but she lived in the sun just like any other wolf.

Her body tensed with the need to come. Her hands at her breasts sent sparks of pleasure down to her clit, and the stroking of Roarke's cock through the entire length of her channel sending feedback all the way to the top of her head. She worked her hips against him, harder, faster, driving toward that peak.

He reached between their bodies and flicked his fingers across her clit.

Spasms shook her body. Lilah gasped her air, her hands clenching against the table. Her nails scored long rents in the wood, and she screamed, as her orgasm swept away her reality and replaced it only with the feel of his cock plowing into her, the scent of sex on the air, and the never ending waves of pleasure that had her writhing and shaking on the table like an out of control beast. Her bitch raised her muzzle to the sky and howled. In the back of her mind, the vampire hid from the sun. Hot. Too hot.

Roarke thrust through her orgasm, his long, solid strokes not giving her even a moment to catch her breath. He rode her hard, the table rocking against the floor, her cries and his grunts filling the air, no doubt audible to Adrian upstairs. She smelled him, her vampire, his musk on the air, the scent of sex and blood that never failed to drive her wild. This time, laying in the sun, her bloodsucker could only whimper as her pussy creamed and her werewolf gave her exactly what she wanted.

His pace quickened. Her heels dug into his buttocks, and she sat up with the need to feel more of him. Her breasts crushed against his chest, the springy hair teasing her already sensitized nipples. Her hands wound around his neck, fingers tangling in the hair at the nape of his neck. Beneath her, cream pooled in a sticky, sex-scented puddle.

Roarke cupped her ass. He slammed into her. His breath blew hot puffs over the side of her neck. He claimed her lips. She welcomed the invasion and tugged at his hair to make him go deeper, take her harder. Wordless cries became grunts of passion, and in that moment, Lilah knew what it meant to be an alpha bitch. She ruled Roarke, the fluttering of her muscles along his cock taking him to the edge of release. She whimpered. Her own orgasm hovered close, too close, and she held it off long enough for him to thrust into her one more time.

He roared with the strength of his release, his cock pumping hot seed deep into her womb. She clenched her muscles, the feel of him so intimately inside her was the final straw that sent her tumbling after him. She tore her lips from his and screamed. The shrill, high sounds of passion echoed in the room.

Slowly, his hips stilled. Thrusts became tiny twitches and jerks of over-sensitized muscles. He held onto her, his hands stroking through the sheen of sweat on her back.

"Mine," he chanted over and over again. "Mine."

"Yours," Lilah panted, heedless of the effect her words might have on the vampire upstairs. "Always yours." She snuggled against his chest, his cock still half-hard inside her. Gently, he scooped her into his arms, and though his shaft slid from her, she still felt as deeply connected to him as she'd been before. He carried her up the stairs, to the bedroom where the vampire lay. She sensed Adrian's coldness on the sheets, his lack of heartbeat and breath unable to tell her if he really slept. She brushed her hand down his arm and tried to tangle her fingers with his, but he remained lifeless. She squeezed his hand and turned to Roarke's warmth. Draping herself across the wolf, she breathed his heady aroma. Things didn't get much better than this, she thought as she fell into a deep, sated sleep.

~* * *~

In the dark, Adrian stared at the ceiling. Next to him, Lilah's body curled against him. Her warmth seeped through skin and bone, touching his heart. He remained perfectly still. Just past dawn before he had fallen asleep, he'd heard her rutting with Roarke. Only it wasn't rutting. It was something deeper, something more powerful than he'd ever experienced with her, and it killed him to be on the auditory receiving end of it. On the other side of Lilah, Roarke spooned her. Their combined heat nearly drove him from the bed.

Yet, he remained with the knowledge that in her sleep, Lilah had migrated toward him. He blinked his eyes and welcomed the siren song of the moon rising outside the window. Finally, it seemed that Roarke had what we wanted, some equilibrium to the pack and no attacks on Lilah from the werewolves. Adrian preferred to handle the vampires himself. He had the contacts, and probably most important of all, he was a vampire. Trying to get Roarke into the Immortal Council's presence would be like trying to convince a three-year-old to eat broccoli. He frowned.

His stomach rumbled with hunger. He'd told Lilah he'd replenish their food supply though with everything that had happened he hadn't had a chance. Swinging back the blanket, he rose to his feet, the slight light-headedness telling him he'd gone too long without feeding. He tugged on his jeans and hurried downstairs with the hope that there might be one bag of blood in the fridge.

Luckily there was. He microwaved and drank it in record time. Red blood cells dispersed through his veins. Energy poured through him. Eyes darkened red, the hunger of needing more blood upon him.

A window crashed in the living room.

Adrian tensed. No alarms sounded, and he cursed the wolf's foolishness in thinking he was safe in his own community. Keeping to the shadows, he crept from the kitchen following the sounds of the intruder and the smell of vampire. His nose wrinkled, and he recognized the member of The Party who'd tried to crash their werewolf meeting last night. Apparently, The Party refused to give up.

Adrian launched himself across the room. He tackled the vampire, sending him to the ground with a muffled thump. Behind him, two more vamps stood at the window. One wrapped a scarf around his hand and punched the glass again. Shards rained all over the carpet. Still low on blood, Adrian tried to avoid them.

He went for the knife at the intruder's belt, needing a weapon of some kind. Kicks and punches were all well and good, but without shedding blood, the vampire wouldn't die. His fingers closed around the cool grip. The vampire twisted and yanked the knife away. The cool muzzle of a small gun pressed into Adrian's side.

"Back away. We just want the woman," the vampire said.

Having no choice, and outnumbered now that the window had been broken wide enough to admit more of the intruders, Adrian did as the vampire ordered. Hands in the air, he stepped back. He dared not gaze upstairs, dared not hope that Lilah or Roarke might have heard the scuffle and come down to investigate.

"Where is she?" the vampire said.

"Not here." Adrian stopped with all three vampires within his field of vision. The first one, the leader, held a gun, as did a second vampire. The third boasted brass knuckles with sharp razor blades, obviously intending to let his fists do the talking. He pulled a Zen-like mentality into his body. He could do this for Lilah.

"I think you're lying," the man said. He raised his nose and sniffed the air. "Sure smells like wolf sex."

"Maybe it does." Adrian shrugged. He stepped forward, his gaze never leaving the leader of this small group. "And maybe you're a bit disgusted that you think it's hot." His attention darted below the man's belt, where his body proved Adrian's words right. He turned his attention back to the vamp.

"Shut up," the vampire snarled.

Amateurs. With preternatural speed, Adrian rushed the lead vamp. His fingers closed around the barrel of the pistol, pointing it towards the ceiling. The gun fired. The bullet tore through tiles and insulation, raining fluffy tufts of building material down on them. He knocked the vampire backwards, rolling as a bullet grazed the air next to his shoulder. Pulling the vamp's arms above his head, he slammed the fists into the floor. The vamp released the gun.

Adrian surged to his feet. He shot the fallen vamp once in the chest, the bullet piercing his heart. The vamp groaned, and Adrian whirled and caught sight of the second one. He dropped the weapon, backpedaling to get away from the lethal vamp with bloodlust in his eyes. Adrian snarled and shot again, through the vamp's heart. He crumpled.

Adrian flicked his attention to the third. Upstairs, he heard Lilah and Roarke shuffling around, the pounding of footsteps on the stairs, the hushed tones of worried voices. This was his fight, not theirs, and he intended to finish it.

"You tell The Party that Lilah's untouchable. She belongs to me, and she belongs to the pack. Whatever your plans for her, you drop them right now."

Moonlight glinted on the razors running along the vamp's knuckles. He clenched and unclenched his fists.

Lilah appeared in the doorway. She pointed her gun at the first downed vamp and fired, then the second. Grey matter and blood sprayed onto the carpet. Roarke appeared behind her and scowled.

Adrian shrugged and stepped forward.

"Mikhail told us you'd fight for the woman, but she ain't worth it." He raised his fists. "Let's go!"

Adrian fired.

The man staggered back, his bulletproof vest stopping the bullet.

Adrian snarled. He raised the gun higher.

"Wait!" Lilah's voice cut through the tension. "He mentioned Mikhail. We have to know what he knows." She aimed her gun at his head.

The vamp looked from Adrian to Lilah, then back again. "Bitch, you ain't going to shoot me."

"Want to make a bet?" She dropped the gun and fired a round into the man's knee.

He staggered, his leg giving out. He didn't fall, though pain created deep lines around his lips and eyes.

Adrian watched the werepyre he loved. Sometime between when Mikhail had turned her, and she'd come to him as an innocent, vulnerable childe and now she'd turned into a lethal killing machine. He wanted to blame it on Roarke and the werewolves, the feral nature of the beast coming to the fore. In truth, he knew his brother was to blame. Running for your life tended to jade a person, and at the moment, looking at Lilah's dispassionate eyes and firm set of her jaw, she was as jaded as they came.

He loved her and seeing her like this killed him.

"It doesn't matter. He doesn't know anything." Lilah said.

Roarke stepped behind her, his hand on her shoulder. "Know what you're doing, baby. Once we kill them we can't get them back." The wolf didn't look at Adrian, and he snarled to think that she trusted the wolf for guidance more than him. After all he'd done for her. His hands were still, though his entire body vibrated with the force of his anger.

"So tell me, do you know anything?" Adrian asked. He stepped forward, one step, two, until he stood less than a foot away from the intruder.

"No," the vamp said. "Kill me."

"Oh, that'd be too easy." He lowered the gun and fired again, taking out the vamp's other knee. He watched as the vamp fell to the ground, writhing and screaming in pain. A small, sick tendril of satisfaction wove through Adrian. He'd taken down the vamp. He'd kept Lilah from bloodying her hands even further. Her bullets in the fallen vamps simply were mercy killings, a way to keep them from a long, lingering death. "I can shoot a little higher if you like," Adrian said, moving the gun just to the left of the vamp's groin.

The smell of spilled blood filled the air. Adrian's stomach rumbled, his bloodlust rising to an uncontrollable point. He glanced at Lilah and willed her to stay away. Leaving the job of killing the intruder to her sickened him. It went against every grain of civility he'd ever been given, yet, his hands shook like leaves on the wind, his mouth watering for a taste of blood. The vampire's blood.

With a snarl, he hurled himself onto the fallen vamp. The gun clattered to the floor with a dull thud. Wrapping his fingers around the vamp's wrists, he slammed the back of his hands to the carpet, keeping the razor blades from his skin. Teeth sank into flesh, and Adrian drank.

Hot, coppery blood filled his mouth. He swallowed, his throat convulsing with the need to pour more and more of the nutrients into his system. Fresh, clean, untainted by drugs or alcohol, this vamp treated his body like a temple, one Adrian desecrated with his hunger. Beneath him, the vamp moaned, blood loss giving way to pain. The flow slowed, though didn't stop.

At last, the vamp twitched and laid still, body pale, gums and lips nearly white from the loss of blood. The flow slowed to a trickle, then a drop, and then ended. Adrian raised his blood-stained lips and licked the last of the vamp's life force off of them. Strength filled his body, and he arched his back and grinned, revealing elongated canine teeth. He turned and looked at Lilah.

She hovered by the door, Roarke's arms wrapped around her. She looked pale, starved even, and Adrian rose to his feet. He stepped over the fallen vamp and strode to her. "Feed," he ordered, his blood-red eyes locking gazes with hers. He sensed the hunger in her, felt it gnawing at her stomach. He smelled her arousal, knew if he unfastened her jeans, he could slide his fingers along her creaming slit and test her readiness. His dick throbbed, full and hard on the blood he'd drunk.

He stopped in front of her and trailed his finger along the artery in her throat. Her pulse fluttered between his touch. "Drink," he ordered, sliding his hand along her cheek and tangling his fingers in her hair. He hauled her forward, her lips to his bare chest. She mewed and her fangs sank into him.

Adrian groaned. He cupped her ass, hauling her against his hard length. Rocking his hips, he let her know exactly what he wanted, and she curled her fingers convulsively against his arm. He unfastened her jeans and shoved them down her hips. Grabbing her panties, he ripped them from her, and then thrust his fingers between her legs. Slick cream coated his fingers.

He ripped open the button on his jeans and shoved down the zipper, freeing his cock. Lilah's mouth worked against his chest. She drank from him, the action so intimate he looked over her shoulder to see what Roarke thought. The wolf stood there, chest heaving with his panting breaths. An erection bulged his jeans, and his hands clenched into fists at his sides. This time, he watched and ached with the wanting.

Adrian spread Lilah's legs. She couldn't drink him dry, not after the way he'd gorged himself on the vamp. The smell of offal from the bodies filled the air, and he should have been disgusted. Instead, the blood pumping through his veins drove his need to a fever pitch. His cock slid along her labia, and she moaned, never losing a drop of the precious blood.

His cock head found her opening, and with a flex of his hips, he shoved into her warmth. Her muscles clenched around him, and Adrian cupped her ass, holding her for his fucking.

Chapter Twenty-Three

So hot, so tight, Adrian thought the top of his head was going to blow off. He plunged into Lilah. Her drinking slowed, though her lips never left his chest. Her tight sheath gripped him, her muscles working along his length. Tiny mewls escaped her throat. Her fingers clenched him as she struggled to hold on.

She felt so damn good in his arms. Her rear filled his hands perfectly, two handfuls of flesh he squeezed and kneaded. His balls hung between his legs, full and tight. With Lilah wrapped around him, and his cock buried inside her sweet cunt, he knew he'd found heaven. The tight fit of her channel with her legs tangled in the jeans only made it that much better.

The base of his spine tingled. Lilah whimpered, and his finger slid through her juices to bring them to her back entrance. He pressed his finger against the tight ring of muscles. Slowly, oh so slowly, as her moans escalated and her muscles tightened around him, he slipped his finger inside. Fore and aft he filled her, adding a second finger and stretching her to fullness.

Adrian lost himself in the glory of Lilah's body. Her tongue sealed the wound on his chest, her lips trailing kisses between his pectorals. Her lips and teeth nibbled him, death by a thousand bites, and as he brushed the opening to her womb with the head of his cock, he knew, then that it didn't matter how many times she took Roarke, how many times she lived as a wolf, he'd be hers, thoroughly, utterly, and forever.

Lilah came like an exploding rocket, her cries filling the room. Her muscles clamped around him, massing, working him to the brink and beyond. She shuddered in his arms and with one, final thrust, and buried himself to the hilt inside her. Seed welled from his balls, rushing forward and exploding from him with such force he thought he'd stumble to his knees. Only the strength of the woman in his arms kept him from pitching forward.

With a roar, he came. His hoarse shout filled the room, undoubtedly heard by those outside through the broken window. Roarke remained in the doorway. He stared at them, his cock in his hand. He stroked himself, and Adrian buried his head in the crook of Lilah's shoulder to fully inhale her musk. Between Lilah taking the excess blood from his system and the physical release easing his need, the bloodlust no longer burned in his veins.

A grunt announced Roarke's climax.

Adrian lowered Lilah to the ground. His cock slipped from her, yet he didn't release her to refasten his jeans. She rested her forehead against his chest, her panting breaths cooling his overheated skin. After long moments, she grew steadier, and she reached down to pull up her jeans.

"You guys have to stop ripping clothing off of me," she muttered. "Pretty soon I won't have any left."

"That's the idea," Adrian muttered, and over Lilah's head, he caught Roarke's answering grin.

"Who were those guys?" Roarke asked.

"The Party. It's time we went to the Council and put an end to this once and for all." Adrian stepped away and looked at the dead vamps. "If we drag them to the back yard the sun will take care of them."

"And the stains in my carpet?" Roarke eyed the splatters of blood and brain tissue dubiously.

Adrian shrugged. "Maybe those too."

Roarke shook his head and grabbed the first body. He carried it through the dining room and opened the patio doors, dumping the body into the backyard. Adrian followed, hauling the husk of the vampire he'd drank from and dropping it next to the vampire Roarke had brought out. The wolf returned with the last body, all three dead vamps lined up like a row of destruction. Together, Roarke and Adrian returned to the living room to find Lilah standing there, staring at the stains in the carpet.

Adrian wrapped his arms around her and pulled her against his now-warm chest. Roarke hugged her from the other side, sandwiching her between them. Lilah trembled like a deer, her gaze fixed on the stains of blood and brain matter on the floor.

"They're gone now. I'm going to make contact with my informant, and then we're going to the Immortal Council. This will be over one way or another very soon," Adrian whispered to her.

Lilah shook her head. Roarke murmured comforting words to her, the syllables not quite forming complete sentences. She relaxed between them.

"I have a piece of plywood in the garage. I want to board up the window before we leave." Roarke slipped his arms from around Lilah and stepped back.

Adrian nodded and snuggled his woman closer to him. He wanted to hold her, just for a moment, and then he'd call his informant to find out the current location of the Immortal Council. He had no doubts that he'd done nothing but put a band-aid on their problems for now. Without being checked by the Council, the Party would continue to come after Lilah. He kissed the top of her head.

"I'm going to make my call from the den, sweetheart. Do you want to come with me?"

Lilah nodded.

Wrapping his arm around her, he led her down the hall to the one room in the house where he suspected she felt the safest, the alpha's den. She sank into a chair in front of the desk, and Adrian went behind. He picked up the phone, his gaze never leaving her, and punched in the number from memory. The phone rang.

He looked at the woman he loved, curled up on the chair. With her legs tucked beneath her and her hand tucked beneath her chin, she looked like a lost waif. His stomach clenched. If his brother wasn't already dead, Adrian swore he'd kill him himself.

On the other end of the phone line, the Reverend answered. "Adrian, I'm so pleased you called. Tell me, do we have you to blame for the alpha's new position on vampire-werewolf relations?" He chuckled low in his throat, amusement trickling through the phone line.

"I'd like to think so, but I believe it probably has more to do with Lilah than with me. I need to know where the Council is right now. The Party attacked again this evening. I want Lilah safe, and I wanted it yesterday." Adrian shifted in his chair and shuffled on the desk for paper and pen.

"I can give you the location and advise them you're coming. Your reception and how it proceeds is up to you," he said.

Adrian nodded. "Fair enough." He scribbled down the address to the Immortal Council, and after exchanging a few more pleasantries, hung up the phone. He turned to Lilah. She sat relaxed now, whatever horrors having gone through her mind faded now. "You okay?" he asked.

She nodded. "Thanks. I don't know why that bothered me but it did. Guess I've never literally blown anyone's head off before." She twined her fingers with his, the simple gesture letting Adrian know that no matter what had transpired she was going to be all right.

He didn't quite know what to say, so he settled for squeezing her hand before releasing it to pick up the phone. Moments later, he had a reservation at a fancy hotel nearby. When visiting the Council they needed to show the extent of the FitzReal name and prove that they belonged there. He planned to obtain a new wardrobe for Lilah, especially as she so eloquently put it, they kept ripping her clothing off. And for Roarke, as well. The wolf must look, and act, his best.

Adrian motioned for Lilah to follow him out of the den. He found Roarke in the living room, finishing the repair on the window. The wolf drilled in the last screw, then unplugged the tool and wound up the cord. A large piece of plywood covered the center window, protecting it from further damage. "Once we get back, I'll have a new window installed. You get the information you need?"

Adrian nodded. "Yeah, I want to leave tonight. Do you think we can be ready?"

Roarke wiped his hands on his jeans and nodded. "Give me an hour."

"Good. I'll start packing." Adrian hurried upstairs, Lilah following. Less than an hour later, they were on the road with Roarke driving. He took one look at the destination, grunted, and buried the accelerator in the floorboard. They'd arrive before dawn, but just barely.

The drive passed mostly in silence, with Lilah sandwiched on the front seat between the two men. As soon as they reached the hotel, Adrian bundled her inside, leaving Roarke to bring in their bags. He drew her scent into his nostrils, knowing what they would need to do before their arrival before the Council. He waited until Roarke arrived, followed shortly by the bellboy and the bags. Then, he closed the door beside them and gestured them to the seating area of the large suite.

"Before we go in front of the Council all three of us will need to make love again. When we appear before the Council it will have to be united, our scents mingled as much as our interests, our bodies and our souls. They'll ask for no less, especially given your recent actions Roarke." Adrian spoke carefully, slowly, as if he were verbally crossing a minefield rather than speaking to people he knew.

"Why my actions?" Roarke asked. "All I did was state that I was going forward with a new era in vampire-werewolf relations. I'd think they would be happy a few less wolves hated them."

Adrian nodded. "And I'm sure they are. However, you do not speak for the Luna Council nor did you have your governing body sanction your actions. In the eyes of the Immortal Council, that makes you a rogue to your people. They do not like those who don't follow established procedures." He inclined his head. "They're very old fashioned."

"I see, but not so old fashioned that they don't mind knowing we fucked each other. I think, vampire, that your governing body is as fucked up as ours." Roarke laughed.

Adrian grinned, Roarke's infectious laughter spreading, and soon, Lilah joined in with the laughter. Their laughter was a cathartic release, and he suddenly felt so much better about meeting the Council. The sound subsided, and Adrian found himself pulled towards sleep by the rising sun outside. He rose to his feet and went into the bedroom with the large bed dominating the room.

"When did you want to do this?" Lilah asked. She swiveled on the couch, her legs tucked beneath her, a beguiling smile on her face.

"When we wake up, right before we go. I'm going to shower and go to sleep. I suggest you guys do the same. We're going to need our strength." He turned and slipped into the room.

Preparing for what was to come, he called down a standing order to the concierge for some suitable clothing for the three of them. He crawled naked into bed, the fine, Egyptian cotton sheets smooth as silk against his skin. He listened to Roarke and Lilah's soft murmurs. She laughed, the husky notes hardening his cock.

"We need to wait for tonight. That way we're at our best." She kissed Roarke and then he watched as she went to the bathroom. The shower started, and he imagined her standing naked beneath the spray. He caught the drops of water sliding over her skin with his tongue, drinking from her as if she were a fountain. The image stayed in his mind, even as sleep pulled him under.

~* * *~

Lilah knew waking up sandwiched between two muscled men had to be the most sublime feeling in the world. She laid with her breasts pressed against Adrian's back, her arm flung around his waist. Her hand splayed across his abs. Roarke spooned her. His cock nestled perfectly between her buttocks, his hand cupping her breast. His chest rose and fell with his deep, even breathing.

Lilah grinned. Time to make sure Adrian woke up with a smile. Leaning forward, she nibbled kisses along his shoulder. Gentle love bites left a trail of marks down the back of his triceps. She sucked on the skin of his inner elbow, and trailed her tongue over his biceps. She bit into the fleshy muscle, her canines elongating to leave tiny, red points. She licked the drops of blood and purred her pleasure. No inch of his shoulder, from his deltoids down to his elbow and back again went ignored. Adrian groaned and rolled toward her.

She rose onto an elbow to kiss his chest. Roarke's hand slid from her breast, and he shifted on the bed. His lips brushed the middle of her back, and then his hot body covered hers. Lilah closed her eyes and savored the feel of a hot mouth trailing over her skin. She sought, and found, Adrian's nipples. The tiny nubs stood at attention, begging for her mouth. She swirled her tongue around one, feeling him stir as she woke him. Walking her fingers over his stomach, she stroked his cock, base to tip, rubbing her palm of over the head to play with his foreskin. His hips lifted, and a smile curved his chiseled lips.

Lilah flicked his nipple with her tongue. She toyed with it, pretending their positions were reversed and Adrian had has talented lips on her breast. Against his arm, her nipples hardened, the tiny points abraded by the dusting of hair on his arms. Her hips moved restlessly, the musk of his arousal surrounding her, drawing her closer to him. She pulled his nipple into her mouth and sucked long and hard.

Adrian reached for her. With his left arm trapped between them, the fingers of his right hand stroked her cheek and speared through her hair. It tumbled around her shoulders. The soft bed and ultra-fine sheets beneath them created the perfect place for seduction. If the Council wanted their scents on each other, than that's exactly what the Council was going to get.

She released his nipple, stretching across his chest to lave the other one. Roarke caressed her body, his gentle touches stroking along her spine, her sides, her buttocks, and thighs. It seemed he touched her everywhere, stroking her nerves to tingling life. His lips followed the path of his hands. His tongue followed her spine, tracing the bump of each vertebra with exquisite slowness. She purred against Adrian's skin and arched into Roarke's touch.

He shifted on the bed, the momentarily loss of his touch, made up for it by his stiff rod pressing against her and his hands reaching around to palm her breasts. Lilah moaned. Her need rose, sated by the blood she'd drunk, and yet, fueled by a need to taste Adrian again. She followed the hair between his pecs down to his abs, and then lower, until she nuzzled the base of his cock.

"Suck me," he groaned.

Lilah's husky chuckle answered for her, as she worked her way across his abs. The wound from where she'd drunk last night called to her, and she placed an open-mouthed kiss against the twin red marks.

Her nails stroked along his thighs, moving to the outside, then to the inside, so she could touch the sensitive skin behind his sacs, and yet, she left his cock and balls alone.

Roarke focused his attention on her back and buttocks. His tongue snaked along her crease, pressing against the puckered ring of muscles, before continuing its journey. Spreading her legs, she silently begged him to taste her cream and tongue her clit. She drew in a shuddering breath, knowing Adrian lay awake, yet almost unmoving. Both hands fisted the blanket. His body thrummed, strung tighter than a guitar string, and as she danced her fingers across his abdomen, she intended to play him like a maestro.

Roarke's tongue found her slit and licked it from front to back, then back to front.

Lilah ground her teeth together against the urge to bite. She rocked her hips against Roarke's face, wanting to watch him and wishing the hotel had a large mirror as she nuzzled the top of Adrian's cock, then slowly, oh so slowly, she wrapped her lips around the tip and she swore she heard him groan,. She sucked gently, her hand fisting around his shaft. She pumped as she tongued his slit. His salty flavor burst on her tongue. Her eyelids fluttered closed, and she moaned.

She slid him deeper into her mouth, her hand eventually being replaced by her lips. She stroked him with her tongue, following the vein from base to tip. The knot of nerves just beneath his head called for her to plunder it with tiny nips. A salty pearl emerged from the tip, and she licked it up, murmuring about how good it was.

Roarke thrust his tongue into her vagina.

Lilah's back bowed. Her mouth slid from Adrian's cock, and she screamed as ripples of pleasure coursed through her. Big hands covered her breasts, one Roarke's, one Adrian's, and she realized he'd released the sheet to do so. Her cream dripped down her thighs, and she bent her head to Adrian's cock. Her hair swept along his stomach. With a grin, she stroked it across his taut shaft, the silken strands falling around him. Then, she took him in her mouth once more.

With Roarke at her cunt, he made love to her with his mouth. Tongue and teeth stroked and played across her clit and labia. Her muscles clenched, and this time, she grabbed a handful of the comforter to keep from spiraling out of control. Drawing deep breaths through her nose, she took Adrian as deep as she could, and when he started to slip down her throat, she vibrated a hum against his head.

She worked her hips, wanting to feel Roarke pounding into her as she made Adrian come with nothing but her kiss. Focusing her attention on him, she drew her lips up and down the length of his shaft. She imagined him in her pussy, filling her, stretching her, the head of his cock finding that place high and deep inside with each thrust. She whimpered as Roarke added a finger on her clit to the tongue in her cunt.

Fuck me. Take me. Mentally, she begged for his cock, needing the thick weight of him inside her. His tongue kept her hovering on the edge. The muscles fluttered around him. Her clit throbbed, slick and swollen. "Please," she begged as she released Adrian's cock. "Please."

"I want to watch you fuck her." Adrian's husky voice startled her into stilling her motions. She turned her head and looked at him, his eyes glowing with hunger. His parted lips revealed elongated canines.

Looking at him lying there, Lilah thought she'd never seen a sexier sight.

"We both have to come inside her." His statement took her breath away.

Lilah swallowed hard and looked over her shoulder at Roarke. He moved away long enough to reposition his cock at her entrance, and grabbing her hips, he thrust home. She screamed.

"Suck me," Adrian ordered, reaching down to cup his balls and offer them to her.

"Yes," Lilah hissed. She bent her head to his shaft and drew it swiftly into her mouth. Reaching between his legs, she fondled his balls, rolling them in the palm of her hand. The wet sounds of her sucking combined with the slap of flesh against flesh. The heady aromas of their entwined scents hung in the room like the fragrance of ambrosia. She rocked back, feeling Roarke take her, remembering the way he mounted her in wolf form in the alley, and wanting it again. This time, she wanted to feel his cock knotting inside her, binding them together.

Roarke reached around and stroked her clit. He pinched it between his thumb and forefinger, a jolt pleasure-pain rolling through her.

She thrust her buttocks against him, wanting to be taken, harder, faster, higher. Roarke's grunts filled the air. Adrian remained silent, eyes watching them. Lips parted, he focused on the sight of Roarke's cock disappearing into her channel only to emerge glistening with her juices. He spoke one word.

"Now!"

That command, delivered with all the hunger in his voice, sent Lilah shuddering over the edge. She screamed, the ripples starting in her sheath working their way outwards. Her nipples tightened, the buds so hard they hurt. Every inch of her skin hummed, and then she tilted her head back and screamed as Roarke slammed into her once more. His head hit her sweet spot, the friction simply too much to bear. Convulsing, she released Adrian's cock from her lips and simply clung to the bedding. Bracing her arms, she tried to ride through the undulating waves of pleasure, and finally, she slumped forward, with Roarke still buried deep inside her.

He thrust once more, then stiffened, and came. His come filled her, gave her a sense of completion that had her twitching into another release. Beside her face, Adrian's cock pulsed, hard and ready, roped with veins. The vampire moved from beneath her, then pulled her up to the bed and flipped her onto her back. He braced himself between her spread thighs and thrust home.

Lilah screamed at the brutal taking. She wrapped her arms and legs around him, ankles locking behind his back. She clenched her fingers into his shoulders, her hips rising to meet his harsh thrusts. His mouth pressed against the side of her neck, his fangs sinking into her skin. He sucked her blood, and she did the same, biting him and uniting them in a circle of life and death far more intimate than any the wolf had ever experienced.

His blood flowed to her, hers to his. His cock filled her, the driving thrusts taking her higher and higher. She cried out, another orgasm sweeping her away. Her jaws locked on him. Stars erupted behind her closed eyelids. And still, Adrian fucked her.

Oh hell, she never imagined it could be like this. Sweat and semen, blood and cream. The world titled on its axis. Vertigo pushed her down, around, until she spun around and around. Maybe it was the blood loss and maybe it was the raw power coursing through her veins. Either way, the world spun.

Adrian stiffened above her. A hoarse shout erupted from his lips at the same time his cock twitched deep inside her. His come mingled with Roarke's, the two men marking her as intimately as they could. She came again, the sheer power of their possession pulling her under once more and blackness blurred the edges of her vision.

When her vision cleared, she once more found herself cradled between Roarke and Adrian. Both men looked down at her, satisfied smiles on their faces, which she was sure matched the one on her own.

"Welcome back, sweetheart," Roarke said. He kissed her on the lips.

Adrian leaned over and kissed her as well. "Yeah, welcome back. You ready for the Council."

Lilah grinned. "Bring 'em on."

"That's my girl," Adrian said.

Lilah watched as he and Roarke left the bed and dressed. Her stomach fluttered, and she hoped things went as well as Adrian expected.

Chapter Twenty-Four

Walking into a room full of important vampires, still reeking of sex with both her lovers wasn't how Lilah imagined her visit to the Immortal Council. Yet here she was, dressed in a form-fitting black sheath that left her back bare and had a slit from her hip to the floor. The stiletto heels she wore felt awkward. With Adrian on one arm and Roarke on the other, the men supported her.

Roarke looked resplendent in his tuxedo. His sun-kissed hair and tanned skin contrasted with Adrian's paleness, and she felt as if she walked between the sun and the moon. Perhaps, she did. After all, her wolf and vampire each had their own worlds, and luckily for her, they combined. Adrian appeared every inch the aristocratic old vampire in his tux, and she saw hints of the vamp she'd originally been attracted to beneath his icy exterior.

The floor reminded Lilah of the pitch dark of the night during a new moon. Black marble flecked with silver gave the illusion of stepping out into the cosmos. Thick black hangings hung on the wall, and no windows marred the dark space. Overhead, a domed ceiling, also hung with black velvet, absorbed the sound and light. In the middle of the room, six vampires sat on chairs hewn from obsidian.

Three male and three female vampires provided the only spots of color in the room. A black female vampire, her skin as dark as the room itself, wore a crimson dress with a high, buttoned neck and flowing sleeves. The hem covered her feet, and she sat like a waterfall of blood upon her throne. Next to her sat a male in a loose silk tunic and baggy pants in a golden yellow. He looked like a ray of light, like the sun on a cloudless sunny day. A female wearing a green dress similar in cut and style to the woman in red, sat next to him, and next to her sat a male in another flowing, silk outfit, this time in the deep blue of the ocean. Looking at them, Lilah saw the elements.

Behind them, a male and a female sat dressed in white. The male's outfit matched those in color, the female's dress of a similar cut. However, where the room absorbed the light, their white garments illuminated the space around them, glowing so bright she had to look away.

Adrian stepped forward. He bowed, his obeisance so deep his forehead nearly touched the floor.

Lilah followed suit, with Roarke also bowing.

"Adrian FitzReal, why do you seek an audience with the Immortal Council? What do you hope to gain here for your female and her wolf?" No individual council member spoke, yet the voice reverberated around them as if it came from everywhere.

Lilah shivered.

Roarke reached for her, clenching her hand. Cold sweat beaded on his palm. He openly started, part in disbelief, and partly in fear. She wondered what the Luna Council looked like, and if it mirrored this one at all to cause him to be so startled.

"I seek amnesty for my female, Lilah St. James. Though brought into our world without permission, she has done nothing to those who did not seek her harm. She did not ask for her infection, and yet, has found herself pursued from both sides. She has a haven in the Northwoods Pack. I ask that the Immortals also provide a haven for her as well." Adrian kept his voice level, his gaze averted from those in front of her.

Her skull buzzed. In her mind, she saw a mirror image of the six who sat before her, only mentally they shifted through her memories, leaving no stone unturned. Light, fire, earth, and water, the elements raged through her mind, with the white light of the two shining above it all. She gasped.

"Ahh, she knows we're in her mind, as does her wolf." Once again, the room shook with the force of the Council's combined voices.

Lilah saw Roarke nod.

"I have nothing to hide," she said. She didn't defer to them like Adrian. Instead, she stared at the two in white, knowing somehow, telepathically, they controlled everything that happened to her. "You see everything." She threw her mind wide open, noticed that the woman in white gasped, her eyes growing wide, and then with a slam, the sextet dissipated from her thoughts.

Lilah staggered back.

Adrian's hand caught her elbow. Roarke clenched her hand, keeping her from falling.

"Everyone has secrets," the woman said. "Especially one such as you. We do not trust your wolf, just as your wolf does not trust us." Whether she spoke about Roarke, or Lilah's inner bitch, she didn't know, and suspected that the woman was actually referring to both.

"My wolf trusts you," Lilah replied. She released her men's hands and stepped forward. She didn't fall to her knees in obeisance. In the dress, it wouldn't be practical. "There are others like me. If I survived, surely others have as well. Wouldn't you want to bring peace, use me to bridge the gap between your worlds? My wolf," she gestured back to Roarke, "has already declared his pack at peace with the vampires. He made Adrian his Second. You have spent many centuries warring with one another. Wouldn't you rather spend your time in peace?"

"Lilah," Adrian snapped.

"It is true," the woman in white said. "She is a strong one, and though you did well Adrian FitzReal to bring her here, you play the games of politics that all immortals play. This woman, she still thinks like a mortal though she has more time than she realizes. She speaks the truth. She speaks plainly, her candor as refreshing as a clear mountain stream. Let us be honest. We sanctioned an attack on Lilah St. James' life just as we sanctioned attacks on any werepyre's life. Until the two races can come to peace, we suffer none who have been used as spies and warriors to live. Your brother did well going to The Party. They seek to harness the werepyre's strength...their ability to walk in the sun. Their scent may be different, but the untrained wolf or vampire thinks nothing of the horrors it hides. So we ask that they all be killed."

Lilah's hand flew to her mouth. The woman spoke with a finality that sent shivers down her spine. Surely, after coming this far they didn't mean to kill her too. Her heart beat a staccato rhythm in her chest. Her mouth went dry, and she swallowed to try and muster saliva.

"But not you."

Lilah's sigh of relief was audible in the chamber.

The woman in white cracked a smile. "You straddle the worlds. We ask that you work for the Council, our liaison between the werepyre worlds and our own. Stay. And there will be no further sanctioned attempts on your life." Her smile revealed a hint of fang, and Lilah knew, if crossed, this woman could be far deadlier than Lilah ever imagined.

She glanced at Roarke. His impassive expression revealed nothing. "What about my pack. I am the alpha bitch of the Northwoods Pack. I will not abandon them." She reached out her hand for Roarke to join her.

He did, his steps echoing against the marble floor.

She reached for Adrian. "And my lover, he who completes my vampire soul. Will you leave him out of this bargain as well?" Lilah arched an eyebrow.

"You are in no position to bargain with us, werepyre, though you try anyway," the woman said. "The wolf goes back to his pack. Adrian FitzReal shall stay and aid you in walking in our world, as he should have aided his brother."

Adrian flinched.

So that was it? Lilah stared at the Council, their stony gazes filled with contempt for her and her companions. She'd taken all the risks in coming here and received little reward. Their offer intrigued her, but if it meant being away from the Northwoods and Roarke. She frowned and glanced at him.

Roarke scowled and released her hand.

Lilah curled her hand around his biceps, needing to feel that connection between them. When the Council said nothing further, she suspected they were done.

"The offer has been made. You have until sunrise tomorrow to decide." Once more, the voices echoed in her head and all around.

Adrian released her long enough to bow, and Lilah curtseyed as the dress would allow. Roarke bowed stiffly, his scowl deepening as Adrian gripped her arm, then turned and led her from the chamber. His shoes stomped on the floor.

Big oak doors closed behind them, and once more, they were alone in the antechamber.

"Surely you're not thinking—"

Lilah pressed two fingers to Roarke's lips to silence him. "Not here. Not with them around." She jerked her elegantly coiffed head back to the twin doors.

With a grunt, Roarke hauled her forward. He set a commanding pace, and in her stilettos, she almost tripped and fell, except Adrian was there, his hand on her elbow, nearly lifting her feet off the ground in an effort to have her keep up with them. Like he had when her world spiraled out of control when she'd been turned. He found her in the abyss, hauled her out, and then, showed her the way to the light she could never have again.

Until her infection.

Oh hell, deep in her bones, the place where her childhood dream to become a doctor and save third world children from diseases curable and incurable lived, she wanted the job with the Council. It belonged to her, would give her opportunities she'd never before had a chance to grasp. It felt...right. And it would push Roarke away from her.

Tears stung her eyes, though she told herself they were from her rough treatment and not the breaking of her heart. Carried out to the truck, the door opened, and she was helped inside as unceremoniously as overstuffed shopping bags. Adrian stepped into the backseat, and before the door closed, Roarke started the truck and squealed tires out of the parking spot. Not the most decorous exit to their all-too-official meeting.

She puffed small bursts of air as the truck squealed around corners and scared motorists in small compact cars to the other lanes. A muscle in Roarke's jaw twitched. Her fingers shook as she curled them around the seatbelt. "Roarke?" She asked.

He ignored her query.

A hand settled on her shoulder. Adrian's. She looked over her shoulder at the vampire. His soft eyes told her it would be all right, when the reality stared in the face with a starkness that had her shaking in her three and a half inch heels. She reached up and patted his hand, letting him know she appreciated the gesture. But first, they had to deal with Roarke.

The thought of losing him squeezed her chest so tight she feared she'd be unable to breathe. Her wolf howled, called to him, and yet he slammed the truck into park and bounded out of the cab without even looking at her. A tear squeezed free of her eyes. His actions told her he thought she'd already made the decision, and it didn't include him.

Hadn't that been exactly what she'd done? Lilah's hand trembled as she unfastened her seatbelt. She opened the door. Before she could attempt to wriggle to the ground on her own, Adrian's hands circled her waist and lifted her down. His hand on her arm, he helped her into the hotel, where the empty lobby mocked her. In his mind, Roarke was already gone.

Adrian pushed the button for the elevator and when the doors dinged open, led her inside. She blinked like a zombie, not quite certain of anything, except she had to talk to Roarke. She had to explain to him and find a way to make this work for both of them.

"He doesn't understand," Adrian whispered as the elevator slid to a stop on their penthouse floor. "I'm sorry."

"I'm not," Lilah looked up at him, her eyes stinging with unshed tears. "I'll make him understand. There has to be a way to work this out. I'm just not sure what it is yet."

Adrian said nothing, only led her to the room with a stoic presence that told her, no matter what happened, he'd be there.

~* * *~

Roarke stared out the patio doors at the twinkling lights of the city and wished the moon didn't rise so full and welcoming in the sky. He lifted his face to the rays of light that bathed his skin even through the glass and resisted the urge to howl. He'd seen the way Lilah looked when the Council presented her with the option to work with them as a liaison between the werepyres and the vampires. He shook his head. They'd offered her the job of her considerably-longer-than-his lifetime on the condition that he'd go. In the world of fantasies, his love would trump anything the Council did. He doubted that would be the case.

He fisted his hand and pressed it against the cool glass. Bowing his head, he turned away from the light and tried to gather the ragged edges of his thoughts. He heard Adrian and Lilah enter. Their mingled scents, still detectable, twisted his stomach into a thousand knots. What he'd had with her had been wonderful. He feared it wouldn't be enough.

Roarke Connelly never walked away from a fight. He straightened, took one last look out the patio door before whirling to face his lover and her vampire. For a moment, his gaze found Adrian, his Second. Pity shone in the vamp's eyes. Roarke snarled. He didn't need anyone's pity.

"Roarke." Lilah breathed his name as if it were the very air she needed. Her glassy eyes bespoke of tears she wouldn't shed. So she'd made her decision. He stared at her, dispassionately, some part of his mind aware that if he wanted to change her mind this wasn't the way to do it. She stepped toward him and stopped. "Roarke?"

His throat worked convulsively. "You'd be a fool not to take their offer. I know you're interested in learning more about others like you, and if it kept the Council from sanctioning threats on your life..." Roarke shrugged. "I won't stand in your way."

"I want you to." Her soft admission tightened around his heart.

His gaze flew to her face. "What? No, Lilah, don't be stupid." Inside, his heart broke with the thought of walking away from her.

"I'm not being stupid. You are. Damn it, Roary you always were too hardheaded for your own good," she snapped.

The childhood nickname reminded him of ties they shared far closer than those of alpha and bitch, of the shared youth and of dreams and fears never achieved and never realized. Suddenly, he was the surly young man trying to take care of everybody and cursing his father's disappearance, and she was just a human. Only Lilah had never been just anything. A sad smile curved his lips. He stepped forward, arms reaching for her, and he pulled her into his embrace.

Pressed against his chest, her pliant body molded to his. Her unique scent, part wolf, part vampire, surrounded him, seeped into his pores and clung to him. It entrapped him with the knowledge that he'd always want her for his own, and she'd forever be tied to the world of the vampires as well as his own. He breathed a shuddering breath.

"She's right," Adrian said.

"I'd have thought you would have wanted her all to yourself." Roarke closed his eyes and nuzzled her hair.

"I do, but then again, so do you." He shrugged. "So I guess we have to share."

"I never was good with sharing," Roarke admitted.

"Neither was I," Adrian barked laughter.

"I don't want to go back to the Northwoods without her or my Second."

"I know. The Council has spoken. Go against their wishes and you'll court not only your own death but Lilah's and mine as well. Perhaps even most of your pack. They don't take lightly to being crossed. We're fortunate we even got to meet with them. They could have just killed us where we stood. You've sensed their power." Adrian loosened the tie at his throat. He shrugged off his jacket and unhooked his cufflinks.

"Yeah, pretty freaky shit."

Against his chest, Lilah laughed. "So is the Luna Council like them? You looked surprised when we first saw them."

Roarke nodded. "Yeah. Maybe now I know why vampires and werewolves fight so much. We're too similar to get along." He released her and cupped her shoulders. Stepping back, he tilted her chin so she looked at him. "Do you really want to do this? Not just because they'll quit trying to kill you, but because you really do want go through with this."

Lilah nodded, her eyes wide. "I do. I'm sorry. Remember when I was a child and I was going to become a doctor to save those kids they show on television."

"Yeah." Roarke hated the gruff emotion clogging his voice.

"That's how much I want to do this. I feel like I'm needed. Like maybe, this is all fate or something. I was born to do this job, even if I was born a mortal." She flattened her palm on his chest. Beneath it, he knew she felt the staccato beat.

Roarke stared at her. Deep in his heart, her words made sense. And the last thing he'd want to do is to hold her back from something she wanted. Yet, the idea of her working with the Immortal Council chafed. The Luna Council had a say in werepyres. His people remained taciturn on the idea. Would it be possible that Lilah could be a liaison to both? He covered her hand with his, warming the chill skin with his heat.

"I love you, Lilah. I don't want a long distance relationship. I can't bear the thought of going back home without you there. Of lying in bed at night and knowing he's holding you, loving you, and I can't just because his people said so. Don't do this me. Don't do this to us," Roarke pleaded.

Lilah bit her lower lip. He leaned forward, and nipped the full pout. Drawing it into his mouth, he suckled it. The gentle tastes lead to more, until he cupped her buttocks and brought her against him. Lilah twined her arms around his neck, her mouth mating with his. She opened to him and welcomed his tongue in her mouth.

She tasted like heaven. He clenched her full cheeks in his hand, needing to feel her pliant body against his. He plunged his tongue into her mouth, drinking from her, tasting her, hoping like hell he reminded her exactly what she'd be missing if she took this job. A soft moan emerged from her lips, and he swallowed the cry like a greedy wolf.

He ended the kiss. His panting breaths matched hers, his alpha tensing with the desire to mount his mate. "Make love to me, Lilah. Let me knot inside you and tie us together." It was tantamount to a marriage proposal, and Roarke knew it couldn't have come at a worse time.

Lilah pressed her face against his chest. She smoothed her hands beneath his jacket, sliding it from his shoulders. Reaching up, she unfastened his tie, then the top two buttons so she could slip her fingers past the placket to touch his warm skin. "You know if I do that I won't be able to let you go." She stepped from his embrace and sank to the plush couch. She refused to turn her head and look into the open bedroom door and see the bed where they'd all made love.

Adrian moved, one minute standing near the door, the next behind her, his hands on her shoulders. She reached up and covered them, looking up and smiling at his comforting gesture. Damn bloodsucker.

Roarke sat down next to her, so close her leg pressed along the length of his. He unfastened his cufflinks, got as comfortable as Adrian, and prepared for battle. "That's why I want you to do it. You're my mate. You have to know what we have is good. I love you."

Lilah hiccupped. "Please," she sobbed. "Don't do this to me."

Her heart was breaking inside just like his, and Roarke wished he could sweep the shards away and start anew. "You're choosing the vampire over me, Lilah. How do you think that makes me feel?"

"As bad as I do knowing that I'm going to have to leave you behind," she replied. "But I have no choice. I'm tired of running, tired of fighting for my life. And this is something I can do. There are other werepyres out there. Who knows how long they've been running? Shouldn't I selflessly put my feelings aside if I can help others? Isn't that what you do as an alpha?"

"Yeah, until I didn't do that, and look what happened. Oh God, what a fucking mess." Roarke dragged both hands through his hair. He looked at Adrian. "What do you think about all of this?"

"The decision is Lilah's to make," Adrian answered.

"You self-righteous bastard. I didn't ask you that, I asked you what you think about this? Are you just giddy as hell that she's finally getting rid of the wolf?" Roarke barked at him. Anger boiled inside him, making him want to rail against something, to pound and scream and yell until he finally got the bile out of his system. Right now, Adrian made a perfect punching bag, and he knew he was the bastard for using the vampire.

"No," Adrian said. "I'm not a man to share, but if it's what she wants, then I'll abide by her decision. I like you, wolf. I respect you, and not just because you made me your Second." He squeezed Lilah's shoulders.

"How long?" Roarke asked. Between the impassible wall of Adrian's nonexistent emotions and the rock of Lilah's determination to do this job, he knew he had no choice. Tomorrow morning, he'd leave for the Northwoods. He wondered if he'd ever see Lilah and Adrian again.

"I don't know," Adrian said. "We won't abandon you. It may take a few months before our duties will let us get away. We will return to the Northwoods. I'll see to it."

Coming from Adrian, Roarke knew the promise would be as good as he'd get. He turned to Lilah, not wanting to spend his last hours with her fighting. "What do you want, honey? What can I do for you?"

Lilah turned tear-stained cheeks to him. "Just hold me."

Roarke held open his arms, and Lilah burrowed into them. He embraced her, drawing her into his strength, his warmth, as if he could envelop her like a cloud and keep all the bad things away. He rocked her, the words of a childhood song springing to mind. Nuzzling her hair, he sang to her, the soft words about a lost pup finding its way home making his eyes sting. "Never fear. The pack is here. Daylight's gone and the night has come. Never fear. The pack is here. We will keep you safe and warm."

Silently, Adrian slipped from the room. Roarke watched him go and appreciated the vampire giving them time alone. Over and over again, he crooned the song, hoping she knew the true meaning behind it. The pack never left one if its own alone. And for as long as he lived, Lilah would be his pack. The ritual, and his love, made it so.

Chapter Twenty-Five

Roarke stood at the foot of the bed. Outside the sun crested the horizon, the pull of the outdoors and light making him step toward the open door. Lilah lay tangled in the sheets, one hand outstretched toward his empty side of the bed as if she sensed he was already gone. The other hand lay pressed under Adrian. The vamp lay on his side, an arm flung across her breasts, the other pillowed under his face. In sleep, even the sleep of the undead, he looked like he could take care of her, that he loved her.

She still hadn't said she loved him. His throat constricted, and he backed out of the room before he did something stupid like tear off his clothes and crawl under the covers with her. "I love you," he whispered, and then he hurried away.

The hotel room door closed with a definite click, his key card left on the bar along with a paper containing the number to the Pack and to Jason. Time to buy a cell phone, he mused, though he'd avoided the technology before. He liked to be accessible when, and where, he wanted to be bothered. With Lilah separated from him, he wanted her to be able to contact him around the clock, if necessary, and made a mental note as soon as he returned to Northwoods to get a cell phone, and then get one for her and the vamp.

With just his duffel bag slung over his shoulder, Roarke strode from the hotel. He told himself he was doing the right thing that he wanted what Lilah wanted, even if it meant throwing him from her life. He slung the bag on the passenger seat beside him and sat behind the wheel. Resting his hands on the molded plastic, he stared up at the top floor of the expensive, exclusive hotel at which he'd never have been able to get a room without Adrian, then put the key in the ignition and turned it. His hand didn't shake.

He backed out of the parking lot. Moments later, he turned from the driveway and he looked in his rearview mirror until the hotel faded from view. Already an empty place settled in his chest where his heart used to be. Until Lilah returned to fill it, he knew he wouldn't be whole. He would be alpha of his pack. Though, without her, it meant damn little.

~* * *~

Lilah sensed Roarke's absence before she even opened her eyes. Her hand tingled from where Adrian laid on it. She winced as she pulled it out from beneath the dead weight of his body. Sitting up, she stared at the orange glow from behind the curtains. An emptiness filled the hotel room and she shivered.

She'd made the right decision. Ending the attacks, or at least the sanctioned ones, on her life meant she could work toward a future. A place where perhaps werepyres were tolerated, accepted even. A chance to deal with the highest echelons of vampire society, and maybe, someday, werewolf as well. She pulled on a thick terry-cloth robe and padded barefoot into the living room. Roarke's white keycard sat on the bar, damning evidence of her decision. She picked it up, pressed it to her lips, and swore she still smelled his scent on it. She went to the patio doors and peered outside.

His truck was gone.

She choked back a sob, reality hitting her with the force of a two-by-four. Sucking in a harsh breath, she bit off an anguished cry. A burst of expletives flew from her lips. She lacked time for this. Clenching the card so tight in her hand it left creases, she held it to her chest for a moment longer, and then flung it across the room. She stormed into the bathroom. Shedding her robe, she stepped beneath a scalding shower. She had a job to do. One that saved her life.

By the time she scrubbed clean and stepped out of the shower, Adrian had wakened. She heard him moving around in their suite. Wrapping the towel around her body, she started to comb out the tangles in her long hair. Adrian paused in the doorway.

Lilah looked her fill of his naked body. From the strong, muscled legs to his cock, which hardened beneath her gaze, across his flat stomach to broad chest, up to his chiseled features, and white, blond hair, he was her vampire's soul mate. At least she didn't have to give him up. She chastised herself for the selfish thoughts.

"You okay with this?" he asked as he strode into the room.

"Yeah." Lilah winced as the comb caught in a tangle of her hair.

"Here, let me." Adrian took the comb from her hands. Gently, he used his fingers to unravel the worst of the snarls in her hair. His deft fingers soon had the worst of the tangles resolved, and they slid easily through the silky strands.

Closing her eyes, Lilah gave herself over to his soothing touch. Beneath the fluffy towel, her nipples pebbled. Heat blossomed between her thighs. Roarke hadn't even been gone twelve hours and she was ready to tumble with Adrian. Did that make her a traitor? She sighed and relaxed. She'd slept with him before, surely it made no difference now that Roarke was gone.

"Thanks," she said as she straightened.

Adrian brushed a kiss across her cheek. "I laid out your dress for you on the bed. I'll be ready in a moment."

"That's because you don't need all the work that I do to make you beautiful. You're a vampire, one of the beautiful people." She winked, taking the sting out of her teasing words.

"You're gorgeous. Next to you, I'm downright ugly." He brushed another quick kiss across the pulse fluttering in her neck, then stepped into the room where the bathtub was and started running a shower.

Lilah flushed at his words. She rubbed her fingers over the spot Adrian had kissed and wondered how quickly they could reunite with Roarke once more.

~* * *~

Where Adrian found the clothing, Lilah didn't know. She smoothed her hands over the short designer suit. The pencil skirt ended just above her knees, the jacket tailored to skim her curves. Her heels, not as high this time, made her look professional. With her hair clipped back away from her face, except for a few framing tendrils, she might have looked like a powerful businesswoman.

Again, Adrian led her to the large oak doors that marked the Immortal Council's chambers. She stopped before them, her thoughts going to Roarke. Was he back in the Northwoods? Did he take over as alpha of the pack? She nibbled on her lower lip, then mindful of her carefully applied makeup, stopped. She glanced at Adrian. "I'm ready," she lied.

Adrian lifted his hand to the doorknob, and the heavy doors swung open under their own power. The six vampires, far older than any she'd ever seen before, still sat in their same configuration. Had they even left, she wondered, then as she felt the telltale buzz of them in her mind, banished the thought. She strode forward, head held high, arms loose, and forced, if not a warm smile, then at least a trace of one onto her face. Adrian walked next to her, his strength like a beacon to her.

"Have you thought about our offer?" the woman in white spoke again, the sound coming from the front of the chamber.

Lilah looked at her and smiled, wondering what kind of an honor it was to be singled out by a member of the Immortal Council. She inclined her head. "Yes, I have." She glanced at Adrian and drew a deep breath. Having Roarke gone when she woke gave her time to think. The ride over in the limo the Council sent made her miss the big truck with its too high steps and loud exhaust. "I accept your offer with one condition, Roarke is allowed to stay. You ask that I work with the werepyre community. Just like them, I am both vampire and werewolf. Adrian balances out my vampire. Roarke is the mate to my wolf. You cannot ask I turn away from the pack and my wolf, any more than you, yourselves could deny the nature of your vampires. I will do as you ask, but only if you honor both sides of my nature."

Adrian looked at her. "Lilah! We didn't talk about this."

She held up her hand and shook her head. "Because it's my life and my choice. I refuse to live it only halfway."

"Even if it means putting your life in danger?" This time the Council spoke in her mind, their words reverberating with the weight of a death sentence.

"Yes!" Lilah answered without hesitation. "My life will be in danger anyway. Do you think everyone in the vampire or werewolf community will be happy with what I have done? With what you have done?" She laughed, the idea that these powerful vampires thought they could defy centuries of thought absolutely hilarious. Talk about being on a power trip.

Adrian stepped away from her.

Lilah's stomach sunk. She knew it was a ballsy move to make these demands after the offer had been tendered on the table. In the back of her mind, she supposed she should have discussed it with him first. Silly her to think that he'd support her decisions. She forced her attention away from him and back to the Council. She'd expected better from him, and now she stood here, without his support.

"Your bold statements come from the heart." The woman in white smiled. "So few of our people even have a heart anymore. It does not beat so they feel it does not exist. I have forgotten how refreshing the passions of those close to mortality are. We cannot allow you to go back to the pack."

Lilah gaped at the Council. Shock rooted her to the floor. "You mean you're going to hold me prisoner." She turned to the door. The Council sickened her. Walking out meant taking her chances with those who wanted to kill her. She'd have lost Roarke, Adrian, and any hope of protection. At least she'd be free. She stepped forward.

"Lilah, wait!" Adrian called. "Don't leave. You're going to lose it all."

"I know!" She yelled at him. "I have no choice. If they deny me Roarke, then they've denied my werewolf half. Do you really think the werepyres would want to work with a Council who hates half of what they are? I know I sure as hell don't." She wished she had a handbag, a clutch, anything to hurl at him and try to vent her frustration.

"Listen to the vampire," the white woman's words halted her flight.

Slowly, Lilah turned. Her heaving breaths and pounding heart echoed horribly loud to her vampire, and she imagined they must be a deafening roar to the vampires. She drew in a shaky breath to steady herself.

Adrian stepped toward her. "I don't like it either, but this offer is all we have. We can't turn it down." He held out his hand.

Lilah went to him, clasping his offered hand in both of hers. "Last night I stood before you and told my wolf's mate that I felt like I had to do this. That hasn't changed. I still feel like this is what I need to do. I just won't deny myself to do it." She released his hand and stepped back.

Whatever happened, at this moment, she knew she'd made the right choice. She looked at the Immortal Council and wondered if any of the six had ever faced decisions such as this one. Whether they came into power through lineage or earned their position, she didn't know, and, at the moment, it mattered little. They were piss poor leaders if they cared so little about those under their control. She let her hands fall to her side and when they said nothing, slowly turned back toward the door.

She placed one foot in front of the other, thankful for the lower heels that made walking easier. She forced her head high, her shoulders square. The slow tapping of her heels against the marble floor sounded like a death march. And Lilah knew it was her own.

She drew even with the doors that once again swung open as she neared. Her foot hovered just over the threshold.

"Do you know what you're doing?" the woman in white asked a final time.

"Yes," Lilah replied without turning around.

"Why?" The question hovered around her, spoken by all six of them, and yet, not in her mind.

"Because I love him!" The answer burst from her. "I love them both." She slammed her foot down and spun. "There, are you happy? I love them both."

"The question is, are you happy?"

Lilah blinked at the woman. "I was until you tried to take Roarke away from me," she said. "Yes, I am happy."

The female vampire smiled. "Good," she said. "Then your alpha is free to join you. This position requires someone balanced with both sides of her nature. I wanted to be sure you were ready."

Lilah breathed a sigh of relief. Giddy laughter bubbled up in her throat, and she wasn't sure whether to give into it or not. "Thank you," she said, tucking back the laughter. "Thank you." She held out her hand to Adrian, needing his touch. "Let's go find my alpha." She nearly dragged him out of the room in her haste.

The limo took them back to the hotel, waiting until they were inside the building before pulling away. Adrian's quiet demeanor worried her. In front of the Council, he'd been quick to turn aside. She feared he might be leaving her now that she'd made her choice. She clenched his hand, trying to convey how much she needed him.

"Did you mean it?" he asked when the elevator door closed behind them.

"Mean what? When I said I loved you? Of course, I mean it. I love you, Adrian, with all my little immortal vampire heart." The grin she'd plastered on her face when the Council gave her leave to find Roarke grew bigger.

She flung herself at him and wrapped her arms around him. The elevator slid to a stop just as her lips found his. She tumbled him against the wall of the elevator. She kissed him, letting all the love, all the emotion she held inside pour through her. Adrian cupped the back of her head. Slanting his lips across hers, he thrust his tongue into her mouth. A masculine groan rumbled through his chest, and to Lilah, it felt like coming home.

His fingers tightened in her hair, dislodging the clip. It clattered to the floor of the elevator.

The door slid open.

A throat cleared outside the doors.

Lilah pulled away, breathing heavily. She slid from Adrian's body and stepped back. She looked to see who had interrupted them and gave an excited squeal. Roarke stood by the elevator doors. She ran forward, almost twisting an ankle on her high heels. She grabbed onto him as if she expected him to be a figment of her imagination and plastered her lips across his. The sloppy kiss deepened as Roarke groaned and opened his mouth. He swallowed her whole, his tongue delving past her lips to penetrate her. His hands slid down her back, and when she wriggled against him, his cock thrust against her stomach.

"You came back," Lilah gasped as the kiss ended and she dragged in gulps of air. "You came back."

"I couldn't stay away." His gaze settled on Adrian, standing behind her. "I, uh, left my room key inside." He grinned.

Lilah blinked. They needed a key to even reach this floor, and she wondered how he managed to be waiting for her, and then she didn't care anymore. She kissed him, long and hard, then at Adrian's scowl, grabbed his hand and pulled him into their room. She pushed Roarke down onto the couch, then straddled him. She freed his t-shirt from his jeans. "So why did you come back?" She flattened her palms on his chest. Inside, she wriggled like an excited puppy, her wolf yipping and barking as she ran around and around, her tail flagging in the air.

Adrian sat beside them.

"For you," Roarke answered.

"Well good, because I turned down the job for you." Lilah slipped her arms from her suit jacket and dropped it on the arm of the couch. She reached for the buttons of her blouse.

Adrian covered her hands with his own. "Shouldn't we tell him all of it?" he asked with a wink.

"All right," Lilah relented. "I told the Immortal Council if I couldn't have you, then I didn't want the job. I told them I love both of you. You're each a part of me. I threatened to walk out. Almost did. But they said I could have the job and you too." She wrapped her arms around his neck. "Isn't it great?"

"A fucking miracle," Roarke muttered against her neck. "You meant it. You love me?"

Lilah playfully smacked his shoulder. "Of course I love you. You're my alpha. You always have been. And now, I have you, Adrian, and a job I can do to help vampire-werewolf relations. I can't wait to begin." Happiness filled her like the shining light of the sun. She reached out to Roarke and Adrian, clasping their hands in one of her own. Inside, her hungers roared to life, and yet, each of the men grounded them.

She kissed first Roarke, then Adrian. Finally confidant with who and what she was. An alpha's bitch. A vampire's lover. Working with the Vampire Council. Adrian laid her out over their laps, his hands removing her clothing. Lilah laid back, content with the way things worked out. She had the rest of her possibly immortal life to worry about the Council and their plans. She was safe. She had the men. A werepyre couldn't ask for anything more. Tomorrow night, she suspected the call would come to return to the Immortal Council. For tonight, she had other hungers to feed.

About the Author

Mary commutes between her dream home near the Mark Twain national forest in Missouri and her current residence in Iowa. She lives with a menagerie of animals including an opinionated horse and a cat that was a dog in past life. When not writing spicy tales of erotic romance, she enjoys writing science fiction and fantasy, spending time with her horse, and enjoying the outdoors. Lucky for her, her partner (hero) shares these same passions, and usually both of them can be found in their respective dens writing.

Website – http://www.marywinter.com/

Monthly author newsletter – http://groups.yahoo.com/group/marywinternews

Reader's Chat Loop – http://groups.yahoo.com/group/marywinterchat

If you enjoyed HER HUNGERS, you might also enjoy...

Tales of the Darkworld Book 3: Fire Season

By Lex Valentine

http://www.pinkpetalbooks.com

available in electronic and print format

Black dragon Holden Antaeus isn't looking for a mate. His life is filled with family, work, and dating. Women adore him and he's never short of offers for sex, but a relationship isn't something he's interested in. When Holden's brother Sean hires a new executive for Antaeus International, Holden's whole world, and everything he's ever believed about himself, is blown to bits. Garret Renquist is a green dragon, intelligent, witty, bi-sexual, and hot for Holden. Despite the fact that Holden is positive he's heterosexual, the moment he meets Garret, something happens inside him. What follows is a journey through stereotypes and ingrained beliefs as Holden struggles with the fact that his destined mate is a man.

Prologue

Alfred Stone leaned back in the sauna, casually adjusting a white towel over his naked lap. His voice sounded as casual as his demeanor, but to his one man audience, the tone rang more warning bells than a three alarm fire.

"I am Magia. My job is to ensure that nature's intended matings actually occur."

Sean Antaeus stared at his best friend in shock. "You have got to be joking." Nothing in his life had prepared him for the words Alfred had spoken. It wasn't so much what Alfred had said about Sean's younger brother, it was what Alfred had revealed about himself.

The Darkworld held people with power and powerful people. Sean had been living in a dream world thinking that Alfred, as the head of the Funeral Directors Guild, was merely a powerful person. Now, he knew the truth.

"Sean, I wouldn't have told you if I didn't think you could handle the information. My job isn't always easy. Your family has been especially hard. In fact, I need Marius' help too. His family is going be just as tough." Alfred's brow crinkled with worry as he spoke.

Sean arched a sardonic brow at him. "So you're letting Marius in on the secret too?"

A sigh escaped Alfred.

Sean thought it sounded rather dramatic and long suffering, which made him feel like he'd walked into some kind of set up.

"If you knew what I was up against, you wouldn't ask me that," Alfred replied in a morose voice.

Now, Sean knew he'd been played. Maybe not a lot, because at the core of it all, he knew instinctively that Alfred had spoken the truth, but Sean also could tell when he'd been manipulated. After all, he was a master of manipulation himself. *Took one to know one.*

"So you're telling me that both Diandra and I were the victims of your...gift?" Sean put his friend on the spot.

Alfred shifted uncomfortably on the sauna's seat. "Not victims, Sean. Recipients of a power that managed to keep you from fucking up your life. If it weren't for me, do you think either you or your sister would have ended up mated? Both of you were so stubborn and arrogant, refusing to see the truth, not wanting to be seen as weak."

Alfred made a rude sound and his gaze locked with Sean's. "If I hadn't butted in and used my gift to help you, both you and Diandra would be single today and unhappier than you could ever imagine," he said solemnly.

Sean bit back his own sigh. He couldn't imagine. His life would be awful if he didn't have his mate and wife, Careen. Yet, getting to the place where he'd accepted that he had a mate, a woman he loved beyond everything else in his life, had been a particularly rough road. The same had held true for his sister Diandra. Her path to love and marriage had been every bit as rocky. Now, Alfred made it seem like neither he nor Diandra would have managed to mate without a nudge from Alfred's power.

"Please tell me that you didn't pick our mates," he growled, feeling unnerved by everything Alfred had told him.

"Of course not. Those are nature chosen. But it's my job to ensure that those who are resistant become...more amenable to having a mate." Alfred smiled, something Sean knew he rarely did. "I smooth the path in any way I can without disrupting the natural flow of a mating."

Sean's brain raced as he absorbed Alfred's words. "And now you're telling me that Holden is in trouble?"

Alfred nodded solemnly. "A lot more trouble than you and Diandra put together. I need your help, Sean, or your brother will be unhappy until the day he passes to the Afterlife."

"Fuck." Alfred had him. Sean loved his younger siblings fiercely. He would fight anything that threatened their lives and happiness.

"So you're in." Alfred looked at him expectantly, triumph already shining in his eyes.

This time Sean did sigh. "Yeah. I'm in."

He shook hands with Alfred and realized that he'd sealed a pact of duplicity and manipulation as he did so. Luckily, being Machiavellian was second nature to Sean, and he bet Alfred knew that fact quite well.

Chapter One

The first to arrive, Holden slipped into his seat and opened his leather covered notepad with irritation. He disliked rah rah meetings. Despite all the team building pep talks, things always went back to the way they had always been...with his oldest brother Sean wielding his iron fist and micro-managing while he and his other brother Declan struggled not to let Sean overwhelm them.

In Holden's opinion, corporate life had been worse while Declan had been gone. During Declan's tenure at a European conglomerate, Sean had refused to replace him. Instead, Holden's oldest brother had taken on acquisitions himself in his brother's absence. Sean had gone crazy buying up whatever he could. Declan had a lot more finesse and savvy when it came to choosing the funeral homes and cemeteries that offered the best value. The company needed Declan's firm hand and cool head when it came to acquiring new businesses and Holden had been relieved when his brother returned to Antaeus International.

Declan's return to the company heralded the end of their sister Eden's term of employment in the corporate world. Her contributions to the company were myriad, but all of them had been tainted by her unhappiness in that environment and Sean's determination to keep her there. It had all come to a head not long after Declan's return. Eden had ditched her marketing job at Antaeus International, packed up her cameras, and headed to New York City. Within a few months, she'd become the fashion industry's new hot photographer, making her name shooting nearly naked men in designer underwear. Sean's fury knew no bounds over her defection and both Holden and Declan had borne the brunt of it.

The door opened and a muscular man with unruly black curls entered the room. Holden cocked one brow up at Vahid Delrey, his brother Sean's right hand man and the company's Chief Operating Officer. Vahid had also been Eden's live-in boyfriend for two years prior to her departure from all things Antaeus. Holden had always been amazed that Vahid had retained his cool demeanor, his deepest emotions, if he had any, masked from everyone when Eden had dumped him. Not for the first time, Holden wondered how Vahid had ever gotten together with his free-spirited sister. They seemed like such polar opposites.

"This is another attempt at a team building meeting, isn't it?" Holden asked as Vahid took the chair opposite him.

A dry chuckle escaped Vahid. "You know Sean. He may suck at something, but his determination won't let him stop trying to master it anyway."

Holden felt his lips curl in a derisive smile. "My brother is a force unto himself that's for sure."

Now, Vahid's brows rose. "Nice way of saying he's an arrogant ass."

The door whooshed open and the subject of their conversation strode in with Declan and another man behind him. Holden's nose twitched. The scent of spearmint assailed him.

"Thanks for the compliment, Vahid," Sean said smoothly, a sardonic expression on his hawkish features.

Declan took the chair at the foot of the table, seating himself on Holden's left. Sean took the chair at the head of the table. The spearmint scent intensified as a man Holden didn't know took the seat beside Vahid. More staff rushed in to join the meeting, but Holden found his gaze caught by the newcomer. Intense green eyes gazed back him, an indefinable emotion churning within them. Holden had no clue as to the man's identity, but an odd sense of familiarity pricked his awareness as he stared into those enigmatic eyes. It was as if knew the man, but couldn't place where or how.

The green gaze shifted as a tall, blonde woman strode into the room. Dressed in an unrelenting black suit and matching silk shirt, her pale hair twisted into a neat chignon, Emily Carrington looked like a fashion model until one noticed her stern visage. As one of the most powerful people at Antaeus International, she held the company's purse strings in her long-fingered, capable hands. The new man smiled at her as she took a seat beside him. Her expression turned smug and the new guy's identity dawned on Holden. The wunderkind of the death care industry's financial sector, Garret Renquist.

Sean and Emily had somehow managed to lure Garret from his position as the head of finance for Stone Mortuary Services, a job he hadn't even held very long. Alfred Stone had hired him away from the biggest British mortuary conglomerate in the hope of turning him loose on the Funeral Director's Guild's financials, a big project that Alfred had spearheaded as the head of the FDG. Instead, Sean and Emily had whisked the whiz kid to Antaeus International. With an internal smirk, Holden briefly imagined the acquisition of the stock market genius taking place over a round of golf. His brother Sean golfed regularly with Alfred and Marius Granville of Granville Cemetery, the oldest cemetery in their part of the Darkworld. Holden figured the three powerful men brokered all kinds of industry related deals during those golf games. Something told him that Garret Renquist might just have been one of those deals.

"Let's get started," Sean said from the head of the table. "This will be a short meeting anyway since we're all leaving."

"Leaving?" Holden asked, startled. What the hell was his brother up to now?

Sean's intense golden stare turned on Holden. "Yes. Leaving. I'll get to that in a minute."

Holden watched as his older brother's hawk-like gaze settled on the new guy. "Has everyone met Garret? Garret Renquist is our new Chief Investment Officer. He'll also be working in the capacity of Budget Director under Emily, which means he'll be working with all of you on your budgets. He comes highly recommended and has a great reputation for increasing a company's investment returns. If you haven't had an opportunity to introduce yourself to him, I suggest you do so over the next four days..."

Sean's voice trailed away and Holden mentally braced himself. He knew that tone. Sean was up to something that would probably irritate the hell out of him. His brother's suggestion that everyone introduce themselves to Garret was a thinly veiled order. Since Eden's departure, Sean regularly did things that he knew would force his younger brother out of his comfort zone and push the limits of his patience. In the past, Holden had always bounced back from Sean's Machiavellian power trips. Lately, he found himself beyond angry when his brother's machinations involved him.

Turning his gaze to his notepad so his brothers wouldn't see the anger beginning to simmer inside him, his nostrils flared as the scent of spearmint wafted toward him again. Who the hell smelled like mouthwash?

"I'll be closing this meeting in a few minutes, but we will reconvene tonight at six over dinner at the Gargoyle Resort. You are all to go home and pack. We're headed out to the mountains for a retreat."

Holden's head shot up and his eyes met his older brother's. A gleam of triumph lit Sean's amber eyes. Holden's jaw tightened. Sean had made his feelings clear a few weeks before regarding the woman Holden had been dating. Since Sean had never interfered in his sex life before, Holden had been surprised that he'd even mentioned her. He'd brushed off his older brother at the time. Holden really didn't give a shit whether Sean liked who he was fucking. It was none of Sean's business and it wasn't serious anyway.

Now, however, Sean's machinations had pissed him off and cost him money. Holden had cleared his calendar for two days so he could have a long four day weekend. His intent had been to spend those days in a sexual stupor at an exclusive spa in Santa Barbara. The steep deposit he'd put down with his reservations for two would now be lost, and the woman he was seeing would require placating. Fury rose within him. The loss of the money didn't irritate him so much, but the thought of having to soothe Gina's ruffled feathers made Holden furious with his oldest brother. Even though Gina had a tongue that could lick all day, she also had a rather bitchy attitude that showed up when she didn't get her way. Thanks to Sean, Holden would now be the recipient of the bitching rather than the licking.

"This will be an opportunity for us to work on some team building and strategizing. It will also give you all a chance to spend some time with Garret to see how he can help each of your departments maximize your budgets."

Sean's smile widened as Vahid got up and handed out brochures and packets to everyone. Holden opened his folder and stiffened. Sean had paired everyone up, forcing them to share rooms. Sean and Declan were together. Vahid shared with Todd Ryan, the Chief Technology Officer and Holden's draw was...the new guy. His head shot up and his gaze collided with Garret's intense stare. A little smile quirked up one corner of the man's mouth. That little smile kicked Holden's irritation up a notch. He frowned, wondering what it would take to get Vahid to trade with him.

Holden's eyes tracked Vahid around the table. When the head of Operations returned to his seat, he cocked a brow up at Holden. His smirky expression dashed Holden's hopes for a trade. Vahid obviously knew that Sean had put the new executive with his youngest brother for a reason.

Fuck! Anger tore through Holden at his brother's little games. Grinding his teeth together, he eyed the itinerary included in the packet. All the rah rah stuff was there and, even worse, there were scheduled strategizing sessions between each set of partners. Great, now he had to talk business with the finance geek all weekend instead of spending his time getting blown and fucked by the hottest woman he'd dated in a year.

The law degree and MBA hanging on his office wall had made Holden the company's General Consul and Chief Legal Officer. He dealt mostly with contracts and the mergers that Declan arranged. Anything related to litigation got shuffled off to a firm on retainer. Holden answered directly to Sean, but spent most of his time working with Declan. Looking at the itinerary for the next four days he couldn't believe Sean hadn't paired him with Declan. It made better sense to him because he and Declan were in the middle of some delicate takeover negotiations with an Australian company. He didn't have any strategizing to do with the bean counter, Holden thought with annoyance. Pairing him with the whiz kid had to be yet another Sean Antaeus production.

Holden watched Sean close the meeting. An odd glow of triumph lurked in the golden depths of Sean's eyes. Holden's dragon senses pinged. A triumphant Sean wasn't necessarily a good thing for the members of his family. He jerked his attention from his brother and gathered up his things, fury propelling him out of the board room. Fuck Sean. Maybe he'd just not show up at the retreat. That would teach his brother.

The scent of spearmint caused his nostrils to flare. He turned his head to find that Garret Renquist had followed him out of the board room. His frown deepened.

"I gather you're unhappy about being paired with me."

Visions of a cool woodland waterfall flitted through Holden's mind at the sound of the British accented baritone. Holden didn't know why it hadn't dawned on him that Garret was British. The man had come from a British based company.

Holden stepped into his office and Garret followed. Holden shut the door and waved the financial whiz kid toward a chair. As he sat down behind his desk he noticed that Garret's green eyes flickered over the wall of certificates, awards, and degrees. For a moment, Holden again had the sense that he knew the man. The spearmint scent apparently came from Garret. Holden's office smelled like a bottle of mouthwash.

"You're the General Consul." Garret's clipped British accent made the words sound almost accusatory, though Holden knew that wasn't his intent.

With a nod, he gestured toward the wall of plaques. "I went to Harvard Law School. I wasn't top of my class, but close." He smiled a little and joked, "All the Boston beauties kept me from studying too hard so I missed out on the top three spots."

Garret's eyes glowed a little and his mouth quirked up in the same smile he'd displayed in the board room. "I've been to Boston. There are a lot of good looking women there. It's a very academic town, isn't it?"

Holden nodded absently. Something about the spearmint scent bothered him, but like the sense of familiarity he had when he looked in Garret's eyes, he couldn't quite place it. He studied the man before him more closely. They had similar builds and were about the same height. Garret stood perhaps an inch taller and he appeared to be a little leaner than Holden. His chestnut brown hair was cropped close around the back of his neck but fell over his forehead with a wave in front. He had a boyishly handsome face, but his reserved demeanor made him look rather stern. Holden wondered if the golden boy of the stock market ever had any fun. He certainly looked all business.

With a mental shrug, Holden studied the man's very green eyes. They held an open expression, but Holden felt sure that behind that expression, Garret Renquist was quite guarded. Had he been the new guy, he'd be totally on his guard.

"I'm not unhappy about being paired with you. I'm unhappy about the whole weekend," he explained, reaching out to grasp his pen, twirling it absently in his fingers. "For one, my brother Sean likes to play at being the puppet master, making us all dance on strings. For another, I had plans."

Two beats of silence followed his words. Then Garret's eyes clouded, the emerald green irises darkening. Holden figured the man didn't like the idea of Sean being a manipulator. It sure as heck wasn't something he'd want to know about his boss's boss on the first day of a new job. He felt a little sorry for Garret now. He'd obviously had no idea what Sean Antaeus was like when he accepted the position at Antaeus International.

"Look, we'll just have to make the best of it, as we do with any of these team building things Sean springs on us. I'm sure we'll find something to work on during the strategy sessions," he said easily, hoping he hadn't scared off the new guy. Sean would kill him if he did.

One of Garret's brown brows arched up. "You don't think we're a good match?"

Holden blinked at the man's odd choice of words. "There's not a lot of interaction between my department and yours. I work more closely with my brother Declan. Declan works with Emily. I'm not sure why Sean put us together."

Garret's mouth quirked knowingly as if he had knowledge Holden didn't. Resisting the urge to shift uncomfortably in his chair, Holden snuck a glance at the guy. He sat there cool as a cucumber, his expression enigmatic, while Holden could barely keep from fidgeting.

Holden looked down at his hands then and dropped the pen he'd been twirling. When he raised his head, his gaze collided with Garret's. The scent of spearmint intensified and a nervous sweat broke out on the skin between Holden's shoulder blades, making his clan mark itch. He sucked in a breath as realization hit him.

"You're a dragon."

Garret nodded, the enigmatic expression giving way to amusement. "Your natural enemy. I'm a green."

Holden made a rude sound. "The dragon clans haven't fought in a millennia. And even then, there was nothing natural about it. All the wars were about power. Not color or clan. Legend says we were all one color in the beginning. Our natural enemies were humans, not each other."

A huge smile broke out on Garret's face. "You're a purist."

Holden's stomach lurched. Geez, the man had the most brilliant smile he'd ever seen. He shook his head. "I'm a realist. Dragons were not born to kill each other. We were never each other's natural enemies. Humans on the other hand instinctively want to be rid of any being stronger than themselves. Their fear drives them."

Both of Garret's brows rose, but his smile stayed intact. "A psychology major."

"Biological Anthropology." Holden grinned, beginning to relax. Maybe the weekend wouldn't be so bad after all. In fact, it would be perfect if he had a victim. "Hey! Do you play...?"

"Tennis," Garret finished for him with a nod toward Holden's college trophies. "Although not in your league."

"That was years ago. My reflexes aren't so fast anymore. I sit at a desk all day after all."

Garret's brow cocked up again. "You don't look so out of shape."

Holden shrugged. "I'm not, but I don't play much anymore and to stay at the top of your form you have to play every day. I had the skill to go pro, but not the drive. I like working for my family." He grimaced. "My brother is a pain in the ass, but I wouldn't work for any other company."

"Your brothers, this company...Antaeus is a powerful name in this industry," Garret said quietly. "I was flattered that Alfred wanted me for the FDG and Stone. I was floored when Sean said he'd pay me more to come here."

Holden laughed. "I'll bet Alfred was tweaked. He's one of Sean's closest friends so I'm sure he gave my brother an earful, but the rest of us would never know it."

"Strangely, Alfred took it all very calmly, as if he had expected it to happen."

Holden prepared himself for the sense of familiarity when he met Garrett's gaze. "I'm sorry if I gave you the impression I was pissed at having to share a room with you."

Something indefinable flickered in Garret's eyes. He rose from his chair. "It's all right. I've been feeling a bit out of my element today so I overreacted." He turned toward the door. "I'll see you up at the resort. Maybe we can get in a couple of rounds of tennis while we're there."

Holden smiled. "I'd like that. Welcome to Antaeus International, Garret."

The other man looked back over his shoulder. "Thank you." A brief smile flashed across his face and then he was gone.

Holden sat staring at the closed door for long minutes, the scent of spearmint lingering faintly in the office. The anger he'd felt at Sean's manipulations had fizzled during his conversation with Garret. He should know better than to get pissed anyway. It never changed anything. Holden had never known anyone to get his way more than Sean.

On his way to the elevator, he ran into Declan. "Nothing from Australia?" he asked.

His brother shook his head. "Not yet."

They both stepped into the elevator. As the door closed, Holden said, "Why did Sean stick me with the new guy?"

Declan shrugged. "Why does Sean do anything? Everything is about control with him."

"Has he messed with your private life too?" Holden's gaze sharpened as he looked at his older brother.

"What private life?" The words were cool and sardonic with a bitter edge.

Sympathy washed over Holden. His older brother had a huge thing for Elysia Granville, one of the most powerful women in their industry. However, she was engaged to the industry's biggest asshole, Austin Stone. Holden didn't understand how such a smart woman had ended up with such a monumental jackass. A woman like her belonged with a man like his brother, not a weasel like Austin.

"I gather Sean's little jaunt to the mountains is interfering with your plans," Declan said, his voice rumbling out of his broad chest.

Holden looked up to find his brother's expression filled with understanding. "Yeah. It's gonna cost me a bundle too between the deposit on the suite at the spa and keeping Gina from being disappointed."

Declan's eyes twinkled. "Buy her an expensive bracelet. She's mercenary enough to be placated by rocks."

The elevator stopped at the underground garage and they headed toward their assigned parking spots. "Why do you and Sean think that's all Gina wants from me?" Holden grumbled as he watched his brother's tall form move toward his Mercedes.

Declan shot him an amused glance over the roof of the car. "Because it's obvious?"

Holden grimaced. "Money isn't the only thing she wants. She likes my cock too."

His brother grinned, white teeth flashing in his tanned face. "Well, she should. Especially when the man attached to the cock buys expensive presents. Just watch it with her, little brother. She wants the gold ring with rocks and you just want to get your rocks off."

Holden walked over to his SUV. "Yeah, well, she can want the ring, but that doesn't mean she'll get it. I'm not the marrying type."

"Neither was Sean." Declan laughed and unlocked his car, the headlights flashing as the alarm disarmed. "I'll see you at the resort. Good luck appeasing Gina."

As Holden drove to his condo, he pondered his brother's words. He knew Gina wanted to marry him. He knew she was dazzled by his job, his money, and his good looks. He also knew that a woman like her would never fit in his family. For all their money, the Antaeus siblings were all about home and hearth and true mates. Holden wouldn't dream of marrying a social climber like Gina. A woman like her could never be his mate. Maybe Sean's interference wasn't such an inconvenience after all. Although left with only his hand to see to his sexual satisfaction, being rid of Gina and her demands was more of a relief than he'd wanted to admit.

Holden's condo was in a high rise condominium complex only two blocks from the beach. He drove into the underground garage and parked in the space reserved for the penthouse. His footsteps echoed in the cement structure as he walked to the elevator. Thoughts echoed in his head too. Everything from Declan's bitterness to Sean's manipulations to the prospect of kicking Garret's ass at tennis. The weekend was starting to look up.

In the elevator, he punched in the security code that took him to the penthouse level. The elevator opened onto a foyer that had but one door, his. Unlocking the penthouse door and automatically disarming the alarm, Holden stepped into his home. From his living room, he had an unparalleled view of the coast in both directions. His expensive, but comfortable furniture softened the starkly modern architecture. It was a bachelor's home, not meant for entertaining in spite of its size.

Holden jerked off his tie and jacket, tossing them on the brown leather couch. In the kitchen, he pulled open one side of the huge brushed aluminum refrigerator and took out a bottle of water. As he drank, he eyed the crayon drawings stuck to the refrigerator with magnets. His sister Diandra's twins were the only Antaeus offspring. He, Declan, and Eden were unmated. Sean and Careen hadn't had any children yet. Holden figured his brother wouldn't have kids until all his siblings were mated. It was a very Sean way to go about things.

For himself, he didn't even wonder if he had a mate. He didn't particularly care. Kids and a white picket fence and the kind of woman who would want that life were so not his style. On the other hand, society type women and career women weren't really his type either. People with that kind of driven personality irritated him which is why he was no longer pissed at missing his weekend with Gina. He really only had one use for her and now that he realized it, he was too nice a guy to continue fucking her when he didn't even like her.

As he headed for his bedroom, Holden wondered if Garret Renquist was the driven type. He didn't seem that way, but it was tough to tell with wonder boys. Things seemed to come so easily to them that if they were driven, those around them never noticed. Holden opened his packed suitcase and changed some of the items so that now his clothing was more suited to a mountain business retreat rather than a beachside spa. Once the suitcase was ready to go, Holden picked up the phone and called the exclusive jeweler his family always used. He ordered an elegant ruby bracelet to be delivered to Gina that evening and headed down to his car.

He figured he'd call Gina while he drove so she'd know he wasn't lying to her about having to go to the mountains. It was going to be an uncomfortable call, so doing it while driving also gave him the excuse of the call dropping if he got tired of listening to her rage or whine. The more he thought about how unpleasant the call would probably be, the more he just wanted to be rid of her. And so, when he was halfway up the mountain pass on the way to Gargoyle Resort, Holden found himself breaking up with Gina over the phone.

She whined. She raged. She cursed him in Italian. And then he hit a dead spot and the call dropped. Sighing with relief, he shut off his cell phone. The remainder of the drive to the resort relaxed him and by the time he arrived, Holden looked forward to playing tennis with Garret. He loved tennis and rarely got the opportunity to play anymore. He hoped Garret played well enough to challenge him.

Holden's shared suite turned out to have two bedrooms and a well stocked wet bar in the sitting room between the two rooms. Since he was the first one there, he picked one of the rooms and unpacked. As he stowed away his suitcase, he heard the door open. He walked into the sitting room to find Garret standing in front of the door, taking in his surroundings.

"It's a two bedroom suite," Holden said with a grin. He gestured toward the door across from him. "That one's yours."

Garret returned his smile and picked up his suitcase. "Thanks."

"Can I get you a drink while you unpack? It's an hour until dinner and there's a fully stocked bar here. No mini bottles." Holden's nose twitched as the spearmint scent reached him. He'd never smelled cologne like that before.

"That would be great. Just a glass of red wine if they have it, please," Garret replied as he walked toward his room.

Holden heard the sound of Garret opening his suitcase and then the closet door. He searched through the wet bar's stock of alcohol looking for wine and found a full size bottle of Merlot and one of Cabernet Sauvignon. The Merlot was a decent vintage and he decided he'd have a glass. He pulled out a corkscrew, expertly removed the cork, and poured two glasses before ambling over to Garret's bedroom door.

The British man had his back to Holden, putting folded shirts in the dresser. Holden noticed absently that they were dressed similarly in khaki slacks and polo shirts. Without the suit jacket covering his torso, it was obvious that Garret was taller, yet leaner, with a narrow waist and broad shoulders.

"Here's your wine. They had a decent vintage of Merlot. Surprised me," Holden said as he watched Garret finish unpacking. The whiz kid had an elegance of movement that was graceful in its economy. Certainly not what he expected of a bean counter.

Garret stowed his suitcase, turned, and took the glass of wine from Holden, their fingers brushing briefly. A frisson of awareness trickled down Holden's spine at the touch of Garret's warm hand. Something about him affected Holden physically. First, there was that odd prickling of his clan mark that he'd felt earlier and now the touch of their hands made him feel flushed. Not to mention that damned spearmint scent that assailed his nose.

Magia. The thought flashed through Holden's mind and he wondered if Garret was more than just a green dragon. Sometimes dragons had magical abilities, but usually those that did belonged to the community of Magia rather than the dragons. He wished he understood what unsettled him so much about the other man.

Abruptly, he turned and walked back into the sitting room, opening the slider to the balcony. He stepped outside into the crisp mountain air and sat down on a comfortable patio chair. Garret followed him and took the chair on the other side of the small table.

"This is a very tolerable Merlot."

The smooth British accent caused Holden's clan mark to prickle yet again and even though they were outside, the spearmint scent was just as strong as it had been inside. Holden didn't understand why the man had such an odd impact on him. Again, he wondered whether Garret was Magia. It would certainly explain his reactions to the guy. His annoyance at being unable to figure out Garret rose.

"So how are you settling in?" he asked abruptly. "Are you looking for a place to live?"

Garret nodded, his eyes twinkling a little as if he had a secret. "Yes. Something with a view of the coastline, rather more modern than not. Nothing I need to spend time keeping up...that sort of place," he replied.

"You should look around my neighborhood. There are lots of very nice condo complexes like that. In fact, I can ask my association manager for a list of availabilities if you'd like." Holden couldn't believe what had just come out of his mouth. He didn't need the new guy living in the same building! Not that he could take the words back now...

"Thank you. I would appreciate that very much."

Garret's cool, even tones set Holden's back teeth to grinding silently, although for the life of him, he didn't know why. "I'll call her this weekend and have her fax a list to you at the office," he muttered, lifting his wine glass to his mouth and gulping down half the contents.

The emerald eyes of his companion glittered knowingly. Frustrated by how the man unsettled him, Holden knocked back the rest of his wine and rose to his feet. "It's almost time for dinner. I'm going down to the restaurant."

Garret's expression turned sympathetic as if he knew how Holden felt. He didn't speak, but those uncanny eyes watched him like a hawk. A muffled sound of exasperation escaped Holden. "I don't get you," he ground out in a low tone that expressed his frustration. "Are you Magia or what? Cause I'm all edgy and weird around you and I don't know why. My clan mark is prickling. You smell like a pack of spearmint gum. Every time I look at you, I think I know you from somewhere, but I can't place where! What the hell is going on?"

The glow in Garret's eyes intensified as he rose to his feet, facing Holden. "Think about what you just said to me, Holden," he said quietly. "Think about what those things might signify. I'm not Magia, but as far as you're concerned, I'm something far more rare and important."

He walked over to the sliding door and then stopped, looking back at Holden. "Open your mind, Holden Antaeus. Life doesn't always fit in neat little boxes or compartments. Things happen for a reason."

Garret stepped into the sitting room, disappearing behind the blinds. Holden stared at the empty doorway for long moments. Emotions tugged inside him. Even though Garret had gone inside, Holden could still smell his spearmint scent. His eyes narrowed thoughtfully. That scent...his dragon lore came rushing back to him and his jaw went slack with shock.

Holy shit! No fucking way!

He shook with reaction, his fingers clutching the empty wine glass convulsively. It couldn't be true. It wasn't possible. Somehow Sean had set him up. His brothers were punking him, playing him off against the

British man somehow. The guy was probably some tennis stud who would kick his ass six ways from Sunday the moment they took their rackets out. Yet, how could they have manufactured his scent and Holden's reaction to that scent?

Holden stormed into the suite, fumbling a little with the door and the blinds. As he stumbled into the sitting room, Garret turned, his hand dropping from the handle of the suite's door. Their eyes met, Garret's sympathetic. Holden knew his expression was wild with disbelief. This couldn't be happening!

Garret sighed loudly and turned his back on the door, facing Holden fully. "It's not as complicated as you think, Holden," he said quietly. "I don't know why either. I just know it *is* and I recognized you right away. What you do with the knowledge, how you deal with it, is up to you, but you cannot change it unless one of us dies."

A growl began deep in Holden's chest as fear took hold of him. "Something's wrong!" he burst out, his emotions wildly overwrought.

Garret shook his head. "No. Something's very right." He moved, crossing the room swiftly to stop a few inches from Holden who wanted to recoil but somehow managed not to. His voice when he spoke was soft, but firm. "Holden, you're my mate."

4901845

Made in the USA
Lexington, KY
13 March 2010